Marion Zimmer Bradley's

Sword

and

Sorceress

29

Edited by

Elisabeth Waters

SWORD AND SORCERESS 29

Edited by Elisabeth Waters

ISBN-13: 978-1- 938185-39-7
ISBN-10: 1-938185-39-0

Trade Paperback Edition

November 2, 2014

A Publication of
The Marion Zimmer Bradley Literary Works Trust
PO Box 193473
San Francisco, CA 94119-3473
www.mzbworks.com

ACKNOWLEDGMENTS

CONTENTS

INTRODUCTION

by Elisabeth Waters

Recently, each year when I write the introduction to the latest *Sword & Sorceress*, I wonder if Marion Zimmer Bradley actually started a new trend or was simply early in picking up on a change in the world. This year that feeling is particularly strong. I believe that Disney's best-selling movies are a fairly good guide to the social norms of their time, and seeing *Maleficent* was a real eye-opener, especially as *Sleeping Beauty* was the first Disney movie I remember.

When I was a little girl, "when you grow up and get married and have children" was all one word. In the environment I lived in, girls remained virgin until they married. "Until death do you part" in the marriage vows meant just that: your parents and your friends' parents would be married to each other until one of them died. It was a sheltered world, a world in which you could believe—at least as a child—that life was like the Disney movies your parents took you to see. You would grow up, find your true love, marry him, and live happily ever after (without the singing animals to do your housework, of course—too bad, we could really use those).

Slowly, however, even Disney's view of true love has become more realistic. In 1991 *Beauty and the Beast* featured a heroine who cared more about books than most of the people around her, and while she married the Beast in the end, at least she got to know him first—none of the idiocy of "love at first sight." Ann Sharp and I saw the movie together, and we both had the same reaction: "Forget the handsome prince; we'll take the library!"

By 2007 things had really changed. In *Enchanted* Giselle starts as a stereotypical 1950's Disney heroine, complete with

7

small woodland creatures helping her to dress, before she is magically sent to real-world New York. The prince follows her, but "true love's kiss" is a running joke through most of the movie, until it is needed to save her. It's at that point that they discover that the prince is not her true love. She has changed, and so has he. And no earlier Disney movie had any dialogue like Queen Narissa's comment to the (male) lawyer clutched in her draconic claws, right after Giselle stuck a sword in her: "It's the brave little princess coming to the rescue. I guess that makes you the damsel in distress, huh, handsome?"

Last year's *Frozen* and this year's *Maleficent*, however, really challenge the myth of "true love's kiss." In *Frozen* the handsome prince is only pretending to love Princess Anna; when his help is really needed, he attempts to kill both her and her sister. It is the sisters' love for each other that saves them both. And Maleficent's curse can be broken by true love's kiss only because she believes that there is no such thing. She's wrong; true love does exist—it's just not always where you expect to find it.

Next year Disney is redoing Cinderella, and I'm really looking forward to seeing what they're going to do to it now, sixty-five years after their previous version.

I think that all of us want to live our version of happily every after. True love, however, is not the only thing in life—or, in our case, in fiction. There's also magic, adventure, and humor. Every year we get more stories demonstrating that. I hope that you will enjoy this year's crop.

THE POISONED CROWN

by Deborah J. Ross

Speaking of *Enchanted*, here's a very different story of a step-mother unwilling to pass the crown to the rightful heir. At least she doesn't send him to New York.

Deborah J. Ross writes and edits fantasy and science fiction. Her most recent books include the Darkover novel, *The Children of Kings* (with Marion Zimmer Bradley); Lambda Literary Award Finalist *Collaborators*, an occupation-and-resistance story with a gender-fluid alien race (as Deborah Wheeler); and *The Seven-Petaled Shield*, an epic fantasy trilogy. Her short fiction has appeared in *F&SF, Asimov's, Star Wars: Tales From Jabba's Palace, Realms of Fantasy*, previous volumes of *Sword & Sorceress*, and various other anthologies and magazines. Her editorial credits include *Lace and Blade* (2 volumes), *Stars of Darkover*, and *Gifts of Darkover* (June 2015). When she's not writing, she knits for charity, plays classical piano, studies yoga, and rehabilitates service dogs.

Spring came late to Errinjar, capital of the kingdom bearing the same name, and for days on end, storm clouds obscured the sun. Damp penetrated the wooden walls of the poorer districts, in which was situated an inn often frequented by soldiers too old or crippled to work. In one of the few private chambers, a meager fire subsided into a heap of ashes. A woman of middle years but with a soldier's strong build sat before the hearth, carefully facing the door, wrapped in a palace guard's cloak. At the sound of footsteps outside, she reached for the sword that lay, still sheathed, at her feet.

"Venise, it's me. May I come in?"

"You need not ask."

The latch lifted and Jessyr, Prince of Errinjar, entered. Venise relaxed against the back of the chair, for Jessyr was the one of the few people in the city against whom she need not be on guard. She had held him when he was but a few hours old, taken up from the body of the mother who died birthing him. The king had met her gaze, each of them astonished at seeing his newborn and only son. The memory still had the power to melt her heart.

When Venise moved to rise, Jessyr protested, "Please, do not overtax yourself on my account. I recently learned how ill you've been." Nevertheless, Venise got to her feet. "Please," he said again.

Venise sensed the distress behind that single word. "Tell me," she said, managing a smile as she sat down.

He responded with an engaging smile. "You were the most loyal of my father's guards..." His voice broke, and Venise imagined him thinking, *I miss him so much!*

He doesn't know. He must never know.

"I needed to see for myself how you fared," he said. "I would have visited earlier, had I known where you were. I thought you might have returned home—Garranja Province?"

"No," she said. "I've been here."

On the day Jessyr's stepmother, the dowager-consort, had been declared regent, Venise had resigned from the palace guards. Princess Emilianara of Caratha could not by law and custom be crowned queen, but that did not prevent her from putting her own people into positions of power and forcing out everyone else.

I should have done more than resign. In the throes of the lung fever, Venise had almost come to plunging a dagger through her own heart—the same dagger the king had given her on the night they first lay in each other's arms. She had taken it out, run her fingers along the length of steel, and felt for the space between her ribs. In the end, she had trusted the fever to do its work. It had failed her.

"What brings you to my door, Your Highness?"

"Jess. Call me Jess, as you used to do."

Venise capitulated. "Well then, Jess. What can I do for you?"

"I've come to ask a favor."

With one hand, Venise indicated the poor quality of the room, silently questioning what she could offer him.

He lowered himself to the edge of the pallet bed. "You served my father—as advisor as well as palace guard. I want you to do the same for me."

So like his father, coming straight to the point. Venise restrained a sigh. *I've got to stop thinking like that. Brinnar is gone and I must live what remains of my life without him.*

"As you see, I'm hardly fit for duty," she pointed out.

"Not my physical protection. At least, I hope it won't come to that." He shifted on the wooden frame. "I need people I can trust, people with experience and wisdom—now, rather than waiting for my coronation."

Venise nodded, thinking how many others would care only for the pomp and luxury of the throne and not the responsibilities it carried.

"The thing is—" and here, Jessyr leaned forward, elbows on his knees, "—I'm not entirely sure the coronation is actually going to take place. Every time I ask about preparations, my stepmother puts me off. Says not to trouble myself about it. Or gets irate that I'm questioning her competence as regent."

Venise thought that if Emilianara was fobbing the heir to the throne off with arguments like that, she deserved to have her competence questioned. "So you're determined to prepare yourself as best you can."

"No." He shook his head. "As best as *we* can."

A feeling stirred inside Venise, one she'd thought was gone forever. Brinnar had had a gift for bringing people together, even those who had been his adversaries. Her answer was already decided.

"You will, of course, be given quarters in the palace," Jess said.

"I will, of course, decline the offer." At his questioning look, she explained, "If you do need a bodyguard, I'll bed down in the outer chamber of your quarters—" *or across your threshold, as Brinnar used to joke,* "but as that is not yet the case, it's best that I am free to come and go, and observe."

"You probably won't want to wear your old uniform then, even with a badge of my personal service?"

She would need a reason to be in the palace without having to explain her position to every cadet she encountered in the hallways. "I'll take the badge," she said, "and have a word with the captain."

"Done, although the old captain retired just after you did." Jessyr named the replacement, a man Venise didn't know well but thought reasonably competent.

After Jessyr took his leave, Venise gazed into the glow of the embers for a long time.

That same day, Venise resumed her sword practice and began walking in the city. Her body needed the exercise to recover strength after her illness, but more than that, she needed to reacquaint herself with the world beyond her chamber. Last night's storm had passed, leaving the day fresh and mild. Despite the new paint on the shops and the ribbons in the manes of the ladies' horses, Venise noticed an unease in the streets. It was not unusual for country folk to make their way to Errinjar during the winter months, but too many of these people looked like foreigners—Zalloans, by their complexions. Venise had learned soldiering in the border skirmishes there, until Brinnar's treaty brought peace.

The closer Venise got to the palace, the more angry mutterings she heard. At the head of a rough procession marched a man in formal robes, some kind of clerk. There was a ruckus at the front gate, where the clerk was questioned by the palace guards before being admitted. Most of the crowd dispersed, leaving only a scattering of men. Venise walked up to one of them, a thin, haggard older fellow. On the side of his neck, she recognized the tattoo of a Zalloan adult, a man of standing.

"Grandfather," she asked politely in the Zall tongue, a bit awkwardly because she had not spoken it in so many years, "can you tell me what's going on?"

The old man's expression softened, but not the hollows around his eyes. "We want only what was promised us, aid in times of hunger."

Brinnar had hoped to stabilize relations between the two kingdoms by promising food during the harsh Zalloan winters. "I don't understand," she said. "Why was the treaty not honored?"

The man glanced toward the palace gate. "We took up a collection, more than we could afford, and hired a scribe to write our words down. A petition, he called it."

Petitioning the dowager-regent to fulfill her late husband's promises? It made no sense that Emilianara would refuse to help Zalloa, for her own people, the Carathans, were closely related, even in the design of their tattoos. Venise recalled the Zalloan expression of wishes for health and peace, and they went their separate ways.

~oOo~

The next day, Venise presented herself to the same palace gate she'd used while on active guard duty. She wore her best clothing, and that was none too good, the leather jacket and pants being scuffed with wear, but her sword was impeccably clean and sharp. One of the guards, the son of her old captain, recognized her and would have admitted her even without Jessyr's badge. The other man was new.

"You thinkin' to rejoin?" the unfamiliar guard asked.

Venise shook her head. "I'm here on special assignment, nothing more. I'm done with the old life."

Taking her leave, Venise hurried along the familiar back stairs to the wing of the palace housing the royal quarters. Jessyr had kept his old suite, down a wide hallway from the spacious quarters once occupied by his father.

Dismissing his attendants, Jessyr led the way into the inner sitting room. "Any trouble? Would you like a drink? Or is it proper to offer you one?"

"No, no, and of course, it is not. I'm on duty, even if I'm not in uniform."

"Please sit down, anyway. You've been out on the streets, I suppose. And heard about the petition yesterday?"

Venise nodded, but remained standing.

"My stepmother's in a fury, at least that's the palace gossip. I heard it from my valet. *She's* not talking to me about it. Or wasn't. I hope this evening's dinner will mark a change. She's been hinting she's willing to go forward with coronation plans, or at very least include me in discussions of matters of state."

A short time later, Venise found herself standing a half-pace behind Jessyr's left shoulder in the royal dining hall and trying not to remember how Brinnar preferred simple meals in his own quarters. The table was sumptuously set for twelve, and the hall bustled with servants and personal attendants.

Venise didn't know most of the dinner guests, except for a general who had been past retirement age when she had left soldiering for the palace guards. She'd heard about the priestess and also the two brothers from important trading families, but had never seen them in person before. She noticed who looked and spoke directly to Jessyr and in what manner, who deferred to Emilianara, and who maintained his own position.

They're all her puppets, or soon will be. The realization made Venise sad that Brinnar had married such a creature. That marriage, like everything else he'd done, had been for Errinjar's sake, for the secure border that an alliance with a Carathan princess brought. *Well, almost everything he did.*

Venise noticed, too, the deftness with which Jessyr maneuvered the conversation to the topic of his having achieved his majority, the age at which he was entitled to take the throne, all the while partaking only of those foods his stepmother had first eaten.

"Well, my dear," Emilianara said to Jessyr in the pause before the dessert wine, "you must be impatient to take up your new duties."

Venise saw the shift in Jessyr's posture. He was thinking that at last his stepmother was going to agree to the coronation.

"Of course, you must ascend to your father's throne at the proper time," Emilianara continued, gesturing with her wine glass. The fine crystal caught the light from the banks of candles. The wine was red and very dark. "The people expect no less. The *gods* expect no less."

Around the table, heads nodded. Stewards poured more wine.

"I will strive to be a worthy successor," Jessyr said.

"That you have already attained wisdom at such a young age speaks well for you, my dear. But you are indeed young, and a young person must seek counsel from those wiser and more experienced. Don't you agree?"

Carefully, Jessyr said, "I agree that good decisions come from discussion and deliberation."

"Even the choice of advisors must be made under the guidance of one's elders. This is why I have created your advisory council." Emilianara indicated the assembled guests.

Venise noted that all eyes went not to Jessyr but to Emilianara. *She's waiting for him to agree.* And there was no way Venise could warn him not to. This wasn't one of those occasions when a person—certainly not the young heir to the throne—could acquiesce for the sake of politeness or expediency, and then change his mind. In this company, his next words would amount to an oath.

"I am honored by the very great service you offer, stepmother," Jessyr said. "My father always said that a king is measured not by his own wisdom but by that of the people he surrounds himself with. I will begin as I mean to go on—by selecting my own advisors."

Emilianara set down her wine glass and fanned her face with her fingers. Venise's gorge rose, as it sometimes did in the moment before a fight.

"I would not presume to dictate what you must do," Emilianara said with a laugh like crystal tinkling. "I have only your best interest at heart, my dear. I merely sought to present you with the best candidates...for your approval, of course."

With each repetition of *my dear*, Venise wanted to wring the other woman's neck. She was taken aback by the intensity of her anger. Other than making Brinnar's private life a misery, Emilianara had done nothing wrong. Why then did Venise feel sick in her belly, as she did before a battle? Why did her hand move to draw steel, here at the royal dinner table? She came back to herself a moment later, as Jessyr was reassuring the dowager-regent that he would give her suggestions the consideration they merited.

Jessyr said nothing until the door to his suite was closed, although he was ashen and sweating. He waved away his valet, saying that he would call for assistance when required.

"I don't think we've heard the end of this," he said.

"I doubt the dowager-regent will give up just because you have said, *No thank you*," Venise observed. "You did well to avoid antagonizing her with a public refusal."

"I've learned *that* lesson well enough. When she realizes I won't accept her lackeys, the real trouble will begin."

"I have always followed the advice to pick your battles carefully," Venise said, taking the chair he gestured her to. "Save your best troops for the critical points and always keep something in reserve. Avoid committing too many of your resources at the beginning, unless you mean to overcome all resistance in a single bold move. Do you understand what I'm saying?"

Jessyr frowned. "That I should go along with what she wants until after the coronation?"

"No, not that! But if some of her candidates are tolerable, give her a small victory. I know something of a few of her choices and can make inquiries—discreetly, of course, and from sources I trust—about the others."

Jessyr paused, reflecting. "General Paniagua does not strike me as nearly as pernicious as the baron."

"I agree, as long as you do not depend on him for military advice."

"For that, I have you!"

Venise shook her head. "I have fought as a soldier, true, but never directed an army."

"Let us pray I never have need, then."

"Indeed." Venise hesitated. Jessyr knew about the Zalloan refugees, but perhaps he did not realize how dangerous the situation was and how quickly it might escalate into conflict. Wars usually boiled down to one side needing what the other side had, and there was no more potent motivation than hunger.

"I will deal with that when I am king," Jessyr replied when she explained her concern.

"Jess—Your Highness—I do not think it wise to wait so long. If Zalloans have already made their way here, confident that their petitions would be heard, how many more at home are growing more desperate every day? And how will they respond when their countrymen return empty-handed? We spoke earlier about *choosing battles carefully*. I think this is one problem that must be solved before it becomes a battle."

"Even if it means confronting my stepmother while she still holds the regency?"

"Not confronting. Discussing...compromising. Especially if you are willing to accept one or several of her suggested advisors, you will be in a position to demand something in return, that something being fulfilling an existing treaty."

"I can call upon my father's memory, I suppose," Jessyr said.

"Whatever arguments you make, think of bargaining in the market. One party gives a little, the other offers a bit more in exchange for some other concession."

"You've just described my father's council meetings! Since you advise me to do so, I will see what can be done. But I want you there with me. You don't have to say anything or explain why you're there. I want to make a certain—shall we say, *point*—with my stepmother."

~o0o~

As good as his word, Jessyr lost no time setting up a meeting with Emilianara. A few days later, they gathered in one of the chambers Brinnar had used for conferences, its mullioned windows overlooking a garden courtyard. Jessyr and Venise arrived early, moved Brinnar's chair into a corner, well away from the central table, and rearranged the remaining, identical chairs. Emilianara arrived shortly thereafter, with cortege of lady attendants, secretaries, and servants. If she was angry at being barred from sitting in Brinnar's place, she hid her reaction well.

The discussion opened smoothly with the topic of Jessyr's advisors, with each side giving a little here and there. Venise wondered if she'd judged Emilianara too harshly. The dowager-regent seemed to have Jessyr's best interests at heart, even if the two of them did not agree.

Jessyr turned to a new subject. "I understand that a petition was presented on behalf of Zalloan farmers, and that refugees are entering the city, yet no aid is provided to them."

"Who told you that?" For the first time, Emilianara's composure slipped.

"Is this not true? And why did you not inform me?"

"Yes, it's true there was a petition, some nonsense about beggars, but truly, such a spurious, unimportant thing, I hardly thought it worth bothering you."

"These people call on us to honor my father's treaty, one that has kept peace with Zalloa all these years, and you think I shouldn't be *bothered*? Do we not have sufficient food in our granaries?"

"Your father was a generous person, but perhaps less wise in the ways of the world than a king ought to be. We must take care of ourselves first. If the Zalloans have mismanaged their own resources, they cannot expect us to pay for their mistakes."

"Hunger makes people desperate," Jessyr said. "And the Zalloans are not to blame for the harshness of their climate. My father was right to have compassion for them, when our own lands are so fruitful."

"Who put such ideas into your head? If we feed these people, more will come, and more after that. Next they will demand homes here, and work, as if they are entitled to it. No—" she held up a hand when Jessyr would speak, "—we must hold firm, defending what is ours. If the beggars will not leave peacefully, we must get rid of them by any means necessary. Sweep them from our borders before it is too late!"

"Stepmother, what are you saying? That we should use force against starving people?"

"If we do not put an end to this menace, we will be overrun! Do not let your soft heart overrule good counsel in this matter, my dear. This is why you must surround yourself with counselors and be guided by them."

Jessyr glanced over his shoulder at Venise, a lapse quickly corrected, but not before Emilianara noticed. Venise, facing her, saw the faint narrowing of her eyes. Then Jessyr sat up straighter. "That will never happen when I am king. I intend to not only honor Brinnar's treaty, but to send seeds and tools to Zalloan farmers, to help them feed their own people better."

"What! That is outrageous, irresponsible—"

"Stepmother, I know you have done your best to preserve Errinjar from one king to another. But nothing in the regency permits you to change such an important policy, not without overwhelming cause."

Emilianara's glance flickered to Venise, then back to Jessyr. "The *overwhelming cause* is the protection of the kingdom against ill-conceived whims concocted under the influence of ignorant advisors."

"That is your opinion, and you are entitled to it, as I am to mine." Jessyr stood up, shoving his chair back so that the legs scraped on the wooden floor. "It is just as well that I will shortly become king, so that such matters do not create discord between us." With a short bow, barely low enough to avoid being rude, he strode from the room. Venise followed without glancing back.

Once away from the chamber, Jessyr slowed his pace. "What do you think?"

"I think I should start sleeping across your threshold."

~o0o~

As lengthening shadows heralded the end of the day, Venise returned to the inn to collect her belongings and settle her accounts. She didn't like leaving Jessyr, despite his protests that he would be safe enough in his quarters and had work to do, researching the legal requirements for the coronation ceremony. Venise made sure Jessyr's quarters were guarded by men she knew and that they understood exactly what she'd to do them, should any misfortune befall the prince.

After packing up the few articles of clothing she wasn't wearing, her field surgery kit, and several keepsake oddments, Venise returned to the palace. The guards at the soldiers' gate were different from the ones she'd encountered before. Both were too fair-complexioned to be Errinjaran, and the one who ordered her to halt spoke with a Carathan accent. They were probably part of Emilianara's entourage when she'd arrived here as Brinnar's bride.

"I'm on special assignment," Venise explained, shifting her pack so that the prince's badge was visible.

The senior of the guards looked even less friendly than before. "You're the one they call Venise?" When she nodded, he said, "You're to come with us."

"So you say. I answer to Prince Jessyr."

"And *we* answer to the dowager-regent. Until the boy is crowed, her word is law, not his."

Emilianara wants to see me? This couldn't be good. Nevertheless, Venise relinquished her pack and sword, keeping only Brinnar's dagger. The guards did not discover it and she didn't offer. The senior guard escorted her to the same room where she and Jessyr had met with Emilianara, only this time the dowager-regent occupied Brinnar's chair. Documents, scrolls and ledger books, some of them quite old, covered the table's surface. At Emilianara's gesture, her two maid-attendants, secretary, and the guard left the room. She regarded Venise with an expression of undisguised loathing. "I know who you are."

Venise offered a bow, not a lady's curtsey. "Your Highness, I was once a palace guard, and before that, a soldier of Errinjar. Now I serve Prince Jessyr."

"What you did in the past is of no account. I recognize your influence in the misguided actions of the prince. You have put yourself forward, causing him to reject those more capable. Your interference will bring disaster to this kingdom. I ought to have you executed for treason!"

Venise had known the other woman disliked her and certainly would suspect anyone who tried to help Jessyr. But...*treason?*

"I said I *ought*," Emilianara continued after an overlong pause, "but I am a reasonable woman. Perhaps you acted out of a genuine desire to be of service. The best way to do that is to leave the prince to the care of proper advisors. Your services are no longer necessary."

"That is for Prince Jessyr to say."

"You presume too much, *harridan*." Emilianara used the insulting term for a woman soldier. She lifted her hands from the table, where they had been curled into fists. Her fingers fanned out, then curled.

Acid stung Venise's throat, but she'd fought through worse sickness. She set her teeth together, estimating how long it would take her to draw the hidden dagger and how she might use it or, failing that, how many ways she could kill the other woman with her bare hands. The nausea receded.

Emilianara lowered her hands. Her face, always pale, had gone even whiter, so that her lips looked very red. "Since you labor under the delusion that you take orders only from the prince, I will see to it that *he* understands the situation. You have his interests at heart? Then consider this: until Prince Jessyr submits himself to the counsel of advisors I have approved for him—those who *in my judgment* are worthy of the post—he will never be anything more than a prince."

~o0o~

Venise went to retrieve her belongings from the guard station, reflecting that these days, the palace was more dangerous than the back alleys of the city. Emilianara had no intention of surrendering her own power. If she could not rule as queen, she meant to do so through her control over Jessyr. What would she do and to what lengths would she go, if he refused to submit? He looked to her, Venise, for advice, and she had none to offer. She saw no solution, no way of forcing the coronation to proceed against Emilianara's will.

With these thoughts heavy on her mind, Venise made her way to Jessyr's quarters. He announced his intention to find the Zalloan petitioners and offer them aid from his personal resources. "At least a token, so they will be assured the treaty will be honored once I am king," he said "My stepmother won't help them, and they can't live on air and promises." He pointed to her worn pack. "That will be perfect." He dumped the contents on the carpet and began filling the pack with a jeweled belt, a vest of silk brocade, a box of sandalwood set with silver wire and onyx, a half-dozen rings wrapped in silk scarves, and various other articles.

Venise pointed out that wandering about the city at night

carrying such valuables, with only one guard, was foolhardy.

"I'd agree," he said, buckling the pack again, "if the guard was anyone but you." He slipped his arms through the straps. "How do I look?"

"Ridiculous, not to mention a target for any thief of even modest competence. If you're determined to do this thing, let me search out the petitioners' representative and set up a meeting in a safe place."

Jessyr made no move to set down the pack. "How soon can you do that?"

"Two or three days, most likely."

"Two or three days in which these people are going to feel even more angry and betrayed?"

Venise folded her arms across her chest. "You've made me responsible for your safety and now you propose to disregard my advice?" When it was clear he would not relent, she added, "At least, leave the valuables here. Take something small to offer as a token of your good intentions. And wear something less noticeable."

He glanced down at his clothing, which was subdued by princely standards but far too costly for walking about the city. Venise rummaged in her belongings and found her spare shirt and pants, patched but reasonably clean. With the addition of her cloak and his oldest boots, he no longer resembled a prince. If the guards at the side gate were suspicious, they said nothing. After all, that peculiar looking young man, an actor no doubt, was *leaving* the palace, not trying to break in.

They combed the areas of the city where foreigners found lodging, and asked at taverns and a few brothels, much to Jessyr's delight. He bought a skin of wine, although Venise told him not to waste his money. Although they encountered a few Zalloans, those had resided in the city for some years and claimed to not know about the petition. Jessyr wanted to keep looking even after one and then another of the taverns closed. Venise persuaded him that a search during daylight hours, when stockyards and stables were open, might be more fruitful.

They had not gone very far, still within one of the less savory districts, when Venise became aware that they were being followed. Here the narrow, twisting streets were little better than alleys. There were too many places a man could hide, and too many ways to be trapped. The only light came from a second story window, most likely the upper room of a tavern.

Venise grasped the hilt of her sword and drew it partway. Adrenaline sharpened her vision and hearing. The next moment, three men emerged from the back door of the tavern and rushed toward them, swords drawn.

Shouting for Jessyr to stay clear, Venise closed with the first assailant. She feinted, slashing at the level of his eyes. He checked himself and tried to spin away, but she was ready for him, pushing past his greater reach. She pivoted, spiraling down and then out with her sword. The blade sliced neatly through the tendons behind his knee. He screamed and went down, even as she sped past him.

The second man was better prepared. His sword flashed in the overhead light, and Venise recognized the distinctive Zalloan shape. He came at her, his blows falling, one after another, so fast that all she could do was fend them off. Her ears rang with the clash of steel against steel. At the first slowing of his attack, she launched her own. His defense was as quick as his offense had been. Her body moved from old habit, the years of training in overcoming the disadvantage of her lesser height and strength. She felt the tug and release as her sword pierced leather—then flesh—

He dropped so suddenly, she almost fell over his body.

Jessyr shouted something. Venise glanced up to see the back of the third attacker as he sprinted down the alley. The man she'd hamstrung was gone, too. She crouched beside the fallen man. His shirt laces were loose, revealing a neck and chest slick with blood. She couldn't tell where she'd cut him, but he was still alive.

"Jess! Bring the wine!"

The next moment he was beside her, handing her the skin he'd wasted his money on. Venise rinsed the blood away with the wine. Jessyr handed her a wad of cloth, a silk scarf by the feel of it, to wipe down the skin.

Venise didn't see the wound at first, only the tattoo on the side of the man's neck. At first, she thought it was a typical Zalloan mark, given to boys when they passed their manhood rites. But even in the poor light, she could see how the design was smeared. She wet the handkerchief and scrubbed harder. Yes, there was a symbol, but it wasn't Zalloan. It had been altered to appear so.

Now Venise saw the wound, a deep cut near the side of the skull. As she watched, the blood flowed sluggishly, only oozing. She felt the change in the flesh beneath her hands, that terrible, sudden stillness.

Jessyr bent over the body, peering at the tattoo. "Wish there were more light, but I think...sweet gods, that's a *Carathan* mark."

Venise rocked back on her heels. Yes, Carathans could pass as Zalloan if people didn't know them well. That tattoo was *meant* to be seen. If Jessyr survived the attack, the Zalloans would be blamed...and if not, Emilianara would never have to worry about his coronation—Emilianara, who had brought her own entourage of loyal Carathan soldiers with her.

"What do we do now?" Jessyr got to his feet, sounding less steady than Venise had ever heard him.

Venise took a moment to wipe her sword clean. "I'll send someone to collect the body. As for the rest, I don't know, except that we dare not wait for the dowager-regent to try again."

"You're officially promoted to bodyguard." He attempted a laugh. "But you are right. She means to prevent me from becoming king, so that is the only way to stop her."

"Can you do that? She is regent, after all."

"Remember when you left me in my quarters while you got your things? I put the time to good use, delving into historical precedents. Because I'm now an adult, I can crown myself. It has to be in public and I have to use the crown of Errinjar, but all the ceremony isn't necessary."

"And do you have the crown?" Venise asked as they headed back to the palace.

"No, but I know where it is."

~o0o~

Dawn was breaking when Venise and Jessyr arrived back at the palace. The guards lounging inside the side doors recognized her and decided she was returning from yet another eccentric errand for the prince. Jessyr had sense enough to keep his head down and his mouth shut.

They climbed the narrow, dark stairs used by servants and emerged into a carpeted hallway leading to the royal residence quarters. A short distance away, the hallway branched and another door opened on a second set of stairs leading to the tower housing the king's private library. Jessyr, full of pent-up tension, took them at almost a run. The stairs ended at a door of polished, carved wood. It was locked, but the simple mechanism yielded to Venise's dagger. As it clicked open, sparks shot out from the contact of steel and lock, and Venise caught a whiff of something burned.

"You're a woman of many talents," Jessyr said.

The room inside was filled with natural light from tall, narrow windows. A reading table and high-backed chair occupied the center, along with a free-standing chest with many drawers. Jessyr went to the chest, opening first one and then another of the drawers. Venise walked about the room, peering out the windows and studying the wooden panels of carved hunting scenes. As she passed one in particular, her stomach lurched and she tasted acid at the back of her mouth. The queasiness was most likely a delayed effect from the exertion of the fight, so she forced herself to ignore it.

Moving to the other side of the room, Venise began pulling out books, looking for hidden compartments. She found several, none of them locked, and all filled with silk-wrapped stacks of letters and journals. These might be interesting, if not valuable, but she had no time to examine them.

She looked around at the sound of Jessyr bitten-off exclamation. "Look—" he pointed to an empty space in the largest drawer. "That's the right size for the box it's kept in, and by the ring of dust, it's been removed recently. *She's* taken it."

"It'll be tricky searching her own quarters," Venise said.

Jessyr shook his head. "She wouldn't keep it there. She has so many maids and lady-attendants coming and going, it's hardly a secure place."

"Does she have a place only she would go? A boudoir? A study? An intimate sitting room?"

"I'm afraid I don't know. Most of the time, I was happier when she wasn't around, so I didn't care where she went."

Venise looked again at the stairs. They ended here, but she had the impression that the library wasn't at the very top of the tower. The angle from the windows had been wrong for the height. She circled the room and came to a halt before the wooden panel where she felt nauseous. Swallowing hard, she ran her hands over the carving. When Jessyr asked what she was doing, she explained her theory that there might be another chamber above this one. "A room that no one knows exists would be perfect for hiding things," she added.

Looking pale, Jessyr added his efforts to hers until at last, something clicked behind the panel and it swung open, revealing a spiral wooden staircase. As they went up, the air tasted flat and the sound of their breathing echoed strangely. They emerged into the center of a workroom. Shelves lined the walls, holding vials and bottles, scales, and canisters.

A square of black silk was draped over a bulky item on the largest table. Jessyr lifted the cloth to revel the crown of Errinjar.

When he moved to take it, Venice grabbed his hand. "Not until we understand what she's doing here. We don't know what she's done to it."

"The crown of Errinjar is pure gold, *king's-gold*, and cannot be tainted by evil." When Jessyr lifted the crown, his face regained a little of its natural color.

Still doubtful, Venise examined the crown. It looked very much as it had when Brinnar wore it, except for a groove running inside the main band, in which rested a circlet of twisted wire. "What is this?"

"I've never seen it before, and Father showed me the crown many times. He said it was far heavier on the head than in the hand."

Venise tipped the crown this way and that, peering inside. She prodded the circlet with a finger, but it was firmly lodged in its groove. It wasn't meant to be removed, at least not easily. She tried again, pressing it in different directions.

A set of short barbs shot out from the wire, pointing inward. Venise was so startled, she almost dropped the crown. The barbs were short, but their tips were needle-sharp.

"Be careful!" Jessyr cried.

"Don't worry, I'm not scratched. But I think...here, take a look."

Closer inspection showed the barbs to be hollow and filled with clear fluid that had a faint, pungent smell. Venise had no doubt that the pressure of setting the crown on a man's head would be enough to trigger them. As to what might be carried in those sharp, hollow points...

"Either by a formal coronation or the old tradition, I cannot be king without wearing this crown," Jessyr said. "And unless we can remove the circlet, I will never be king if I do."

"Will you hear my advice, my prince? The dowager-regent may have anticipated your plan, or she may have prepared the crown in the event circumstances forced her to agree to a formal coronation. Either way, you must become king, so best do so on your own terms. Take the crown away with us now."

"You think we can remove the circlet and make the crown safe? I may become king then, but she'll know she's been discovered. She'll try something else, and we might not be lucky a second time."

"Not if you trust me now."

~oOo~

Since dawn, a crowd had been gathering in the plaza below the king's balcony, until the place took on the air of a market festival. Purveyors of food and drink set up their stalls around the periphery, while children selling ribbons moved through the throng. Flute-players and drummers played merry tunes.

From the chamber behind the balcony, Jessyr peeked out at the mass of people. He wore a robe of white silk, stiff with embroidery, and a cloak trimmed with snow-eagle feathers, that only a king might wear. "I didn't think there would be so many."

"It's a good thing to have half the city as your witness." Venise had been taut and wary all day, ready to counter any last minute trick by Emilianara. The greatest peril, when all might be undone, still lay ahead. The crowd below didn't concern her, but the other people in the room did. Some were palace guards that she and the captain had hand-picked; she trusted them, but only so far, and so she wore not only her sword, unlovely though it was, but two daggers and a throwing knife. Her dress uniform felt too loose in some places and too tight in others; it was new, from the palace guard stores, and she hadn't had the chance to get it altered to fit properly.

Several of the advisors Emilianara had put forth, those whom Venise judged least pernicious, had been admitted, as well as ambassadors from Zalloa and Caratha, two senior judges of unimpeachable integrity, and a distant, elderly cousin of Brinnar's mother. The bishop had been notified, but as he would not be performing the ceremony, he had considered his presence superfluous. Of Emilianara herself, there was no sign.

"Ready?" Venise murmured.

"The first duty of a king is to be ready."

Before Jessyr could step onto the balcony, however, the door at the other side of the chamber burst open and Emilianara strode in. She was dressed in a faintly martial style, the bodice of her gown cut like a general's jacket, complete with feminine versions of epaulettes. Even her skirts, normally lush and full, were of simple design. She rushed up to Jessyr, Carathan guards on her heels, and halted only when Venise moved to intercept her.

"You're really going ahead with this—this—pretense?" she demanded.

"No pretense, stepmother, but a legitimate ritual, as every Errinjarn knows."

"For that, you need the crown. Do you have it? Where? Let me see it!"

What, so you can tamper with it again?

"It is safe enough," he responded temperately. "You are, of course, welcome to observe the proceedings."

"My dear, I want only what is best for you and for this kingdom, that was entrusted to me." Once again self-assured, Emilianara gestured toward the crowd below. "There is no need for this primitive show, when I am prepared to arrange a properly dignified ceremony."

Jessyr's eyes narrowed, as if he were thinking, *You had your chance.*

"My lord," Venise said, "your people await you."

"After you, stepmother," Jessyr said with a courtly bow. "Unless, of course, you would prefer to remain inside."

Emilianara lifted her chin and proceeded to the balcony. When her Carathan guards started to follow her, Venise blocked them. "You gentlemen had best remain here. I myself will vouch for the dowager-regent's safety."

Emilianara had taken a position to one side of the balcony, clearly aware that by her presence, she gave the ceremony her blessing. At a gesture from Venise, Jessyr emerged, and the crowd grew silent, as if holding their collective breath. He came to stand in the very center, beside the low, cloth-draped table that Venise had prepared.

"In ancient times, the rule of this land did not pass from father to son," Jessyr began, pitching his voice to carry as far as possible. "There was no fancy ceremony, no need for a bishop to bless the occasion. The man—or woman—who wore the crown was chosen by popular acclaim. By the will of you, the people of Errinjar." He paused, and the crowd grew even more attentive.

They are his, as they were Brinnar's. As I am his.

Jessyr lifted his arms. "What say you, people of Errinjar? Will you have me as your king? Will you accept my pledge to work for friendship with our neighbors and for justice here at home?"

The answering *YES!* drowned out anything else he might have said. Venise couldn't help grinning as she knelt at his feet, pulled aside the cloth from the table, and drew the crown out from the shelf beneath. Out of the corner of her vision, she caught the Emilianara's unreadable expression. Then Jessyr lifted the crown, recited the oath handed down from the earliest days of his ancestors, and placed the crown on his own head.

He stood there, arms outstretched, while wave after wave of jubilant cheering arose from the plaza. Then he swayed, turning slightly towards Venise. His eyes were closed, and trickles of blood ran down his head from the edge of the crown. His body crumpled on the balcony floor. The joyful sounds from below died down into muttering.

"Treachery!" Emilianara screamed, her cheeks livid. "Vile treachery!" She rushed to the center of the balcony, exactly where Jessyr had stood. "People of Errinjar, your king lies dead, slain by Zalloan sorcery! For months now, they have been invading our city, disguised as refugees. You know this to be true, for you have been accosted and harassed by their outrageous and baseless claims. I tell you, this assassination is only the beginning of their evil designs—next, they will seize your farmlands, your livestock and goods. They'll strike deep into our sacred land, secure in the belief that Errinjar lacks a strong ruler!"

She paused, gathering herself. "They are wrong! Errinjar is not weak and leaderless. Since Brinnar's death, *I* have kept Errinjar safe! Now *I* will teach the Zalloans the meaning of fear! I will lead our army across their land, set their own fields ablaze, and crush their cities into rubble! We will never need to fear them—or anyone—again! In the name of Brinnar and all you hold dear, will you have me as your queen?"

Mimicking Jessyr's gesture, she spread her arms wide. Cries of astonishment swept the crowd. Emilianara, turning, let out a shriek. Behind her, Jessyr had gotten to his feet. Trickles of blood still marked his forehead, but his eyes were clear and his voice steady.

"Treachery indeed, stepmother. But not from Zalloa." He seized her shoulders and spun her around, so that the people might see her face. "Here is the traitor, the one who refused to honor my father's treaty, condemning our friends across the border to starvation—the one who disguised her own agents as Zalloan assassins and sent them after me—all so that you would hail her as queen and war-leader! The one who tampered with this very crown. Now you have seen! Now you know her for what she is!"

"Carathan witch!" someone shouted, and others took up the cry. "Burn her! Hang her!"

But these people were still Jessyr's, as he was theirs, and they quieted when he held up a hand. "Justice will be served—*the king's* justice!—at the proper time. Go now in peace."

With a final round of cheers, they did so. Venise took command over disarming Emilianara's men and securing the dowager herself. Venise did not know what Jessyr had in store for his stepmother, but it would be neither cruel nor ineffective. A physician attended to Jessyr's head wounds, which were no more serious than pin pricks. Venise had seen to it that the fluid inside the needle barbs was thoroughly washed out and the tips clipped to only graze the skin.

The circlet was removed and set aside as evidence against Emilianara. After that, a swarm of attendants and well-wishers, from lords and stewards down to valets and ambassadors from Zalloa and Caratha, vied for Jessyr's attention. Venise watched from a distance. It wasn't until well past nightfall that she made her way back to Jessyr's suite to gather her belongings. She wasn't sure where she'd go—back to the inn, most likely. Her work here was done, Jessyr was crowned, and Emilianara no longer a danger. She hadn't thought she'd miss the palace, but the thought of never sitting with Jessyr again left her with a feeling akin to grief.

To her surprise, Jessyr was finishing his dinner, ordinary fare, and a second place had been laid for her. He gestured for her to sit. As she did so, she tried and failed to find the words to say goodbye.

"I expect you to stay on," Jessyr said. "I mean, I would like you do. I *request* it—as your friend, not as your king."

"Thank you for the honor, but you have a palace full of guards and an entire kingdom from which to choose your advisors. I can't believe—I hardly think—that you need me any longer."

Jessyr set down his eating knife with a clatter. "You wouldn't have said that if my father were asking."

He knows. He has always known.

Cheeks suddenly hot, Venise shook her head. "What service would you have of me, then? Take over as captain of the palace guards? I'd be terrible at it—I'm not made to command so many others. Sleep across your threshold? Can you imagine the gossip! Sit among your councilors, making rude remarks?" She rolled her eyes.

Jessyr stopped her with a touch on her hand. "You are the closest thing to a...a big sister that I've ever had. You helped me when no one else would have, and not for your own personal gain. There's no one else I trust as I trust you. So I want you to stay on as my friend. Live in the palace or anywhere else you like, I don't care. Just don't leave me. I'm not ready to do this alone."

You are the son I will never bear. You are all I have left of Brinnar. Even as Venise thought it, she knew it was not true. Jessyr was more than a copy of his father. In time, he might become a great king.

Friend. It was as good a title as she could wish for.

HEARTLESS

by Steve Chapman

Here is a new story about Princess Shada. I supposed that some day she will grow up and become less impulsive, but in the meantime she keeps finding still more ways to get into trouble.

A lapsed musician and engineer, Steve Chapman lives with his wife and daughter at the New Jersey shore. His fiction has appeared in the prior four volumes of *Sword & Sorceress*, and recently in Prime Books' anthology *Handsome Devil* and in *Penumbra eZine*.

A faint and flickering silhouette slipped between the towering oaks of the Archon's Grove. To the untrained eye, there was no one there, nothing to see. To Shada it was clear that someone possessed of at least minor sorcery was sneaking into the spiritual heart of St. Navarre an hour before sunrise.

Sword in hand, Shada gave silent pursuit. She hadn't come looking for trouble. Okay, she'd been planning to sneak into the College of Mages when she had been expressly forbidden to do so, after a shouting match with the Archmage and getting confined to her quarters.

But her friend Micah, a student at the College, was in trouble, and Shada couldn't sit in her rooms fretting. She'd been headed for the secret tunnel that ran from the Grove into the College when she'd sighted the hooded figure moving through the trees. No one was allowed in the Grove after dark.

Shada came around a big oak and stopped dead. Ahead, atop the stone memorial at the Grove's center, the intruder had opened a portal.

It was an oval of liquid black eight feet tall, shimmering in the moonlight. He stood before it, hands in purposeful motion.

Portal-conjuring required serious chops. Shada's mouth went dry. She could be stalking a real mage.

Her swordsmanship meant little to a wizard able to disintegrate at twenty paces. She was out of her depth.

A shape appeared within oily circumference of the portal. The small hairs rose at the base of Shada's neck. Her quarry was portaling something inside St. Navarre's enchanted walls. There was no time to get help. She had to collapse the portal before whoever, *what*ever, came through.

She sprinted forward.

The hooded mage turned toward her, his hands making fast, cutting motions. The telltale glimmer of a coming spell sparked about his wrists. She had seconds to close the gap between them—

The air shimmered. Shada's blade slashed his forearm—and he vanished. He'd conjured not an attack, but an escape. Without his sorcery to power it the portal faded away.

A branch snapped. Shada spun about.

A slim girl dressed in black skidded to a halt at the end of Shada's blade. She was unarmed, her eyes large and dark beneath short brown hair.

Shada pressed her steel against the girl's throat. At least she'd netted the accomplice. "Who was that? What was he doing?"

The girl struck the sword away with the flat of her hand, so fast that Shada couldn't react, then dropped to the ground, her legs sweeping around to take Shada's out from under her.

Shada leapt them and angled her blade. "Not bad. But I have a sword and you don't."

The girl rose. Her left hand came at Shada's face. As Shada moved her blade to block the girl flowed sideways, her left leg snapping up into a kick that caught Shada under the right arm.

Her hand went numb; the sword fell.

She scrambled backward, a second kick just missing her face. The girl was incredibly fast. Panic roiled Shada's stomach.

She slipped her dagger from its sheath—

A kick smashed her wrist, sent the blade flying.

Shada barely got her arms up to block a flurry of chops. She tried to maneuver for a kick, but the girl gave her no room. She blocked a punch at her eyes, a kick aimed under her ribs.

Then realized she'd only done so because she recognized the pattern of attack.

"Miss Delerium's three by eight?" Shada was drilled in identical techniques three times a week.

The girl pulled her punch.

"You train with her. In the Citadel. So do I." Shada softened her stance. "So why are we fighting?"

"Princess Shada?" The girl bowed in apology. "I didn't recognize you."

Her words were respectful, but Shada sensed a snarl beneath them. The girl shouldered past her to examine the portal's residue.

Shada wasn't used to being brushed off by her subjects, even if they were able to beat her up. Study with Miss Delirium meant the girl must be with the Scarlet Guard or one of St. Navarre's Great Houses.

She crouched low, running fingertips over the blackened surface. "Mages are disappearing. From the College."

Shada again felt the fluttering of panic.

"This intruder was my only lead." The girl's voice shook with anger. "Another minute and I'd have learned what he was planning. Thanks to you, *your highness*, I'm back to square one."

~oOo~

"He's no novice. A couple handwaves and the portal tensor was up and resonating." The hard girl's name was Lyra. She was sixteen years old and worked for Nistil Murane, St. Navarre's ancient spymaster.

Shada thought she knew everyone in the Citadel. A girl spy her own age, an accomplished student of Miss Delerium's to boot? Lyra was apparently the most interesting person ever, and Shada had heard not a whisper of her.

"He didn't pick up your tail?" Murane, scarecrow-thin and possessed of an unsettling stillness, stared without blinking.

"No, sir." Her hair brushed and face clean, Lyra was barely recognizable as the hellion Shada had fought the night before.

35

With her dark eyes and sharp features, she was pretty in a severe, vaguely frightening manner. She wore a dark tunic and tights and seemed unable to smile.

Sir Gregory had summoned Shada to Murane's offices in the heart of Citadel, where no natural light penetrated. They were lit by torch and candle, as if to emphasize their secrecy. Shada assumed that she and Lyra were to be disciplined. But though Murane queried every particular, he did not seem skeptical of Lyra herself.

"Yet you allowed him to escape before revealing the nature of the summoning," Murane said.

"Princess Shada scared him off."

Shada felt her face redden. "I stopped the summoning."

"Before I could identify the summonee." Lyra raised her voice. "I had the situation in hand—"

"You would have had plenty in hand if some monstrosity had come through." Shada was crap at royal imperiousness, but gave it her best shot. "You didn't even have a weapon."

"I didn't need one to kick your ass."

"I was just getting warmed up." Shada's pulse raced. But fighting with Lyra would get her no closer to finding Micah or the intruder. "You said mages had disappeared from the College. Who?"

Lyra looked to Murane. He nodded.

"Prestidigitators Hubrix and Caul haven't been seen for weeks," Lyra said. "Two of our most powerful sorcerers, gone. The Archmage is stonewalling. They've got a problem they don't want anyone to know about."

"A friend of mine, a student, is missing as well."

Lyra turned back to Murane. "If the princess isn't going to have me executed can I get on with my job?"

"You insisted the disappearances were part of a larger puzzle, Lyra." Murane stood. "The Archmage denied it, and denied us entry, but your intuition has proven accurate."

Lyra bowed her head.

"The matter is yours to unravel. Do so promptly."

Shada was stunned. Far from being punished, Lyra was

being...*assigned* to deal with the threat? "What about me?"

Murane blinked. "I'm a mere spymaster, Princess. I wouldn't presume to instruct you."

"Whereas I'm glad to," Gregory said. "Shada, I told you to avoid the College and stay in your chambers. You disobeyed me on both counts."

"But I was right!"

"Yes. Bravo. Well done. This was because your father worries for your safety and I was concerned you might impede Murane's investigation."

"I saved Lyra's life," Shada insisted. "Even though I want to kill her now."

"Murane's investigation has been wrecked, you've been beaten black and blue, and it falls to me to inform your father." Gregory grimaced. "Konran will escort you back."

~o0o~

Alsdair Konran, six feet tall, blond hair falling over his forehead, was Shada's Shield, her personal bodyguard. And he was pissed. He marched Shada to her quarters in stony silence.

"Sorry about slipping out last night," Shada ventured.

Konran offered her nothing.

Shada had more important things to worry about than his bruised ego. It was completely unfair that Lyra was solving the mystery while Shada was grounded. She'd overheard enough of her father's council meetings to understand that dangerous enemies surrounded St. Navarre. She'd trained herself to defend her people. For her trouble she'd been instructed to take greater care in brushing her hair prior to receptions and sent to her room.

Missing mages constituted an existential threat to the city. She needed to get to that tunnel.

"Konran, I've got to go back."

The big guardsman grunted. "Gregory wants you locked up a fortnight. I'm pushing for a month."

It was truly remarkable, Shada's ability to piss off her Shields.

"The princess is coming with me." Lyra stepped from the shadows. "You know who I work for."

"Like hell." Konran examined her. "I could break you like a

37

matchstick."

Lyra spread her hands. "Come try."

Konran was nearly twice her size. She was unarmed. Yet he hesitated.

Shada realized it was in the way Lyra carried herself, an utter physical confidence that radiated from her every motion. This girl was never sent to her room.

"Fine. Murane can take it up with Gregory." Konran stalked off.

Shada drew a deep breath. Relief battled with embarrassment that she'd required rescue. "Here to assassinate me?"

"You wish." Lyra brushed mortar dust from her tights. "My services cost coin. I don't think anyone's that bothered about you."

"You challenged a Scarlet Guardsman. You must be bothered about something."

"I know you could have slipped him," Lyra lied. "But time's tight and I need your help."

Shada felt her mood shift at this unexpected kindness.

"It struck me after you left," Lyra said. "You know a way into the College. That's why you were in the Grove last night."

Shada nodded. "There's a tunnel, to the dorms."

"I don't have time for any princess crap," Lyra said. "But Murane said you're the problem princess nobody can wrangle."

"That's me." It would likely be chiseled on her tombstone.

"Want to find your friend?" Lyra almost smiled. "Even though you were ordered not to?"

Shada sighed. "I'm always ordered not to."

~o0o~

The tunnel was barely five feet high. Shada felt a twinge of claustrophobia as her head scraped the low ceiling. She wore an illumination disc on her wrist, throwing silver light over Lyra's shoulder. In front, without a weapon, Lyra moved noiselessly forward, unbothered by anything but her mission.

This was the focus and courage to which Shada aspired, and only occasionally managed.

"How did you become a spy?" she asked.

"My village was destroyed in the border wars. Murane's Order takes in orphaned children, trains those that show promise. I was a spy before I was anything else."

"You don't have family? I'm sorry."

Lyra halted. "We're here."

Shada followed Lyra up into an empty chamber, its walls and floor constructed of obsidian tile. They were inside the College.

Lyra listened at each entrance. She signaled Shada to join her at the third.

"We catch a student, alone," Lyra whispered. "Drag him down the tunnel and get some answers. If we come across more than one, stay hidden. Two spellcasters at once—they'll shred us."

Shada didn't need to be told of the dangers of spellcasters. Her heart beat so loud she was surprised it hadn't roused half the college.

They took a right turn, then a left, without seeing a soul. It wasn't just Micah who'd gone missing. The entire wing was deserted. The air felt thick, mossy. A deep, faraway thrum vibrated through the floors.

Shada ran a hand along the wall. The stone was moist, as if fevered, and strangely striated. She allowed a sliver of light to escape the illumination disc.

Tiny filaments, red as summer roses, webbed the surface of the wall.

She released more light. Scarlet threads covered the wall, floor, and ceiling, converging on a door at the end of the corridor.

It was locked tight. Lyra went to work with a pick. Tumblers turned. "Ready?" she asked.

Shada felt intensely unready. Whatever lay beyond the door was unnatural. Sorcerous. But Lyra didn't seem scared, so Shada drew her blade.

Lyra kicked the door open.

Scarlet webbing stretched across the walls, ominous tangles hanging in the corners. In the center of the web sat a glistening mound of muscle.

Her breath coming too fast, Shada recognized the shape from her anatomy tutelage. It was a human heart, but enormous. And it was beating, its mammoth thrum rumbling the stone beneath her feet. Veins spilled outward, creeping under the door and along the corridors.

"Caul and Hubrix." Lyra pointed to dark shapes held against the ceiling in a mass of veins.

This was sorcery powerful enough to ensnare St. Navarre's greatest mages. Shada willed herself to stop trembling before Lyra noticed.

"They're still alive." Lyra tried to pull apart the veins holding Hubrix. The instant she touched one a dozen snaked towards her. She leapt back.

Approaching footfalls echoed through the open door

Shada's heart skipped a beat. There was nowhere to hide. "Run?"

"Too late." Lyra moved flush with the wall, signaling Shada to do the same. Shada flicked off the disc.

A hooded figure stepped over the threshold. Lyra dropped low and kicked out. She pinned him as he hit the floor, her left hand interlacing with his right, her right foot pinning his left hand. Unable to move either hand, he couldn't cast.

Shada flicked back his hood with her blade. "Micah! Lyra, Let him up."

Lyra glared. "He's a mage. He can kill us with a gesture."

"This is my friend."

Lyra released him, but didn't look happy about it. Micah sat up. He was tall and skinny, with soft brown hair that fell tangled to his shoulders. Shada thought of Micah as handsome, but now he looked pale and underfed.

"Sorry." Shada crouched beside him. "We didn't know who you were."

"Shada?" His gaze snapped into focus. "What are you doing here?"

"Nobody's heard from you in weeks. The College stonewalled me."

Micah's laugh was harsh. "You're here to rescue me?"

"She is," Lyra said. "I'm here about your colleagues." She nodded to the suspended mages. "Why is there a giant, beating heart here?"

"You need to go," Micah said to Shada. "You have no idea what's going happening."

"So tell us," Lyra said.

"Who's your violent friend?" Micah eyed Lyra. "She's cute. Can I paralyze her?"

Lyra crossed her arms. "You can try."

"Stop it, both of you," Shada said. "Micah, talk to me. Where is everyone? What is that thing?"

"The wing's been cleared." Micah rubbed his right wrist, and Shada suddenly felt ill.

She shoved him against the wall, her arm against his throat. She knew, even before she pulled back his sleeve to reveal the bandage on the wound she'd cut the night before.

Micah was the intruder who had opened the portal.

Lyra's big eyes got bigger.

"You're my friend and I love you." Shada felt hurt, betrayed, and very much wanted to hit something. "But you will tell us *everything* or this is going to go badly for you."

"The princess is your friend." Lyra moved in close. "I'm not. Talk, or she won't be able to protect you from me."

"I could," Shada said. "But I won't."

~o0o~

"I was failing." Micah sat slumped against the wall, his gaze fast on the beating heart. "The exams, the castings, were too difficult."

Lyra rolled her eyes.

"Last month Hubrix took us to Jancynth for field study. I met a woman there."

Shada felt herself blush.

"Ri's a healer. She gave me a crystal to strengthen my castings. As instructed, I brought it into my casting space and applied seven drops of my blood. The next morning it looked bigger, though my conjurings weren't any better. Soon it was the size of a pumpkin and looked like a heart. It began beating.

"Ri couldn't explain what had gone wrong. I tried to destroy it with a conjuring. No effect. It kept growing, catching insects, mice in its veins and ingesting them. Hubrix and Caul worked up an Annihilation casting. But it backfired, and the veins got them. They're alive, but unconscious." A pause. "I think it's draining their magical power.

"The Archmage is baffled; Hubrix and Caul were his experts. Ri said she'd help if I'd portal her through. I was bringing her in last night, when you attacked me." Micah sighed. "I've been stupid. I'm sorry. But I'm trying to make it better."

Shada understood what it was like to have acted stupidly, to try to put it right. She felt for Micah.

Then she hit him in the face.

"Ow! What the hell, Shada?"

'You're holding back." She understood Micah would be desperate to pass the exams. But his story didn't make sense.

"You really are crazy."

"Something you should maybe remember."

Micah looked furious. And also terrified.

"There's a giant beating heart that eats mice and paralyzes mages growing in your room," Shada said. "You got it from a 'healer' you know nothing about. And you're going to portal her inside our walls? Have you lost your mind?"

Micah looked as if the possibility had just occurred to him.

"He's under an enchantment," Lyra said. "Micah, your mind's been clouded. How do you contact Ri?"

He pointed to a pewter-framed mirror on the near wall. "She gave it to me, a permanent casting."

Shada inspected the glass. A real magic mirror. Its surface shimmered.

"Micah, you have company." The woman's voice, honeyed and amused, came from the mirror. "Feminine company. Should I be jealous?"

Shada's reflection dissolved. Staring out at her was an ageless face, violet eyes framed by silver-white hair.

"Princess Shada. I was beginning to doubt you'd ever turn up."

"I don't know you." Shada couldn't look away. Her neck felt like a band of frost.

"I am ancient history, forgotten. Your ancestors slaughtered my people and took our caverns beneath this cliff for their own. I am the Enchantress Rionach, and I am pleased to meet you."

Shada knew the name. One of the long-lived sorcerers who had thrived in the wilderness around St. Navarre before Shada's people had rebuilt the ancient city two hundred years ago. But Rionach had been defeated by the College of Mages decades before. "Rionach is dead."

"Merely patient." The woman smiled. "Shada, you carry a dagger. Cut open the palm of your left hand and let your blood fall upon my beating heart."

"Yeah, right." But Shada felt a sharp pain. The wound across her left palm had been made by the knife in her right. She squeezed her hand shut and blood fell upon the heart, which she now stood beside.

Muscle steamed where the blood fell. The beating accelerated.

"My broken heart has begun to beat anew," Rionach said. "But it cannot truly grow without the blood of old."

Shada tried to pull her arm back, but it was encased in the same band of ice that had her neck. She felt a terrible vertigo, as if she was being shut out of her own body.

Lyra reached for her, and froze.

"No interfering, valiant Lyra. Busy yourself breaking the fingers of your right hand, one by one."

Shada watched in horror as Lyra took her right index finger in her left hand and snapped it backwards.

"Stop it!" she cried.

"Don't get distracted, Shada," Rionach said. "Take the dagger and carve along your forearm, deep into the wrist."

Shada's hand moved independently of her will, pushing the tip of the blade into her arm. This cut would kill her. She tried to throw her body right or left, but couldn't move.

Another *snap.*

Lyra grunted as she broke a second finger—and broke free of the enchantment. She tackled Shada, pulling the blade away—

~oOo~

Suddenly Shada was sprawled in the cool grass of the Archon's Grove, under a full moon. Lyra knelt beside her. Micah stood above them, gasping for breath.

Shada put pressure on her bloody palm. "What just happened?"

"I teleported us out. Like last night. Once Lyra broke Ri's enchantment, I could move." Micah turned to Lyra. "How did you break it?"

"Murane teaches a technique for resisting torture." Lyra carefully wrapped her broken fingers. "Use the pain as a lens to focus your mind. No fun, but aces at bucking enchantments."

Shada trembled. She'd been moments away from killing herself. She could still feel of dagger's cool tip against her skin.

"That's Rionach's heart in your room, Micah," Lyra said. "It's a Trojan Horse enchantment, right? Her sorcery can't penetrate our walls, so she tricks someone into bringing a seed of it—of her—inside."

"The crystal," Micah snarled. "I'm a fool."

"She enchanted you." Shada stood. "You couldn't see what was happening."

"I guess she picked the stupidest student." Micah looked miserable.

"Rionach wanted my blood. She picked you because we're friends. She knew I'd come after you."

Micah snapped his fingers. "Royal newborns are baptized in the cavern waters, with the old magic of Rionach's people. Your blood has to power to make her heart even larger, more powerful."

"All our mages will end up like Caul and Hubrix." Lyra winced as she tied off her hand. "While the rest of us get ingested like the mice."

A scream echoed across the oaks from the College. Then another.

"What can we do?" Shada felt faint with panic. Rionach hadn't gotten much of her blood, but it apparently had been enough.

"Micah, your blood first animated the crystal?" Lyra asked.

He nodded. "Seven drops."

"Give me your dagger," Lyra said to Shada. "I can stop this."

Giddy with relief, Shada passed the weapon. Lyra took it by the hilt, tested the weight.

"Sorry," she said to Micah, and shoved the dagger into his gut.

Shada caught Lyra's wrist and deflected the blade so it only sliced through Micah's flank. She twisted hard. The knife dropped. Micah howled in pain.

Shada clamped her free hand on Lyra's other wrist, pulling her close so she couldn't kick. "No."

"Micah's blood animated Rionach's heart." Lyra spoke calmly. "He's her link to it. If he dies, she dies."

"We'll find another way."

"Hubrix and Caul, our greatest mages, couldn't find another way. I'm sorry, Shada. This is how it has to be."

Micah sat in the grass, examining his wound. He would live, if Shada could wrangle Lyra. "I'm sorry," he pleaded. "Under the enchantment I couldn't think."

"It isn't his fault." Shada kept her gaze locked with Lyra's.

"Doesn't matter." Lyra sounded regretful. "This is how we can stop it. One life for the thousands in St. Navarre."

Lyra tensed her arms, testing Shada's grip. The spy was slight but built entirely of lean muscle. If it came to a fight, Shada knew who'd win.

"Micah's a good man," Shada said. "We can't just kill him,"

"I can." Lyra pulled her arms further apart. "I'm an instrument. I do what has to be done."

Shada's arms ached. Lyra's wrists were slipping free.

The words formed in Shada's mind. She hadn't spoken them since her twelfth birthday, since she learned their corrupting power. Everyone expected her to use them. They wanted her to. Their denial was a point of pride, the thing that made her who she was. "I command you: stand down."

These words would disable any subject, and Lyra was less than her subject. As a member of Murane's Order, Lyra was an oath-bound instrument of Shada's family.

Lyra paled. "You agreed to no princess crap."

"I didn't try to fix your hair or make doilies."

Lyra's arms went slack. "You're soft."

"You're heartless."

"I'm necessary." But Lyra flinched. "And you're going to get every one of your subjects killed."

Shada felt the sting of her words. But it was worth Micah's life.

"She could be right," Micah said. "Killing me might break Ri's connection to her heart."

"One more time: we find another way." Shada had to work quickly. Saving Micah would be little satisfaction if Rionach's heart ingested them all by dawn. "She enchanted us through the mirror. We need to even the playing field. Can you bring Rionach here? Physically?"

Micah considered it. "I can open the portal and throw a Gathering spell. Pull her through. But she'll still be able to enchant you."

"Not if I stab her first," Shada said. "Lyra, will you help me?"

"Why don't you just command me?"

"I'm *asking*."

Lyra studied the memorial. "We need to hit her the instant she comes through."

"See the cool things you can do when you don't murder your mage?"

The screams from the College grew more frequent as Micah bowed his head in concentration. An oily, black sphere appeared above the memorial, growing into the full portal.

He flung his right hand forward. Scented air poured through the gateway, a human shape taking form.

Micah had Gathered Rionach.

Shada's grip tightened on her blade. Lyra tensed beside her.

A wave of air knocked Shada off her feet. She was scooped up as if by a fist of wind and drawn headfirst into the portal.

~o0o~

Shada lay on a floor of cast iron, in what looked like a furnished cave. Her head ached. Her hand was empty.

Micah lay unconscious beside her. Lyra was nowhere to be seen.

"When in doubt, attack." Rionach stood ten feet away, Shada's sword at her feet. "You're predictable, Princess. Knowing that a Gathering is coming, it's little effort to reverse the casting."

Silver hair cascaded past the enchantress' bare shoulders. Beneath a sheer violet dress her body was covered in silver tattoos that swam like schools of fish across her flesh. They crowded her face, danced across her forehead and along her jaw.

Shada's dagger was tucked up her sleeve. She had to get close enough to use it.

"My heart is ingesting your mages." The enchantress gestured to a mirror, the twin of Micah's. It showed the scarlet chaos of Micah's room, screams echoing through the frame.

Shada stood up on trembling legs. Micah's spell had failed. She tried to clear her mind and *think*.

"With her mages gone, St. Navarre will fall." Rionach touched the glass and drew away fingers dipped in scarlet. Silver tattoos scurried along them to feast on the blood at their tips. The enchantress was drawing the power her heart collected from the mages through the glass.

The mirrors, not Micah, were her link to it.

Shada tried to lunge for the mirror but Rionach's gaze rooted her to the spot. She felt her presence behind her eyes, taking control of her muscles.

"Blood of mages is good." Rionach smiled. "Blood of you is better."

Shada stood frozen at the center an iron disc rimmed by a canal—an instrument for collecting her blood. A cold fist of fear twisted in her gut.

Lyra stepped from the shadows. Her eyes were blank and her mouth tight, as if an unbearable tension had hold of her jaw.

"Ferocious Lyra." Rionach caressed her cheek. "Take the princess' dagger. Bleed her out."

The spy stepped on to the iron disc. The frost holding Shada's legs rose to fasten her arms. She could barely turn her head.

"Lyra, no." Shada hated the crack of fear in her voice.

"She hates you," Rionach said. "A creature of privilege, playing at swords."

"Lyra, fight her." Shada couldn't beat the enchantment. Why did she insist Lyra could? Because Lyra was serious, where she was not? Because Lyra was hard enough to murder Micah? "You can break free."

But she couldn't. In Micah's room she'd used her pain to break free. Here she had nothing.

Lyra drew the dagger from Shada's sleeve.

Shada fought back tears. Lyra was right; she was too soft.

At her feet, Micah had woken. He took in Rionach, Lyra and the blade. Caught in the enchantment he understood what was happening, but didn't look scared. He gazed up at Shada and simply nodded; as if he had every confidence in the world she could save them. She had, after all, just saved his life.

And she hadn't saved Micah's life just to let them all die here.

She flinched as the blade sliced into her shoulder.

Lyra struggled with the knife. She couldn't stop it, but was able to keep it away from Shada's vitals.

She cut across Shada's arm. Shada gasped as white-hot pain encircled her.

"Use it," Lyra grunted.

Shada understood. Use it as Lyra had used her broken fingers. Shada focused her thoughts and narrowed the entire world to the hurt surging through her body. Everything else fell away. There was only the pain, and the knife that she required.

Lyra stabbed her again.

The frost shattered.

Shada forced a scream from her throat and grabbed the knife from Lyra's hand.

Rionach threw a protective casting over herself.

Shada pivoted and threw the dagger into the mirror. A web of cracks crept outward from it, and then the glass shattered.

Rionach shrieked.

Her connection to her heart was severed. The color drained

from her flesh. The silver tattoos fled, pouring across the floor at her feet. She fell forward and the tattoos feasted on her flesh like rats upon a carcass.

Within moments there was little left of the enchantress.

~o0o~

Shada was at the healer's when she heard.

She sprinted past the Guardsmen, down the tower steps, and through the Citadel gates, racing along busy docks to find the *Flying Larkspere*.

The merchant schooner was ready to sail, the morning sun low and blinding. Minutes later Lyra appeared, a bag slung over her shoulder.

Shada blocked the gangplank. "Where are you going?'

"You know where I'm going." Lyra wouldn't meet her gaze. "Or you wouldn't be here."

In the days since Rionach's death and the deaths of a dozen senior College faculty members, St. Navarre hung suspended. Something terrible had happened at the College but no one outside the Citadel knew exactly what.

Then word came down—the King wanted the Archmage out. His lie of Rionach's long ago death had backfired disastrously. The remaining sorcerers agreed he would go, but only if retired with honors. Someone else had to be blamed for St. Navarre's near miss with destruction.

It turned out to be the fault of a young member of Murane's Order. The spy was nobody, so there could be no unpleasant aftershocks from her public shaming.

Exile. The ugly word hung between Shada and Lyra.

"You're a hero," Shada said. "I've told everyone who would listen."

"Let me pass, Princess." Lyra studied the planks beneath her feet. Above billowing sails, gulls wheeled and cried.

"You know this is wrong." Shada wanted to punch someone, probably her father. "We can fight it together."

"My orders are to go, Princess."

"Stop calling me that." Shada stamped the boards in frustration. "I'm your friend."

"An instrument doesn't have friends."

Shada took a breath. "I could command you not to."

Lyra finally met her gaze. "I believe you have too much integrity, Shada, to do that to me."

She was right, of course. But Shada wasn't going to let this stand, either. She stepped aside. "I'll speak with my father. This is unfair and you know it."

"Don't you dare." Lyra flushed. "I do my duty. No one said it would be fair. I don't do what I do because the people I work for are good, or right. I do it because I have nothing else. It's all I *am*. Please, don't take that away from me."

Shada felt her anger dissipate into confusion.

"I know you mean to help." Lyra put a hand on her arm. "But you can't help what I am."

What Lyra was, Shada had thought she yearned to be.

Lyra started up the gangplank, and then turned. "I'll be in Dathos, working for hire. Should you have need of me, Shada, send word. I'll be yours to command."

I don't want to command you, Shada yearned to say. But there was no point.

So she sat on the dock, watching the *Flying Larkspere* vanish into the sun-drenched horizon.

WITCH OF STONES

by Rebecca G. Eaker

Moira has a gift she despises and a sister she envies. This is not the "happily ever after" she expected, but with a few changes, she may get the life she really wants, instead of the life she thought she wanted.

Rebecca was born and raised in Richmond, Virginia, and she now teaches in Henrico County in the suburbs of the city. She has spent the last five years teaching tenth and twelve grade English. She says that she can't see herself doing anything else (except, in an ideal world, holing herself up with her MacBook and writing endless numbers of best-selling novels). She may very well get there.

She added the following to the biography she sent in this year: "And most importantly, in August of this year, I married the love of my life, Dan, whom I have been with for going on four years. In a way, my relationship with him is a lot like the characters, Moira and Finn, who appear in this story—Dan has helped me to see things about myself that I had never seen before. This story is for him."

Congratulations, Rebecca and Dan. We wish you a long and happy life together.

Moira stood with crossed arms and tilted head before a tall block of white-veined, gray speckled granite. The stone—simple, unrefined—exuded possibility. For her, it was a blank canvas.

With the grace of a dancer, she reached toward the corner of the granite and, whispering a word, trailed her fingers several inches down the edge. As her fingers glided over the surface, the edges of the granite began to crack and then to crumble, bits of dust and fragmented stone cascading to the floor. She slid her hand toward the front of the granite and down the other side, more bits of stone slipping away. As a cloud of granite dust plumed up around her, she saw a human face emerging from the stone, eye-level with her own. It was exactly as she had envisioned.

She smiled, satisfied, and stepped back a moment to observe her work as the dust settled. The face was what that of a goddess should be—soft, delicate features, with a sharpness about the eyes that suggested fortitude of spirit, fitting for Goddess Winter. The statue was one that the town had commissioned Moira to create, an homage of sorts to the Goddess Winter, a festival in whose honor quickly approached. Moira cared little for the Four Goddesses themselves, revering them more for their mythology than any sort of actual divine power. Instead, she simply wanted to create something beautiful.

She reached again to the statue and, with hands cupped around the stone, made soft curving strokes, shaping a long, narrow neck, sloping shoulders, and two full breasts. With fingers spread, fan-like, she bid bits of stone to fall, and she carved out folds of fabric. A flowing robe embraced the Goddess, and a hood draped about her shoulders. Moira brushed her fingers down both sides of the Goddess's face, and curling tresses of hair emerged from the stone.

All around her, a cloud of dust floated about the room, settling onto every surface. The debris did not bother her; in fact, as it settled onto her clothes and hair, chalky and dry on her skin, the debris, like the stone, became an extension of her. Moira lost herself in her work, in discovering the features of the Goddess from the granite.

A knock on the door startled her. Moira looked up to see her sister standing in the doorway, waving her hands at the dust as if it she might shoo it away.

"By the Goddesses, Moira," Felicia said, coughing, "how do you breath in this mess?"

Moira withdrew her hands from the half-formed Goddess. She flicked her fingers, beckoning the granite dust to settle, which it obediently did, forming clouds which migrated to gentle heaps on the floor.

"Well, good morning, Felicia," Moira said, embarrassed at

being so lost in the stone. "Come see my work."

Felicia wrinkled her nose and picked her way over toward her sister, hiking up the skirts of her rose-colored dress and balancing on tiptoes. She stood beside Moira and observed the granite.

"What do you think?" Moira asked.

Felicia pursed her lips. "She's not exactly how I picture Goddess Winter. She's looks very...seductive."

"Why can't she be?" Moira asked. Hands on her hips, she shifted her weight. "Just because she must herald cold, dark winter doesn't mean she can't be beautiful and alluring."

"There is nothing alluring about winter. Most things die in winter."

"You being a Witch of Flowers, I suppose I should have expected that answer," Moira replied. "But consider poor Goddess Winter. I understand how underrated she must feel. There's nothing much alluring about being a Witch of Stones either."

"Let's not start this again."

Moira turned to her sister and sighed. It was always the same, this tension between them. Moira knew this was her own fault, the result of years of thinly veiled jealousy. Daughters of a witch, they had grown up knowing they'd be witches in their own right. Moira had always imagined herself well suited to the beauty of Flowers; how devastated she'd been when, in her teens, she discovered herself a Witch of ordinary, mundane, unremarkable Stone.

"Say what you will." Moira gave a half-hearted, one-shouldered shrug. But even then, she began to doubt. She knew her ability to create beauty out of mere stone was impressive—after all, she kept the shop in the village stocked with trinkets of stone: small statues of the Goddesses, jewelry boxes, bowls and plates and vases. People came from all over the kingdom to buy her wares. Just three months ago, the king himself had asked her to craft an homage in stone to his late wife; supposedly, it now sat in the courtyard in one of his castles. But this statue was something different. It was public. Everyone would judge her for it. She wondered if her vision of the Goddess of Winter was wrong. Suddenly this statue seemed foolish, indulgent.

"Well, it's your project, isn't it?" Felicia replied, rocking forward on her toes as she observed the statue.

Moira bit her lip and moved away. Snatching a tattered sheet from a table nearby, she covered the statue with it. She would have to revisit it later.

"Are you leaving soon?" she asked Felicia, who had stayed overnight as she quite often did. Moira's home was both a convenient resting place for Felicia as she carted her own wares from village to village, as well as an opportunity to check in on her little sister. Moira might want to deny it, but no amount of jealousy could veil the fact that Felicia cared deeply for her.

"I think so," Felicia said. "It's long ride home, and I need to start on my winter gardens. But I'll be back next week for the Winter Festival; I'm providing a few decorations for it myself. Can we get out of this dreadful dust?" Felicia, coughing again, scurried out the door, skirts hiked to her knees. "I can hardly breath in here."

Moira followed, shaking her hands through her hair and patting her clothes to dislodge the dust. At her command, it fell behind her in a straggling trail. She closed the door to her workroom. "You can stay longer if you want."

"I would. But I told Ivan I would be home today." Felicia cast a backward glance at her sister as she walked down the narrow hallway to the front of the house.

"Of course. I forgot how domestic you are these days now that you're married." Moira shrugged, following her into the living room. It was a large space, filled with furniture that Moira had shaped from white marble. She had covered everything with pillows in brightly colored fabric—yellows and blues and greens. In the afternoon sun streaming in from the windows, the marble gleamed. Several large mirrors hung about the room, reflecting the light—a trick she'd learn to make her stone house seem warmer. And Moira realized, somewhat ashamed in the presence of her sister, just how many pots and vases of flowers, large and small, were scattered about the room. During the warm months she kept them full of wildflowers; now, they were filled with only remnants of summer, just a few dead twigs and leaves.

"It's different when you have someone to go home to," Felicia said and absently moved toward the door. A large, waist-high vase of pale gray marble sat there on the floor. Tall, billowy flowers cascaded up and out of its opening, but their tiny white petals had long since begun to droop and wither. With a touch from Felicia's fingers, the flowers petals spread and bloomed, as if stretching after a long sleep. This was her gift as a Witch of Flowers.

Moira turned away. She remembered the day Felicia had discovered her Craft. In a meadow as they picked flowers, Felicia had found she could make them bloom with a whispered word. She'd twirled about the field with joyful laughs, daisies springing up beneath her feet, laughing all the more, no doubt, because it was no secret that's what her sister had wanted more than anything. For Felicia, who had always been plain compared to Moira, it was a victory.

Moira paced a few steps to the window, realizing her fists were clenched, her nails digging into her palms. Stretching her fingers, she took a deep breath and leaned on the sill. Outside, she could see two horses approaching, pulling a wagon behind them. It would be the shopkeeper and his men, coming to bring supplies for her and pick up her wares for the village.

"You know," Felicia said, coming to stand by her sister, looping her arm through Moira's. "You should think about settling down yourself."

Moira rolled her head in her sister's direction. "I don't want to settle down. It's not so bad, being alone."

"You say that, but I know it's not true," Felicia said, turning her gaze back out the window. "You need a good, strong man in your life. What about Finn?"

"What *about* Finn?" Moira asked, withdrawing her arm. She gawked out the window at the shopkeeper as he hopped down from the wagon, followed by two of his workers. He saw her and raised a hand in greeting.

"He's nice enough."

"Our relationship is merely professional. He sells my wares in his shop in the village. He comes every few weeks to pick up merchandise and brings me things I need. That's all. Besides, he's not my type."

But Felicia saw her blush and nudged her with an elbow. "You're impossible."

Moira only shrugged.

"Well." Felicia huffed. "I suppose it's time for me to go."

Moira followed her sister in silence as she walked out through the front door and to the barn beside her house. Felicia had already saddled her horse, and it waited for her nearby. Together, the sisters walked the few steps to the fence of gray stone that surrounded the house, Felicia leading her dappled mare. Moira pushed open the iron gate.

"Take care," Felicia said. "It's been good to see you, if only for a little while." She embraced her sister and then climbed up into the saddle.

Moira smiled and nodded, watching as her sister disappeared into the distance. She didn't mind Felicia's visits—so long as they were brief—but was always glad when she departed.

Moira turned and, wrapping her arms around herself in the brisk air of almost-winter, wandered back to the front of the house. The shopkeeper and his men were unloading several wooden crates from the cart, stacking them by the front door for Moira to sort through when she pleased.

"Morning, Moira." Finn greeted her first.

"Hello, Finn," she said, not looking at him. Something about him always warmed her, stirred a longing for something she knew she could not have. He was not an extraordinarily handsome man: his nose was too big and a bald spot shone through his thinning blonde hair, premature for a man not even in his thirties. But there was something about his smile, something about the way he grinned at her as if she was the only woman in the world. She supposed he smiled at all women like that.

"Did you bring everything I asked?" Moira asked, rubbing her arms against the chill.

"Should all be here. Candles. Some dried herbs. Some apples

freshly picked from Farmer Nathan's crop—probably the last of the season. Oh, and that fabric came in finally."

"What about firewood?"

Finn paused for a moment, surveying the growing pile of boxes. "No, sorry. I must have forgotten that."

"It's all right."

"I'll bring it by this evening," Finn offered. "If that suits you."

"Of course. Thank you." She lingered outside for moment longer, as Finn and his workers resumed unloading boxes. She wanted to say something, to get his attention. She wanted to stand close to him in the chill air and feel his heat. But she knew a man like Finn could never belong with a woman like her. In the village, everyone liked him, respected him, came to him for advice. His shop was a gathering place in the town, where travelers stopped to purchase supplies, trading stories and gossip and news with the villagers. He deserved a beautiful woman on his arm.

"You okay there, Moira?"

Moira blinked, so lost in thought she hadn't realized she'd been staring. Finn leaned against the stack of boxes nearby with his hands, half bent over, grinning at her.

Nodding, she smiled weakly and turned away, retreating back into her home.

Inside, she closed the door, catching her reflection in the mirror across the room. What had happened to her these past years? As a teenager, Moira had been well aware of her emerging sensuality, of how other women coveted her gold-tinted hair and blue-gray eyes, how young men stared too long at her full lips and round breasts. She had imagined herself well suited to the beauty of Flowers or to the mystery and grace of Wind. Or perhaps the elegance of Rain. She'd had dreams of being something remarkable, unforgettable. And here she was now, unable to even get the attention of a man she had liked for a long, long time.

Moira stepped closer to a mirror near the door, pulling away the pins that kept her hair in a tight coil at her neck. She shook her hair about her shoulders and stared at her pale reflection. She wished she could be beautiful again. She wanted to go back to those days when she was fifteen years old, before she came into her Craft, when she was lovely and desirable and flirted with boys. She wanted to wear jewels and makeup and brightly colored dresses. But when she had come to this village two years ago on her eighteenth birthday—mostly to escape Felicia—she had decided to look the part of a Witch of Stones. She wound up her hair and wore browns and grays, the colors of river stone. What place did beauty have with idle rocks?

Moira paced over to the vase of flowers that sat on the floor, tracing the petals with her fingers. How was it fair that Felicia— plain, dun-haired, gray-eyed Felicia—should command the beauty of Flowers? Why did she have everything and Moira nothing?

She clenched her fist and the stone vase crumbled, earth and dirt and white petals tumbling onto the floor. She ground her heel into the petals and, turning, stormed away to her workshop.

~oOo~

Hours later, Moira wavered before another tall block of granite, this one a deep gray with black freckles. The old stone, her first attempt at the Goddess, cowered in the corner, still hidden by the sheet. She had moved it there shortly after Felicia left, waving her hands carelessly in its direction. It had shifted backwards across the floor at her beckoning, inches at a time, until it was virtually out of sight. It was easy enough to ignore now.

Moira touched the new stone with her fingers, trailing them downward to etch a face from the granite. Pushing her fingers back, she formed waves of hair, then pulled her hands down so that it fell in straight ribbons to the new Goddess's square shoulders. With both hands, she bid a high collar to form around the Goddess's narrow neck, a row of buttons down her chest: a warm jacket for the Goddess Winter. Moira scooped a handful of dust from the floor and smeared it around the Goddess's neck, and it solidified into the shape of a billowing scarf.

She stood back to survey her work. The new Goddess looked like an ordinary woman, nestled in her coat and scarf. She could be anyone, really.

Moira sighed as a knock resounded through the house. Brushing dust from her clothing, she wound down the hall to the front door. She opened it and found Finn leaning on the doorframe.

"Hello, Moira," he said, smiling. "I brought you that firewood. Okay if I stack it on the far side of the house?"

"Yes, thank you," she said, following him as he stepped back outside. She watched, lingering just outside the door, as he carried logs in his arms from the wagon to the side of the house. He made several trips, his breath forming small, transient clouds in the air. She liked to watch him work, to see the strain of his shoulders, the strength in his arms.

"It's getting cold out, I'm afraid," he said, glancing skyward as he rounded the house from his final trip. "Might even snow."

"Just in time for the Winter Festival," Moira said, following his gaze to the ashen sky.

He clapped his hands together, ridding them of debris from the firewood. "Speaking of the Festival, how's that statue coming?"

She looked away. "Oh, I don't know."

"I'd love to see it," Finn said, blowing into his hands.

Moira felt the flutter of panic in her stomach. She didn't want anyone to see the mess she was making of the statue, much less Finn. "It's nothing, really. Nothing worth seeing." She shifted back inside the doorway, her hand searching behind her for the knob. She started to close the door and called over her shoulder, "Thanks, Finn."

He caught the door with his palm. "Come on, Moira. You could at least invite me in. We're friends, aren't we? It's cold out here and a slow ride back to the village."

She looked back at him, the tip of his nose and ears pink from the cold. Reluctantly, she opened the door and stepped aside. "Come in then."

Finn smiled and followed her, closing the door behind him. He glanced around in a casual, familiar way. "It always amazes me how warm and bright your house is, even though it's made of stone. You're a real artist, Moira."

"Thanks, I guess," she muttered, lingering uncomfortably by the door.

Finn shrugged off his jacket. "This is the part where you say 'Gee, Finn, why don't you have a seat' and offer me some hot tea."

Moira smiled despite herself and lifted her eyes to his face. "Of course. Have a seat, Finn. I'll be right back." She hurried down another hall to a storage room and fished out a bag of tea leaves. Triumphantly—and nervously—she returned to the living area to put a kettle on the fire that already burned in the hearth.

Only to find Finn was gone.

"Finn?" she called. Confused, she surveyed the room, sure she hadn't heard the front door open. Then she realized exactly where he had gone.

Striding a few steps down the hall, she found him standing in the middle of her workshop, surveying the second half-formed Goddess statue, peering into her face as if she might speak to him.

Moira felt heat rise to her face, a mixture of anger, embarrassment, and shame. She regarded her workshop as an intensely personal space, home to half-finished projects and fancies. Everywhere throughout the room, blocks of stones of many colors and sizes were scattered about in a sort of organized chaos—they sprawled across the floor or were stacked on top of one another or tumbled across the dozen tables that were spread haphazardly against the walls. Unfinished projects pervaded the space: here a set of plates and bowls, here a dragon statue with only one wing, here a necklace and a bracelet, a trinket box and some vases, some river stones, a chair and a basin. The floor, littered with mounds of dust, showed Moira's footprints. In the overcast sunlight drifting through the skylight, everything seemed enveloped in a pale haze.

She couldn't help but feel that for Finn to be here—in all the mess that was her workshop—was like exposing her innermost secrets.

Moira took a deep breath to compose herself and walked

toward him, dropping the bag of tea leaves on a table as she passed. She clasped her hands tightly in front of her. "I suppose you don't want tea, then. It is usually considered polite, however, to ask before inviting yourself into someone's private rooms."

He gave her a sly look from the corner of his eye as she came to stand beside him, and she found it impossible to stay angry with him. "Lighten up, Moira," he said. "I just wanted to see your work, that's all. You're so secretive."

Moira wrapped her arms about herself. "Well, since you're here, you may as well tell me what you think."

"She's lovely," Finn said, but Moira could tell he wanted to say more.

"But?"

"She seems so traditional. I somehow expected something more. Something different. I see your work more than anyone. And this doesn't seem like you somehow."

Moira sighed and crossed the room, leaning her hips back up against a worktable. She stared at the statue, but it did not look much better from a distance. "I admit, I'm having some trouble."

"Tell me about it," he offered.

"My first time carving her, I wanted her to be beautiful. But I thought I was trying to make her into something she's not. So then I tried this."

"Why can't she be beautiful?"

"Because winter isn't beautiful."

"You think so?" Finn stepped across the room to her and, crossing his arms, leaned back against the table with her. They stood, side by side, surveying the statue. "Haven't you ever seen a fresh snowfall before anyone's walked across it? It's so perfect and undisturbed. Or the ice crystals on tree branches? I think that's beautiful."

Moira looked at him, surprised. "I hadn't thought of that before."

Finn nodded toward the covered statue. "Let's see the other one."

Moira shrugged and, reaching toward it, pulled the sheet down. Dust billowed up about her feet.

Finn blinked and smiled widely. "She *is* beautiful. I like her much better than this grandmother over here."

"So what do I do?"

"You do whatever *you* want," Finn said. "Trust yourself, why don't you?"

Moira looked back and forth between the statues, suddenly hating them both.

"Are you actually even going to go to the Festival?" Finn asked abruptly.

She shrugged, plucking a palm-sized river stone from the table behind her and rolling it between her palms. "I haven't decided."

"You know, you've lived here two years now and hardly anyone knows your face but me. People ask me about you all the time. They want to know about the mysterious Moira, Witch of Stones."

"I know. I just...I'm embarrassed sometimes." Without thinking, she began to mold the river stone in her hands, bits of grit falling to the floor.

"Embarrassed? Embarrassed, Moira? Of what? Everyone loves your work. Look! They commissioned you for this statue!"

"I know that," she said, lowering her head. She rolled the stone a bit more in her hands until petals emerged and a stem. She held a daisy now in her palm, delicate and small. "But I never wanted to be a Witch of Stones. I want to be something beautiful, like a Witch of Flowers. That was supposed to be me. Not Felicia."

"Felicia has it easy you know—she works with something already beautiful. She doesn't have to *do* anything. If you think about it, what you do is far better. You make something beautiful out of the ordinary."

"Not really. It's just a cheap trick, see?" she said, holding the stone flower out to Finn. "It only *seems* to be beautiful. It's not really. It's only stone." She closed her hands and pressed them together until her palms cupped only dust.

Finn looked away, shaking his head. "Forget all that, Moira. I want you to come to the Festival." He paused, glanced at her from the corner of his eye. "And I want you to come with me."

Moira pushed off the table and paced a few steps away. "Finn—"

"I'm not taking no for an answer this time. You make every excuse in the world not to see me." His voice was low and steady. "It's like you think you're better than me or something."

Moira pivoted back to him, hands clenching and unclenching as she struggled for words. "It's not like that, Finn. It's just the opposite. You don't belong with all of this, this hideous mess." She gestured expansively at her workshop, at the stone. "No one does."

Finn sighed, turning away abruptly and striding toward the door. "I have to go."

Moira followed him wordlessly down the hall and back to the front door, biting the inside of her cheek. Outside, he paused, looking at the sky. The gray clouds had lightened, now soft and pale, looking pregnant with snow.

"It's starting to flurry," he said. He stepped toward the wagon and his horse, dusting flecks of white off the mare's back. "I have to get back."

"Finn, wait," Moira said, lingering behind him. She swallowed the lump in her throat. "Are you...are you mad at me?"

He paused, looking over his shoulder at her. "No. But I hate that you're so miserable you can't see your own worth." He climbed onto the wagon, taking the reins of his horse in his hand. "Goodbye, Moira."

Watching him go, Moira felt a chill. For once, just once, she wanted him to sit with her at the hearth while the night sank in. She wanted to be near him when the cold snow fell harder. More than anything, she did not want to be alone. But she simply turned away and said nothing at all.

Back inside, she sank down in a chair by the window, feeling tendrils of cold creeping into her home from the edges of the window. Wrapping herself in a blanket, she leaned her elbow on the arm of the chair, head in hand, and watched the world outside turn to white.

~oOo~

The snow fell for hours. And Moira sat, perched in her chair, gazing steadily out the window, rising only once to stir the fire in the hearth. Outside, the tiny flecks of snow flurry transformed gradually into fuller flakes, falling faster and faster. Sky and earth blended together—a single shade of winter gray—fading into a dusky haze and finally to night.

Moira tired to see as Goddess Winter might see, to see and feel the beauty of winter's gift. She studied and squinted. But she saw only snow, and she felt only a bone-deep cold.

She considered forgetting all about the statue. In fact, she considered a great many things as she sat in the quiet darkness: why she constantly denied Finn's attention, why she locked herself up on in a house on a hill away from everyone, why she so envied Felicia, why she didn't just give up on being a Witch of Stones if it bothered her so.

"Is it true?" she muttered to the darkness. "Am I miserable?"

But, lifting her head, looking around the dimly lit room, she knew she could not leave this. She did not need to see with her eyes each corner of her house—the walls and furniture and vases of stone—to know its value to her, to know how much she had poured into crafting her home and her life. Being a Witch of Stones was not the path she had expected, but she loved being what she was. She loved this house. She loved standing in her workshop, hair tangled with grit and dust, skin coated with a fine, powdery layer. She loved making something from nothing.

It was not the gift of Flowers. But it was a gift, nonetheless. Somehow, she had to accept that.

Then, struck with a thought, Moira rose hastily and lit a lantern. In her workshop, amid her stacks stone, she felt most whole, most alive. Perhaps in the snow, surrounded by winter, she could better understand the Goddess. She slipped on her boots and ventured outdoors, the new snow crunching beneath her heels.

She inhaled the cold dry air, her chest aching as it filled her lungs, and held the lantern high. A gust of wind enveloped her, numbing her nose and fingers and ears. Snowflakes—white blurs clouding her vision—clung to her eyelashes, while a gentle layer of snow lighted on her shoulders. She shuddered at the cold caresses the flakes left on her neck. The world was still in the way it only can be in the snow, everything enveloped in a gentle hush.

Moira stood within her circle of light for a time, watching the illuminated flurry of snowflakes spiral down around her. They fell in a flutter of twirling chaos, like hundreds of dance partners in a whispering, frenzied waltz. But the magic was in the breaths of wind that shifted everything at once, changing the direction and slant of the snowfall. It was a dance both sporadic and synchronized, a dance the snow conducted to a melody all its own.

Nestling her lantern in the snow, she turned her face upward so that the snowflakes kissed her cheeks. She flung her arms wide and spun about, swaying with in the silent melody of the snowfall. When Moira stopped spinning to catch her breath, she found herself laughing.

This was it. This was the cold, quiet beauty of winter. And it was an unexpected beauty, she realized, just like the beauty of her Stones.

Moira rushed inside, hopping down the hallway as she hastily stripped herself of first one boot and then the other. She caught a glance of herself in one of the mirrors, her cheeks flushed with the chill, snowflakes still in her lashes and glistening in her hair. She smiled at herself and rolled up her sleeves, marching off down the hall toward her workshop. Now, she had the answer.

~o0o~

Days later, Moira trod down the path to the village. The snow had mostly melted and now she hopped around puddles, careful of the hem of her skirts. She wore a deep blue dress, one that complimented her eyes and one that she had not dared to wear since she became a Witch of Stones. Her hair she let fall down her back in its naturally curling locks. And she paid homage to her Craft with a necklace of smooth, round river stones strung together. Looking in the mirror before she left, she felt like herself for perhaps the first time since she'd become a Witch of

Stones. She knew that she looked beautiful.

Now, she walked straight-backed and confident down toward the village. It was the day of the unveiling of the statue.

Earlier, before she'd gotten dressed and readied, a dozen or more of Finn's workers had retrieved the statue, heaved it into a cart and lugged it down to the village square with a laboring team of mules. She could have done it herself, but Stone moved slowly—even at her summons—so it was just as easy to let Finn's workers handle it.

She had been disappointed that Finn had not come himself, but she knew the village would be teeming with activity because of the Festival; he would be in the midst of it all. And so she went now to fetch him. She was done hiding from him.

The path wound down from the hill on which her house sat and, in a quarter mile, she approached the edge of the village. She knew little of the village itself—with its dirt roads, simple wood buildings, and cobblestone square—but she had visited Finn's shop before. It lay a few streets down the main road around a busy corner, just beyond the square. Moira navigated through the masses of people who had gathered in the streets for the Winter Festival, found Finn's shop and, after taking a deep breath, she stepped inside.

People filled nearly every square inch of it, laughing and talking and sipping hot cider from mugs. She felt a touch of anxiety, having so rarely come down to mingle with the villagers. But almost immediately, she spotted Finn and waved a hand above her head to catch his attention. He looked at her, raised a hand in return, and sidled through the crowd toward her.

"Hello, Moira," he said, thrusting his hands casually into his pockets. There was a flash of surprise in his eyes as he observed her but, other than that, she could not tell what he thought. "I half expected you wouldn't come."

"Well, here I am," she said, knotting her fingers together. The confidence she had felt on her way down to the village wavered. But she smiled at him as steadily as she could. "The statue unveiling should be shortly. Will you come with me to see it?"

His neutral expression broke then, and he grinned at her, the same warm smile as always. "I thought you'd never ask."

And looking up at him, seeing his smile, Moira wondered if, perhaps, it *was* a smile just for her. Maybe all along, she'd just refused to see it.

Finn offered her his arm, calling over his shoulder for one of the workers to mind the shop. Then, arm in arm, they made their way through the crowd to the village square.

She could count on one hand the times she'd been there. It was a simple cobblestone pad in an open space between the buildings of the town, a place where people gathered for all occasions. On a pedestal in the center, the statue stood, veiled with cloth. Already a crowd had gathered to see it. Moira noticed that people turned to look at her, whispering and pointing, but she held her chin up. Reassured by Finn's presence at her arm, confident in her work and herself, she was unafraid and unashamed.

They made their way to the front of the crowd. Moments after they took their place, Moira heard someone call her name, and she looked up to Felicia pushing through the throng of people.

"There you are!" Felicia exclaimed. She gazed at Moira's face, narrowing her eyes, surely noticing but not commenting on the change in her. Her eyebrows shot up when she saw Finn.

Moira lifted one shoulder in a shrug, a smile tugging at the corners of her lips. "I'll tell you all about it later."

"I expect you will," Felicia said, nudging her with an elbow. She gestured toward the statue. "So this is it then. How did it turn out?"

"Exactly like I wanted her to," Moira said and meant it.

And when the statue was unveiled some minutes later, Moira heard the crowd inhale collectively. The Goddess Winter stood, all in flawless white marble. Her features were soft but strong, and her hair trailed wildly and ethereally down her back like a flurry of snow, tiny glistening snowflakes woven in among her locks and lighting on her lashes. Her robe, textured like fur, hung loosely about her, exposing perfectly round shoulders and one long, slender leg. She balanced on one foot as if mid-step in some wild dance, arms reaching skyward, hands cradling snowflakes. With her face upturned to the heavens, she looked as if she reveled in the snowfall. She was celebrating the winter, celebrating herself.

Moira felt the eyes of the crowd search her out, smiles spread across every face she saw.

Even Felicia, standing beside her sister, breathed a sigh of awe. "She is stunning," Felicia said and Finn, seeming speechless, nodded in agreement.

Moira gazed upon her work, liking the way the bright white marble shone in the sunlight. Turning to her sister, she grinned and said, "I know." She doubted anyone had ever seen a Goddess Winter so beautiful.

CHOSEN ONES

by Amy Griswold

There are many, many fantasy stories about people being chosen by magic for some task or other. But this one doesn't turn out the way you'd expect.

Amy Griswold has been a fan of science fiction and fantasy ever since she first watched Star Trek at an impressionable age. With Melissa Scott, she is the author of the Victorian fantasy/mystery novel *Death by Silver* from Lethe Press, featuring detective Julian Lynes and metaphysician Ned Mathey, and the upcoming sequel *A Death at the Dionysus Club*. She has also written several Stargate Atlantis and SG-1 tie-in novels, including the Stargate Atlantis: Legacy series (with Jo Graham and Melissa Scott) and *Stargate SG-1: Heart's Desire*. Her first sale to *Sword & Sorceress* was "Caden's Death," in *Sword & Sorceress 25*. She lives in Chapel Hill, North Carolina, where she writes educational test materials as well as novels, and tries not to confuse the two.

The night before the offering, we couldn't resist trying to decide which of our daughters would be the chosen one.

We had camped in the lee of our wagons, spreading out our bedrolls while Myrtale made our dinner. She was the best cook among us, having run an inn with her man until a fire took him. I took the bowl of stew from her gratefully and ate it with the flat bread she had cooked over the fire's ashes.

The girls sat together to eat, huddled together in a whispering knot as if at a harvest fair. There were five of them, tall and short, brown and fair, and every age from ten to thirteen. We had put our heads together all the way to the city trying to puzzle out what the Corn Mother might be looking for in her offering. The best we could say was that all the chosen girls were the daughters of widows and not yet wed themselves, and that wasn't much to say.

Across the fire, our guards were silent as ever, two burly soldiers who might have been mute for all we knew. The sorceress who had chosen our girls sat beside them, bending her head over her food, the Corn Mother's tree inked on her forehead darker than her graying hair. We were close enough to the city now that people had begun giving us gifts as we passed; the sorceress wore a crown of white flowers that had been handed her by a shy girl younger than my Lethe, and the guards were sharing a jar of wine offered by a pair of ragged mendicants who wore no shoes.

"My Ana is a fine weaver for her age," Kalliste began cautiously, casting a glance over at the long-legged girl who was teaching one of the others a game of knots with the ribbon laced between their hands. "She has a good eye for colors already, and I've been teaching her to thread the standing loom."

"I doubt she'll be chosen as a sorceress just because she can weave," Olympe said impatiently. Olympe was a city woman, a philosopher's widow and a scholar herself, and was used to speaking among men. It showed in her frankness and her tendency to speak up when it might have been better to hold her tongue. "At least my Silvia can read and write."

"So can my Lethe, if it comes to that," I said, as Olympe needed reminding from time to time that she wasn't the only woman among us with any learning. "My man was a merchant sailor, and I kept his accounts for him, and learned my Lethe her letters and numbers as well." I didn't mention that I could also steer by the stars and trim sail, and that Lethe could do a tolerable job of both, as I doubted a sorceress needed to do either.

"It can't be reading and figuring that they're looking for," Myrtale said practically, sitting down heavily with her own bowl. "Any number of girls can do that. And surely all the girls born in the temple can, and I hear they never choose any of them at the offering."

"They marry well, though," Colubra said. She was an

apothecary's wife and a midwife herself, dark and clever and brisk, and made little pretense of having been happy in her marriage. "A sorceress's daughter will never lack for choice."

"You didn't do too badly for yourself," Olympe said.

Colubra snorted. "If you like a man who prefers sitting up drinking with his friends to coming to bed and doing anything useful there. It's a wonder he ever produced Toria, and that's all that I'll say about that." Kalliste blushed hotly, her pale cheeks flaming red, but Myrtale laughed.

"Some might say that's ideal," Myrtale said. She shrugged at Olympe's frown. "Well, a man's a bit of a nuisance, isn't he? And I'm fortunate in my Bria, but I lost three stillborn before her, and I've no desire to start all that again."

"I never found my man a nuisance," I said. The grief was a dry lump in the back of my throat, like something I'd swallowed that wouldn't go down, bitter as the bread was savory in my mouth. He'd been dead scarcely a year, long enough for me to tire of living on the grudging sufferance of his kin, so that I agreed eagerly to bring Lethe to the temple when the sorceress came calling.

"Nor did I," Olympe said, more kindly than I'd thought she was capable of. "Was it the winter fever, Patrice? That's what took my husband. A sorceress came down from the temple, but all she could do was ease his passing."

"It was pirates," I said. "We had a cargo of wine and woven cloth, and we were running low in the water, so it was clear we were heavy laden. They came up on us in the dark and boarded. My man killed half a dozen before they cut him down." I could still see him falling, gone limp and sightless before he hit the deck. "I killed two myself." I had my long knife still with me in my bedroll, not because I thought I would need it on the road, but because I had carried it always aboard ship and felt naked without it now.

"Good for you," Kalliste said fiercely, taking me by surprise. I'd put her down as rather a tame goose. "We had a cargo of tapestries lost to pirates, and the man who ordered them said he wouldn't pay for what he hadn't got—that was a hungry year."

She rubbed at her fingers as if feeling sharp bones through their healthy flesh.

"They say they're going to send sorceresses on some of the king's ships, to do something about all these pirates," Myrtale said.

"They say a lot of things," Olympe said skeptically.

"All I care is that they say all the girls we bring can stay in the temple and get an education there, even if they're not chosen," Colubra said. "I'd like my Toria to train up to some trade. I expect I've saved more lives at the birthing stool myself than my man ever did with all his potions."

She looked up at her brown, slender daughter, who was laughing at some silly story another was telling. "I'd rather that for her than being chosen," she said quietly. "They stay in the temple so long before they let them go forth as sorceresses. I heard it was twenty years."

"It can't be much less, as you never see a young sorceress," Myrtale said. "But you're right. The most important thing is to see them well taught and well wed, and to get a roof over our own heads in the meantime." The fire that had taken her husband had taken her inn and half her village as well, leaving her wandering the roads with her daughter until the sorceress had found her. You'd never have known it now, as neat as she kept her borrowed clothes and as little time as she spared for self-pity.

"Perhaps even marry again," Kalliste said. "Someone must want a sorceress's mother."

"The Corn Mother forbid," Myrtale said fervently, and the general laughter put an end to speculation for the evening.

Lethe came back to sleep at my side that night, all restless energy, twisting in her bedroll until I said, "Be still, child, we'll see tomorrow."

"What if I'm not good enough?" she said, her voice small and tight. "Or smart enough, or brave enough, or..."

I kissed her hair to stem the flood of words. "You're a good brave girl," I said. "They can't expect any more of you than that. You're good enough for me, and that'll be true no matter what tomorrow brings." I settled her down in the curve of my arm, and after a while we slept.

I woke before dawn, unsure what had woken me besides the unfamiliar stillness of the ground beneath me when I was used to sleeping aboard ship. Then I saw the two men in their rough clothes bending over our guards in the dying firelight, rifling through their gear. One was skinny and ragged, and the other short and ragged, and it seemed to me I'd seen them on the road. The guards never stirred, though I could see them breathing, and abruptly I remembered the wine.

I reached in my blankets for the knife. Lethe stirred beside me, opening wide eyes. I put a hand hard on her shoulder to still her, and stood up, striding into the firelight. "Oi! Get you gone!" I said, hoping that would be enough to wake the sorceress, and that she hadn't shared in the wine herself.

One of the men laughed. "We're scared, right enough," he said. Colubra was awake, shaking the sorceress by the shoulder, and the woman was stirring under her hand, though slowly.

"So you should be," Myrtale said, and she had a stout stick in her hand. She gave me an approving glance, and that steadied me. Her girl had a stick in her own hand like she meant to use it, her chin up. "I've turned enough drunkards out of my inn in my time."

The skinny man lunged at her abruptly, a knife in his own hand, but Myrtale swung her stick hard and knocked him back. The short man made for the nearest of the girls, and I yelled and went after him.

He pulled a knife, but he didn't much know how to use it, and I knocked it aside easily enough. He waved his knife wildly, leaving himself wide open, and I pressed him back against the wagon hard with my own knife at his throat.

"Drop the knife," I said, and after a moment he did. I'd never had to offer quarter before, but I knew the right words to say. "Now beg mercy," I said.

His voice was scornful. "Won't."

"I'd recommend it," the sorceress said quietly, coming up behind me. Colubra was steadying her with one arm, but the woman still had a power about her that I could feel crackling over my skin. It made all the hairs on my arms stand up, and my braids begin unknotting themselves, as if the hair on my head was straining to grow.

She spoke a single word that sounded as though I ought to know it, though afterwards I couldn't say what it might have been. The trodden grass under the man's feet began to straighten and grow, little creepers reaching up to twine around his ankles and then strengthening to thick vines that seemed strongly rooted in the earth. He swore and twisted away, but couldn't break their grip.

"Do you want him dead?" I said, as hard as I could, though I wasn't sure I could do it like that, in cold blood.

"That depends," the woman said. "Do you ask for the mercy of the Corn Mother?" Her voice was calm and curious, but I could see that the vines were still tightening around his legs, and climbing higher.

"I do, I swear, I do," he stammered out. "Beg pardon, lady."

"Then get you gone," she said, and the creepers and vines that held him released him at once, falling into a withering tangle at his feet. He ran stumbling away, after his fellow, who had fled already, bruised and battered under Myrtale's assault.

There was silence for a moment, and then Myrtale leaned on her stick and laughed. At once all of us broke out laughing, the laughter near tears that comes with great relief. The sorceress put a hand on my shoulder for a moment.

"That was well done," she said. "Now, Colubra. What ails our guards here? I expect you'd know better than I."

Colubra bent over one of them and smelled his breath. "Poppy juice in the wine, I expect," she said. "If they're breathing still, I should think they'd wake by dawn."

"Suppose we have our breakfast, then, and wait until they're fit to stir," the sorceress said. I made as if to put the knife away, and she said aside to me, "And you might keep that handy, Patrice, while we're still on the road."

It was high noon by the time the wagons rattled up the road into the capitol. Olympe looked around like she was steadied by seeing familiar sights. The rest of us gawked and stared more openly than our daughters, who were hiding in their wagon torn between the desire to look and the fear of being stared at. None of us women had much fear of being stared at, and we looked our fill, and caught the flowers and ribbons that were occasionally thrown our way, though none of us reached for any more proffered jars of wine.

The temple rose high and gray on the hill above the city. When the wagons stopped, we clambered out, stiff from the road, and followed the sorceress into a chamber where we could wash and put on our best clothes. Myrtale and her daughter had nothing better than what they were wearing, that being borrowed already, but we did the best we could by the girl, weaving the ribbons we'd caught into her hair while the other girls divided up the flowers.

"It's time," the sorceress said at last, and we followed her out into the paved courtyard. Lethe clung to my hand as if she were a tiny child and not a great girl of twelve, and my heart was in my throat.

It was very quiet in the courtyard. I had expected a festival, with more flower-throwing and a happy crowd, but there were only a row of women in quite ordinary dress, one bearing a cup of something dark, which she handed to the sorceress who had accompanied us all this way on the road. In the center of the courtyard, a stone statue of the Good Mother watched over us, a sculpted figure of a young tree sprouting from one outstretched hand.

"We called you because the Corn Mother needs you, and so does her land," the sorceress said, quite simply. "Some of you will not be chosen today, but that does not mean she does not need you, only that your path is a different one." All the girls were barely breathing, Lethe with her shoulders squared, Ana and Bria clinging to each other's hands. "You will have teachers here in the temple, and a home among us until you are ready to make your way in the world."

The sorceress stepped forward and took Silvia by the hand, the plain girl looking up at her with wide, serious eyes. Olympe caught her breath, and then let it out as the sorceress kissed the girl solemnly on the forehead. "Go with the Corn Mother's blessing," the sorceress said. One of the waiting women took the girl by the arm, leading her away across the courtyard, and I understood then that she was being dismissed.

There was a murmur of mingled disappointment and excitement from the others. The sorceress kissed Kalliste's daughter, and then Myrtale's, and blessed them both as she dismissed them. The girls clung to each other's hands hard as they crossed the courtyard, and the women who led them away spoke kindly to them and stroked their hair.

Toria and Lethe stood looking at each other, neither daring to speak. The sorceress smiled at them both, stroked Toria's brush of hair back from her face, and then pressed a kiss to her forehead. "Go with the Corn Mother's blessing," she said.

Colubra and I both gasped, but neither girl made a sound. Lethe stood as if stunned, her eyes very wide. Toria took a few steps across the courtyard and then turned back to look at her, jealousy clearly warring with curiosity.

The sorceress laid her hand on Lethe's shoulder for a moment, and I couldn't breathe as she kissed Lethe's brow.

"Go with the Corn Mother's blessing," she said.

"But..." I began, but Lethe was already running off across the courtyard. The expression as she turned to go was relief, not misery, and I wondered how I'd escaped realizing before now that her fears were more of what would happen if she was chosen than of what would happen if she were not.

"Do you find them all wanting, then?" Olympe demanded, and for once I was glad of the steel in her voice. She stepped forward, and all of us seemed to welcome her speaking for us, as the only one who wasn't too in awe of the temple to raise her voice here. "A strange thing, when it was you who chose them."

"I chose," the sorceress said, and dipped her fingers into the cup, wetting them with ink. She extended them toward Olympe, who froze, and seemed unable to move even as the sorceress traced the shape of a tree on her forehead. "And I think I chose well."

"I don't understand," Kalliste said. The sorceress turned to her, and traced the tree on her forehead, dark as night against her fair skin.

"The land needs its protectors," she said. "Strong women, clever women, masters of their crafts. Women who have loved and shed tears of grief without growing bitter. It would be a wise woman indeed who could look at a child of thirteen and see all that in her future. Far easier to look at a woman of middle years and see her for what she is."

"Everyone knows you choose innocent maidens," Olympe said, a note of outrage in her voice.

"Sometimes what everyone knows is wrong," the sorceress said gently. She turned to Myrtale, who stiffened, her throat working.

"Bria isn't my own daughter," Myrtale burst out, as if as afraid to speak and even more afraid to stay silent. "Not one of mine ever drew breath, not one. But then this beggar girl came in the inn one day, just a scrap of a thing willing to sweep floors for her keep, and then after the fire...she was all I had."

"She had no one, and you were a mother to her," the sorceress said. She reached up with inkstained fingers and traced the tree on her skin, and the tears came into Myrtale's eyes. "As you have brought a hundred children into the world besides the one you carried in your body," she said, turning to trace the tree on Colubra's dark forehead.

She turned to me, and I held out my hands to ward her off, my throat tightening. "I'm nothing like an innocent," I said. "I've killed two men. I would have killed that one who tried to rob us on the road, if he hadn't begged quarter."

"Only a child can be innocent," the sorceress said. "But a woman can learn when to be merciful." She traced the tree on my forehead, and I felt a new power rising up within me, deep and wild and beyond any command I knew yet how to give, like being borne up by the great surging swells of a wine-dark sea.

Myrtale laughed aloud, and I followed her gaze downward. Between the stones of the courtyard, grass was sprouting, straining up green beneath our feet.

"I see that we had better begin your lessons without delay," the sorceress said, a little dryly. "I warn you, it won't be easy to learn to use what you've been given."

"We're none of us afraid of hard work," I said. "But I expect you knew that already." And we followed her into the temple, ready to begin.

WARMONGER

by Robin Wayne Bailey

They say you can't go home again. That's not precisely true. It would be more accurate to say that when you go back, it won't be the home you remember. Sometimes it's better to stay away and simply keep home in your memory.

Robin Wayne Bailey is the author of numerous novels, including the *Dragonkin* trilogy, the *Frost* series, *Shadowdance* and the Fritz Leiber-inspired *Swords against the Shadowland*. His many short works have appeared in magazines and anthologies, including previous *Sword & Sorceress* volumes, and his newest book is a collection of poetry entitled *The Geometries of Love*. He's a former president of the Science Fiction and Fantasy Writers of America and lives in Kansas City, Missouri.

Basheba stood shivering ankle deep in snow, her slender blade dripping with first blood as she glared at the Winter-Troll that blocked her path. Its pale wrinkled skin and silvery beard rendered it nearly invisible in the blizzard. The creature had risen up from the drifts with a howl of fury, and only instinct had saved her.

The thin gash across its furry stomach was barely a scratch to the monster. With fangs bared, the beast advanced toward her. She ducked its powerful arms, her heart pounding as she leaped outside of its reach and tried to strike again, but her doe-skin boots slipped in the snow, and her point missed its mark. Finding her balance, Basheba turned to fight again.

The Winter-Troll roared a terrible challenge that echoed among the peaks of the Gray Mountains. The sound seemed to go on forever. Basheba choked back her fear. Running from the monster was useless. She stood her ground as it raised shaggy arms.

Basheba's gloved fingers touched the clasp of her cloak. It was desperate, but she snapped the heavy, fur-lined garment at the troll's eyes. It recoiled, and Basheba flung the cloak over its head. Taken by surprise, the beast faltered and howled again. With one sweep of its arm, it flung the cloak away.

It was the chance Basheba needed. She attacked, driving her blade halfway to the hilt in its guts and kicking one booted foot up into its immense groin before she backed away. The troll shrieked in pain and bent forward as blood spilled between its fingers.

A simultaneous rush of panic and triumph seized Basheba. Gripping the hilt of her sword with both hands, she chopped once, then twice at the beast's offered neck. Blood stained the snowy mountainside. She struck a third time, putting all her fear and anger into the blow, and a gigantic bearded head fell into the snow. Its eyes blinked and continued to stare at her. A sound rattled through its ruined throat.

Basheba watched the life fade from huge white eyes, then shook back her dark mane of hair. The icy wind blew upon her exposed skin and falling snow churned about her, but still warmed by the heat of battle, she barely noticed. Her heart pounded, yet little by little, her breathing slowed and she calmed.

"We need fewer trolls," she muttered.

A sudden strong gust of wind blew down the side of the mountain. The driving snow stung her flesh. Shielding her eyes, she gazed upward into the maelstrom toward the mountain peak, which still seemed far away. Wiping her sword clean on the dead troll's pale fur, she sheathed the blade, then recovered her cloak of leather and fur, and put it on again. The cold penetrated through her wet, doe-skin boots. She felt the first tingling sensations that warned of frost-bite.

Suddenly, she heard a cry, a small sound that echoed from deep in the mountains. She wondered if it was Malcolm. The blizzard had separated them an hour or more ago. Lifting her head, she called his name and listened. Her only answer was more echoes.

Basheba scowled and took out her frustration on the troll's corpse. Grabbing a handful of beard, she flung the bloody head around and around, and then let go, sending it flying down the mountainside. It disappeared into the snowstorm, and if it ever hit the ground, she couldn't tell it.

Once more, she called for Malcolm and listened to the echoes, but the snow was filling her ears and making icicles in her hair. Basheba dared not linger. Drawing a frigid breath, she tugged up her fur-lined hood and started up the mountainside again, putting one heavy foot in front of the other, certain that she had long ago lost the path.

The shrieking wind changed its note, and the driving snow slammed against her from a new direction. Daring to peek from beneath her hood, Basheba spied a rocky outcropping to her left, a rough overhang of stone with space beneath to take shelter. She made for that and, cramming her body into the narrow space, began scooping handfuls of snow to build a fragile wall around herself. Now, the worst of the wind and ice could not get at her.

It was, at best, a place of brief rest. Her fort might keep at bay the storm's ravage, but it could not keep out the cold. If she stayed long, she would freeze and die. She rubbed her gloved hands together, wiggled warmth into her toes and ate some snow. Then, just as she thought to relax a little, she saw it—staring back at her through her hastily made wall, caked in the snow, a human skull, its eye sockets black with death, the remains of a shattered helmet still upon its head.

Basheba jumped, banged her head on the ceiling of her stony shelter and scrambled back into its deepest corner. Her heart hammered as she stared at the obscenity. It seemed to laugh at her, to mock her fear. Basheba didn't like being mocked. Cautiously, she eased her sword from its sheath and poked the point through the skull's right eye. The socket cracked. Basheba cursed under her breath, then kicked at the skull, dislodging it. Her snowy fort crumbled, and the wind swept in.

No matter. She hadn't come all this way to hide in a storm. Sheathing her sword, she crawled out of her shelter to face the elements again and whatever lurked in them. Too many lives depended on her, too many people she cared about.

Never care for anyone. It made life easier, she had told herself before, but she kept forgetting her own lesson. Gathering her cloak tight around her, she called across the white wasteland. "Malcolm!" The echo faded quickly in the screaming snow.

Glancing upward toward the mountain's unseeable peak, Basheba resumed her climb. She hadn't gone far when she slipped and fell. Something made a loud *crack!* At first she feared it was her arm, but once that shock wore off, she dug into the snow and found pieces of bone. Lots of bones and lots of skulls. Among those, she also found weapons. Putting a gloved hand to her mouth, she turned in a slow circle, fearful and gasping. Some army had passed this way before. She stood upon a killing ground.

For a moment, the moaning in the wind took on a new significance. Slowly, she picked up an axe from the snow, judged its balance and its weight, and fought down her superstitious terror. It wasn't ghosts she heard, just the keening storm. Still, she clung to the axe and tucked it beneath her cloak.

She hadn't gambled on the storm. Neither had Malcolm. The skies had been cold, but clear, when they passed through the northern gates of Kresh and marched side by side across the frozen fields into the Gray Mountains. Only once had she looked back to note their footprints marking the long way.

Malcolm, though, he looked back often, his bitter gaze following their footprints back through the gates, his eyes red and tearful and filled with anger, as if he could see his wife and daughter still watching in the rough hands of the guards.

Basheba's thoughts wandered as she moved among the frozen bones and weaponry. Tales of war between Kresh and Condor had reached her half a world away. For a while, she put the stories aside, yet they gnawed at her. She had known her share of war and battle. Over the days and months as the tales grew worse, she found herself dreaming of the mountains and wondering if she had any family left.

Malcolm had been all, only Malcolm with a wife and daughter.

A half-glimpsed shape drew Basheba's thoughts back to the present. Something shuffled through the storm off to her left. Gripping the axe with one hand, putting her other hand to the hilt of her sword, she froze and watched. A second shape moved through the blizzard, then a third. Breathless, Basheba watched them. *Three Winter-trolls!*

The beasts had not seen her yet. Basheba thanked her luck. Cautiously, she knelt down, then stretched out on her back. With her hood close about her face and the axe upon her chest, she began to scoop snow around her body, concealing her form beneath a freezing white blanket.

Through narrowed eyes, she watched the shaggy beasts draw closer and prayed they could not hear the thumping of her heart. She might have beaten one troll, but never three. As the first troll stepped over her feet, she clenched her teeth to prevent them chattering. The second and the third nearly stepped on her.

The snowfall filled her eyes. Buried, afraid to move, Basheba remained still. Only when the cold became too much did she sit up and shake herself. The Winter-trolls had moved on. Dusk had segued to darkness, but the storm had not abated. She was alone on the bleak landscape, cold and shivering.

Basheba stared back down the mountain slope. The snow had filled in her tracks, obliterating any evidence of her passage. In the dark of night, she held no real hope of retreating. Nor could she merely stand still, for that meant a freezing death. Left with but one choice, she gripped her axe and climbed. The lives of Malcolm's wife and child depended up her reaching the summit.

Katrina and little Triana—mother and daughter, so alike in appearance. Basheba had remembered Katrina as young and beautiful, even flirtatious. The iron gray in her hair and the deep crow's feet around Katrina's eyes had startled Basheba.

No more, though, than Basheba's sudden appearance had startled Katrina. Malcolm's wife had stared at her with slow recognition across a bread-baking oven, her expression turning from surprise to fear. A door quickly slammed, lanterns dimmed, and Katrina's hand on Basheba's elbow hurrying her into the gloomiest corner of the small home—the memories pelted

Basheba with as much force as the wind-driven snow. And Triana, whom Malcolm called his *Little Snock*, the gods only knew why, looking confused as she clung to her mother's aprons with flour-smeared face and hands.

Basheba could hear Katrina's whispering still in her head. "Why did you come back? You don't know what you've done! Why did you ever come back?"

Now Malcolm was lost, probably dead in the storm. Maybe the trolls had gotten him, or maybe he had fallen. Maybe he had just fallen asleep. Her brother was no warrior, only an unpretentious potter who worked clay and kept to himself. Basheba had to admit that she barely knew him. She hadn't recognized him at all when he walked in a few moments behind her. She had tried to tell herself then that it was only the dimmed light. It wasn't the light, however—it was the years between them.

The way up the mountain dictated itself even in the storm. The open slopes were behind her now. Icy walls of stone and sharp juts rose on both sides of her. Finding another outcropping, she paused again out of the wind to rest for a few moments, but the cold penetrated her furs, and a growing sense of guilt compelled her forward.

As she stepped out of her narrow shelter to resume her ascent, her axe scraped on stone, causing sparks that lit up her hooded face. The unexpected light dazzled her eyes. For just a moment, she saw a figure in her path—*Little Snock*, but it wasn't flour that smeared her tiny face, it was rime and ice.

Basheba dismissed the vision with a short laugh. With only memories and hallucinations for company, she was going to die here. Soon, she would be just another pile of frozen bones, like the bones crunching beneath her boots, like the skulls laughing at her as she stepped over them.

She scraped her axe upon stone deliberately, causing more sparks. Let the trolls see her and come.

Her legs were past fatigue, and her feet tingled with frostbite. Though she gripped the axe tightly, she hardly seemed to feel its handle. The weight of ice accumulating on her cloak make her walk bent over. Sometimes she stopped to catch her breath, but the air only burned her mouth and nostrils.

Then, the wolf blocked her way, and its eyes shone with hunger. At first, she thought it another hallucination, but when the creature sprang at her, she reacted without thinking. The axe came up and carved a gash in the wolf's shoulder. It howled, contorted in mid-leap and landed on all fours. It snarled and regarded her with greater caution before it sprang again. Basheba moved also, but too slowly this time. The creature slammed her to the snowy ground; its claws dug into her furs and its jaws strained for her throat. Tangled in her heavy cloak, she still brought the axe up hard under the wolf's chin. It retreated again, and somehow she found her feet.

Rage and fear overtook her. Basheba drew her sword. Doubly armed, she met the wolf's next attack. The lighter sword slashed across its snarling throat, and as it twisted away, she swung the axe in a wild arc. Blood poured upon the snow as the wolf stumbled. For a moment, Basheba lost all reason. She didn't count her blows, but when she stopped, the wolf was dead at her feet.

She gasped, staring at what she'd done. Then, she knelt down, removed her stiff gloves and thrust her hands into the creature's wounds. She gasped as the warm blood stung her frozen fingers. It felt like putting her hands in fire, but she did what was necessary.

Then, after a little while, she carved a piece of muscle from the wolf's carcass and chewed it. The blood tasted coppery and bitter, but she choked the meat down, grateful for the nourishment and the energy it brought. When she was finished, she washed her mouth out with snow. She regretted that there was not time to skin the wolf properly, yet one more thin pelt wouldn't have done her much good.

The wind screamed more fiercely than ever as she resumed her march to the summit. She tried not to think of the skulls and bones that littered the mountainside, the remains of men who had attempted this trek before her, men blackmailed into undertaking an ill-fated quest under threat from their queen, the Queen of

Kresh. She tried to resist superstition, but she heard their voices in the wind, their rage in the storm. She clutched her hood closer, hoping to muffle the angry wailing, and for the sake of Malcolm's wife and daughter, she pressed on, blackmailed as those men had been.

The rocky trail changed. It became a true path now and soon rough-hewn stone steps emerged. The steps were immense, as if carved for the feet of giants, and snow made them treacherous and slick. Basheba started up the unnatural cascade, unconsciously counting the steps and thinking of Malcolm.

She remembered the look on his face when he first saw her in his home, how joy had turned immediately to fear, how he had echoed Katrina's very words. "You shouldn't have come back! Oh, my sister! You shouldn't have come back!"

My sister.

After fifteen years and too many battles, Basheba had come home to Kresh to find her family, to learn if any of them still lived. In a world of constant war, she had held little hope. Still, weary and lonely, she had followed her heart. It had led her with only a little effort to Malcolm, grown up and handsome, a husband and a father, and he had cried, "You shouldn't have come back!"

The driving snow slackened, and the wind died away. The blizzard passed. A soft powder fell upon the mountainside as Basheba continued to climb, and then even that ceased. She stopped to marvel as the clouds broke apart. A three-quarter moon bled light upon the staircase, and the snowy ground sparkled.

In the moon's glow, Basheba climbed faster, sensing that her destination was near. Her heart raced. A warrior going into battle, she prepared herself to face the unexpected, no matter that she barely understood the stakes. In a moment with her guard down, the soldiers of the queen had taken her too quickly, and Malcolm and his family, too. She hadn't even been able to fight back with Triana, *Little Snock*, standing so close.

The guards of Kresh had noted the arrival of a strange warrior, overheard her inquiries, and followed her. By coming home, Basheba had endangered her family. In little time, the soldiers dragged them to the court of the Black Queen. Draped in shadows and diamonds, her face unseen, the Queen spoke to them from her throne.

"You have been chosen, she said as she pointed at them, like so many before you. Go to the Gray Mountains to the Palace of the Moon and bring me the Demonfang, that I might use its power to smite Condor and all others who would oppose me."

Malcolm had clenched his teeth and said nothing while Katrina sobbed. Without even a chance to kiss his wife goodbye or hug his daughter, he and Basheba were marched to the Northern Gates where they were given weapons and packs and pushed into the cold wasteland.

The memory angered Basheba. Later, her brother had told her a little more, how the Black Queen had become obsessed with a legendary weapon, how she had sent soldiers at first, then criminals, and finally any able-bodied man, into the mountains, always taking their families hostage to insure their service.

Basheba thought of all the bones she had tread upon in the snow and repressed a shiver.

A thin wisp passed over the moon, and the light dimmed. When it shone bright again, she found herself upon the last step at the edge of a plateau. The flat, snow-covered surface shimmered. She stood at the top of the world and gazed over the side into black valleys, at the shadowed peaks of lesser mountains. The sight took her breath away.

Yet, a more amazing sight greeted her when she turned. An imposing structure seemingly made of ice and moonlight rose up on the farthest edge of the plateau. Smooth, crenelated walls reached up into the sky. Slender towers and minarets soared to impossible heights. In all her travels, Basheba had never seen its like.

The Palace of the Moon.

Gripping her axe in one hand, drawing her sword with the other, Basheba strode toward the structure. Her boots crunched in the snow, and her shadow ran before her. Again, she heard Malcolm's words in her head. *"Witch or goddess?"* he had told her, *"or something else? No one knows who built the palace— the legends never say who lives in it."*

Her hands tightened on her weapons as she advanced. Nothing moved among the crenellations. No other shadows stirred on the smooth snow. A patch showed in the palace wall directly before her. A doorway, maybe, or a gate. She set her course for it.

The wind died away to nothing. Beneath her heavy garments, the hair on her neck stood on end. No wind on such a high mountain? It wasn't natural. But then, nothing about Gray Mountain seemed natural. Fighting a growing fear, Basheba continued toward the gateway, and as she got closer, she perceived a black, shapeless thing near it. Slowly, as if hearing her footsteps on the crisp snow, the shapeless thing moved. A gloved hand appeared from deep folds of fur and pushed back a hood.

Basheba stared in disbelief as Malcolm looked up, his face white, tears frozen on his cheeks. "Brother!" she gasped, dropping sword and axe as she threw herself down to embrace him. His gaze locked on her face, and his eyes took a moment to focus.

"I knew you would make it." He spoke in a hoarse whisper, as if the cold had numbed his speech. "You were always the best of us, Sister." His joints creaked as he lifted his arms and wrapped them around her. "The little fighter, the little warmonger who beat the boys at everything."

Fighting back tears, Basheba pressed her face to his. "I only wanted to come home, Malcolm! I was tired of fighting!"

Malcolm stroked the back of her head as he held her. "I know, I know," he answered gently. "I couldn't believe my eyes when I saw you in my house."

"I'm sorry!"

He shook his head. "It's not your fault. I've—I've waited here to tell you that." Malcolm gave a weak laugh. "I couldn't get in anyway."

Basheba leaned back to look at her brother. No blood showed in his face, no color in his lips. Without regard for her own safety, she whipped off her cloak and added it to his. Then, holding him close, she rubbed his cheeks and arms in a desperate effort to warm him. "Malcolm!" she shouted. "Get up! Stay with me!" She felt him slipping away. Malcolm really had waited for her. She tried to pull Malcolm to his feet. "Look!" she said. "You beat me here! You beat me!" But Malcolm didn't move. "You're all I've got!" she cried.

His gaze fixed on her face. His voice was barely audible. "You've got more family than you know," he whispered. Then, the smallest smile turned up the corners of his lips. "I'm glad you came home, Basheba."

Her name faded as her brother died in her arms, one more casualty of the Gray Mountains. There was no way to bury him or get him back down to Kresh. His bones would lie here among all the others. Yet he, a mere potter, had made it all the way to the Palace of the Moon.

Basheba lurched to her feet, blind with rage. With all her might, she lunged at the gateway. It refused to open. She pounded with her fists and called challenges. Still the gates remained sealed. A snarl on her lips, she seized up her axe. Every muscle in her body strained as she swung the blade. The edge left not a mark, but she swung again and again, determined to chop her way inside.

"Come out!" she called, and finally exhausted, she sank to her knees, dropping her axe, and begged. "Let me in. Whoever you are, let me in."

The gates eased open just wide enough to admit her. Basheba looked up and got slowly to her feet. For a moment, she thought of taking up her axe and reclaiming her sword. Instead, she stepped over the axe, leaving it in the snow. Half numb, she walked inside.

A harsh voice spoke from the icy gloom. "Have you come to attack me and steal from me like all the others?" It was a woman's voice, but filled with age and power.

"No," Basheba answered. "I came because I loved my brother—and if you really existed, to ask a question."

The gloom subtly brightened, though Basheba could not say

how. No fire sprang to life, no candles or lamps. She stood in the presence of magic. A figure appeared in the shifting light, a contradictory shape that stood bent with the weight of years, yet with a child's youthful face. "A question?"

"Why?" Basheba asked. She found herself glancing away, unable to look for long at her host, whose form shifted randomly and always in contradictory ways. But the creature looked at her, and she felt the weight of its gaze. "What is it you have that the Black Queen of Kresh so covets? What is the *Demonfang?*"

The creature chuckled, its voice turning masculine. "That is three questions," it observed. "But I have not spoken with anyone for a long time, and your company amuses me. You have the look of a warrior and the heart of one, yet something is different about you." The creature made the slightest of gestures. "Allow me to thaw your bones before I send you on your way again."

The air began to warm comfortably, chasing the chill from Basheba, who also perceived the gateway closing behind her.

The creature spoke again. "The answer to your first question is *why not?* There are many forces at work in this world. They are all capricious and most are malicious. You are covered in blood inside and out. All humans are, even when you deny it. It's your nature." The creature changed again, its form straightening as its face took on the aspect of death. "You already know the answer to your second question. Might as well call her the Mad Queen, for she is that. She desires an ultimate weapon to vanquish her enemies, but such as she never lacks for enemies. As soon as she vanquishes them, she makes more. That is her nature."

Basheba tried yet again to look directly at her host, but the strange figure seemed to slip back into darkness. Suddenly, she thought that perhaps the creature did not really want to be seen. "I'm sorry," she apologized, diverting her gaze again.

"You are quite civilized for your kind," came the almost musical response. "Now to your third question, and then you must go back to your own world. "The *Demonfang is* a small thing, a trifle actually, at least in appearance. Yet, it is exactly the weapon Kresh's queen desires. It is older than time, and its true powers are unknown even to me. Indeed, its powers may change with the holder. This much I know, however—whoever holds the *Demonfang* becomes invincible."

"That's why the queen wants it," Basheba said under her breath. "She wants to use it to crush Condor. Then who would be next?"

The creature shook its head. "I've answered three questions, but no more. Time for you to go, Warrior. Take up your weapons, for the path down the mountain is no less treacherous than the ascent."

Basheba felt herself pushed gently away. She had more questions, wanted to know so much more, yet she thought it wise not to resist. *Back to your world*, the creature had said. *Your world.* The gateway opened and closed, and Basheba found herself outside the palace in the bitter cold once more. She wondered if it had all been a dream.

Reluctantly, she reclaimed her cloak from her dead brother and donned his, as well, for extra warmth. Grief stabbed her heart as she looked upon his body, but she picked up her weapons. As she pushed her sword into its sheath, she also made a strange discovery. Her weapons were three now. A slender jeweled dagger hung upon a belt around her waist.

By some strange instinct, she knew its name.

~oOo~

The guards at the Northern Gate saw her approaching. More guards were summoned as she entered Kresh. They surrounded her with eyes full of suspicion and awe and escorted her directly to the Queen's Court, which was a long, low chamber lit with braziers and sconces. Still more guards flooded in behind her, and the queen's entourage turned out as well to see the only warrior who had ever returned from the Gray Mountains. In truth, Basheba knew, they turned out to see the prize.

The guards stopped halfway into the chamber and parted into two ranks, two lines reaching all the way up to the throne. For some long minutes, Basheba waited patiently, her thoughts on Malcolm, his words playing in her head. *I'm glad you came home, Basheba.* His last words didn't make her smile. There had been time to think as she descended the mountain, and time to reflect. *You have more family than you know.*

The Black Queen stepped out of the shadows just into the edge of the light. She sparkled with the cold fire of diamonds. Her eyes shone with a different fire. "Do you have it?" she demanded without so much as a welcome or congratulation.

"Yes," Basheba answered. The crowd broke into gasps and murmuring.

"Well, give it to me!" The Black Queen extended an insistent hand.

Basheba listened and observed and touched the clasps that held her cloak and her brother's around her shoulders. The garments fell to the floor. Basheba countered the demand with one of her own. "Bring out Katrina and Triane, the wife and daughter of my brother, Malcolm."

The Black Queen scowled. "They were of no further use to me, and so they are dead. I never really expected either of you to succeed where so many others had already failed." Her voice rose to a shriek. "Now show me the *Demonfang!*"

Basheba smiled to herself and brushed her fingers over the dagger she wore. The Black Queen did not recognize the weapon she so coveted. For a long moment, she studied the woman in all her diamonds, the woman who had killed Malcolm and Katrina and *Little Snock.* She had never found time to ask her brother about that odd nickname. It didn't matter now.

You have more family than you know.

Basheba drew back her shoulders and spoke up. "Why are you hiding from me, Isabella?" she said. "Malcolm was not my only sibling. Step into the light, Sister, and let me hear you welcome me home."

The Black Queen faltered and put one hand on the throne. Then, she stepped into the light of a brazier. Basheba regarded her with a measure of sadness. Isabella might have been beautiful but for the madness and rage that contorted her features. Basheba wondered briefly how her sister had become the queen of Kresh, but that didn't matter now, either.

"One last time," Isabella ordered. If she recognized Basheba, she gave no sign of it. "Give me what I desire or my guards will take it from your corpse! Give me what is mine!"

"No," Basheba answered.

The Black Queen sneered. "Then die, Sister. You've been gone a long time. Your life means nothing to me."

The guards moved toward Basheba, but they had neglected to take her weapons. She raised the axe and drew her sword. At her side, the *Demonfang* purred like something alive, and Basheba felt a cold satisfaction. She moved through the chamber like a storm, dealing death to guards and soldiers and to anyone else who came within her reach.

When she was done, Basheba looked over the carnage toward the throne and her sister, who cowered behind it. "This power will never be yours," she told Isabella. "Set your dreams aside and run. Never let me find you again."

"You shouldn't have come back!" Isabella screamed.

"I've heard that before." Basheba turned away from her sister and looked to the handful of courtiers who still remained. "Choose another queen," she advised. "Kresh deserves better."

"You, Warrior!" one of the courtiers dared to call. "Be our new queen!"

Basheba answered with a bitter laugh as she gathered up her cloaks. Disheveled and drenched in blood, yet unscathed, she left the court, made her way through half-remembered streets where she had played as a child, and departed the city. Kresh had nothing to hold her, and her place was on the battlefield.

That was her nature.

GIFT HORSES

by Samantha Rich

"Don't look a gift horse in the mouth" is an old saying, and most times it's good advice. There are, however, a few times when it's not.

Samantha Rich is a nonprofit professional who grew up on *Sword & Sorceress*, MZB, and genre fiction in general. She lives in Maryland with a (bossy) cat and a (nervous) dog. This is her first fiction publication.

Khalla stood in the doorway and watched the sun fill up the stableyard. She checked the angle of the light against the guidestones in the distance, the spire at the top of the temple, the line of the earth at the horizon. They told her what she already knew; there were still weeks until highsummer.

Last night the moon had told her the same. Still weeks to go. Patience. Braid and tie and pin, count the hours, bide your time. All will be well.

From the corner of her eye she saw Perrin, Lord Rymon's chancellor, step from the entry to the great hall. She moved back into the shadows of the stable itself, her breath hitching in her chest. She had been at the keep nearly a year, since just after last highsummer. She'd learned to fear Perrin more than the rest by far.

Lord Rymon himself was no threat. His legs and hands were too twisted with age for him to ride or fight. Among her people, he would have been valued for his wisdom, given a place close to the fire and extra bits of meat. She might even have liked him.

Here, at the keep, she only hoped that he would die faster and easier than Perrin.

She turned back to her morning chores. She had fed the horses before she stopped to look at the sun and now they were all nearly done with their feed, snuffling softly as they chased to the corners of their feed bags for a last missed kernel. She walked down the row of them, her hands gentle on their flanks, checking each one over for injury. They must all be unmarked, glossy hide and strong bone, bright eyes and good tendon.

They were holding up well. She whispered in their soft-pricked ears, promising them a turnout later in one of the keep's rolling pastures. Despite the fences that kept them bound, there was enough room for the horses to stretch their legs and shake the dust from their hooves. Bound but not pinched, she would give the keep that much credit.

The sun had almost reached the threshold of the stable. Over the next few hours it would make its way down the aisle to touch the far wall. Khalla had one more task before then.

She returned to the first stall and set to work, checking the neat, tiny braids in the horse's mane and forelock. Each braid was bound tightly at the end in extra horsehair, with a small wooden charm threaded and pinned in place over the binding. Khalla re-plaited the braids that had softened, re-bound those that threatened to slip, and double-checked every pin. The horses whuffled softly in her ears and brushed soft noses against her neck and shoulder, still and patient for her ministrations.

Khalla sang softly as she worked, the words indistinct and barely audible under her tongue. They were old words, powerful words, and she worked them into every braid and every charm, envisioning them building up slowly in the stones and beams of the building and on the dust of the floor. The sun would bake them there over the course of the day, every day, as it had done for nearly a year.

The turning of a year was a propitious amount of time. Soon there would be enough power built up. She knew it.

~oOo~

The day Khalla arrived at the keep, it had rained. She stood outside the gate soaked to the skin and shivering, holding the reins of her own horse with twenty others arranged in a loose herd behind, the edges held in place by grim-faced outriders.

They were a gift to Lord Rymon, tribute from a newly conquered foe who had always considered themselves a neighbor. He wanted the land they held in settlements from autumn to spring, before they rode out with the herds for the summer. Perhaps he'd wanted the herdland, too, who could say? All that her people knew was that soldiers swept through and they had to ride hard and abandon almost everything to stay alive.

The settlements were burned. A long stretch of the herdland was burned, wildfire chasing at the animals' heels like hellwind. Their choices dwindled until they yielded.

Yielded, surrendered, and offered a gift in tribute: twenty horses and a bondslave-girl to tend them.

"The savages do have the finest horses this side of the Old Sea, my lord," Perrin had said. "They would bring fine new blood into our stock."

Khalla had smiled at them, showing all of her teeth, and Perrin cuffed her on the side the head, giving her her first lesson in the fort's type of humility.

The outriders had gone back to the plains with a note of acceptance of their tribute, a promise of benevolence, and Khalla's horse. She stayed behind with the twenty horses.

The next morning, when the sun broke weakly through the clouds to touch the stableyard, she braided the charms into their manes and forelocks and bound them there.

~o0o~

The moon and the sun continued their careful paces toward highsummer. Khalla groomed and rode the horses, checked them for cuts and bumps, tended them with the care that the people of the keep showed their small chapel and its dusty icons. She cleaned their stalls, oiled their hooves and their bridles, and every morning she tightened the braids and bindings of the charms.

The stablemaster and the ragged band of boys and girls who served as grooms and jacks-of-all-sorts left her to herself, mostly. They brought grain over in great bags and poured it into the well-worn barrels so she could measure it out to her charges, and whenever she needed a rasp for a chipped hoof or a bottle of liniment for a sore muscle, they provided. They watched from the edge of the pen when she rode the horses, and many times she had seen them out by the pasture fence, watching her charges play in the sun.

They didn't interfere, and they never asked about the charms. For that, she hoped that they, too, either escaped or died quickly.

She knew that she was greatly fortunate that Perrin rarely set foot in the stables. She could just imagine if he did; the sharp snick of his hand-knife through horsehair, the charms falling to the dust and ground underfoot, her work made precarious and dangerous and a hundred times more difficult in a moment.

She thanked her gods for their protection daily, and whenever she passed the little chapel she spared a thought for the blank-faced figures depicted in the icons, thanking them for the courtesy of looking the other way.

~o0o~

More days passed, and the sun came almost in line for highsummer. Khalla's fingers were clumsy as she wove and bound the braids, and the horses were fractious, tossing their heads and shifting restlessly in their stalls. When she turned them out to pasture, they ran from the gate to the far end, almost out of her sight, then wheeled and ran back again, jostling each other and tossing dust high into the air. Khalla stood gripping the rail of the fence in her hands, watching them. Their eyes were wild and sweat ran freely from their flanks, dampening the hide of their chest and bellies. Their tails lashed the air, themselves, each other, nearly crackling with static and contained power.

If the sky hadn't been so clear, she would have assumed a storm was rising to bring such trembling energy into the air. But the storm was carried inside the horses, raised by nearly a year of sunlight and moonlight and whispered words, gathering power almost to a peak.

When she walked back to the keep's kitchen for her midday meal, she saw Perrin and the head of Lord Rymon's guard deep in conversation at the edge of the hall. She pressed herself into the shadows and lowered her face, pretending to be engrossed in the cuff of her sleeve.

"There's nothing they can give in tribute that it won't be easier to take," Perrin said. "Fire the grasses, chase them to the river where their villages stood, meet them there with soldiers and put them to the sword. Easy enough."

"Take the livestock and the horses." The head of the guard nodded and shrugged a shoulder indifferently. "What about the wool and fabrics and leather? The nomads are very good with those sorts of things."

"They do wonders with animals, I must agree. Logical enough, being all but animals themselves." Perrin smiled, a twist of the mouth that made Khalla bite down hard on her tongue. "Once we have the stock, we can do our own work with the wool and leather. Their techniques are interesting but hardly required."

"As you say, sir. When do we ride?"

"A week's time." Perrin clapped the man on the shoulder and began walking toward the door, guiding him along into the courtyard. "Lord Rymon has left all this in my hands, you know. Seems like a lovely gift to give the savages for their highsummer."

Khala waited for sixty breaths before she allowed herself to move, forcing her jaw to unclench as she took slow, careful steps toward the kitchen. So things were in motion faster than she'd known. She owed her own gods a twist of sagegrass and a spill of milk in thanks, and the fort's dead-eyed icons one of the candles they seemed to care for so much.

And she needed to hurry on to the last steps of her work. A year less several days would have to be enough power, gods be with her. Gods, sun, moon, and song.

~o0o~

She sat by the window that night in the servant bunks, working by the light of the waxing moon. It was nearly full. Two more days, she knew that in her heart. She had the sun and moon of this place woven into herself now, deep into her skin and bone.

She turned bits of wood this way and that, judging the lines and angles of the grain in the pale light, and then took her knife to it again, shaving away delicate curls of bark and pulp until she had the shape she wanted.

A tiny sword was growing under her fingers, coming clear from the chip it had started as. She would rub a nail over it to bring the flat of it smooth and let iron kiss its surface, and then she would drive a pin through the hilt so steel kissed its heart.

At her side in the dust lay two more swords and the delicate curve of a bow, strung with a single horsehair. Arrows would come the next night, when she'd had a chance to gather twigs from the horses' tails.

A shadow fell across her, breaking the moonlight, and she looked up, her fingers tightening on the knife as she found Perrin looking down on her. The moonlight did cruel things to his face, turning it to a gaunt mask, but the smirk was all his own.

"What are you doing awake, little slave?" She didn't answer, and he reached down, taking the wooden sword from her hand and turning it between his fingers. "Making toys?"

"It's nothing," she whispered, feeling blood bloom between her fingers where she still clutched the knife. The other servants were asleep. Perrin had no reason to be here, and no one would suspect he was. She could lunge and slash, right now; she could cut the artery in his thigh, or his throat, she could—

She couldn't leave the horses.

She eased her grip on the knife and took a breath. "It's nothing, sir. Just a way to pass the time when I can't sleep."

"Well. Have a care, girl." He snapped the sword in half between his fingers and dropped the pieces to the dirt. "You might prick your finger."

He walked across the room as slowly as a ghost and faded into the night, seeming to take some of the moonlight with him. She had to blink frantically and count her breaths to slow her heart before she could see again.

She wiped the bloody knife on her trousers and studied the broken halves of the sword. Well. She could cut those up into slivers for the arrows, at least.

She took another woodchip from her pocket and began to carve again, letting the edges taste blood this time.

~oOo~

Two nights later she stood in the doorway, watching the moonlight make its way across the stableyard. One hand was full of a tangle of horsehair and wooden charms, cut neatly away from the horses' manes and forelocks.

The other hand held steel pins, and her pocket bulged with delicate wooden weapons, kissed with iron and blood.

She turned back into the stable and walked down the aisle again, stopping at each stall to weave a new braid, bind it off, and pin a weapon in place. A sword here, a bow and delicate charmed arrows next, an axe. Smooth wooden discs, rubbed to a sheen with boiled leather, were tied on with a single hair, each one a shield.

As she finished each one, she kissed the horse between the eyes and touched the point of her knife there, still dark with her own blood.

When each horse was ready, she went back to the stableyard, sitting down in the dust with her back to the closed doors, and waited.

She sang, too softly for any ears but her own and the gods', and waited for the sun to rise. When it was high enough to touch her face, she closed her eyes.

When she opened them, the stable door opened behind her, and the warriors came out.

PLAUSIBLE DENIABILITY

by Cat & Bari Greenberg

Speaking of undesirable gift horses, here's a story about a woman who survived one. Cassandra, as you may know, was cursed by Apollo. She had the gift of prophecy, but his curse made everyone disbelieve her. She told the Trojans not to bring a large hollow wooden horse left by the Greek army inside the city's walls, but they didn't listen to her.

Cat and Bari Greenberg are a married writing team. Bari is an engineer by day and writer by night and this is his publishing debut. Cat was previously published under the name Sandra Morrese (*S&S 11, Four Moons of Darkover*, and *MZB's Fantasy Magazine*) and by day works part-time for a greeting card company. In addition to fiction, they also write filk songs together which are recorded by their band, The Unusual Suspects. They currently have two albums out from their studio, Mountain Cat Media. They live in St. Louis along with four cats and a dog.

Unfortunately, Bari passed away from a heart attack on August 17, 2014, so he won't see his story in print, but it's a part of him that still lives on.

The queen stalked closer, her face a mask of rage. She gripped an axe still dripping the king's blood from its ornate blade. The younger woman stood simply watching her. She didn't run, or cower or scream; there was no point. This was all expected.

She had warned the king, but of course he hadn't believed her. No one ever did. But this time, she was pleased he hadn't listened. For once, the curse had worked in her favor.

"I am not your enemy, Clytemnestra," she said quietly, looking the older woman in the eye as the queen raised the axe to strike. "And I am already dead."

Queen Clytemnestra paused, held by the younger woman's

steady, direct gaze.

"I have nothing," she said. "I am nothing. I have been raped, beaten and held against my will by the same man you just executed. I owe you thanks for that. From where I stand, he got better than he deserved."

The Queen's eyes flickered. This was clearly not the reaction she expected. The axe lowered.

"Kassandra, Princess of Troia," she said, "my late husband's war prize."

"Troia is destroyed, my family slain. I no longer have a birthright, *or* a home." She kept her eyes locked on the Queen's as she continued. "I have done you no wrong, nor do I stand here by choice. Am I to blame for Agamemnon's deeds? I beg of you one mercy: say I am dead and let me go. I wish only to disappear and live out my life in peace and anonymity."

Kassandra watched the blind rage leave Clytemnestra's eyes. The head of the axe lowered slowly to the floor; she then released the handle. The clatter of gilt wood striking marble echoed like judgment through the hall.

"There has been enough death in this house," Clytemnestra said. She clapped sharply and a guard appeared. "The king is dead, as is his concubine. This is Eurayle, a servant of the princess. We grant her mercy, but banish her from Mycenae. Escort her out of the city at once."

Kassandra bowed deeply, then wrapped her travel cloak tightly about herself, hiding her face and hair, and the fine gown no servant would own, as she followed the guard.

She was alive. She was free. But free to go where? Do what? Her thoughts skittered like beads spilled on marble. Belatedly, she realized the guard was talking.

"I'm sorry," she said softly. "What did you say?"

"Which way? North gate or south?"

"I...have no idea. Which direction would you suggest?"

Did she see pity in his eyes?

"Go north. There's been trouble on the south road. A caravan's heading out. You could buy passage with them."

~o0o~

Kassandra walked the northern road overwhelmed and dazed by her escape. She'd seen her own death, yet here she was, walking safely away from that grisly fate, although history would say otherwise. That meant the futures she saw *could* be changed!

The irony of the name Eurayle did not escape her—it meant "wanders far," a subtle message from the queen. Which was fine, it matched her fervent desire to leave more than a decade of horror and tragedy far behind. And all because she said no to a god.

As a priestess of Apollo, Kassandra had learned herb lore and basic healing arts. She was able to barter her skills for a place in the caravan, which had no healer of its own. The days passed in peace and Kassandra felt her previous life fade, marveling at her incredible turn of fortune. She was Eurayle now, who spent her time cataloging the herbs they stocked, determining how much to save and how much could be sold or traded. They stopped in towns for only a few days at a time. She was even learning how to cook.

A different life, simpler yet more labored, but she embraced it. The Achaeans were not her enemy, only their rulers were. These people had not attacked her city or murdered its citizens. They were good, honest and decent. They didn't judge her and no one pried into her past.

~oOo~

She'd had no visions since Mycenae and was just beginning to wonder if she might finally be free of Apollo's so-called gift when she woke with an all too familiar headache.

Most of her visions began with the same dull ache behind her eyes, then flashed a series of dreamlike images, and ended with slight disorientation. Not this one. It slammed her with a migraine fit to fell a Titan, pitching her into a swirling maelstrom darker than Hades. When the roiling mists dissolved into clouds and parted, she was standing on a pinnacle of rock.

One side overlooked a wide ridge with a modest acropolis. In the valley on the other side sat a well-kept small town. As she watched the town, it grew until it became a bustling city branching inland from the sea toward the ridge.

She turned and watched the acropolis grow commensurately magnificent with beautiful polished white stone adorned with colorful frescoes. Throngs of well-dressed pilgrims filled the aisles.

A blast of wind and dust accompanied an earthquake-like rumble, sweeping through the acropolis. The stones became weathered and grayed, pillars and icons toppled, broken, or smashed, walls and roofs in tumbled down blocks or entirely missing. The place was suddenly dark and deserted.

She turned to the valley, expecting to see the city equally devastated. It was changed, but to her astonishment, it was *not* in ruins.

The city was immense! Buildings of every size filled the landscape. Tall buildings of strange design stretched square fingers, reaching for the distant clouds, glittering with bands of silver between tiles of jeweled stone. Lights gleamed everywhere.

The dawning sun revealed smooth streets with colorful, enclosed carts darting along without the benefit of oxen or horses. Whooshes and honks unlike any wind or bird susurrated around her. Bewildered, she turned back to the acropolis.

Throngs of people moved through it again, but not pilgrims. They wore strange clothing of separate pieces, including lower robes that enclosed their legs individually rather than skirting both. There were people of colorations she'd never seen, who must come from lands unheard of.

She spotted a young Achaean girl clutching a toy, asking questions of her mother. They spoke a tantalizingly familiar mix of dialects with unfamiliar pronunciations. But after a while, she made out enough words to guess more and get the gist of the mother's answers. Her daughter laughed in bemused delight. It was quite a revelation.

Mist shrouded everything again, then cleared and she stood surrounded by similar ruins in a lonely bower on a mountain top. The man lying there had a face etched indelibly into her memory, but now it looked gaunt, pale, and anguished. He stretched out an emaciated arm, reaching for something unseen, then collapsed back onto his ancient alabaster chaise. He became translucent, then blurred and transparent, finally dissipating like wisps of steam. Poignant as it was, she couldn't bring herself to mourn.

~oOo~

Kassandra climbed the steps of a temple to Apollo, a place she never thought she would enter again. It was well past when pilgrims normally arrived and the Pythia, the temple's High Priestess, tried to block her way.

"It is late. Come back tomorrow."

"No," she said, brushing past her. She headed for the door of the sanctum, and the Pythia gasped.

"Impertinent woman! You cannot enter the heart of the temple."

The look she turned on the Pythia was implacable.

"I can, and I will. You have the ear of Apollo? Tell him his prophet awaits his countenance." She turned as the Pythia sputtered incoherently.

Her footsteps echoed on the marble floor as she walked the distance to Apollo's statue. He stood carved in stone, naked, a robe draped across his out-stretched arm. She folded her arms and stood as if she, too, were stone.

"I'm waiting," she sent to him, a prayer and a demand.

The light of the setting sun faded, leaving only the flickering torchlight in their sconces. She half sat, leaning casually against the altar. She kept herself awake, knowing his tactics and what he might try if she dozed off. Finally the statue began to glow, soften, and change until Apollo stood before her in human form. Still naked.

"Kassandra, how good of you to visit me. I have not heard your lovely prayers in so very long."

"I decided to pray only to someone I could trust, and you don't qualify."

"I'm wounded," he said, placing a hand on his heart, his musical voice soothing and warm. "So why entreat me now?"

"I bring you a prophecy. It came to me this morning, and I am compelled by your gift to tell you."

"A prophecy? About me?" He was positively elated.

"Oh yes. It was very clear."

"Well by all means, do tell."

She let her face go completely blank. "Belief fades, and with it so do the gods. Your temples will crumble and your followers abandon their faith. You become a memory, then a legend, and finally, no more than a myth, a story to entertain children. It is then you will fade into oblivion forever."

Apollo stared at her a long while before bursting out laughing. "Kassandra," he chided, "you have become a raving madwoman."

She managed the stricken look she'd practiced on the way here.

"I should be angry at your insolence, dear Kassandra, but I have always been fond of you. So, I forgive you and send you on your way." He stopped chuckling then and scowled. "But do not push your luck with me, mortal. Leave my presence and never return."

She bowed deeply. "As you wish," she said in her most humble voice. When she rose, Apollo's statue was again merely stone; the god had departed. She smiled.

"I had a feeling you wouldn't believe me."

Then Eurayle strode out of the temple and into the first shafts of dawn.

THE STORMWITCH'S DAUGHTER

by Dave Smeds

Azure and her partner Coil have successfully fulfilled their mission to rescue Zephyr, the witch's daughter. But there are just a few leftover complications....

Dave Smeds is the author of novels such as *The Sorcery Within* and *The Schemes of Dragons*. His short fiction has appeared in myriad anthologies, including fourteen previous volumes of *Sword & Sorceress*, and in such magazines as *Asimov's SF*, *Realms of Fantasy*, and *F&SF*. His next major upcoming release is *The Wizard's Nemesis*, the conclusion of his "War of the Dragons" trilogy. "The Stormwitch's Daughter" features his characters Azure and Coil, picking up where we left them at the end of "The Salt Mines" in *Sword & Sorceress 27*.

As she so often did, Azure dreamed of the journey between the worlds, unable to quell the vividness, unable to improve the outcome as she could with other repeated dreams.

The dream began where it always did. Coil freed the camel from its hobbles. He rolled out the magic carpet. Azure and Zephyr settled upon it. Coil joined them and spoke the words he never should have spoken.

The carpet rose, carrying them beyond the reach of the Witch of Sandstorms. At first it flew just as it had while liberating them from Salt Town. Ordinary air buffetted their collars and sleeves. Moonglow painted them in shades of ash and silver, and the craters and dark seas of that moon were fixed in the same configurations Azure had always known. The godsmoon hung to the right, pocked and oblong—another profoundly familiar sight given how many times she had been forced to sleep under the open sky during the past thirteen years.

Dave Smeds

Then they entered some other kind of place. It did not seem at first that they had crossed a threshold, because the stars over their heads seemed the same as ever. But when Azure looked down, where she expected to see dark landscape, she only saw more night sky. More stars. The world of their birth was no longer beneath them.

Coil placed an arm over her shoulder. Azure crowded close against him, but she suspected he was drawing as much reassurance from her and he was giving back. He was the one who had made the mistake, and therefore had regret to pile atop his disorientation. The disorientation alone was bad enough. The wrongness of their surroundings tugged at Azure's insides, made her tongue into a slab of lint, kept her even from knowing which way was up and which was down.

The carpet knows, she told herself. *It was made to carry passengers. It will always be beneath.* Time and again throughout the journey she depended on that fact to fend off panic.

The stars faded, replaced by filmy strands not unlike algae waving in a stagnant pond, but of every hue, not just those of nature. Hunks of mountain floated past, disconnected from the ranges to which they belonged. Waterfalls cascaded in the near distance, originating from unseen sources, disappearing into unseen chasms.

Snow speckled their faces, but even as Azure reached to pluck the traces from her eyelashes, a blast of heat as fierce as any she had felt in the Desert of Fumes evaporated the flakes away so thoroughly they did not have time to form into droplets. They were enveloped by scents of startling randomness: Jasmine. Baking bread. Rotting fish. Rainwater.

Eventually even their own bodies became ductile, shrinking and expanding, turned airy then stonelike, growing extra parts. Awareness was the only steady aspect here. Surrender that, and they would surely become just another shred of the chaos, their former selves made unrecoverable.

Time was difficult to measure. They grew hungry, ate food from their packs, and grew hungry again.

The second half was worse. Coil admitted where he meant for them to go, and so Azure understood no matter how tolerable the rest of the actual transit might turn out to be, they were going to the wrong place.

The words. How could he have said *those words*? Without consulting her? They'd only had the carpet a matter of hours. They should have made a plan together. Should have weighed the options. But no. He had said it: "Take us to where the Eleven Gods went."

The scribes all said that when the gods departed, they went to the world of the gentle sun. And that was where the carpet took them. Their surroundings ceased transforming in unnatural ways and they found themselves floating through a sky not too different from their own. Below was a landscape of rolling hills and prairie, woods and rivers, not unlike the terrain of any number of kingdoms Azure and Coil had traversed during their wanderings, all of it lit by, yes, the glow of a sun that she could only describe as gentle, its radiance settling upon the skin rather than searing down, and yet for all that, the air was blessed with a sweet and welcoming warmth.

Yet when the carpet deposited them on a field conveniently trampled by the recent passage of some sort of large grazing beasts, she saw no gods. The carpet had done its job, but the words Coil had chosen had produced a complication. It had been thousands of years since the gods had come to this world. They'd had enough time to tire of it and move on to another.

Azure opened her eyes. She had been awake for some time, though just when the memory had stopped being a dream and become simple recollection, she wasn't sure.

Crepuscular hues swathed the eastern sky, but in the west, the blackness lingered, framing constellations that reminded Azure how impossibly far away she still was from home. The waning gibbous moon displayed no seas upon its face, only craters, and it was alone in the sky, unaccompanied by the dim and irregularly-shaped companion the Twelve Gods had seen fit to move into the heavens above her own world.

Coil and Zephyr lay beneath their blanket on the other side of the campfire. Nestled close. Azure still found it disconcerting to see them together so unequivocally. Coil had always been like her. Never one to form a steady attachment. They were creatures of the road. To form an attachment led to the pain of having to leave someone behind.

Part of the difference, of course, was that they had not left Zephyr behind. She was now their companion. Even so, Azure found it odd that her milk brother had been won over so quickly and so...influentially. Zephyr was too young for him. Not that she was a girl. She'd been a woman when they'd rescued her from the Salt Prince's tower, no matter that Lady Sirocco had characterized her daughter as a girl. She had certainly gone after Coil with a mature confidence. But Coil had never before been drawn to any woman unless she was at least as old as he.

Apparently Azure hadn't known him that well after all. He was a man, and what man would not find Zephyr appealing?

As if he sensed her gaze upon him, Coil opened his eyes.

Azure rolled over and faced the other way.

She heard him rise, stir the embers, add a few small pieces of deadfall atop them. Then he marched past her in the direction of the stream, carrying the cookpot.

He could be gone a while. They'd chosen to sleep far away from water because at this time of year the suckmites tormented anyone foolish enough to bed down near a stream.

The flames ignited. Azure rose and added larger wood. She opened a pack and rooted around for one of their sacks of pearl grit, as they had taken to calling the local porridge grain. She considered the flavor inferior to oats or wheat but the stuff was equally sustaining and certainly easier to prepare. One did not have to smash the kernels with a rolling pin nor soak the potful ahead of time to make them cook as quickly as travellers needed their breakfast to cook.

Her fingers brushed silk. The carpet was folded away in the pack. The enchantment gave it an unnatural sheen, as if it were lit from inside the threads.

They could climb on it this very morning and be on their way home. And would, if she had her way.

But she had been outvoted.

In all the thirteen years since Azure and Coil had become creatures of the road, they had been comrades of equal standing. On the occasions when they had disagreed on what course to take, her opinion mattered as much as his, and his as much as hers. But now they were a trio.

Returning home was their intended final use of the carpet. But it had enough magic left for two trips. Coil wanted the penultimate journey had to be to the place he had intended them to go last time. He wanted the help of the Eleven Gods. And so they had remained for months on the world of the gentle sun, in search of the information they needed. It wouldn't do to simply tell the carpet, "Take us to where the gods are now." Zephyr had explained the carpet would not know where that was unless they supplied it with that knowledge.

Azure didn't want anything to do with the gods. Not after their encounter with Schrae. The legends all agreed that Schrae was the worst, but they said some frightening things about the others. Azure wanted to stay as far away as possible from all of them.

Outvoted.

She snuffed out what was left of the kindling, leaving a glowing bed of coals on which Coil could set the pot when he returned.

"Good morning." The speaker was Zephyr.

"Is it?" Azure responded.

"You know it is," Zephyr said. She rose, blanket wrapped around herself. She nodded in the direction they were headed. The dawn was just starting to reveal a broad, pleasant valley full of farmlands, stone bridges, and hedgerow thickets. Azure could just make out the town in the far distance by the moth light in its tower. In another few minutes the tile rooftops would assume their daylight colors, a patchwork of hues from yellow to turquoise to the occasional vivid green. The denizens here seldom chose colors of nature for their buildings.

"We'll find our answer there," Zephyr said. "I know we will."

The sorceress's daughter moistened a washcloth with a splash

111

from her flask and wiped the eyelash crustiness and dew tracks from her face. Then she began brushing her hair.

Two hundred strokes or more, every morning. Azure knew if she did that to her own hair, in a few weeks she would end up as plucked as a chicken outside a farm wife's kitchen porch.

"You're sure that's the town?" Azure asked. "I thought there was something about a lake."

"No, the lake is beside the monastery. In the hills. Remember what he said?" And in the language of these lands she rattled off three sentences of the conversation they had overheard a month ago, two provinces away.

Azure made out only half the words. She and Coil had always been good at picking up languages. As children they had heard a polyglot of tongues spoken by the visitors to the inn. Yet Zephyr had the advantage here. Most of the locals used a traders' tongue based upon the speech of the Twelve Gods. Zephyr had been required by her mother to study the old scrolls. Half of those were written in that language.

Azure could not bring herself to ask Zephyr to repeat the words at a slower pace.

"This will be a *good* day," Zephyr reiterated. "Soon we will know where the Eleven Gods are. And that will be the end of Schrae. It's what you've strived for all these years. Why do you insist on all this worry?"

The End of Schrae. There it was. The Eleven Gods had killed Schrae once. Why would they not do so again? If they did, Azure's greatest desire would be fulfilled.

Azure would cooperate with the plan. Nevertheless, she could not shake the feeling they should find some other way.

~o0o~

Coil tried to engage Azure in small talk twice during the morning's journey. Her replies were too terse to keep the conversation going. It would take more than small talk to cure her pensive mood.

He, on the other hand, felt increasingly optimistic as they trudged along. After thirteen years of wandering, and months more upon a strange world, their goal was within striking distance.

Before noon they skirted one last farmstead and found themselves standing directly across the river from the town.

A stone barbican guarded the bridge landing, a vestige of the era when the denizens on this side were more bandits than dairymen and hay farmers. Peace had apparently been the rule lately. The portcullis was up and the lone, bored guard on the battlement simply waved them in.

As soon as they crossed, the scene transformed. The air rang with the clang of hammers, the zimming of saws, the braying of drayage beasts. The aroma of roasting sausages and the odor of fermenting mash coursed down the avenue. People were out and about, going about their daily trades or seeing to errands or pausing to share gossip. Many displayed a great deal of skin. This was not a world where people had to take measures against sunburn.

People nodded at them or even waved. The town was on the kingsroad. Travelers arrived on a daily basis.

They did not need to ask for directions. They spotted their destination right where their informant had said it would be. Hanging from the tavern was a sign of three drunken pigs leaning against an oversized tankard of beer, passed out from a night of guzzling.

Coil by now knew enough of the culture to understand the euphemistic meaning of the sign. "Three drunk pigs" was what you affectionately called a trio of fellows who had successfully completed an evening of whoring, drinking, and gambling.

He glanced across the street and found what he expected— another large building, this one with a balcony all along its upper façade. At this hour the balcony was uninhabited, but Coil knew that would change as evening neared. He pictured women leaning over the railing, calling down to passersby to come in and spend some time.

The proximity of the brothel mattered. It meant the tavernkeeper would be keen to hire entertainers whose talents could keep customers in their seats, buying ale and food and playing their games of tumble peg rather than spending their wages across the street.

They found the owner of the Three Drunk Pigs at the back alley entrance supervising the unloading of fresh meat and greens for the kitchen. Judging by the stains on his apron, he was also the head cook for the day.

As always, Zephyr was their spokesperson. She made them known with a soothing and fluent outpouring Coil could not have emulated until he had spent another six months learning the language.

The tavernkeeper's gaze lingered upon the shape of Azure's lips, upon the dimple of Zephyr's smile.

"You two could make more across the street," he told them.

"We could," Zephyr agreed. "But if we wanted to make money that way, we would have inquired there."

"I already have someone booked for tonight. A juggler and a dog. They're very funny."

"So you've hired them before?"

"I have."

"Then your customers have already seen them. They haven't seen *us*. Here's what we can do."

On cue, Coil lifted his sevenflute to his lips. Azure and Zephyr stood beside one another and sang the first stanza of *The Ballad of the Tailor's Cat*. It was a song whose lyrics would have mystified the tavernkeeper if he'd understood them. There were no domesticated cats on this world. Azure and Zephyr sang it in the original Tamian. That was a tongue in which even curses and politician's speeches sounded as though they had been crafted to fit a measure and tone. The tavernkeeper tried to hide how much he was enjoying the novelty of vocal renderings as pleasant to the ear as those that came from instruments, but he gave himself away by letting his mouth hang open to let the music filter in that way as well as through his ears.

"You like?" asked Zephyr when they were done.

He shrugged. "Can't give more than I would've paid the juggler. A meal. A room. A third of the tip jar."

"*Half* of the tip jar," Zephyr countered.

The tavernkeeper paused, but Coil knew the battle was won.

Half of what they'd bring in would be more than two-thirds of what the juggler would have earned, even if he'd brought three dogs and a monkey.

"We'll try it one night, and see," the tavernkeeper said.

Coil gave the man full credit for holding his own. Every word out of his mouth had been a maneuver to bargain down their price. But if he had possessed any genuine reluctance about hiring them, it had been overcome. That was usually the way it went when Zephyr was part of the negotiation.

~oOo~

As suppertime neared and the common room began to fill, Azure finished the bath she had been longing for all week, and descended from their room.

She found Coil was already up on the dais with his sevenflute. Zephyr was out among the tables, conversing with a brawny fellow. She was wearing the outfit she had spent all afternoon shopping for in the town: an embroidered, low-cut blouse, a pleated skirt, and an intricately worked belt of braided lacewheat hung with tassels of polished flintwood. Azure herself would never invest so much effort in crafting her own personal presentation, but she had no urge to mock Zephyr for doing so. The girl had been routinely left completely naked while she had been a prisoner of the Salt Pirates.

Eventually the sorceress's daughter joined them on the stage. She gave Coil and Azure a little nod to let them know the conversation with the brawny fellow had gone as they had hoped.

They began with *The Ballad of the Tailor's Cat*—the full thing, this time. As soon as it was done, the first copper bits and even a few silver links jingled their way into the tip bucket. Azure gave the biggest tipper a grand smile—and found it no struggle to do so. She had never had to sweat so little to earn money as in this realm. She was accustomed to dancing and acrobat routines and to serving as the risk-taker of Coil's knife-throwing act. Here all she had to do is sing. The audience didn't care that they didn't know any of the words.

Things went so well that when they took their break an hour

later, the tavernkeeper happily filled Zephyr's special request. Leaving his nephew to tend the bar, he descended into the cellar and came back with four chilled glasses of dark brew, thick with foam. He set the tray on the table near the stage that Coil, Azure, and Zephyr had temporarily claimed.

"The barkeep's reserve," he declared. "You won't find any better in this valley."

When they'd had a taste, all three of them raised their glasses in salute. Their host chuckled the whole way back to his station.

Zephyr held up the fourth glass and beckoned the brawny fellow. He wasted no time joining them.

"Do I keep my word or not?" Zephyr asked.

"Wasn't you I doubted," he assured her. "Old Pembrohel there hoards this stuff worse than his brother ever did. It's been a whole season since I've had a drop." Their guest tilted the glass to his mouth carefully, making sure to spill none in his beard. Closing his eyes, he savored the drink on his tongue for three, four, five beats.

The barkeep's reserve was a black ale, tapped from the bottom of the vat. It was far more complex than the tavern's everyday beer. The latter was decent enough, but Azure understood why their new companion had waited around for a chance to have a serving of the black.

"This is Coil," Zephyr said. "This is Azure."

The man raised his glass in their directions. "Murten," he said.

"You have strong-looking hands, Murten," Azure said. Having rehearsed the question, she got the sentence out with only a slight stumble. "What's your trade?"

"Teamster."

"Really?" Zephyr interjected. "You didn't mention that before. What kind of goods do you haul?"

"Mostly foodstuffs," he said. "I take supplies to the Curators. They don't have any fields up in those hills. Barely any gardens. They're always hiring me to fetch another load of this or that. The Blessed Scholar and her family have an affection for fresh honey; I put a barrel or two of that on the wagon nearly every time. One of the gods apparently liked honey. I think maybe they eat so much of it to make themselves closer to the gods. As if they aren't already."

Orthuneiae, thought Azure. Orthuneiae was the god who liked honey. It was said the Eleven had taken along hives of bees when they departed. She'd seen beekeepers' boxes across every realm they'd traversed these past months.

Murten seemed perfectly willing to talk about himself. Good. They'd already known he was a supplier of the monastery, but the more new information they could glean, the better.

"We came all this way partly to speak to the Curators," Zephyr said. "But we were too late for Godsday. Now we have to wait eleven months until the next one."

"I'm in the same wagon," Murten said. "It's the only time anyone like us ever sees the Viewers, and only they can talk to the gods. I've been to the keep sixty times or more, and it's only the pantry stewards and warehousemen I get to speak with."

"Not quite the same wagon," Zephyr pointed out. "You didn't have to journey for months to get this close."

"True. You have my sympathy about that."

At that point, the subject of the gods and the Curators was dropped. They couldn't ask too many questions or Murten would begin to wonder why they were so obsessed with the topic. Zephyr went on to ply him with random small talk. He was around for most of the evening and returned as they were wrapping up their set. He was obviously full with the hope of any healthy young man. He took it in stride, though, when Zephyr sent him off with, "We've just met. Talk to me tomorrow. I have to see how dedicated you are."

~o0o~

As they climbed the stairs back to their room, Coil was brimming with cheer. Ideally they had wanted to find a man who would to smuggle them into the monastery. Murten seemed too honest and simple to enlist that way, but they could still make use of him. The conversation had confirmed the monastery was nearby, and Murten would soon visit it. Following him unseen might be a challenge, but it wouldn't be the first time he and Azure had

117

done such a thing.

He was in such a fine mood his caution was as low as it ever went. Entering their room with the women right behind, he headed across the darkened chamber with the intention of lighting the candle on the sideboard. He barely sensed anything wrong before the net landed over him. Men tackled the three of them. All too soon they were tied up.

They had been seized by half a dozen strongmen in dark clothing. Moments later in walked an armored figure. His livery bore the emblem Coil knew was that of the Curators. Murten was with him.

"That's them," Murten said.

Too simple a man? Apparently not simple enough.

The three of them were taken out to the alley and locked into a caged wagon. A tarp was fastened over the cage.

Coil expected a short trip. Just to jail. But it went on and on until finally the wagon tilted this way and that and bumped over stones. They had entered the hills.

Zephyr wormed nearer to him. "You don't suppose they...?"

He grunted his astonishment.

This was hardly the way they wanted to infiltrate the monastery, but when it came down to it, no other available method would have brought them within its walls as quickly.

As the journey went on, he saw this might well have been the *only* practical way to enter the place. They passed through three waygates before dawn. Each time the guards and the wagon were allowed through only after the escort presented himself and said the right password—and it wasn't the same password at each juncture. After dawn, they passed through four more.

Finally, long after sunrise, they stopped. The tarp was pulled off. After he coped with the increase in brightness, Coil saw that the wagon was now parked by a loading platform of a stone fortress. A lake, created by a dam made of the durable false stone only the gods knew how to create, filled the view to the north. The fortress was built atop the cliff of its southern shore.

They had come through a narrow defile. Had they used that road uninvited, archers would have made strawmen dummies of them.

They were untied except for the bonds around their wrists, and marched into the lower levels to a large chamber with a rack and a table laden with whips, flaying tools, and fingernail pullers. A pallid excruciator stepped forward, clad in dungeon vestments that, while recently laundered, were heavily discolored by bloodstains.

This was not promising, Coil decided.

The excruciator frowned at them, as if he had expected to hear a whimper from the women. Clearly he didn't know Azure and Zephyr.

Into the room stepped a bald man in a particularly fine set of leather armor. "Your services will not be needed yet," he told the excruciator. "They're to be brought to the High Curator without delay."

Their treatment changed under the officer's supervision. They were each briefly allowed to step into the privy and were given cups of water to drink. And then, oddly, their feet were washed.

A large squad of men-at-arms took them upstairs. Every one of them was as finely attired as the officer. Nothing less would have suited, Coil realized, because the halls and galleries they passed through were sumptuously appointed. The marble floors were too fine to be traversed by boots tainted by road dust and horse dung. Instead the men wore soft slippers of sheepskin or meadow hare. Coil understood now why his feet and those of the women had been cleaned. He could also see why the monks were also called the Curators. All around were works of art of the highest order. Paintings. Sculptures. Furniture. The gods had moved on, but they were not quite done with this world, because it contained one of their museums.

That indicated the influence of one god in particular: Yixos, the god of Renderings. He had always collected fine works. Some of the things here were surely his own creations. What better way to see this trove preserved and maintained but to leave it in place, tended by the descendants of those who had been the caretakers when the gods were still local?

They came to a library. Thousands upon thousands of books

lined the shelves all around, some of them accessible only by climbing up four levels and then standing on a ladder. Sitting at the great center table was a gaunt, pasty man, his cloak embroidered in gold thread and pinned with a clasp of platinum and sapphire. Beside him sat an elderly woman wearing only a simple wrap, but the fabric was so compellingly live in aspect it made her figure seem decades younger.

"Gracious High Curator. Revered High Scholar," said the officer. "Here are the prisoners."

The High Curator rose, came around the table, and looked his "guests" up and down. "You are not of this world. The gods say people are much the same no matter what world they come from. I see now what they mean."

"Ask them why they've come," the High Scholar said petulantly.

The High Curator sighed. "If it had been up to me, you would have been killed in the town. But my cherished peer has more curiosity than I. Very well. Why are you here?"

He addressed the query toward Coil, who opened his mouth and would have replied despite his lack of fluency, but Zephyr spoke first.

"We come from the world where the gods dwelled before this one. The Twelfth of their number, Schrae, has been restored."

"Impossible," said the High Curator.

"My companions have seen Schrae with their own eyes," Zephyr said. "They can describe her appearance, the pitch of her voice, the way she moves. None of those things is written in the old scrolls."

"Of course it's written," argued the High Curator.

"No," countered the High Scholar. "When she was unmade, so was her chronicle."

"We must speak with the gods," Zephyr reiterated. "If they go on thinking Schrae is dead, they will be unprepared when she attempts her revenge upon them."

"The gods are mighty," the High Curator said. "They're not in danger."

"You haven't seen Schrae," Coil interjected.

The gaunt man narrowed his eyes at him.

"It's almost the hour of The Viewing," the Blessed Scholar said. "Perhaps that's a sign."

The High Curator's frown did not go away, but eventually he threw up his hands. "Take them to the barracks," he told the guards. "Cut off those bindings. Feed them a meal. Clean them up a bit. Bring them to the Viewing Hall just before the visitation is to start."

To Coil, Azure, and Zephyr he said, "Even if you're telling the truth, you're fools to want the attention of the gods."

Things had switched from promising to dreadful to promising so rapidly in the past twelve hours that Coil didn't trust their luck, but he was almost trembling with hope as the guards did as their master commanded. The remaining wait passed excruciatingly slowly, but in due course they found themselves in the Viewing Hall.

The place proved to be one of the highest chambers in the entire edifice. All along the north side much of the wall was open, displaying the lake to beautiful effect. But it was the large panel of dark glass embedded in the west wall that caught Coil's attention. And seemed to have the attention of everyone in attendance.

The High Curator spared the captives only a brief inspection. "We call it the Window of Their Regard."

He gestured to the officer, whose men moved Coil, Azure, and Zephyr over near the open wall, away from any of the doors. Coil estimated the potential fall over the edge to be two hundred feet or more to a shoreline of jagged rocks. There was barely any rail.

Gags were thrust in their mouths and fastened tightly in place with cords behind their necks.

Silence fell over the chamber. And all at once, the dark glass panel was no longer dark. It was as if it had become a window in truth. Coil saw an exquisite courtyard with a rectangular pool, a banquet laid out upon a table in the background, servants standing near the entrances. He distinctly heard the sound of a breeze ruffling through palm fronds and the muted cacophony of distant, unseen gulls.

Coil did not feel the breeze, though, nor smell salt air. That and the light reflecting off the glass confirmed the rectangle was not an opening to this other world, but only a depiction of its sights and sounds.

On a divan in the foreground reclined a man of striking proportions and a countenance so attractive Coil's mouth might have fallen open were he not gagged.

Yixos. Unlike Schrae, images of him had not been purged from the old scrolls. As expected, he had not aged in the slightest in the thousands of years since those portraits had been created.

"Your requests, Great One," the High Curator said. Two stewards in white livery placed a large painting immediately in front of the window.

Yixos studied the painting intently. He took his time. The High Curator and all the others simply waited where they were. Finally Yixos gestured. The painting was moved away, and a steward stood in its place, holding an urn that appeared to have somehow been fashioned out of a single huge agate.

Yixos smiled. "Spit in it," he said. His voice proved to be as mellifluous as his face was handsome.

The steward spat. And out of the urn came a bloodcurdling human cry that dribbled off into a whimper.

Yixos chuckled. Then he lifted his hand, "Save the rest for the next time."

"Great One," the High Curator called out politely. "A moment, if you will."

Yixos lowered his hand. Blinked. "Yes?"

"Three strangers are here. They say that have urgent news from the place you occupied before you came to live among us on this world."

"News? From the Godsblight? We are done with that place, Curator. Kill them. Trouble me no more with this."

And with that, the window went dark.

Coil had been prepared for a challenge in presenting their case, but he was stunned to have no opportunity at all.

Suddenly Zephyr was pulling him in the one direction where

guards were not blocking their way.

"Jump!" she cried.

Burnish had taught Coil not to hesitate when his life was on the line. Even though his instincts told him he was committing suicide, he followed Zephyr's example and launched himself over the low railing into space.

~oOo~

If Azure had been given any proper chance to guess what Zephyr was up to, she would have leaped as well. But two large, strong guards seized her before she had completed her first step toward the open wall.

Just before her companions plunged out of sight, she saw Zephyr fling a compact bundle of silk.

The carpet. How had she even had it? It had been hidden away in a secret pocket in the back of Coil's pants, right beneath his belt. He had put it there before coming down to the common room of the tavern for the performance, not wanting to risk leaving it in the room. Later their ambushers had been far too interested in confiscating the purse full of tips than in exhaustively searching Coil's person.

An assortment of guards and stewards rushed to the rail. Several cried out in astonishment. Soon Azure could see what they saw: The carpet, bearing Coil and Zephyr, was gently rising upward. It paused at the same height as the Viewing Hall.

A young, spry-looking guard shucked off his breastplate and greaves and evaluated the distance to the carpet. He chose not to jump. The carpet was floating a little too far away.

"Fetch the archers!" roared the High Curator.

Azure could only stand there, held tight, and gaze at Coil, who gazed back at her wide-eyed.

Zephyr reached for the cuff of Coil's pants, retrieving the tiny fold knife he'd hidden there. She cut loose her gag. She touched the woven roc. Azure of course could not hear the destination she uttered, but the carpet began moving, carrying Coil and Zephyr away over the lake.

As always, the magical conveyance moved slowly at first. Azure heard the archers burst into the room. She counted their steps to the rail. Her mouth went dry.

The arrows sailed upward. "Hah!" one of the bowmen cried in satisfaction.

But the carpet was speeding up. As the arrows came down, every one of them fell short.

They were safe. Azure laughed. They were safe.

The High Curator shook his fist as the carpet and its passengers as they receded toward the narrows of the lake and turned up the river canyon, vanishing from view. His hand was still over his head when the carpet reappeared in the distance, climbing skyward.

And disappeared in a shimmer.

Azure blinked. Her smile died.

The High Curator stalked over to where she stood trapped by the guards. "We have *you* at least."

The officer unsheathed his dagger and offered it. The High Curator started to reach for it, then shook his head.

"No. Too quick. We'll follow the ritual."

He made a dismissive gesture remarkably like the one Yixos had displayed. Azure was handed over to a squad of female guards who hauled her down to the dungeons, pulling her along more roughly, she decided, than the men would have done.

The one on her right, a stout woman with positively fishlike eyes, was in a talkative mood. "A ritual execution! You know how we do that here? If you were a man, you'd be hung at dawn from the great plank over the lake, body left there until the carrion birds have picked the flesh from your bones. A woman? She goes off the plank, too, but right into the lake with weights tied to her ankles. At sunset. Won't be long until you're at the bottom, knowing your lungs won't hold out. And only the fish to witness it."

Her escort took such delight in the description Azure was surprised by a glimmer of what might have been kindness once they reached the cell. The woman took out her fingernail knife and severed the cord holding Azure's gag in place.

"Say your prayers," she murmured. "But be careful which god you pray to."

The woman locked the dungeon door and marched away. Two of the squad remained to stand guard in the corridor.

The walls crowded close, made of unpolished stone and foul with the traces of the prisoners incarcerated there over the ages. Aside from a slop bucket on the floor and a tin cup of water on a ledge, the only feature was the tiny window, heavily barred. It provided a view of the lake, an example of punitive architecture, confronting Azure with a vantage of her grave to be.

She had always prided herself on being the sort of person who only wept at the suffering of others. Nevertheless her throat grew raw, her body trembled spine deep, and she began to blink uncontrollably. Out of anger, not self-pity. Betrayed by a witch's whelp. Left in the stronghold of enemies with no weapons and nothing with which to bargain. And so very, very abandoned. For thirteen years, Coil had always been there, but he could not help her this time. The shimmering disappearance meant he and Zephyr were committed to a journey between the worlds. They couldn't turn around until they got to where they were going. Just the outbound transit would take longer than Azure had left to live.

The anger was toward herself. Her instincts had told her not to go along with the plan. Why had she not fought for her position?

Because she wanted to kill Schrae, and there had been at least a small chance the plan would lead to that goal. She'd *let* herself be outvoted, because her need for revenge had overcome her wits.

There was no comfort to be had. Azure found it a relief when the jailors opened the door and she was hauled back up and marched out onto a long, wide plank.

The High Curator didn't even bother to attend. Perhaps to do so would dignify the event more than he wished. The only resident of the monastery who seemed to view the occasion as exceptional was the small man who tied the weights to her ankles. He knotted the leather in intricate ways. It was clearly his art. Azure had no doubt she would be unable to untie his workings in the meager time she would have before she drowned, even if they had left her hands in front of her. Which they had not. They were tied behind her, and the little man had taken just as long with those knots.

But they did not re-gag her. That might be enough to save her.

Finally all others retreated back behind the railing. When the last glint of the gentle sun flashed along the horizon, the landward end of the plank was lifted, and she tumbled off the distal end.

She didn't give them the satisfaction of a scream. She did gasp at the speed with which she dropped. Twenty body lengths—whoosh. And she hit. The gasp helped her, though. Her lungs filled to capacity just before she reached the water.

Hard as she entered it, the water slowed her momentum and she struck bottom softly. When she opened her eyes, she saw what good luck that had been. She had landed on the decayed corpse of a previous victim, but so gently the rib cage had not been shattered, leaving her feet uninjured and better still, propped above the mud. Nearby lay other skeletons, some of their broken bones jutting upward like spikes on a rampart.

Her bonds were tight, but her captors had not understood how supple she was, and how much she had trained her body. She bent herself over as few people would be able to do and began chewing at the cords connecting her ankles to the weights.

Somehow she managed to keep most of her air from escaping around her teeth, but even as the first ankle came free, she didn't know how she was going to last long enough to free the second.

Suddenly something began blocking the light filtering down from above.

~oOo~

While floating there outside the Viewing Hall, staring at the guards holding Azure, all Coil could think about were ways to attempt to free her. When Zephyr began pawing at his pant cuff, he realized she was going after the hidden fold knife, and he was awash with hope. Yes. They could travel to a spot not far away and come back to rescue Azure—though that made him worry the monks would kill her right away, and that in turn overwhelmed all other thoughts for as long as it took Zephyr to cut off her gag and say, "Take us to Yixos."

If he hadn't been gagged, he would have screamed at her. He didn't even get ready to dodge should the archers get in place in time to threaten them.

What had she done?!

She handed him the little knife, but did not wait for him to speak. She reached into her blouse and pulled out a tiny bottle of what he had always thought was one of her perfumes. Certainly he had seen her dab a bit of its contents on her neck from time to time, and it had smelled wonderful upon her. Now she poured it all out. The glistening track of fluid spread down from her collarbone to her sternum. As soon as he had thrown away the gag, she pressed his face between her breasts. The aroma, as compelling as ever, washed over him.

"All will be well," she murmured. "All will be well. When the Eleven Gods see us arrive they will be so intrigued they will *have* to listen to our story."

"Azure..." he murmured.

"All will be well," Zephyr repeated. "You don't need anyone but me. I will help you kill Schrae. We don't need Azure. I am enough. It's what's meant to be."

She lifted his head back and gazed intently into his eyes. For the first time since he had known her, he saw the forgeglow that was so much an aspect of her mother's eyes.

The potion was fogging his mind worse than any liquor he'd ever had. The things she was saying actually sounded reasonable.

So he removed himself from their reach. He shoved her away from him and somersaulted backward....

Off the carpet.

He didn't actually know whether the lake was still below or not, but he was glad to see it was. The height from which he was falling, though—that was alarming. He had grown up diving from the village bridge, and put his best skill into the plunge, but even so, the impact nearly knocked him unconscious. Pure animal craving to live made his arms and legs work, bringing him back to the surface.

He cleared the water from his eyes just in time to witness the speeding carpet, and the tiny figure of Zephyr upon it, shimmer and vanish from the sky.

Yixos would kill her, of course. She'd earned that, he supposed.

~oOo~

When Azure realized what was blocking the light was Coil, swimming for her with all his vigor, she stopped chewing and held on to what little air she had left.

His fold knife was already in his hand when he reached her. He went right to work upon the tethers holding her ankles to the weights.

Her chest was aching worse than it had when Schrae's great spider carried away her mother. It took very little time for the blade to cut the leather, but it seemed like more. As soon as she was loose, Coil gripped her beneath an arm and kicked like an otter. As did she.

All she cared about was reaching the surface, but he still had his wits about him. He guided them toward the underpinnings of the monastery. When their heads finally popped up, they were close against the cliff in its shadow, out of easy view of anyone above.

Her lungs filled so abruptly they hurt in a whole new way. Somehow she managed not to cough so loudly the noise would echo up to her executioners' ears. Coil let her concentrate on her recovery. Meanwhile he carefully sawed through the bonds on her wrists.

When her arms were free, she threw them around him, even though the action nearly dunked them both.

"*Now* do you admit I was right?" she whispered in his ear.

"Haven't had time to think about that. I've spent the past few hours diving off a flying carpet, infiltrating a fortress, finding out what they were going to do with you, and arranging to be close enough to reach you when they dropped you off the plank."

"Think about it now."

"Very well. Yes. You were right."

He grinned. She grinned.

He let the moment have its weight, then he added, "I think we're out of view here, but over there would be better." He helped her swim over to a place where the rock hung over them more completely. When they got there, they discovered a natural shelf ample enough that they could sit on it, side by side, their heads and shoulders out of the water.

"It will be dark soon," he said. "No moon until later. We should be able to slip away. By sunrise we'll be far from here."

While they waited, he told her what had happened on the carpet.

"She must have been using that potion on me from the beginning," he concluded.

"She was her mother's daughter," Azure observed. "How did you manage to resist there at the end?"

"Takes more than a perfumed cleavage and magic to make me lose my way."

She wished it were not so dim already under the overhang. She wanted to savor the twinkle he always got in his eyes when he knew he'd done well.

"Coil?"

"Yes?"

"Thank you."

"You're welcome."

"It really *was* remarkable, now that I consider it. I don't suppose you've also managed to come up with a way to get us off this world?"

"I'm afraid I have not. But if we're trapped here, at least we're *both* trapped."

"Yes," she agreed. "There is that."

They sat in silence while they waited for the darkness to reach its full. As the night breeze kicked up, she started to shiver. The water was so much milder than other lakes she had found herself in, but it *was* runoff from mountains. Some of it might even be snow melt, though she had yet to see snow upon any peak of these latitudes of the world of the gentle sun. She placed Coil's arm over her shoulder and nestled against him.

His warmth took her shivers away.

SHINING SILVER, HIDDEN GOLD

by Catherine Soto

Lin Mei was supposedly taking a vacation from the caravan business to spend the winter with a friend. The visit, however, took Lin Mei to a valley that was a major trading route with the land of Hind to the south, so it behooved her to keep her eyes and ears open.

Catherine Soto lives in San Francisco but her heart is in China. She sold her first story to *Sword & Sorceress 21*, and she has been writing about Lin Mei and her brother ever since. When not writing or at the obligatory day job, Catherine hangs out at the Asian Art Museum or explores the various ethnic neighborhoods of her adopted city. At the present she's working on a novel about her characters and hopes to be finished early next year.

"Anshazhe?" Lin Mei asked. The woman seated opposite her on the yak-hair mat merely gazed back at her. "I have heard of them. They are usually found within the Empire."

"I have also heard of them," the woman replied, stopping to take a sip of tea, "and that you have occasionally had dealings with them."

"Not in any friendly manner," Lin Mei responded. Her mind was racing. What was this all about? The woman, whose name was Pakchen Dgorge, smiled slightly, setting her tea down on a small tray. She was a tall dark attractive woman, slender in the manner of the mountain people, with long black hair brushed back and held in place with silver pins. She wore a plain green silk robe devoid of ornament.

"So I have heard," she replied. "Your experience may be of value, since it seems that these 'anshazhe' have been reported outside the borders of the empire."

"They are mercenary spies and assassins," Lin Mei replied, her words carefully chosen and spoken, "rarely approached, or hired, by those not involved in the affairs of the Great Lords. I doubt most people would even know how to contact them. May I ask who has reported them?"

"Two of my herdsmen said they spied black-clad men clambering among the rocks on the hillside," Pakchen replied casually. "When they were approached the strangers vanished in a cloud of smoke."

"Anshazhe sometimes use clouds of smoke to cover their escape," Lin Mei said carefully, "along with other tricks. They are known for subterfuge and deceit."

"I have heard that also," Pakchen replied. She looked at Lin Mei for a moment.

"Would it be appropriate for me to ask for your assistance in looking into this matter?"

Lin Mei looked back at her for a moment. "Would it be appropriate for me to question those herdsmen?"

"I see no reason why not," Pakchen replied.

Lin Mei looked through the open door to the veranda, where her cats, Twilight and Shadow, lay quietly in the half-slumber they favored. It was getting dark.

"Perhaps I can talk to them tomorrow?" Lin Mei asked.

Pakchen nodded. "I will arrange it," she said.

Lin Mei thanked her and left, the cats padding along behind.

~o0o~

Alone in her quarters Lin Mei sat down on a mat and pondered the meeting she'd just had. She had met Pakchen Dgorge earlier in the season at the Taiyung silk fair, when Lin Mei had helped her deal with a somewhat complicated and messy domestic matter that had involved dark magic and mysticism. After the fair had ended Pakchen had invited Lin Mei to stay with her in her homeland for the winter, now that the trading season was over.

"By all means, go," Shin Hu had told her. "We can manage without you on the journey back to Kendar. There is only the silver and gold to guard." Lin Mei nodded, understanding.

Compared to the silk they had brought out on the journey to Taiyung, gold and silver were a more compact, if heavier, load, involving fewer pack animals and a consequently shorter caravan, easier to guard. She was learning the running of a caravan guard business under Shin Hu and had spent many frantic days and nights helping him manage the small town on the march that made up a trade caravan.

"You can use the rest," he said with a smile. "Rejoin us in Kendar when the spring comes." And then the smile was gone.

"And keep your eyes and ears open," he went on. "The kingdoms of the Yarlung-Tsangpo Valley are wealthy and powerful, and they are an important trading route with the land of Hind to the South. Whatever you can learn would be of great value." She had nodded again, eyeing him, wondering if he was aware of her role as an occasional secret agent of the Empire.

And so she had come to this strange kingdom in the high mountains. She had skirted Tifun, entering the Yarlung-Tsangpo Valley through the narrow passes where it abutted the Empire. Bounded on both sides by towering peaks shrouded in clouds and with the ice-cold waters of the Yarlung-Tsangpo rushing down between them, the land of Pakchen Dgorge was verdant and cool. Kingdoms of varying size dotted the vast length of the central valley, all fiercely independent. The land ruled over by the Pakchen-Kalden clans was one of the largest, as she had discovered upon her arrival. And a wealthy one, as Shin Hu had said. Long and narrow, the Valley ran east and west the length of the mountain chain and was relatively easy to defend, so the lucrative trade between the Hind and the lands to the north was easily controlled.

~oOo~

Lin Mei looked around at her quarters. Hardwood pillars supported a red tile roof overhead. More hardwood supplied the flooring and furnishings. It was common here, but all that exotic hardwood would have sold for a fortune to the north. Her practiced eye spotted rosewood, aromatic sandalwood, mahogany, ebony, and teak, in addition to the silk hangings and silver utensils all about. She recalled talk of the rich silver mines of the Valley, reputed to be a major source of the land's wealth.

It occurred to her that if anshazhe were truly in the area, there was certainly enough to interest whoever might have hired them. She checked her sword and matching daggers, making sure they were close to hand as she blew the lamp out and pulled the silken quilt over her.

~oOo~

Dawn came damp and clammy with a thin drizzle of rain. Lin Mei opened her eyes to a gray light coming in through the oiled paper that covered the narrow windows high on the walls. On her return from the privy she found servants had brought barley bread and meat stew and a mug of buttered and spiced tea, as well as some pieces of dried meat for the two cats. Picking up a pair of chopsticks she set upon her meal with relish, while Shadow and Twilight gnawed on their scraps nearby.

The morning rain had turned to a fine mist as she finished. She let the two cats know they would not be needed for the moment and dressed for the day in wool and leather, with a raw wool cloak as a rain cover. She thrust her sword and daggers into a woolen sash.

Two men were waiting for her on the veranda. One she recognized. Palden was a master of the lance, which he carried loosely in one hand, and one of Pakchen's four husbands. By now Lin Mei was familiar with the customs of the mountain people and their rather flexible ideas of marriage and family, and Palden had been a valuable ally in the Taiyung matter. She trusted him.

The other man was another matter. Tall and slender, youthful looking despite the graying hair bound up and covered with the hat of a court noble in the Imperial Capital of Chang'An, he wore the red silk robe of an Imperial official, incongruous in this land of towering mountains and rushing rivers.

"Shien Ng," Palden said, introducing him, "of the Imperial Court." Lin Mei gave a short bow, adequate in such an informal setting.

"I am honored," she said. "It is a pleasant surprise to meet one of your splendors so far from the Imperial Court." The man smiled down at her.

"My mother's ancestors came down from the mountains in ages past to serve the August Throne," the man replied with the faintest of smiles. "The Son of Heaven has graciously permitted me to return to these ancestral mountains to spend my retirement here in study and contemplation."

"The Son of Heaven is indeed most gracious," Lin Mei replied courteously. She saw Palden out of the corner of her eyes. His face was still and bereft of emotion. So he didn't believe a word of it either. Good; she would talk with him later.

"May I be permitted to see these herdsmen?" she asked. Palden smiled.

"That is why we are here," he said. He turned and led through the compound, which sprawled down the hillside. Pemako was nearby, a rather sizable village, with a small temple of red-painted wooden pillars topped by a blue tile roof near the center. Palden led them in a short walk to the temple, passing throngs of townspeople going about their business. The men were uniformly clad in dark brown and utilitarian clothing, but the women favored bright colorful clothing, and quite a few wore elaborate silver ornaments. Lin Mei was intrigued at so much wealth among the common people, more than she would have expected in most places. She commented upon it to Palden.

"We are not as wealthy as many cities of the Empire," he said. "But we are not poor either. The people are allowed to keep most of what they produce. A strong and healthy people make for a strong and healthy kingdom."

"Would that all other kingdoms were governed by rulers so wise," Lin Mei replied. "I note that the women wear much silver. No gold?"

Palden laughed. "We are not like the people of Hind."

"They wear gold?" she asked. He nodded.

"Especially the women," he replied. "In Hind a young bride must bring a golden dowry to her wedding. The larger the dowry the more prestige accrues to her family. Some of those dowries rival those of a great lord's daughter in the Northern lands."

"Truly some people are strange," Lin Mei replied. Palden

laughed at that too.

At the temple they found the two herdsmen waiting for them under the eaves. They stood and bowed as she and the two men approached. Pakchen introduced them as Choden and Duga.

"Pakchen Dgorge has requested the aid of this young woman in the matter you two reported yesterday," Palden told them. "Tell her what you saw." The older of the two men, Choden, spoke first.

"Up on the hillside we saw three men, all of dark, from head to foot, standing on the hillside," he said, pointing up. Lin Mei's eyes followed his grimy finger upward to the hillside, noting the rock strewn expanse of green just barely visible through the mist.

"What do you mean by 'all of dark'?" she asked.

"They were dressed in dark, even their heads were covered," the old man replied. Lin Mei saw the younger man was frowning.

"What did you see?" she asked him.

"There were three dark figures on the hillside," he said, his voice diffident. "They were hard to see, and when we approached to see who they were there was a cloud that suddenly hid them. When it lifted they were gone."

"A cloud," she asked. "Not a puff of smoke?"

"It was hard to see," he replied quietly. Lin Mei looked at them. Simple herdsmen and villagers, they would give little more.

"Thank you," she said. "I may talk with you later." She and her companions stepped away from the villagers and looked up into the mists. Abruptly she made up her mind.

"I want to take a closer look at that hillside," she said, settling her sword and daggers in her sash. She saw Shien Ng hesitate. "I will not take you away from your study and contemplation," she told him.

"I will return to my studies," he said, turning and walking away. Palden smiled at the man's retreating back.

"So," she asked him as they started up the hillside. "Who is he?"

"A distant cousin of the Pakchen clan," Palden replied. "He

appeared last spring with a small party and his tale of retiring to his ancestral mountains. He brought gold and silver to pay for his house, and a small retinue. So far he has not caused too many problems." He paused for a moment. "He is a loyal and trusted servant of the Son of Heaven." Lin Mei looked up at him in understanding. So Shien Ng was a spy, and her hosts knew of it, or at least suspected.

"I am glad to hear that," she replied, an answer that could have several meanings. The rest of the ascent passed in silence.

At the spot indicated by the two herdsmen they found nothing. Both Lin Mei and Palden were practiced at reading sign, but the ground told them little. She spied recent tracks of deer and other wildlife, obviously made after the night's rain, but nothing more.

"Choden and Duga," she asked, "what kind of men are they?"

"If you are asking if they are the sort to imagine things, or make up fanciful tales, I have to say they are honest and reliable men," he replied, "or at least, as honest and reliable as any other men." She laughed at that. She was beginning to like Palden. They turned at started back down.

At the base of the hill she stopped for a moment. There appeared to be some sort of commotion at the lower end of the compound, and her experienced eye recognized the return of a caravan. There were more human porters than she would have expected, and heavily-armed guards surrounded the area, all given a wide berth by the surrounding crowd. She noted the porters carried small packs but still seemed to be carrying heavy loads, and stayed especially close to the guards.

"Has Shien Ng expressed any interest in the silver mines of the Yarlung-Tsangpo Valley?" she asked. Palden looked down at her for a moment.

"He might have," he replied slowly. "They have come up in conversation on occasion. Why do you ask?"

Lin Mei thought carefully for a moment before answering. "The court at Chang'An is reputed to live in lavish style," she replied. "So the court would be interested in additional sources of revenue."

Palden's face hardened. "They are not the only ones interested in additional revenue," he said. "Hind to the south and Tifun to the north have also expressed an interest on occasion. So far they have not ventured too far into the valley of the Yarlung-Tsangpo." Lin Mei looked up at his rangy height, noting the casual and easy manner in which he carried his lance.

"I can see why they would not," she said. He smiled grimly back down at her.

"I have some matters to attend to," he said. "If you should need anything, do not hesitate to ask for it."

"I will," she replied, and went back to her own quarters. She had been mildly startled upon her arrival a few days prior. She had expected a small village or town with only a few score people, but the size and opulence of the seat of the Pakchen-Kalden had surprised her. The main building, where Pakchen and the immediate clan resided, was a full three stories high, of white-washed stone and tile roofed. Her quarters were in one of the lower corners, reserved for occasional guests, she suspected, and in size and furnishings would have rivaled the home of a high official in the Empire, or in any of the kingdoms she had travelled through in her career as a caravan guard. And the common people she had seen so far seemed well-fed, well-clothed, and contented.

She entered her quarters to find Twilight and Shadow staring at her. "Too wet to go outside?" she asked. Shadow made a face, Twilight merely looked pitiful. She left the sliding door open just enough to let them slide through and go under the veranda for their late morning routine while she settled into the mat and brewed herself another cup of tea.

It was good, but with a smoky aftertaste that hinted at an origin to the south, most likely Hind. That too added to the picture she was forming in her mind of a wealthy and established kingdom, all the more surprising in this mountain fastness. In the Empire's view of things all the other lands around it were peopled by barbarians and were in some way or other subservient to the Son of Heaven, but she had learned that the lands outside the Empire were often of a high culture and had their own views of their relations with the Empire.

There was a tapping on the floor on the other side of the inner sliding door. "Enter!" she called out. A serving girl, young and pretty, entered, bowing low.

"The lady Pakchen desires your presence at her midday meal," she said.

"Please tell lady Pakchen that I am pleased and honored to attend upon her." The servant girl bowed low and left. Lin Mei looked out the door as Shadow and Twilight entered. The sun was still rising, she had time to bathe and dress.

Pakchen was waiting when she arrived at the main hall, along with two of her husbands. Palden and Tsering were brothers, along with Sousom, a boy too young to assume the duties of an adult. He was still with his family in their own home further up the valley. The fourth one, a cousin, was away on business at the moment. Lin Mei bowed low as she entered.

"I am honored by your wish that I attend upon you," she said. Her hosts bowed back.

"We are honored by your visit to our poor home," Pakchen replied. "Please accept our hospitality." Lin Mei settled down on a mat reserved for her as servants brought in trays of food.

It was all good, if simple. The meal began with more hot buttered tea. There was meat stew and barley bread. Lin Mei mused that such food would strengthen people against the mountain climate. Soon enough the meal ended and the trays were cleared away. More tea was brought.

"The last of the trading caravans arrived soon after you left to visit Pemako," Palden said as soon as the servants were gone. "They brought the latest news."

"I would hope the news was favorable," Lin Mei replied.

"The army of the August Throne met the horde of the Yarlung Khan in a battle near Dunhuang," she said. "Both sides claim victory but people note that the Khan has returned to Tifun and Zhi Tse Meng, the commander of the Imperial Army, is encamped on the plain outside Dunhuang."

"Then that is good news," Lin Mei said, feeling only slight relief. Her brother was away serving with the Imperial armies, but victory for the August Throne did not necessarily mean he was safe. She offered up a silent prayer for his safe return.

"What did you determine on your morning visit to Pemako?" Pakchen asked suddenly. Lin Mei took another sip of tea to gain a moment to gather her thoughts.

"In my experience," she replied carefully, "anshazhe prefer the night and the darkness for their activities. And they are not usually seen unless they want to be. Also I was puzzled by their being seen above Pemako. If they are in the area I would expect they would have the most interest in the residence of the ruling family."

"You suggest their appearance there be part of some deception?" Pakchen asked.

"It could be," Lin Mei agreed.

"Shien Ng spoke well of you," Pakchen said unexpectedly. The remark startled Lin Mei, although she managed to hide her surprise.

"I am pleased," she said, "that one such as he would do so." Shocked was what she really felt. The officials of the Heavenly Court looked down on those involved in trade. They also looked down on those who bore arms. And they especially looked down on women in general. And Lin Mei was all three. On the other hand, perhaps he would have been reluctant to offend his hosts by speaking ill of another guest.

"Shien Ng is a loyal and trusted servant of the Son of Heaven," Tsering spoke up. Lin Mei looked at him, his words hanging in the air between them. Out of the corner of her eyes she saw Pakchen and Palden looking at her, their faces impassive. She let out her breath slowly.

"I am certain that he is," she said. Her mind raced back to a visit she and her brother had paid to the Taktsang lamasery. The abbot there had alluded to their role as sometime agents of the Imperial secret service. Tsering was also a monk, although released from his vows so that he might participate in his family duties as one of Pakchen's husbands. How much did he know?

"I have met many such in my travels," she added.

"I am certain you have," Pakchen said with a slight smile. She sat back on her heels, setting her small tea bowl on the mat beside her. "Please forgive my rudeness, but we have important business matters to attend to."

"I thank you for the meal, and your pleasant company," Lin Mei replied formally and left.

~oOo~

Alone in her quarters she pondered the meal and conversation she had just had. It had obviously been more than just a simple meal. She thought about the sudden reference to Shien Ng.

In her experience retired scholars and court officials normally returned to their home villages. That he was most likely a spy was obvious, which explained why Pakchen's family had given him quarters in the compound, where he could be watched.

And the way they had mentioned him, bringing him to her attention, was interesting. She sat back on her heels, lost in thought. She had met Pakchen, and Palden, when they had been attacked by a Rolang, a corpse re-animated by the dark magic of one of her other husbands, who was now serving a life sentence meditating as a monk in a cave high above Taiyung. She had been present during the affair because her host, Dorpak Champa, had wanted her available and on hand to help resolve the domestic drama. Now she wondered if Pakchen's invitation had been inspired by similar motivations.

Abruptly she made her decision. If she was there to help resolve another crisis, then she should earn her keep. Arising she stuck her sword and daggers in her sash and left, sending a thought to the cats to rest. From long experience they knew that meant possible action later, and they settled down onto the mats, paws decorously tucked under them. Not that they needed an excuse to nod off to sleep.

She started with a stroll about the compound, noting all the activities she observed. It was all normal enough, with herdsmen, farmers, and tradesmen going about their daily routines. Women wandered about, gossiping and spinning thread as they walked, nodding to her graciously as she passed, the young girls giggling and covering their faces as the outlandish stranger went by. In the building where the forge and smithy were located she chatted with the smith, a wiry older man named Tenzin. She made small talk about other such places she had seen in her travels. The rest of the day revealed nothing out of the ordinary in the compound.

The next day she strolled about the town of Pemako. There were herdsmen, farmers, tradesmen and artisans. Women carded wool and spun thread, weaving it into various types of cloth. A visit to the temple proved productive.

After a small donation and the purchase of a few sticks of incense which she lit before the images against the far wall she engaged the priest in conversation.

"This is indeed a happy kingdom," he agreed when she remarked upon her day's observations. "The Pakchen and Kalden lords are wise and benevolent."

"I see the women wear much silver," she commented, "but no gold. I have found that gold is often found in mountains. Is this land different?"

He smiled. "These mountains produce both gold and silver, but in truth most of the gold in these lands comes from the lands west of Tifun, and most of the silver come from the land of Hind, to the south."

Lin Mei's ears pricked at that, although she was able to mask her thoughts. "I am told that the young women of Hind must bring a dowry of gold to their wedding."

The priest made a small face. "A barbarous custom," he said. "Their lust for gold does not earn merit. Here young women bring useful items to their marriage." She agreed with him and dropped a couple more coins in the brass collection box before leaving.

A purchase of a silver bracelet bought a few moments of conversation with an artisan, which yielded the information that in Hind silver and gold traded at a ratio of fifteen to one, well above the rate found in Tifun and the Empire. A suspicion was forming in her mind.

Back in her rooms she ate a light supper and saw to it that the cats ate as well, then lay on her mat and took a nap, Twilight and Shadow doing the same.

It was night when she awoke. She dressed in dark blue

clothing. Her sword and daggers went in her sash. Silently she and the cats went out into the night.

The sky overhead was dark with clouds that promised rain later. Lamps lit the windows of Pakchen's quarters on the second floor. She noted that the first floor quarters allocated to Shien Ng were also lit.

Silent as mist, she and the cats climbed the steps to the veranda and spent a few minutes at the door. Her human hearing gave no clues as to any activity within, and when she melded her senses to those of Twilight and Shadow she learned nothing more. Looking about to make sure there were no watchers, she teased open the oiled paper window with the point of a dagger and looked inside. There was no one in sight. She lifted both cats and dropped them inside through the wooden bars, then sat down and let them explore the interior.

She didn't know where the strange power that allowed her to use their senses as her own had come from. She had found them as orphans in a deserted temple, so she simply attributed it to some magical or heavenly source. Whatever its origin, the ability had proven valuable through her tumultuous life.

A few minutes of feline prowling about convinced her that Shien Ng's rooms were empty. Silently she recalled the cats, catching them as they leapt down from the window and led them to the rear door of the building.

There were no guards there. Made of heavy timbers and secured with a heavy brass lock, it was apparently not a door that anyone felt needed guarding. No one had anticipated Lin Mei. A few moments with her lock picks and she and the cats were inside.

The hallway was unlit, dark and musty. With the cats leading the way and providing superior night vision, she followed the corridor into the building to where it crossed another corridor.

And there the cats stiffened, sensing danger. She recalled them, flattening herself into a doorway. Twilight and Shadow crouched down into the space beside her. Down the hall she heard a small party passing by. Twilight stuck her head out of the doorway just enough for Lin Mei to catch a glimpse of black-clad armed men led by a taller man, also in black.

Lin Mei pursed her lips and let out a silent whistle. So the retired scholar and court official did not disdain weapons after all. After they had passed she sent the cats ahead as scouts. At the intersection they all turned left and descended a flight of stairs to another heavy wooden door. The wick on a butter lamp on the wall still smelled of smoke. A few moments with flint and steel and it was alight once more. A moment with the lock picks and the door swung open with only the barest of creaking sounds.

After what she had learned she was not really surprised to see the room piled high with gold. Bars and ingots were neatly stacked on the floor. Sacks of jewelry and other ornamentation lay by them. Small sacks filled with what appeared to be coins lay on heavy wooden tables.

It was so obvious now. There were no silver mines. Gold went through the mountains to Hind. It traded at favorable rates for silver, which went north to Tifun and the Empire, and was traded for more gold, also at favorable rates. Profit flowed both ways, all of it accumulating in mountain storerooms like this. The hair on the back of her neck rose, not so much at the sight of all that wealth but at what it represented.

Here was the wealth of an empire, held by a kingdom she could ride across in a day, enough wealth to pay armies, bribe kings, and tempt the avarice of an Emperor. It was the last that concerned her. If word of this made its way back to Chang'An, the recently victorious armies of the Empire would not be discharged. They would come south into the long narrow valley of the Yarlung-Tsangpo, where their tactics of mass envelopment would not work. Men like Palden, used to fighting in these mountains, would shred an Imperial army trapped between the deep and frigid waters of the Yarlung-Tsangpo and the towering mountains on either side. And her brother was serving in the Imperial army.

She wondered if the court knew about this. Someone had sent Shien Ng with his anshazhe, for there was no longer any doubt in her mind that was what they were. She doubted that anyone had told the Emperor, since the penalties for being wrong were so high. Better to inform him of a known fact. So Shien Ng and his party were advance scouts. After all, the anshazhe were hired spies and assassins...

And assassins...

Realization hit her with a cold chill. She turned and ran back up the stairs and along the dark hallway, the cats loping along behind her. At the end another stairway waited, this one leading up to the second floor. She bounded to the top, the cats following.

And there she almost tripped over a pair of bodies sprawled on the landing. There was enough light to identify them as guards, and in their throats she saw the pointed stars used by anshazhe. By themselves they would not have been enough to kill the two men, but their contorted faces showed the stars had been tipped with some fast-acting poison. Blood on their chests showed where dagger thrusts had assured the deed.

She leapt over the bodies, the cats scampering around them, and ran down the short hallway where it made a turn to the left.

There she saw Shien Ng and his anshazhe.

"Assassins!" she shouted, "anshazhe! They are here to kill Pakchen!" Surprised, they turned to look at her. But they recovered instantly, and one whipped out a poisoned star and threw it at her. It might not have missed if Shadow had not already gone ahead and jumped on the man's leg with all claws extended. The anshazhe swore and raised a hand to strike down at the feline form.

And left his armpit exposed. Lin Mei's sword found the mark and she stepped nimbly around the falling form into the room beyond. In the far corner Tsering was covering Pakchen with his body. In the center Palden crouched, long dagger in one hand, his lance in the other, one of the anshazhe already dead in the center of the room. But he still faced two men. Lin Mei backed up and spared a glance down at the man she'd just killed. A glint of metal in his sash caught her eye. She stooped and carefully but quickly pulled out a throwing star. Stepping forward she threw it at the taller of the two men between her and Palden.

Fortune favored her. Shien Ng had just turned to see what was behind him, and the star hit his cheek, drawing blood through the black silk scarf serving as a mask. He swore and stepped back, his hand clawing at the poisoned star.

It was all Palden needed. His lance snapped in and out with the speed of a crossbow being released, and the tall anshazhe fell. That left one, still a deadly assassin, but with Lin Mei behind and Palden before, he fell in the next instant, pierced from both directions.

~o0o~

Later that night, after the commotion had died down and had been cleaned up after, they all met in one of the larger halls on the lower floor. Tea had been brought and sipped. Finally it was time to talk.

"It has been a busy night." Pakchen began, setting her bowl down by her side. Her two husbands flanked her: Palden on her left, his lance to hand and long dagger in his sash; Tsering decorously on her right, in the robe of a scholar and monk.

"It has," Lin Mei agreed. Shadow and Twilight sat in a corner behind her, eyeing them.

"Travelers tell tales," Pakchen went on, "and this will make an oft-told campfire tale when you return to your own lands in the spring."

"Does it need to be? I do not often talk of my adventures."

"But you must," Pakchen said smiling, "all the more so since this rebounds to your credit."

Lin Mei raised a quizzical eyebrow.

"You were restless, were you not? You could not sleep. So you took a short stroll about the palace to settle your nerves. Shien Ng had come to visit us in our quarters and, sadly, he was still there when three anshazhe, hired by parties unknown, attacked us. Fortunately you gave enough warning so that we were able to defend ourselves. Shien Ng, that unfortunate man, was killed by a poisoned star carried by one of the anshazhe. His ashes will be returned to the Imperial court along with a full report of these unfortunate events." She stopped and took another sip of tea.

145

"Is that not so?" she asked.
Lin Mei smiled. "That is so," she agreed.

MENDACITY

by Michael H. Payne

Because she is a squirrel, Cluny is expected—and generally believed—to be a familiar. In fact, she is a mage and has two familiars, one of them human. Making everyone around her believe that he is the mage is an everyday challenge. Having people try to kill her is only an occasional one.

When asked for a current bio, Michael replied:

All previous conditions continue to apply—my library clerking, my church singing and guitar playing, my radio show hosting—but I've also reached the third-of-a-million-words mark with the My Little Pony fan fiction I write under the name of AugieDog while keeping up my daily webcomic, *Daily Grind*, and my weekly webcomic, *Terebinth*. I'm hoping to have the first Cluny, Crocker, and Shtasith novel finished this fall. It willl detail what brought them all to Huxley College in the first place, then cover their entire first year there. As always, hyniof.livejournal.com will have all the relevant ups 'n' downs.

Whiskers tingling, Cluny watched Crocker twiddle his fingers at the little chunk of soap Shtasith had fetched from the bathroom. Steeling herself for anything, she was instead pleasantly surprised when his spell did what it was supposed to, a pile of bubbles sprouting, quickly spreading across Crocker's desk and stacking higher than the tufts of Cluny's ears.

Because, yes, Crocker had always been good at doubling magic—that was what had saved their lives and gotten them into so much trouble during their first trip to the Realm of Fire, after all. But seeing him apply the spell so well and so easily made Cluny quietly proud.

The desk shook, the mounded bubbles quivering with little rainbow reflections from the October afternoon sun shining through the window of their dorm room. Cluny glanced over to see Crocker settling into his chair, Shtasith stretched all black and gold and scaly from one shoulder to the other along the back of his neck, the little dragon's snaky head peering out from beneath Crocker's left ear. "So go ahead," Crocker said, folding his arms.

Refusing to let her tail jitter, Cluny took a breath and poked a claw into the damp, slippery wall ahead of her.

With a pinging tap like a pebble bouncing off a window, her claw went straight through, the surface barely jiggling, and Cluny's pride puffed up even further. If Crocker had tried this same spell last year, Cluny knew, she'd be covered in soapy slime right now. She turned a smile at him. "Works just fine."

The human and the firedrake both had their eyes half closed. "Now try pulling it out," Crocker said.

"What?" Facing the bubbles again, she gave the tiniest tug and had to wince at the magical stresses and strains that ricocheted between her whiskers. "Oh. I see. The spell only increases the tensile strength of the material on the outside. No *wonder* it's giving you so much trouble!" Possible solutions to the problem started dancing their schematics through her head, but, well, first things first. She gestured with the paw not wrapped in bubbles. "If I could have my familiars' assistance, please, we can start working on this."

"Assistance?" Crocker gave one of those sighing sort of snorts he'd been doing so often in the two weeks since they'd started their second year here at Huxley College. At least, it seemed to Cluny that he'd been doing a lot more snorting lately. "Are you saying there's some problems the great squirrel sorceress can't solve for herself? Or that there's something her lowly familiars can do that she can't?"

Steam puffed from Shtasith's nostrils. "Speak for yourself, simian. I for my part have never been lowly, and I feel no particular desire to begin the practice now."

Ignoring him, Cluny shrugged. "A familiar's magic is fundamentally different from a wizard's, Crocker. So yeah, there are things you can do that I can't the same as there's things *I* can do that *you* can't."

All the surliness melted from Crocker's face leaving it looking more usual: round, pale, and blinking. "Really?"

Which got Cluny scowling. "Are you paying attention in class at *all*?"

"Of course I am!" But the way his eyes shifted under his bushy black eyebrows told Cluny all she needed to know. "It's just the professors are always—" He hunched over, scrunched his chin up closer to his nose, and slipped into a rough voice that she guessed was supposed to be an imitation of Master Trevacette, the grizzled old wizard who presided over the sophomore familiars' program. "'You're nothing without your wizards! Don't ever even *think* about trying to forget that!'"

Cluny's tail bristled. Back when she and Crocker had still thought they were a human wizard with an animal familiar, she'd often had to bite her tongue at the professors' talk of a familiar's proper place. So after their adventure in the Realm of Fire had led Master Gollantz, Huxley's magister magistrorum, to conclude that she and Crocker were something unprecedented in the history of wizardry—an animal sorceress with a human familiar—Cluny had vowed that she would never treat Crocker the way she'd seen other wizards treat their familiars.

Master Gollantz insisting that she and Crocker act as if they were a normal pair had made her vow both easier and harder to keep: no one expected Crocker to call her 'mistress' the way all the textbooks said a familiar should, but Crocker refused to let Cluny call him 'master' even when they were pretending. They'd actually started a fad last year, some of the other frosh wizards insisting that their familiars stop being so formal and call them by name.

Of course, Cluny's accidentally gathering Shtasith to herself as a *second* familiar had complicated matters, but she and Crocker had finally gotten it through the firedrake's spiky skull that he was strictly forbidden to call Cluny his mistress. He'd grumbled and groused about it, but he'd finally settled on addressing her as 'my Cluny,' something that worked well enough with the cover story they'd been forced to adopt to explain their new trio: Crocker was a powerful wizard, Shtasith was his *actual* familiar, and Cluny was just a regular sapient squirrel whom Crocker had fixated on as a totem to balance his more-than-slightly disturbed mind.

Not the most elegant of solutions, no, but it did turn away unwelcome attention. After all, the *last* wizard to have two familiars, Esmeralda Stone, had been killed 120 years ago after nearly taking over the kingdom with her army of undead monstrosities, a fact that sometimes poked Cluny awake in the middle of the night as sharp as a shard of nutshell in her gums. Could she be really be as powerful as the legendary Jade Sorceress? And would that power drive her just as insane?

Quickly, she stroked her familiars' magic wrapped around hers, Crocker's as soothing as a blanket across her shoulders and Shtasith's as welcome as a bonfire on a mid-winter evening. "The three of us," she said, finding her voice again and moving her gaze back and forth between Shtasith's reptilian eyes and Crocker's human ones, "we're not like anything the world has ever seen. So a lot of the stupider rules don't apply to us."

Shtasith bowed his long neck. "As you say, my Cluny."

"Yeah, well..." Crocker's sigh this time was a lot less snorty. "I just wish—" He stopped and shook his head. "I dunno *what* I wish." Leaning forward, he rested his forearms on top of his desk. "So what're we doing about these bubbles?"

Smiling, Cluny twitched her whiskers to make the strands of Crocker's strengthening spell glow in various colors. "If you and Shtasith can grab the tertiary layers there, I should at least be able to pull my claw out, and then we can get started on deconstructing the power matrix."

Crocker nodded, and the afternoon actually flew by, Cluny doing her best to show Crocker the problem rather than just fix it for him. He didn't snort either; in fact, there was a air of concentration about him that she usually only saw when they'd gotten themselves into some awful situation—like when Fitzwilliam Goulet had tried to kill their whole study group, or when Mistress Evantrue, the former dean of Huxley's Healing Arts Department, had tried to kill the three of them in her mad quest to tame the Wild Magic she thought Cluny was harnessing....

It had been, she thought as evening started darkening the sky outside their window, a fairly eventful first year.

"Ha!" Crocker slapping the desk brought her attention back. He poked a finger at their latest mountain of bubbles, and with a little ping, the shimmery surface let him pass right through. "And then?" His arm tensed under the sleeve of his wrinkled wizard's robes, and he pulled his finger back out.

A gulping noise like the last bit of water slipping down a drain, and the bubbles just quivered, not a single one popping.

"Ha!" Crocker said again, and he waggled the finger at Shtasith, the firedrake curled on the highest bookshelf above Crocker's bed. "You owe me a pizza!"

"I owe you nothing." Shtasith didn't even open his eyes. "The sun is mere moments from setting, and our bet clearly stated—" His eyes flew open then, and he leaped to all four paws, steam gusting from his gaping jaw. "My Cluny! Sunset! We will be late for study group!"

Cluny stretched and sighed. "It's independent study, Shtasith. That means nobody's taking attendance, remember?"

"But Crocker wished to—!"

"Shut up, Teakettle!" Crocker leaped across the room and wrapped a hand around Shtasith's whole head. "Whenever we get there'll be great, y'know? I mean, why would *I* be in a hurry to get to study group?" He gave a herky-jerky sort of laugh, his magic odd and jagged in a way Cluny had never felt before.

She narrowed her eyes at him. "There something going on here I ought to know about?"

"No!" Panic hovered around him like gnats, but then he took a breath, blew it out, almost seemed to deflate. "Really. There isn't. There *can't* be." He reached for the backpack with all their books and papers in it. "Can we just go?"

Glancing at Shtasith, Cluny had to blink some more when the firedrake avoided her gaze. "Yes," he said, "by all means." And leaping through the air, he settled on Crocker's shoulders.

Her brow wrinkling—neither of them smelled right, and their

magic was rubbing against hers as rough as winter tree bark—
Cluny nonetheless scampered down the front of Crocker's desk,
across the carpet, and up the off-white cotton of his robes into
the right breast pocket. Whatever secret her two familiars were
keeping didn't feel dangerous, so she let it go. "Just let me know
when you're ready to tell me."

Crocker gave a smile. "Thanks, Cluny."

Their nice, brisk walk across campus in the early fall evening
went quickly and quietly—well, except for the whispers that
followed them through Eldrich Park, the semi-wild woodlands at
the center of campus. And not just other students, Cluny couldn't
help noticing: even *professors* gave them curious looks and
started muttering as they went past.

Cluny sighed. The price of fame...

The study group Master Gollantz had gotten them into met at
noon and dusk in Podkamennaya Hall, Huxley's oldest library, a
hollowed-out pile of lichen-covered boulders at the edge of the
Park on the south side of campus. Crocker used his airball spell
to pop the illusion that covered the door, and when he stepped
them all inside, a thousand years of scholarship stroked across
Cluny's whiskers like a sweet summer breeze. Ever since she'd
used the building's accumulated magic to stop Goulet and his
mana flayer last year, it had seemed to her that the library knew
her, that it grinned a slow, rocky grin every time Crocker carried
her into the place.

As usual, Tzu Yin was sitting on the 'Information' desk, a
flannel shirt over her wizard's robe. "You're late, Crocker!" she
called with a grin that was neither slow nor rocky, and she
hopped to the floor, her black hair swishing around her ears.

From her perch in his breast pocket, Cluny could feel
Crocker's heart rate increase. "We were playing with soap
bubbles!" he more blurted than said.

Tzu Yin cocked her head. "Special project, I take it?"

Crocker's swallow seemed loud in the library's dim and
deserted reading room. But his voice was nearly normal when he
said, "Oh, you know us. We've always got *something* going on."

"I'll say." Tzu Yin turned for the stairwell hidden among the maze of bookshelves. "And hello, Shtasith and Cluny."

"A good evening," Shtasith replied, then whispered, "Perhaps, Crocker, you'd like to uproot yourself and follow?"

Crocker lunged forward; Cluny had to dig her claws into the fabric to keep from falling out. The young woman was waiting at the foot of the stairs, and she smiled as they started up, the silence all around strangely electric. "So!" Cluny asked, not quite believing what her whiskers were telling her about the situation. "How's Jian?"

"Great!" Tzu Yin beamed. "He loves that scouring spell you guys showed him." She spread her hands to create a glowing ball, the image of her sparrowhawk familiar zipping around it. "He's found a way to cast it on the air when he's in flight, and it sucks him along in its wake. He's managed some pretty impressive bursts of speed." She flicked her fingers to dissipate the ball. "You all should come over to Powell House and visit sometime, y'know? Let Jian show you his new tricks."

"Us?" Crocker's heart rate shot up again. "To your place?" His extra-salty smell and the general quiver that passed through his magic made Cluny crane her head around and wonder how she hadn't noticed before the way Crocker's feelings for Tzu Yin were practically floating in the air around him. Not that she knew anything about human courtship behavior: was this friendship? Admiration? Love? Lust?

She knew better than to ask about it here and now, though, so she just said, "I'll check our calendar when we get back to the room, Tzu Yin, and let you know when we can stop by."

Crocker started stammering, but by then they were topping the stairs, Podkamennaya's main hall stretching away to their right for almost as far as Cluny could see: ever since her scouring spell had stripped a thousand years of accumulated magical residue from the floor in order to clog Novice Goulet's mana flayer, the shining wooden parquet kept the room from being lost in shadows. The place looked much cheerier, she thought, and she had half a feeling that cleaning it up was the *real* reason the building liked her so much...

The pair of tables under the nearest glowing sconce was

always reserved for their group, and the others were already in their places, some of the most honored students at Huxley College: Enrique and Jeanette, leaders of the academic decathlon team; Meeshele, an amazing musician and the school's prize archer; and Eubie, a magical prodigy a few years younger than the rest of them and the funniest person Cluny had ever met, especially when his stoat familiar Tangle was with him.

Of course, Tangle *wasn't* with him—familiars and wizards followed completely different academic tracks, but part of their cover story held that Crocker needed Cluny and Shtasith with him at all times to stay balanced—and Cluny caught her breath to see Master Gollantz sitting where the tables met, the magister magistrorum's eyebrows looking thicker and stormier than ever.

"Sophomore Crocker—and ensemble," Master Gollantz said, the rumble behind his words a sound Cluny knew too well. "I've news to share with the group, so if you'll kindly take a seat?"

Crocker scrambled for the nearest empty chair, and Tzu Yin slid into the one beside him. Master Gollantz did a bit more glowering, then leaned his elbows onto the table. "I was informed earlier today that Fitzwilliam Goulet is being released from the hospital tomorrow morning."

The air seemed to freeze around Cluny, but that was OK since the questions the others started asking with varying degrees of panic were all the ones she would've asked if she'd been able to open her mouth: yes, Goulet had been found guilty of attempting to murder them all, but no, he wasn't going to prison for it. "The doctors can't find a single flicker of magic left in him." Master Gollantz spread his hands. "Stripping his abilities is the exact punishment the courts would've handed out anyway, so the authorities are remanding him to his parents' custody and closing the books on the case."

Cluny couldn't speak to object the way she wanted to, but Crocker cleared his throat above her and said in a cracking voice, "That seems a little short-sighted to me."

"Indeed." Master Gollantz scowled. "I examined the remains of the mana flayer he built, and the only word strong enough to describe it in my mind would be 'diabolical.' I've expressed my concerns directly to her Majesty, and while she was sympathetic, she supports the Justice Ministry's decision."

"But—" Eubie looked even younger than usual, his dark eyes very wide. "Goulet tried to kill us!"

Meeshele gave a laugh that Cluny guessed was supposed to be full of confidence even though it really just sounded scratchy and rattling. "But how stupid would he have to be to try again without magic? I mean, what's he gonna do? Throw rocks at us?"

Ric patted Eubie's shoulder, but Cluny's whiskers almost wilted under the collective unease settling over the group. The way Master Gollantz's eyes shifted told her he was noticing it as well. "As you say, Sophomore Mtembe, it's unlikely anything will happen, but I felt you needed to know. Your safety is our utmost concern, and several djinni from campus security are outside in case any of you wish to discontinue this evening's session and be escorted back to your rooms."

Eubie jumped at the offer, and Meeshele volunteered to go along with him. "So he won't get too scared," she said, but Cluny couldn't tell which of the two smelled more nervous.

Ric and Jeanette stood, said they'd be fine and that they'd see everyone tomorrow at noon, and that left Tzu Yin seated to Crocker's right, her hands clutching her backpack. "But I was gonna work on my project," she said plaintively, and Cluny had to nod. Tzusy was about the only person Cluny knew who was as devoted to magical research as she was herself. "Besides, Master Gollantz, you said Goulet wouldn't be released till tomorrow! How could he possibly bother anyone tonight?"

Master Gollantz glared through his eyebrows, but his wasn't the next voice that spoke. "I'll stay, too," Crocker said.

Cluny almost knocked herself out of her pocket craning her head back. Crocker shrugged, and Cluny was surprised when Shtasith ride the motion without even the tiniest hiss of complaint. "It's just," Crocker went on, "there'll be the four of us here, right?" He snapped his fingers and turned a big grin toward Tzu Yin. "Heck, since we're not in session, you can ask Jian to come over! Then we can all get some studying in, and it'll be *five* of us in case anything weird happens!"

The smile that Tzu Yin gave then, well, the increased thumping of Crocker's heart behind her made Cluny consider sending a quick message to Hesper, the unicorn currently in charge of Huxley's Healing Arts Department. "Crocker?" Tzusy poked him in the shoulder. "That's the best idea I've heard all week." She turned a pleading look toward Master Gollantz. "We'll just be a few hours, sir, I promise!"

Thinking to tip the balance, Cluny widened her eyes into her 'winsome woodland creature' face. "Please, sir?" she added.

Master Gollantz barked a laugh. "Stop it, the pair of you!" He crooked a finger so sharply, Cluny was sure she could feel it tap her chest. "With anyone else, I'd say no. But—"

"Yes!" Tzu Yin sprang from her chair and practically ran for the stairwell, Cluny's whiskers prickling at the force of the summoning spell that burst from her. "I'll go let Jian in!"

The silence when her footfalls faded pressed heavily against Cluny's ears. She swallowed and forced a smile at Master Gollantz. "Nothing will happen," she told him, though why she felt the need to say it out loud, she didn't know.

As sharp as the imaginary touch of his finger had been, the magister's gaze was even sharper. "With you three involved?" He stood, Crocker scrambling to his feet. "Something will *surely* happen." He headed toward the stairs. "I trust you to handle it, however." And he, too, descended out of sight.

"Goulet." Shtasith voice practically dripped with venom, and when Cluny looked up at him, flecks of red spun in his narrowed eyes. "He was a fool, yes, but not so much of one that he would dare come here in his current state." The little dragon's spiked tail lashed the air above Crocker's right shoulder. "I announce myself to be unconcerned!"

Cluny nodded and focused on Crocker. "So," she said as gently as she could. "You and Tzu Yin."

Crocker flinched, and Cluny tried to make her voice even gentler. "No! I mean, I think it's great, Crocker, that you, ummm..." She didn't know how to put it. "Have feelings for her?" she finished after a long and itchy couple of seconds.

His sigh seemed to deflate him again, and he slumped into his chair. "It can't ever happen, though."

"What?" Grabbing the front of his robes, Cluny scampered up to just below his shoulder. "Why would you say that?"

"I'm a fraud, Cluny, remember?" His magic had gone all spiky against hers once more. "A liar and a fake?"

"Crocker, you're not—"

"Not a wizard." He said it matter-of-factly, but the sourness in his scent told Cluny how much this still bothered him. "And, yeah, I know I have to do all this pretending so you can get your training and we can get ours; I mean, I *really* don't want us going all crazy and turning into a world-devouring freak show like the Jade Sorceress. But—"

Shtasith's hissed another jet of steam from his nostrils. "We would *not* follow that path, Crocker!" He flexed the needles of his claws. "I would tear out our Cluny's throat before I would allow her to fall into such evil!"

"No, you wouldn't," Crocker said just as quietly as before. "You like to think you would—heck, I like to think *I* would. But no." The calm depths of his eyes made Cluny's tail frizz behind her. "'Cause we're a team, sure, but she's the captain. And wherever she goes, we go. That's just plain truth."

Opening her mouth, wanting to deny it, Cluny found that she couldn't, the way their magic embraced her saying it clearly: they were together now and forever.

A swallow bulged Crocker's throat. "It's just another truth I can't tell Tzusy. And if I can't tell her the truth, then, well, then nothing happens between us. Simple."

Cluny clung to the front of his robes, her blood and breath just as frozen as when Master Gollantz had told them about Goulet. Then a whistle rang out downstairs, and she jerked her head around to see a silver-gray projectile not much larger than herself whoosh up the stairwell. "Greetings, all!" came Jian's familiar high-pitched squawk, and the sparrowhawk himself lit on the edge of the table with a flourish of wings. "It's an unexpected pleasure to join you here this evening!"

Laughter from below, the unmistakable stomp-stomp-stomp

of Tzu Yin's boots echoing up the stairs. "Will you wait a minute, Birdy?! Some of us only have feet, y'know!"

Jian rolled his eyes, and Cluny had to grin at Shtasith's extravagant sigh above her. "Ah, the lamentations of the landlocked," the little dragon said.

Tzu Yin topped the stairs, a big grin on her face, and they all settled in to study. Keeping to their usual charade, Cluny brought any books that she needed to consult over to where Crocker was scribbling away at the spellwork she'd given him so she could ask, "This is one of the books on the list, isn't it?"

Crocker would take it, leaf through it, nod sagely, and give it back to her. "Write up a summary, would you, please?"

None of which was technically a lie; the book was indeed on their list, and she would indeed be writing up a summary for her own notes. But that didn't stop her from wincing a little. Tzu Yin was sitting right there at the next table, after all, and knowing now how Crocker felt about not telling her the truth, Cluny wished she could think of another way.

What *really* surprised her, though, as the evening went on, was seeing that Tzu Yin and Jian were actually working the way that she and Crocker were pretending to, Jian holding what looked like one of his own shed quills in the gray sparkle of his magic and jotting careful notes as he leafed through a book from Tzusy's stack of research materials. And as much as Cluny didn't want to bring the subject up—Ric and Jeanette tended to tease Crocker about leaning so heavily on his familiars—three or four hours into their session, she couldn't help asking, "How long have you let Jian do book reports for you?"

Grinning, Tzusy patted the little stack of cards with the bird's meticulous writing on them. "I saw how well it worked for you guys, and I just—" Her eyes seemed to unfocus. "The bond you three have, the trust and the friendship, it's...I don't know. But Jian's willing to try some extra stuff, and so far it's turned out to be really helpful." She shrugged. "Not our fault nobody else wants to see the example you're setting."

A pair of light snores. Cluny turned to where Shtasith lay stretched across Crocker's slumped shoulders and gave a laugh.

"Yeah, well, I'd better get our prime exemplar home to bed."

Jian giggled, and Cluny roused Crocker enough to stuff all their books and papers into his pack. "So!" Tzu Yin clapped her hands. "You're walking me home, right, Crocker?"

Crocker's eyes opened so wide, Cluny figured he probably wouldn't sleep for a week. "Well, yeah! I mean, sure! 'Cause, y'know, it's late and Goulet and monsters and stuff."

"Goulet." Tzusy's face fell. "I tried talking to him a couple times, but he never seemed interested in talking back; I mean, he was quiet like a block of ice is quiet." She shook her head. "I wish I could've done more to help him."

Halfway up Crocker's robes, Cluny wanted to scurry back to pat Tzu Yin's hand, but Crocker was already standing and strapping on their pack. "Yeah, well," he said, "I only ever met him that last day when he, y'know, tried to kill us all."

Tzu Yin scowled, but Cluny quickly asked, "How did your research go this evening?" And that got the conversation moving in less painful directions. They left the old library and started down the path toward Eldritch Park, the midnight sky salted with stars and just chilly enough this early in the autumn to make Cluny know October was here. The woods stood as silently as always, even the scents seeming quieter when they started into the forest's darkness. Cluny noticed Tzusy lowering her voice and found herself doing the same; it just felt like the right thing to do in this place.

And when Shtasith stirred on Crocker's shoulders above her and snapped his head up with a hiss, it made her voice falter even further. "Crocker, my Cluny, Mistress Tzu Yin." He took a big sniff. "We are being observed."

The fur sprang up on Cluny's neck, Shtasith leaping into the darkness. "To the right, Jian!" he cried.

"I see him!" Jian chirped in reply, and Cluny felt the whoosh as the sparrowhawk rushed past Crocker's chest. A yowl rose up among the shadowy trees to their left, and something came bounding toward them from the underbrush, pointed ears and four legs the only impression Cluny got from the thing.

The squirreliest parts deep inside her shrieked, and the force bubble she cast seemed to leap almost unbidden from her claws and whiskers. "What—?!" Tzusy was shouting by then, her hands bursting into radiance, and in the sudden light, Cluny saw Shtasith and Jian swooping towards the pearlescent sphere she'd created, a large and wild-eyed black cat caught inside it. "Is that—?" Tzu Yin gave a gasp. "Polaris?"

Crocker had brought his own hands up by now, so Cluny slipped their usual misdirection spell into place to make it seem as if he was casting the shield. Shtasith had pulled into a hover above the bubble, Jian darting back and forth overhead, but Cluny forced her gaze away from the cat's tight ears and snarling muzzle. "You know him?" she asked Tzu Yin.

Tzusy was glancing around the forest. "Polaris," she said again. "He used to be Goulet's familiar."

"Not 'used to be'!" the cat hissed. "For I still am! I will never abandon him! *Never!*"

"What?" Tzusy snapped an annoyed glare at him. "Polaris, I've seen you around campus with other frosh wizards."

"So?!" Polaris folded his front legs across his chest. "Huxley forces me to play their stupid dating game so I can stay, but I have but one true master!" He threw himself against the force bubble. "And you're the ones who destroyed him!"

Shtasith flicked a claw against the shield, the bubble tolling like a bell and rattling the cat around inside it. "Speak respectfully! Besides, your master destroyed himself!"

"Hold it." Crocker squatted down before the floating bubble, and Cluny caught her breath, the cat's bared claws suddenly much closer than she would've liked. "Polaris? You haven't seen Goulet since they took him away, have you?"

Now that she was so near to the cat, Cluny could almost see the exhaustion hanging around him like a fog. "They wouldn't allow it," Polaris whispered. "They said he wasn't my master anymore, told me to move on, and I...I couldn't...didn't know how...never wanted to..." His voice trailed off, and silence again enveloped their little section of the woods.

Crocker's magic quivered against Cluny's as well, and as much as she didn't want to—"You're serious, Crocker?" she asked, trying to keep their cover story intact. "You think we should take Polaris to Goulet's house tomorrow?"

"What?!" four voices shouted at once, but only Shtasith's jabbed Cluny like a leap into the boughs of a pine tree. "My Cluny!" the firedrake went on. "What madness is this?!"

The surge of warmth from Crocker, though, made her tingle all over, and she let that feeling stroke through her fur as she raised her glance to where Shtasith and Jian were staring at her from above the goggle-eyed cat. "Jian?" Cluny asked, pretty sure she knew the answer but equally sure no one had ever asked him. "How bad is it for you when Tzu Yin comes across campus by herself twice a day for our study group meetings?"

Jian's wings stuttered. "It's bearable," he said after a long few seconds.

"What?" Tzu Yin stepped around the force bubble, left her glowing handprints floating in the air, and took the bird in her arms. "But I thought—I mean, you never said—"

"It's necessary." Jian stroked his wings along the sides of her neck. "We familiars must learn separation to be fully useful to our wizards." His eyes rolled shut, his next words barely audible. "But the lessons aren't easy."

More silence followed, but Cluny could tell from the way the swirling reds in Shtasith's eyes had softened to a more golden-yellow that, while he still didn't approve, he at least understood. Polaris, however—

"A trick," came the cat's wavering voice from inside the bubble. "You hate my master! Why would you reunite us?!"

"Hate him?" Crocker shook his head. "He just tripped over me when he was trying to kill some other people. But I can tell you this." A spell flickered around Crocker's hands, and Cluny barely recognized it as a backward version of the bubble magic they'd been working on all afternoon. "Goulet misses you just as much as you miss him." He rested his hands on the surface of the shield sphere. "So whaddaya say? You'll stay the rest of the night at our place, then tomorrow, we'll—" He stopped, his eyes going wide, and he turned a quick look toward Tzusy. "D'you know where Goulet's folks live?"

Tzu Yin shrugged. "I'll find out before we leave."

"They—" Polaris's ears rose, and that simple action drained about eighty percent of his scariness away, Cluny thought. "They live just down the hill in town; I've been there many times. But—" The hope sparking at his whiskers dispelled the last bit of the panic he'd been inspiring in Cluny. "You'd do this? Honestly?"

"You bet." Crocker's hands flared, activating the odd spell, and Cluny could only blink as he reached through the force bubble, lifted Polaris out, and set him on the path.

"Wow," Tzu Yin said, she and Jian still holding each other. "I mean, with his magic gone, Goulet wouldn't've been able to renounce you and let you go even if he'd wanted to, and, well, it doesn't sound like you're interested in renouncing him."

"I couldn't." Devotion shone from Polaris's eyes. "He needs help, not more isolation."

Cluny nodded. "OK. Tomorrow morning we'll all—"

The familiar gurgle of Shtasith clearing that long, narrow throat interrupted her. "And Master Gollantz? Do we inform him of our plan? In case this highly touching story turns out to be just as highly rehearsed?" He settled onto the still floating but now empty shield bubble and arched an eyeridge at Polaris.

Crocker's magic went cold around hers, and he looked down at her again.

"Hmmm." Tzu Yin tapped her foot. "If Master Gollantz gets involved, this gets public real fast, and I mean 'front page of the papers' public." She shrugged. "Which might not be a bad thing if we're looking to help Goulet."

"No." Cluny felt this all the way down to her bones. "The ranting he did when he was holding us prisoner in the library made it pretty clear that feeling humiliated's what made him snap. So the less of a spotlight there is on this, the better."

A hiss folded her ears, Polaris's whiskers crackling. "Master Crocker! How can you allow such insolence from a creature who isn't even a proper familiar?!"

Cluny froze; had she been acting too 'in charge'? But Crocker just folded his arms. "'Cause she's usually right." He turned to

Tzu Yin. "Can you, I dunno, rig up some sort of time-delayed message? We'll leave here tomorrow at eight, and if we're not back by eleven or something, the message'll fire off and tell Master Gollantz everything."

Tzusy blinked. "Yeah, sure, I can do that." She glanced sideways, blew a breath at the glowing handprints floating beside her, and they went out like candles, the forest's darkness engulfing them again. "Looks like you get another reprieve from walking me home, Crocker." The shadowy place that was her moved, Cluny's eyes adjusting quickly enough to see her brush a quick kiss against Crocker's cheek. "I'll get that message set up, catch a couple hours sleep, and be at your place tomorrow before eight." And she was gone.

Crocker's magic seemed to swell against Cluny's like a balloon pressing a pin, but she wrapped it tight to keep it from exploding; they still had a guest, after all. "Polaris?" She leaned over the edge of her pocket, and in the slight glow of the shield bubble, she saw him still standing where Crocker had set him. "Is this all OK with you?"

Nothing for a moment, then—"Better than OK," he said, his voice a little choked. "I...I don't know how to thank you."

"No problem!" Crocker announced with a clap of his hands; thinking quickly, Cluny used the sudden sound and motion to cover her dispelling the force bubble. "Now! I need to lie down before I fall down, so how 'bout we turn in, huh?"

The walk back to the dorm went quietly, Shtasith staying airborne, the fire of his magic sharp and vigilant to Cluny's senses. Polaris paced alongside Crocker, and the few flickers of emotion that flashed through his typical feline reserve seemed warm and positive. And Crocker, of course, practically floated the whole way. Cluny smiled, picturing herself as the lines that tethered his hot-air balloon to the ground.

In their room, Crocker said, "Make yourself comfortable, Polaris. Bathroom's through there, and if you can find anything in the fridge, you're welcome to it." Cluny scrambled down the front of his robes as he fell back onto the bed, his boots popping off with the shimmer of the unlacing spell she'd taught him. Not even bothering with his socks, he burrowed into the blankets, and to Cluny's amazement, slid immediately to sleep, his magic around her as light and fluffy as chocolate mousse.

Climbing up to her own nest of blankets on the first bookshelf above his bed, she watched Polaris curl himself into the space between the end of the desk and the far bookcase, his back against the wall. She still had more questions she wanted to ask him, but the way his breathing deepened and his muscles relaxed, she got the impression that this was maybe the first easy sleep he'd had in months.

"Rest, my Cluny," came Shtasith's gentlest hiss, and she looked up to see orange swirling eyes on the shelf above her bed. "I shall keep the night watch."

Nodding, she let her familiars' separate styles of magic wrap around her, and when she found herself blinking awake to the early morning sunlight drifting in at the window, she felt rested and ready for whatever might happen. A quick glance showed her the three males still asleep in the places she'd last seen them, and she sent a few gentle nudges along the links connecting her to Crocker and Shtasith.

The two shifted and grumbled. That got Polaris twitching, the cat gasping and leaping to his paws half a moment later.

Cluny fought the urge to do the same. "It's all right, Polaris!" she called down to him. "You're in Terrence Crocker's room, remember? We're going to see your master Goulet later!"

Polaris froze, then turned his head, his eyes wide and staring. "I...I'd been afraid it was a dream," he mumbled.

Tzu Yin and Jian showed up about half an hour later with smiles and a bag of butter croissants. "Our insurance policy's all set," Tzusy said, Cluny more than a little surprised to discover that they had enough plates for everyone. "I also looked up some info on prisoner releases and found that Her Majesty's djinni tend to do their work really early in the morning. So Goulet's probably already home."

Jian, perched atop Tzu Yin's backpack on the floor beside her, fished a folded piece of paper from it, and Tzu Yin opened it with a flare of her fingers. "This is a map of Huxley Grove." She tapped a finger at the familiar irregular shape of the campus in the lower left-hand corner of the page and waved to the more regular gridwork of streets and boulevards that crisscrossed the rest of the surface, her attention fixed on Polaris. "Do you remember Goulet's parents' address?"

"413 Tamarack Road." Polaris's whiskers twitched, and a red dot appeared in the upper right section of the map.

A little frown creased Tzu Yin's forehead. "That's a couple miles." She sighed and stood. "Well, at least we know he'll be there for sure by the time we hoof it over there."

"Hoof?" Cluny waved a paw. "That's OK. I'll just—" She caught herself. "—just have Crocker teleport us."

"Teleport?" Tzusy turned her deepening frown toward Crocker. "That far away? To a place you've never been?"

Cluny pulled her mouth shut. She could've explained the process easily enough, of course, but, well, like Polaris had said so angrily last night, as far as anyone knew, Cluny wasn't even a real familiar. So she *certainly* wasn't supposed to have any knowledge of the more obscure types of teleportation spells.

"Oh, sure!" Crocker was saying. "You just send out a— Whaddaya call it, Cluny? A wave pulse form?"

"Pulse waveform," she corrected before she could stop herself.

"*That's* it!" Crocker snapped his fingers, the sound and the motion drawing Tzusy's and Jian's and Polaris's attention back to him. "See, it reads the lay of the land before you get there and automatically corrects the spell matrix so you end up on a solid horizontal surface instead of, y'know, halfway inside something." He gave a big grin. "Cluny's really good at rooting out these neat spells for me. You just wait, Tzusy, till Jian starts bringing you stuff *he's* found!" He flapped the sleeves of his robes. "So c'mon! Cluny, Shtasith, mount up! Tzusy, Jian, Polaris, gather 'round here, and we'll be off!"

Shtasith had been sitting quietly on one of the upper bookshelves this whole time, his magic hovering around Cluny's with a simmering watchfulness. But now he spread his wings and glided down to Crocker's shoulders, his wings flapping with a little flourish as he landed. "Fear not," he said, and while he was looking at the other three in the room, Cluny could practically feel the warmth of his words stroking the fur between her ears. "All will be well."

Cluny wasn't so sure, scampering forward to hook her claws into the front of Crocker's robes. Because yes, she'd been lying to nearly everyone for almost a year, but with Tzu Yin and Jian and Polaris standing right there looking at her, for the first time, she thought she understood what Crocker had been saying yesterday. How could she really be friends with these folks if she couldn't be truthful with them?

"Right," Crocker said, raising his arms, and Cluny shook herself, huddled down into her pocket, let her whiskers bristle into the misdirection spell she used so often. She spread her claws, plucked the strings of power that lay under reality itself to send vibrations northeast, and when the waveform pulsed back to her, she squinted at Tzusy's map, matched the pattern there to the one she was picking up from the physical world on the other side of town, and nudged a hind foot into Crocker's chest to let him know she was ready.

"Here we go!" he called out, and Cluny triggered the spell, wrapped its energy around all six of them, and popped them through the spaces between space to the corner of Tyler and Tamarack, her whiskers shivering as the air where they appeared rushed back to fill the void they'd left behind in their dorm room. This sort of spell was all about balance, after all.

Tzusy gasped. "Crocker! That was...that was *amazing*! How did you—?!"

"I'll lend you the book." Crocker's heart was hammering in his chest like a bird trying to escape; Cluny leaned back and sent soothing waves over him as well as she could, her own jangled mental state not helping at all. Still, his voice came out more or less normally. "Remind me when we get back, Cluny."

She nodded, took her first breath in what seemed like minutes, and glanced at the neighborhood: single-family homes with well-tended yards under a crisp blue October morning. "The house is 413?" she asked, looking down at Polaris.

The cat twitched and blinked like he was coming awake. "Yes." He lifted his nose and sniffed, his ears springing to attention. "He's there! Please! Quickly!" And he took off up the sidewalk.

Cluny looked over at Tzusy and Jian, and they were looking back at Crocker. A gust of steam, and Shtasith said, "I sense no threats, but I would still recommend caution."

Crocker gave a little laugh. "Yeah, thanks, Teakettle." He started after Polaris, Cluny clinging to the edge of her pocket, her whiskers spread for any hint of magic more intense than she would expect in a nice part of town like this.

"Weird," Tzusy murmured, moving right alongside Crocker, her head swiveling from side to side. "I half expected Goulet to live in some dank and run-down old mansion."

"Tzu Yin?" Jian chirped quietly. "Polaris has stopped."

Focusing forward, Cluny saw the cat sitting on the sidewalk in front of one of the many little houses that lined the street, his tail lashing the sidewalk. "Polaris?" she asked as they came up to him. "Is this it?"

Polaris didn't answer, but it was fear Cluny sensed in the air around him, not anger. "What...what if the master renounces me?" he whispered, his dark eyes wide on the front door at the end of its brick walkway. "What if he tells me he doesn't want me, tells me to go away and not return, tells me to—?"

"He won't." Crocker brushed his fingertips over Polaris's ears, stepped up to the front door and knocked.

Cluny sucked in a breath, Shtasith's magic humming soundlessly around her, and readied her whiskers to unleash as many defensive spells as she knew—

But after nothing happened for several long, long seconds, she forced herself to blow the breath out and take another. Wouldn't do anyone any good if she passed out, after all...

Sighing, Crocker knocked on the door again, and this time it opened to reveal a tall, older man in a button-down shirt and slacks, his aura barely flickering even to Cluny's amped-up perceptions. "Yeah?" the man asked.

"Ummm," was all Crocker said.

167

With an effort, Cluny kept herself from lashing the claws of her hind paws into his chest, put on her 'small woodland creature' face, and gestured toward the street. "Good morning, sir. We brought Polaris by."

"Polaris?" a voice from deeper in the house called out, and Fitzwilliam Goulet himself slid from a door behind the older man, everything about him even more pale and drawn than Cluny remembered from that day last spring.

"Master!" Hearing joy in the cat's voice for the first time made Cluny grin, something dark flashing past Crocker's shins and leaping into Goulet's arms.

The moment floated, Cluny thought, like a soap bubble, Goulet gasping, pulling Polaris close, pressing his face into the cat's black fur, Polaris's eyes curling shut, his body going limp, his purr as loud as a lawnmower to Cluny's ears.

Then the older man cleared his throat. "Come in, then."

Goulet's head snapped up. "What are *you* doing here?" he asked, but the way his eyes skittered around under his brows like leaves in a windstorm, Cluny couldn't tell if he was looking at Crocker or Tzu Yin or all of them when he said it.

"William," the older man growled. "They brought your familiar home. Say 'thank you.'"

"Father, these are—" Goulet stopped, a twitch pulling at his cheek, and held Polaris a little closer. "These are two of the students I tried to kill." His lips curled, and Cluny had no doubt that his glare then was aimed directly at Crocker. "*That* one's the wizard who tore my soul out and destroyed any possibility that I might ever lead a normal life."

"I'm not a wizard," Crocker said quietly, and Cluny nearly froze. "Remember? You tested me when we were sitting there in the library, and I didn't have any more magic than a baby."

"I—" Goulet's eyes widened. "I did. You...you registered a few points above null."

"Impossible!" Tzu Yin stepped around Crocker, her brow wrinkled. "The things I've seen you do—"

"I didn't do any of them." His magic tugged at Cluny, made her look up to meet his gaze. "Did I, Cluny?"

Again, the pressure of their attention—Tzusy, Jian, Goulet, his father, Polaris, all of them turning their various wondering or confused expressions toward her—made her want to chitter, want to scream, want to leap over Crocker's shoulder and run, run, run till her legs gave out. What was Crocker doing?! He knew as well as she did that everyone who'd come to suspect the truth since last spring had tried to kill them!

OK, so maybe Master Gollantz hadn't tried to kill them. And Hesper, she'd actually helped them put together their current cover story after she'd found out. But—

Their cover story. Cluny blinked as the thought blossomed inside her. It wasn't really a story, was it?

"It's true," she heard herself say, and she swiveled herself around in her pocket to look from Tzusy to Goulet. "Crocker isn't a wizard. I'm not a wizard. Shtasith isn't a wizard. It's only when we're together, trusting each other and helping each other, that we *become* a wizard." She fixed on Tzusy's startled eyes. "You told me last night how much better you and Jian are getting things done now that you're treating him like a partner instead of a pet, right?"

Perched on Tzusy's shoulder, Jian gave a little chirp, and Tzusy reached up, touched his claws, the air practically glowing around them. Cluny turned quickly to Goulet and Polaris, still clinging to each other. "And even though that flayer sucked out every drop of the abilities you used to possess, Goulet, now that you and Polaris are together again—" Cluny swallowed, everything she'd learned about the way magic flowed through the mind, the heart, the soul, and the body telling her she was right. "I know you can feel something. I *know* it."

The young man was panting like he'd been running in place the whole time; he clenched his eyes and shuddered, and a shower of light green sparks clattered down from his hair.

Polaris gave a joyful yowl. "Master!"

"But—!" Goulet's voice choked off. He buried his face in Polaris's fur for a moment, and when his head came back up, tears shimmered on his cheeks. "How?"

And as much as Cluny wanted to shrink back into her pocket,

she was pretty sure that wasn't an option any longer. "Humans have one sort of magic, animals have another, and it's only when we come together that we make a wizard." She took a breath, blew it out. "I think maybe they've forgotten that up at Huxley." She reached for the warmth of Crocker's magic, once again smooth and comfortable around her, and for the fire of Shtasith's magic, banked for now but always ready.

"And maybe," Cluny muttered, her whiskers shivering, "maybe it's time somebody *reminded* them."

AMMA'S WISHES

by M.E. Garber

There are a lot of stories about people who are granted three wishes. Very few of them feature people who manage to use the wishes sensibly.

M. E. Garber grew up reading about hobbits, space-travel, and dragons, so it's no wonder that she now enjoys writing speculative fiction, and dreams of traveling the world(s). She used to live near the home of Duck Tape, then near the home of Nylabone. Now she lives near the home of Gatorade. She's a 2013 graduate of the Viable Paradise Writers' Workshop. See her blog, megarber.wordpress.com, for more information.

The door to the Dragon's Beard Tavern slammed open and wintry winds gusted within, twisting Amma's skirts about her legs like the arms of a drunken hero. Amma stumbled, sloshing ale from the tankards on her tray onto her skirts. She glared towards the door, where three men dressed in crimson-edged blacks let the door bang shut behind them.

Damn these fighters. Couldn't they just once enter like human beings?

They swaggered to the far table, ignoring everyone in the crowded tavern. "Stew!" one yelled over his shoulder.

"Wench! Hurry with that ale. We're thirsty men!" a helmed man at the table before her demanded. Those around him roared their agreement.

She slapped the tankards onto their table, careful that the ale didn't slosh over so much as dance within the cups. *What would their mothers think of them, acting like this?* She glared at each man in turn, daring any to speak out. None did.

She turned to stomp back to the kitchen when a great hand seized her buttock. Anger and frustration engulfed her. She whirled, lifting the serving tray high and crashed it onto the helm of the damned dwarf, who sat stunned but grinning like the idiot he was. Amma fled for the kitchen's safety, her heart beating in her throat and her arms shaking, as raucous laughter rang in her ears.

Once through the kitchen doors, she slumped against the wall, letting her breathing drop its ragged edge. The rage that had fed her strength fled, and exhaustion weakened her limbs.

"What's wrong now?" Marda asked, her voice sharp. The innkeeper's wife and tavern cook scooped three bowls of stew and handed them over.

"The same. Grown men acting like boys." Amma loaded the bowls onto her dented tray, pausing as her anger bloomed again. "My six year old nephew behaves better, Marda! What's *wrong* with them?"

The older woman wiped her hands in her stained apron as a tired smile creased her face. Her eyes clouded with memories. "Amma. Child. They're not bad men. My Grumps was one of them for years, you know. We met at a tavern just like this one, and the men back then, they were just the same. They're only showing off for each other. It's what adventurers do."

"I wish they'd do it someplace else, then. I'm tired of it." She turned to leave the kitchen.

"You think it's better at The House of Flowers?" Marda's laugh pealed out into the front room as Amma shoved open the swinging door with her hip. No, servers at the only other bar in Milldale had it worse. At least here she didn't have to turn tricks, as they did. She carried the stew to the newcomers. They tried to impress her, flexing their mighty thews, but she ignored them.

Instead she made her way to the drafty corner table where Forgettable Fillmorr hunched alone over his tankard. The spectacled mage was the only one who treated her like a human, probably because she could snap him like a twig if she'd wanted. On the bench beside him rested a brownish lump: his long-empty loot sack. Now it sported a tiny bulge. The mage sighed as

Amma neared.

"Another ale, Formidable?" she asked, using the name he called himself instead of what others called him.

He startled, then blinked up at her. "Why yes, that would be nice. Thank you, Anna."

Amma smiled as she went for his drink. He always forgot her name. But he said "thank you," and he never slammed the door.

Her smile was wiped away as the door was flung open again, crashing against the inside wall with a reverberating *boom*.

The night eventually ran itself down. The bard in the corner went from stomping tunes to mellow ones, then slid into melancholy ballads that salted everyone's ale with tears. When he slipped out the front door, Amma assessed the nearly empty common room: cider made a slow splat-splat-splat as it dripped onto the floor while Fillmorr nodded his head in time, his eyes owlish and unblinking.

Behind the bar, Grumps rattled the crockery as he wiped at dirty mugs with an equally dirty rag. Amma set to moving the filth around, working her way to Fillmorr's table.

"Formidable, it's time to leave."

He tilted his neck up at her and blinked rapidly. "So soon?"

She nodded.

He gave a little sigh. "Well, I suppose so." He placed a hand on the tabletop and started to rise, but shivered, stopped and sank back down. "Oh! But first, I need to do this." His hand went below the table, and an odd expression crossed his face, as if he concentrated hard on his actions.

Amma leapt aside, afraid he was going to urinate right there. But no. His hand reappeared holding his loot sack, which thumped when he placed it on the table. Still staring at the bag, he spoke slowly. "Tonight, Ennie, I celebrated my last day as an adventurer. I've had enough. I'm going back to Immonsville, to run the candle works there for my aged mother." He raised his eyes to meet Amma's, and they were surprisingly clear. "No one will miss me, and most probably won't remember me. I know they called me "Forgettable," and I am. But you, Essi, you always treated me kindly. To you, I'm giving the last of my adventuring treasures. I bequeath you my padded loot sack, and the last trinket within. It's not much, but its the only way I can express my thanks to you, kind lady."

With that, he rose onto unsteady feet and bowed. She backed away, afraid he might topple over, but he turned and left the inn, shutting the door silently behind him.

Amma looked from the door, back to the brownish lump of sack he'd left for her. It was padded, to mute the sounds of things clinking within. At the very least, it would make a good pillow. Once she'd washed it.

"What's wrong then?" Grumps' voice cut through her thoughts.

She shoved the bag beneath her apron, looping it through the strings to hold it in place. "Nothing. Fillmorr just told me he's leaving."

"Hunh. No surprise there. He never was the right type. Didn't have enough bravado, enough flair. His name fits. 'Forgettable,' indeed."

Gritting her teeth, Amma continued washing up.

~o0o~

By the time cleanup ended and Amma was safely locked within her tiny room, she was exhausted. She didn't care what the sad loot sack contained. She was tucking it away in her clothing box when something heavy bruised her knuckles. Frowning, she upended the bag. A tiny oil lamp of some foreign sort fell out, its brass tarnished and stained.

No wonder Fillmorr didn't want it. He's going into the candle business.

She berated herself for the unkind thought. It wasn't a bad gift, not at all. With a bit of cleaning, it would be fine. To prove it, she wiped vigorously with her sleeve, trying hard to bring forth the gleam of the metal.

With a hiss like sand in an hourglass, whitish smoke billowed from the spout. Amma flung it onto her bed, backing away from the cloud that formed between her and the door. She ran for the window and tried to fling it open, but the old frame was warped, and it wedged after opening only an inch.

174

Maybe it'll be enough to let the poison gasses out. Turning, she put a hand over her mouth and nose and stared at the shape that had formed.

From floor to ceiling, the mist congealed into the form of a burly red-skinned man. He wore outlandish purple-striped pants, and a tiny brimless hat perched on his bald head. Gold winked from both ears, and thick bands of it encircled his wrists, as well. His eyes gleamed like hot brass, not kindly at all. Amma gasped, and shrank to the floor.

"Mistress." His voice was deep, but soft. Gentlemanly, even. The genie bowed.

Amma scrambled to her feet, but remained pressed against the window.

"I come to your call. I am the genie of the lamp, bound to your service."

She'd heard such tales, of course. Working with adventurers, how could she not? But she'd never thought they were real. "You're...going to grant me three wishes?"

"My reputation precedes me. How nice." The genie smiled, but his eyes remained cruel. "This will simplify things greatly. You know the procedure, then? Standard offer—three wishes, no wishing for more wishes, et cetera."

She nodded, and moved towards her bed. "May I?" She indicated the lamp with a bob of her head. He nodded, so she grasped the lamp and placed it upon the wash basin stand, then seated herself on the woolen blanket covering her bed. She stared, silent and still, at her feet.

The genie cleared his throat. "Your wish?"

"I don't know." She shook her head. "I know better than to wish for money—it'll just make more trouble than it's worth. Or fame, for the same reason. Or a dozen other things. So, what should I wish for?"

"What is your greatest desire, Mistress?"

After her ridiculous day, his voice, so calm and cajoling, released some spring within her. She nearly shouted it: "I just want everyone in this damn tavern to behave *properly* for a change!"

"Done!"

An explosion of color, smoke everywhere, but no sound. When it cleared, Amma found herself curled atop her blanket upon her bed. She was shivering in the frigid air blowing in her window. The tiny lamp rested where she'd set it, on the washbasin stand. Just a bad dream. Then why was she disappointed?

Rising, she shut the window, blew out the candle and lay under her blankets. In moments, she was asleep.

~oOo~

The next day found Amma downstairs marveling at the customers coming in the door. Not one slammed it open or closed. They held the door for one another, and swept bows towards Marda and Amma, but their actions were stiff, their motions jerky. They looked like marionettes manipulated by terrible puppeteers. It was hard not to giggle.

Even Grumps, after frowning at the first few adventurers who came traipsing so peaceably within, couldn't slam the tankards down and curse out his frustrations. He was reduced to a wild-eyed rant of "My goodness, but what's come over everyone this evening?" as he paced rapidly behind the bar.

Amma was in heaven. No one grabbed for her. No one yelled at her. No one slammed the door. They all behaved like perfect gentlemen. Once she got over their odd motions, she relaxed and enjoyed the effects of her wish. She knew there was no way she could go back to how it had been.

Word got out. The next day, adventurers were daring one another to step over the threshold, and to just *try* cursing. The following day, they were making wagers on how long certain patrons could stand it. The crowd outside the door and at the windows became larger than the one inside. By the fourth day, no one came inside. No one at all.

~oOo~

Marda and Grumps summoned Amma as she floated down the staircase. They ushered her into the kitchen, which shone with the attention it had recently received.

"It's been six days, Amma. Six days with no business." Grumps' face contorted as he was forced to swallow the curses he wanted to spit out. "I'm afraid we'll have to let you go. We can't afford to keep going with no customers. Please say you understand." His face said he'd like to yell and scream and pound the table. Marda looked like she'd swallowed an overripe egg whole. She patted her husband's hand.

Amma's joy dissolved. Turning tricks would be her only option.

"Just give it another day, please," she begged them. Thinking fast, she added, "It's only polite, after all, to give an employee notice."

Marda's eyes narrowed, and Grumps was shaking his head.

"Without pay, of course," she added. "Just let me keep the room."

"Very well, then. Another day," Marda said.

Amma ran for the lamp. She lifted the heavy brass and rubbed it with her clean skirt. The genie appeared, smiling like a cat that's been in the pantry.

"All's well, Mistress? Your wish was satisfactory?"

"Yes. No! I mean, *I* like it, but no one's coming to the tavern now, so I'm being fired! You've got to tell me how to make this work, genie. This week has been heaven!"

"Sorry, Mistress, but I'm not allowed to interpret your wishes for you, or to tell you how to word them properly. That's against the rules."

"Rules? *You* have rules?"

"My life is filled with rules, Mistress." He lifted his arms, displaying the gold wristlets. They winked in the sunlight filtering through her window. "These bands mark me as a slave to the lamp, and slaves live and die by rules."

Only two more wishes, and the genie couldn't help her. He was already turning tricks.

"Can you drink, genie? I think we have lots in common, and a drink might make things seem better."

She sneaked downstairs and liberated a bottle of dragonberry wine. It was potent stuff, and soon she and the genie—"call me

Gene"—were sharing stories of the ways people took them for granted, talked down to them. They commiserated over glass after glass.

"The worsht of it cometh when they prwomish to fwree me, but I know they're lying," Gene said. He stared into his glass, then upended it, draining the last of their wine.

Amma thought he might be slurring a bit, but she wasn't sure. His statement, though, was an outrage. "They lie to you? To *you*? You're a genie! You should kill 'em all." She waved her empty glass.

"Can't." Gene hiccoughed. "Can't hurt anyone who's owned the lamp, unleth ordered to. Even if I do get fwree."

"If-*smiff*," she said, swaying a little. "When I figure this out, *I'll* free you. I promise." She hugged him, and promptly began snoring, even before her forehead landed on his shoulder.

She woke cradling the lamp against her belly. A headache was splitting her skull in two and sending sharp slivers of agony deep within her eyes. She shut them, gulped down her nausea, and opened them again. The inn was blissfully silent.

She recalled why, and her deadline. She sat up. The room swayed, but Amma forced herself to wash, dress and go downstairs.

Grumps and Marda slumped like drunks in the empty common room. The glare they gave as Amma came downstairs spoke volumes, and Amma winced, knowing they'd never let her stay. She asked anyway.

Grumps shook his head, and his eyes held a desolation she'd never seen in him before. "No. You must go." He met her gaze and his anger flickered to life. "See what happens when you get what you ask for? Nothing good comes from being too picky. Nothing!"

Marda patted her husband's broad shoulder. "If adventurers wanted to behave like proper gentlemen, they'd have stayed home with their mothers," she agreed. "This just isn't natural."

The words snapped in Amma's head, and she knew what to do. "Alright. I'll leave. But I'll be back. I'm going to solve this riddle." She fled upstairs, packed her few possessions in

Fillmorr's loot sack and scurried out the door, which swung gently shut behind her.

Outside, the night's rains had ceased, but the wintry cold remained. Not having coin for the coach to Immonsville, Amma began walking. By mid-afternoon, her hangover was frozen away.

She scurried through the wide streets of Immonsville until she came to a sign showing a robed student holding a lit candle over a book: the Scholar's Candle Works.

Squaring her shoulders, she pushed the door beneath it open. A bell tinkled sweetly. She faced a long counter, which guarded a curtained doorway. The curtain twitched aside, and a man bobbed into view, still reading the book in his hand. It took a moment for Amma to recognize Fillmorr; he'd been transformed into a merchant by the fine clothes.

"Yes," he said, looking up at last. "Oh! It's you, Ammy." His gaze traveled from her to the door, as if looking for the loutish adventurers from the Dragon's Beard in her wake.

She stepped forward and smiled. "Yes, it's me. Formidable—"

He raised a hand, wincing. "No. I'm just Fillmorr now."

"Fillmorr, then. I need your help."

He gave her a sorrowful smile, the one she'd seen from him so often. "I've given all that up now, Emmi. You know that. But I see you're using my loot sack. I'm glad."

"Yes," she said, seizing the opportunity. "That's what I'm here about." She pulled the lamp out and set it on the counter. It shone in the light streaming in the rounded glass window behind her.

Fillmorr admired it. "My, that looks lovely now that you've shined it. It *is* the one I gave you, isn't it?"

"Yes. But it's not just a lamp. Look." She rubbed the cold brass briskly, warming it with her hand. Smoke and Gene poured out.

Gene gave her a wincing look, then saw Fillmorr. He straightened, crossing his arms over his chest, and his voice boomed. "What is your command, Oh Mistress?"

Fillmorr's mouth gaped.

Amma smiled, stifling her laugh by biting a knuckle. "It's alright, Gene. I'm just here to get Fillmorr's help. He's the one who gave your lamp to me."

Gene eyed the former mage, taking in his merchant's garments, his thin frame, and the book in his hand. "You...you were a mage," he said at last. "You found my lamp, and you...you gave it to Amma? Freely?"

Fillmorr lived up to his moniker, at last. He snapped his mouth shut, straightened his spine to stand erect before the towering bulk of the genie.

"Yes. I found your lamp in a troll's treasure heap. And when I gave up adventuring, I gave the lamp to..." he glanced at Amma, "to Amma. I didn't know it...I mean, thought she could use it. *You*. I mean, that she might need it more than I." He flushed and stared at his feet.

The genie shrank to human size, his hot eyes fixed on Fillmorr. "No one has willingly parted with my lamp before. You are unique. Intriguing, even."

Fillmorr burned brighter red. Amma cleared her throat. "Getting back to the situation, then." She explained the problem at the inn to Fillmorr, and how she'd been relieved of her job, and how she was determined to use her final wish to free Gene from his lamp forever.

Fillmorr listened, his face growing more intent by the second.

"So," he said when she'd finished, "you need to get your job back. Why don't you just undo the last wish?"

Amma fidgeted her feet and looked at her hands as they played with the cords of the loot sack. "Well, I *like* it the way it is. I can't go back to the old way. I just can't!" She lifted her head, beseeching him to understand.

They moved to the back room and Fillmorr's mother, a shawl draped over her shoulders, took over the shop. Fillmorr and Amma sat at a small table in straight-backed chairs. Gene hovered in the corner, just below the low rafters, glowing as brightly as the fire in the hearth.

"So, Gene, you can't aid Em—Amma's questions in any way, right?" he asked for the third time. He tapped a slender finger to his pursed lips, staring at the tabletop before him.

Amma sipped her tea, looking from Fillmorr to the nodding Gene and back again over the rim of her cup, her stomach clenched in hope, anxiety, and dread. She didn't want to be yet another possessor of the lamp to wriggle out on her pledge to free the genie, but it was looking more and more likely. She closed her eyes.

"But you can tell *me*, right? I'm not your Master, and honestly, I already gave your lamp away. So you can tell me anything."

Amma's fingers loosened on the teacup, and she nearly dropped it to the floor. She sat it back on the table with a clatter, her eyes never leaving Gene, who considered the question.

He frowned, stuck out a thick lower lip, tugged at it with a beefy hand. His golden bracelets glinted in the light, and the fire in his eyes was banked. He looked to Fillmorr, then to Amma. "I do think you're correct. There is no prohibition against it, if you're not family or romantically entangled. You're not, are you?"

It was Fillmorr's turn to spit his tea. He choked, gasping, and Amma reached out and snatched his cup away.

"No," she said. "Definitely not."

Amma and Fillmorr stayed in the back room, and the genie went to Fillmorr's bedroom; he couldn't speak knowing that Amma would hear his words directly. It slowed things down, but Amma didn't care. They would figure this out.

Fillmorr brainstormed with Amma, then carried messages back and forth. "Forgettable Fillmorr" was long gone as he bustled about, his stride long and his face determined. "The Reward Idea won't work. The gold will lure adventurers to steal it," he'd report. "But what if we...," and they were off again, plotting the next potential wordage.

Again and again, he came back, shaking his head. "No on the Muffling Spell."

"Nope. Not the Politeness Potion, either."

"The Sparkle Dust won't fly."

Amma's heart sank, and her shoulders slumped lower.

Night fell. Fillmorr's mother brought them bread, sliced pork, and cider, and now their empty plates lingered on the table beside her. The cloying scent of old cider filled her with despair.

Fillmorr burst in and threw himself into the chair beside her. "No. It won't work. It just won't," he said. He crossed his arms and scowled, his thin face sour and nasty looking.

He'd have made a fine adventurer if he wore this face all the time.

"There's no solution, Amma." He leaned forward, elbows on his knees and head cradled in his hands. "I'm not smart enough to see it, at least. So now I'm failing even you."

Her blood boiled at his self pity. *He* was failing? What about *her*? She was the one heading to the whorehouse, not him. She slammed her hand down onto the table. He leapt, cringed away and stared at her as if she were going crazy. "What—" she began to yell, but was interrupted when the door creaked open.

Fillmorr's mother shuffled in, her eyes bright. "Still up? Let me just clean away these things, then, dears. Don't mind me, carry on 'chatting.'" And she began the painstakingly slow process of removing the plates from the table between them.

Fillmorr gave her a look, begging Amma to hold her tongue and temper before his mother. Her pulse beat in her ears, a hard drum that slowed only as she concentrated on her breathing.

The old woman shuffled out at last, and Fillmorr breathed out, a deep sigh. "Thank you," he said. "Mother hates rude guests."

She opened her mouth to curse him roundly, but popped it closed with a snap.

"Your mother—" she said. And then, "Marda said adventurers would stay home with their mothers if they wanted to behave." She beamed at Fillmorr. "Don't you see? We need every adventurer's mother behind the bar. Then they'll all behave!"

~oOo~

The door to the Dragon's Beard Inn flew open on blustering winds, and the patrons looked up. The spring storms were bad, and rain lashed inside as two men gusted in, stomping their feet on the threshold. The newcomers looked to Amma, who had positioned herself to be seen, and both men gaped.

"Mama?" one whispered, his face slack.

"Auntie Zim. But how...," the other murmured before trailing off.

The spell engaged, Amma watched as it released them from the vision of their favorite mother figure. They shook their heads, befuddlement and wonder in their eyes, and softly shut the door behind them.

She bustled to their table with a complimentary welcome drink, which wondrously knocked the edge off their shock, and then took their order. She called the drinks out to the big man behind the bar, who wore a vest and breeches. His skin had an odd, reddish cast, and chained to his belt was a pair of thick, broken wristlets, like some foreign trophy.

She'd heard the regulars tell passers-through that if he got angry, his eyes gleamed like molten lava. But most didn't care to incur the wrath of the innkeeper, who strangely reminded each of them of his—or her—own mother. Those who didn't care for that moved to the new tavern across town, The Bad Spell, which Grumps and Marda had opened. The Dragon's Beard was a mellow place, these days, and more profitable than ever.

In the kitchen, Amma gave the food order to Fillmorr, who hummed a tune as he stirred, tasted, and seasoned the various pots. She was glad to see him so happy. "How's your mother, Formidable?"

Gene, his eyes agleam, slipped into the room on silent feet and stalked up behind Fillmorr. Amma kept her gaze directed at Fillmorr, allowing the sneaking to continue.

"I wish you wouldn't call me that," he said. "But she's fine. Loves the new shop next door, too. Says she should've moved here ages ago."

Gene threw his brawny red arms around the thinner man, who gave a muffled, high-pitched shriek. "'Formidable,' indeed!" Gene said, nuzzling his ear.

Fillmorr blushed redder than Gene, then swatted at the former genie with his soup spoon. "I should've thrown your lamp into the sea!" he scolded.

Gene laughed, a deep basso that echoed off the rafters. "Then you wouldn't be one-third owner of the nicest tavern in Milldale."

A thundering crash of the front door thrown open was followed by a bellowing voice demanding ale.

Amma sighed. "Looks like I'm needed in the front," she said. She lifted the bowls Fillmorr had abandoned and carried them through the swinging door into the common room, interrupting the bellower mid-tirade. He stared at her, mouth hanging slack, and with one thick hand, caught the door that was ready to slam shut behind him. Instead, he guided it to snik, ever-so-quietly, into place.

She beamed at him, nodding her delight. It was such a pleasure to work in a civilized place, where people shut the door properly.

DEAD HAND OF THE PAST

by Jonathan Shipley

Jenna is a Church exorcist, which is a dangerous job in itself. But when she and her Knight-Guardian are summoned to the capital, she suspects that the assignment is going to be worse than usual. She's proved right, as she quickly discovers that her assignment is not at all what she was told it was.

In Jonathan Shipley's fifth appearance in *Sword & Sorceress*, he offers a third tale about Jenna the exorcist, this time mixing in royal intrigue with the ghosts of her profession. Since *Sword & Sorceress 28*, he has published a half dozen more speculative fiction short stories, and one of the 2013 horror anthologies to which he contributed won the 2014 Bram Stoker Award for "superior achievement in an anthology." Like Anne Rice, Jonathan lives in a fine, old house in a historic district, but unlike Rice, he doesn't use his own home as a setting for the macabre. Living in an old house can be challenging enough without populating it with ghosts. He leaves all that to Jenna. Jonathan has a web presence at www. shipleyscifi.com and lives in Fort Worth, Texas.

"Are you sure Commander Frant hasn't complained about me?" Jenna asked again as the towers of King's City grew closer under the steady hooves of their mounts. She couldn't imagine any other reason why the Exorcist-General would summon her.

"No." Trayn, her Knight-Guardian, gave a long-suffering sigh. She had asked that same question a lot during the journey. "I would swear on my own blood that he sent a commendation for cleaning up the vengeful ghost at the Commandery. He said he even commended me for my part."

"But the Exorcist-General doesn't summon provincial exorcists to the capital—he just doesn't. It has to be—"

"Jenna, stop," Trayn pleaded. "We may not know why you've been summoned, but your record for successful exorcisms has been outstanding. Trust your record and stop worrying."

She gave up the argument but continued to worry. She was young to be a Church exorcist, commissioned in the field because of natural talent with the dead. She preferred to be invisible to the eyes of the Church hierarchy, in case someone got too curious about her hereditary talent, which was admittedly a little bit witchy. So this summons from the Exorcist-General was more than a little threatening, especially because it said to drop everything, come at once to King's City, and to report directly upon arrival. They were three days on the road, traveling light and making good time on fast post horses borrowed from the Commandery. It looked as if they would reach King's City by late afternoon.

"I've never been here before," Jenna admitted as the city gate loomed up before them. "You?"

"When I was young and stupid." Trayn didn't elaborate.

That was a great opening, but she let it pass. She did wonder, however, what "young" meant in that context. Trayn wasn't much older than she was, a very junior Knight of the Holy Retribution in terms of age. In casual traveling leathers, the two of them looked more like a young couple than Church officer and knight.

As they entered the city, Trayn led the way to a stableyard right inside the gate. "Why here by the gate?" Jenna asked as they dismounted. Doesn't the palace complex have its own stables?"

"It does, but we're not stabling there," Trayn said. "This is better for a hasty departure."

Jenna raised an eyebrow. "Are we expecting a hasty departure?"

"King's City is famous for sudden betrayals and hasty departures." He shouldered his saddlebags worked with the quartered chevrons of his house and started down the street without more explanation.

As they reached the city center and the Great Square opened

around them, Jenna gaped. In size and grandeur, it was greater than anything her upland border upbringing had prepared her for. On all sides stretched the rambling palace complex. Besides the royal residence, the wings housed an abbey, the main offices of the Church, the headquarters of the Knighthood, and the cathedral of St. Kyre. The complex itself symbolized the tight union of Church and Crown that the present kingdom was founded on.

St. Kyre's was directly in front of them, but Trayn led the way to the left, to one of the administrative wings. Jenna was unexpectedly relieved. The cathedral was supposed to be the beating heart of the Church, but she knew too much about St. Kyre himself—bought his sainthood, made an altar service out of cursed gold. Amazing the perspective you get when long-dead spirits tell you the real history of things.

They crossed the square to the entrance of the Church offices where a cleric in neutral gray eyed their traveling leathers and saddlebags with distaste but directed them up the stairs to the offices of the Holy Exorcism. It took surprisingly little time to move through the various offices. Each official seemed aware of her identity and passed them through to the next level without questions.

"It's not usually like this," Trayn murmured in her ear as they passed through another doorway. "Bureaucracy is set up to block people from seeing the higher-ups, not to facilitate it."

Then they arrived at the carven door of the inner sanctum itself. Self-consciously, Jenna straightened her cloak, wishing there had been time to bathe and change before this interview for she smelled of horse and sweat.

As they were ushered in, she glanced about the spacious room with its carved oak paneling and massive fireplace. The cloying sweetness of incense hovered over all. She focused her attention at the gray-haired man behind the central desk. He looked annoyed—or at least impatient.

"Exorcist-General," she began tentatively. "I am Jenna of—"

"Yes, yes, I'm sure you are," he interrupted, adding in a loud voice over his shoulder, "Now I will take my leave." He stood up and walked out the door, leaving Jenna and Trayn exchanging startled looks.

Then there was a distinct click in the corner of the room. The wall tapestry rustled, and a handsome woman of middle years with flaxen hair and pale complexion emerged from behind it. Her gaze went directly to Trayn and lingered there, almost hungrily.

Jenna shifted uncomfortably. Even if he was tall and fine and knightly, that was no reason to be blatantly ogled by a woman twice his age.

The woman crossed the room to stand right before them. "I am Antaria, mistress to the King," she said simply. "As a favor to me, the Exorcist-General summoned you here. Forgive the subterfuge, but I must take great pains to ensure the secrecy of this meeting. This is the court, where politics and poison lurk hand in hand."

Jenna kept a polite smile on her face, but her mind whirled. Court politics—what did she know of that? "I am only a country exorcist, milady," she said. "Probably not the right person for what you have in mind."

"You are exactly the right person," Antaria contradicted. "I have scoured volumes of reports, making sure you are the right person. There seem to be precious few exorcists in the profession who have experience with dead witches."

Oh, the haunting at the Commandery where a long-dead witch had cursed the Commandant. Messy business, but it had ended well enough. "So this is a haunting by a dead witch," Jenna said in her best professional tone. "Recently dead?"

"A powerful curse recently imposed," Antaria said, "and time is not on our side. My son, the Knight-Commander, has been cursed and I *will* have an end to it."

Trayn gasped. "Prince Mikhail has been cursed?"

"And I count on your efforts to free him. I'm sending you to an old, forgotten gather hall."

Multiple surprises here, Jenna noted. A cursed prince and a gather hall, which was an old term for the meeting places of wizardly orders, all of which had been expunged by the Church.

This was starting to feel very dangerous in ways far beyond dead witches, though the pattern of events was coming clear. Witch curses prince; prince kills witch; exorcist summons dead witch for counterspell.

"Go to a clothier's shop called Pucchi's," Antaria continued. "If you enter the alley behind it and walk to the far end, you will see a bricked-up doorway to the left. Place this jewel against it and it will open. Mikhail is waiting for you inside." She handed over a broach, a red stone in a silver setting.

Jenna felt the tingle as soon as she touched it. Definitely magic and very sophisticated magic at that, centering on an empowered jewel. Officially, she couldn't use this. Trafficking with magical talismans still carried a sentence of death, though that was seldom enforced these days with so few talismans still in existence. "Milady, I dare not. No one is allowed—if the Church finds out—"

"Falderol!" Antaria snapped. "This must be done, and I make no apology for dragging you into this. There will be no consequences from the Church, that much I can guarantee. I can call in favors from the Lord Bishop. Now go quickly." She paused with another lingering stare at Trayn. "Good to see you again, Trayn of Harebridge."

"Milady," he answered with a small bow. With a curt nod, Antaria recrossed the room to disappear behind the same tapestry.

Trayn knows the king's mistress? Jenna was surprised. She knew Trayn was noble-born, but had no idea he traveled in royal circles. "I had no idea you were so well connected," she said coolly. "You must find life in a backwater Commandery very dull by comparison."

He shot her a look. "Don't start, Jenna. If I wanted to be in King's City, I would be. But I had my fill of this"—he extended in arms to take in everything around them—"at an early age. Politics and poison were not to my taste. If I had known this was palace business, I would have come in full armor. Now we'd best get moving and allow the Exorcist-General the use of his office."

Practical advice, she realized as they exited to find her

superior waiting impatiently in the room beyond. With the barest of nods, they passed through and continued on until they were well into the winding streets of King's City.

"This may end badly," Jenna said to break the long silence between them. "I may have the gift to hear the dead, but dead witches are the worst to deal with. And a curse? I deal with hauntings and possessions, not curses."

"If it ends badly, it will end very badly." And Trayn fell silent.

It was early evening when they reached the clothier's establishment with the alley behind it. They hugged the wall of the building, looking for the bricked-over entrance. Several times Jenna let her fingers touch the weathered stone, and each time she felt something.

"Are you sensing something?" Trayn asked.

"It resonates like an old, haunted place. Perhaps that's the gather hall, or perhaps it really is haunted. But I'd like to know what we're dealing with before getting too far in."

He gave a snort. "That horse is already out of the barn and far down the road. We've been embroiled in something since the moment you were first summoned."

They found the bricked-over doorway. Trayn pounded at it in several places to check its solidness. "In any other circumstances, I'd say there was no entrance here. But we know better."

Jenna nodded and produced the jewel from her pocket. She pressed it to the bricks. In the dark, it radiated a red glow, and in that glow, the bricks Trayn had been pounding on seemed to melt away, leaving a dark opening. It was by no means inviting.

"Too late for second thoughts," Trayn muttered and wrapping an arm around her, stepped forward into the darkness.

A flash of bitter, airless cold, then the world resumed around them. The place where they were standing was dim, but not lightless. A wall taper burned next to where they stood, and fifty or so paces beyond, a brace of torches lit the cold, vaulted space. A deep subcellar, Jenna guessed from what she could see of the place. It had the unpleasant feel of a dungeon, though it probably never was. There was no pain in the stones.

"Is this natural cold or death cold?" Trayn asked with a shiver.

Jenna closed her eyes and quested with her talent. "Definitely haunted," she concluded, opening her eyes. But a strange sort of haunted, she added silently to herself. The feel of it was different from ghosts she had dealt with.

Then she gave a gasp. A short, stocky figure was suddenly standing before them smelling strongly of ale. "Are you seeing this?" she murmured to Trayn because it seemed too solid to be a ghost.

Trayn shook his head, his hand settling automatically on his sword hilt.

So a ghost. Jenna took a step closer. "Have you come with a message, spirit?" she asked.

It gave a start. "You can see me?"

"I have the Sight," she nodded. "And you are a very strong manifestation."

The ghost guffawed. "I'm supposed to be a strong manifestation. What's the sense of a weak guardian?"

"Guardian?" she asked carefully. "Of this place?"

"No, the Queen's bedchamber," it snorted. "Of course, this place! Ritually bound, blood to stone, to anchor my spirit here. And my kind is more cohesive in death than you humans, so we make excellent guardians over time."

"If not human, exactly what kind are you?" Jenna asked.

"Are you daft? Dwarfkind, of course. What else would you take me for?"

With his build and beard, he did look exactly like a dwarf out of folklore, but that was the problem—dwarves didn't exist. "How long?" she asked. "How long have you been down here?"

The dwarf gave a shrug. "Can't much tell since it's mainly dark and empty. But I'm guessing a long, long time. Not bad having a little conversation for a change. I would ask your name, but I know how rude that is in your circles."

The power of old name magic, Jenna guessed he meant. That hadn't been a consideration since the fall of the wizard-lords centuries before. And binding a spirit as a guardian was old, dark magic that she hadn't encountered before. Barbaric, really. "Do you seek release?" she asked. Standard exorcism question.

The dwarf's eyes narrowed. "What's it to you? Could be that the interloper is trying to sweet talk her way past the guardian?"

That sounded threatening. "We have a right to be here," Jenna said hurriedly and held up the broach with its glowing gem.

The dwarf gave a *hrrmph*. "You'd think with all the recent comings and goings that *someone* would be an interloper, but no—a second key. And I was so hoping for some action." He winked out of sight.

Jenna let go of the breath she'd been holding. She hadn't come equipped to fend off a non-human guardian itching for a fight. That was beyond her experience...maybe beyond the Office of the Holy Exorcism. "It was a guardian spirit, but we're allowed to pass," she told Trayn, holding up the jewel.

They started forward across the cellar and soon reached the wall torches. Between them, she saw the remains of a campfire on the stone floor, and wrapped in a military bedroll next to it, someone was snoring fitfully.

Trayn cleared his throat and announced loudly, "In the name of the King."

The snoring ceased as the sleeper responded with battle reflexes, rolling out of his blankets and to his feet with a fluid motion, sword materializing at the ready. Then with a pained gasp, he let the sword clatter to the floor and cradled his sword hand to his chest. All this happened in a blink.

"Mikhail, we're friends," Trayn said quickly.

The prince recovered his bearing and straightened, standing pale and blond in the torchlight. He seemed young for his role of Prince-Commander of the Knighthood, not much older than Trayn. Confused, he stared at each of them in turn. "Trayn? What are you doing here? Did my mother send you?" Then he gave another pained gasp.

Cursed, Jenna remembered. Her eyes went directly to his sword arm where an ornate metal wristguard sat encrusted with glowing red jewels. More Old High Magic. The hand below the tight wristguard looked swollen and ashen compared with the flesh of the arm above. *He needs to loosen that guard or lose that hand*, she thought in passing—then frowned. Was that the curse?

"Yes, we're from your mother," Trayn answered. "This is Jen—"

Mikhail continued staring at him, wide-eyed and wild. "But now you're trapped here, too."

"Trapped?" Trayn repeated, hand going automatically to his sword. "No, we have a jewel from your mother that lets us come and go through the portal."

The prince gave a bitter laugh and fished from around his neck another red jewel, this one set as a necklace, not a broach. "So I thought as well when I arrived. The first time I tried to leave, I found out differently. We are trapped here together—in this hall and in this dark plot." He gave a sudden cry and flung the jeweled necklace into the shadows.

"Trapped? But we were sent to—" Jenna began, then fell silent as Trayn shook his head.

"Mikhail," he said firmly. "You're cursed, in pain, and running a little wild. We're fine—not trapped. Take a breath and calm yourself, then tell us the story from the beginning."

The prince closed his eyes a moment and breathed deeply. When he opened them again, he was more composed. "My apologies. This infernal place gets to me...and the pain. It's always with me. I have dark dreams of being trapped here forever. So let us begin again. Trayn, old friend, introduce your companion."

"This is Jenna, the Church Exorcist I serve with. She's here to help."

"Is it possible?" Mikhail demanded, turning to her. "You can break the curse?"

Jenna winced, knowing she could promise nothing. "I can try, Highness. I run across many strange things in my exorcisms of the dead. So to the business at hand," she said briskly, then winced at the way that had come out. "I mean, what can you tell me of the curse?"

Mikhail managed a thin smile at her choice of words and held up his sword hand. "A very old talisman from another age. When legend said it would enhance my fighting skill, I was fool enough to believe it. Now it appears I am doomed to live out my days one-handed in constant pain. I fear it will drive me mad long before the end. I was a fool to ever go to Sarosar."

Sarosar? Jenna had to be sure she had heard correctly. That was the last of the wizard-lord strongholds to fall, and the ruins had been interdicted by the Church ever since. It was indeed foolish to go there—she assumed that was the influence of the witch. "May I take a closer look?"

The prince raised his arm. "The ruins of Sarosar were not hospitable. Very haunted." His gaze cut to Trayn again. "You would know that better than anyone."

Trayn nodded grimly.

"I don't understand," Jenna said.

Trayn gave a long sigh. "One of my brothers and I thought exploring ruined Sarosar on the edge of the family holdings would be great sport. He never made it out. One of the reasons I'm no longer welcome at home."

"And no doubt why you are serving below your station as guard to an exorcist rather than an officer of men," Mikhail added.

Jenna blinked, surprised and surprised again by these revelations. She'd had no inkling of any of this.

"After I located this talisman and removed it from its hiding place," the prince continued, "I left quickly. The first night out of the ruins, I had my first good sleep in a while, though my dreams became stranger and stranger until suddenly I woke in excruciating pain. The talisman I was conveying had attached itself to my arm while I slept."

Jenna nodded as she studied the nasty piece of work holding his hand hostage. In form, it looked to like a hungry piece of steel constricting his wrist like a tight mouth. The constrictor seemed to be tempered steel, too small to have arrived where it was, and far, far too small to ever leave, now that the flesh in its harsh embrace was swollen.

But perhaps more significantly, the heavy steel was embedded with glowing red jewels that cast a hellish glow over the purpled flesh. She let her eyes defocus and probed forward, then hastily pulled back. There was both malice and power here, accumulated over centuries and nothing to be trifled with. Whatever that cruel talisman caught in its maw, it would devour. Then she spotted something like a clasp on the underside set with tiny red jewels in the pattern of a coat of arms.

Mikhail groaned and let his arm drop. "The pain," he muttered. "In certain positions, it's greater."

"How bad is it?" she asked.

"Less now," Mikhail shrugged. "At first, it was agonizing. I spent most of the first day writhing on the ground. Then my hand began to grow numb, and I could move again. Traveling back, the torment ebbed and flowed. I am proud to say I only fell off my horse twice incapacitated by pain when there were a dozen more times that I easily could have. Now that I am mostly numb, I feel only a throbbing ache that is always with me. I have learned to move carefully lest I bump my hand, which is like shards of glass piercing my flesh. Such is my situation. Is there any new hope, or do I proceed with the blood bath?"

"Bloodbath?" they asked in unison.

"No, blood...bath. The only possibility my mother came up with was for me to kill someone and bathe in his blood. She was going to send me a thief or a footpad as the sacrifice. I've killed many an adversary in battle, but slaughtering a man like an animal was not a plan I looked forward to. I am relieved my mother sent an exorcist instead. Much better plan."

Jenna kept staring at the glowing wristguard. Blood held powerful mystical properties, but usually that meant the blood of family or self or a hated enemy. She'd never heard that bathing in some random person's blood would break a curse. But she would know more when she brought back the witch who'd activated this curse.

"I doubt that you kept any personal effects of the witch, but the sword that killed her would still carry some resonance of her. Can I assume that sword to be yours?"

A bit of wildness crept back into Mikhail's eyes. "What are you talking about, Mistress Jenna?"

"The dead witch," Jenna said. "The one who placed the curse. Your mother brought me to King's City because I have experience with exorcising dead witches."

Mikhail kept frowning. "I found the curse in Sarosar, as I explained."

"But not alone—the witch was with you?"

"Quite alone, I assure you. There was no witch, dead or otherwise. And you say my mother told you this? I don't know what new game she is playing, but she has told you false."

Now Jenna was frowning, very confused. "Then why was I summoned?"

Suddenly Trayn was at her side, pulling at her arm. "There's been a mistake, Jenna. We should go—now." His voice was strangely grim.

A short intake of breath from Mikhail as he caught the same mood. "Indeed you should. I am not yet so desperate as to abandon all honor, but when the pain comes, I am not myself."

What? On the way across the cellar, Jenna tried to decipher why this mission had stopped making sense. No dead witch and a suddenly anxious Knight-Companion. Lies and danger? But what danger?

The portal wall loomed before them. With a last glance at the prince standing pale and blond across the cellar, she pressed the broach to the wall.

"When we emerge, be prepared to run," Trayn urged softly as they waited. "We've been betrayed, and it may not be over yet." He held his sword at ready. Then he turned with a question in his eyes. They hadn't left the cellar.

Again Jenna pressed the glowing jewel against the stone and waited. Even before the raucous sound of laughter reached her ears, she knew they were trapped.

"Looks like someone underestimated an opponent," the dwarf guffawed. "Might be a sword in your gullet or it might not, but you'll die here all the same. And your brave knights? They're both idiots who think Sarosar is a place to go exploring. No surprise the pale one ended up cursed. House Har'Bre of Sarosar was famous for double-edged talismans." Still laughing, he faded out.

To wither away in the cold and dark with a ghost laughing in her ear. It wasn't Jenna's idea of a good death. She glanced at Trayn and guessed he was thinking along similar lines. Reluctantly, they returned to the prince.

"You don't need to say," Mikhail said as they reached his makeshift camp. "Trust my mother to give only a one-way key to anyone involved in this. I may have sounded touched in the head, but now you're as trapped here as I am."

"Your word, Mikhail," Trayn said, hand on his hilt. "You can not go forward with this mad plot to bathe in blood."

"On my honor, I would not!" Mikhail insisted. "A thief, maybe and no sure thing at that, but a friend come to help me— never."

Jenna's knees sagged suddenly as she finally realized what the two of them were saying. *She* was the blood sacrifice sent by Antaria to break the curse. The dead witch had only been a ruse. "Why me?"

"Your talent," Trayn answered, supporting her as she faltered. "You have the Sight and who knows what else coursing through your being. Antaria must think your blood is witchy enough to conquer the curse." She looked up, wide-eyed and fearful. "But I am here to protect you," he added.

"We shall both protect you, Mistress Jenna," the prince added. "On my honor, I would not hurt you."

The wording snapped Jenna out of her dazed state. There was something inherently silly in a brave knight pledging protection against himself. "My thanks, but none of us have much of a future down here. What was your mother thinking to trap her own son down here? How could she be so cruel?"

Mikhail's mouth tightened. "I have rations for two days. Her thought was after that time, I would either have bathed away the curse or gone completely mad with pain. She would come and see which. I have been twice the fool," he added slowly. "I never fully considered the ruthlessness of certain political ambitions.

More to the point, the son who can not become Heir becomes useless."

Jenna blinked in surprise. The King's bastard was not the Heir, even though he was the eldest of the sons. Then it hit. All this must be about the succession—Antaria plotting in the palace to elevate her son to the Throne...until this curse removed the popular Prince-Commander from the game. Trayn was right all along—this was royal politics of the most dangerous stripe, though the strategies were exceedingly murky.

"So one way, your mother would have you gone," Jenna began, "but—"

"Nothing in this game is simple," Mikhail explained. "First and foremost, my mother wants to see me elevated to Heir. But if I am crippled and half-mad and disqualified for the role, she would just as soon see me disappear entirely. Either I break the curse or rot here."

"As we all rot here," Trayn added darkly. "It seems the only hope for any of us is to break the curse. Any ideas?" he asked, glancing at Jenna. "Being trapped like this makes me feel like a duck stuffed for dinner."

"I still don't understand how spilling the blood of a random stranger could break the curse," she said. "I may have the Sight, but I'm no witch or wizard-lord. There's no particular power in my blood. And yet Antaria specifically summoned me here."

"I should have worn full armor and battle lance," Trayn muttered. "I have stuck to you like a shadow, but this time it wasn't enough to protect you."

She smiled sadly. "You are always faithfully at my side. How could anyone ask—"

"Jenna?" Trayn asked as she fell silent midsentence.

House Har'Bre of Sarosar, the dwarf had said. House Har'Bre...Trayn's House Harebridge with holdings adjoining ruined Sarosar. Could it be? "Highness," she said abruptly. "Sorry to cause you more pain, but may I see the wristguard another time, the underside specifically."

As the prince lifted his arm again, she studied the coat of arms more carefully. She only half saw the other time, but this time she recognized it. Finally something made sense. Antaria didn't want her blood at all.

"Look at the crest," she began slowly. "I've seen those quartered chevrons on your shield, Trayn, every day we're on the road. At some point in history, this wristguard was bound to your lineage. Antaria never wanted an exorcist. She wanted the Knight-Guardian that came with the exorcist. It's your blood, not mine, that can break the curse. So I say we try feeding your blood to the thing."

"What a relief," he said woodenly. "Mikhail will be bathing in my blood, not yours."

Mikhail gave a snort. "I would never raise a sword against a friend no matter—"

"No listen, both of you," Jenna interrupted. "Blood is the key, but Antaria only got it half right. A few drops of the right blood can accomplish more than buckets of the wrong blood."

"A few drops I can manage easily enough," Trayn said, unsheathing his belt knife. "But if I need to open a vein, I'd appreciate a tourniquet ready to go."

"Oh, open a vein and a few more," came a harsh laugh followed by a whiff of sour ale. "Can't have too much blood, I say."

Jenna glared at the stocky ghost. "Not helpful. Do you recognize the cursed wristguard on the prince's hand?"

"Who is she talking—" Mikhail began but Trayn hushed him.

"I know a piece of Old High Magic when I see it," the dwarf shrugged. "Just give it a bucket or two of blood and see if that helps."

"Hell's bells," she muttered as he leered and faded. The dead were notoriously unreliable, especially in matters of living blood, which they would drink like nectar.

"Just a drop, right on the latch," she finally decided. "We'll start there."

Trayn pricked his finger with the knifepoint and pressed the oozing droplets against the latch of the wristguard. For a moment nothing happened, then with a distinct click, the wristguard released and fell to the stone floor with a *clunk*.

Mikhail gasped in surprise and flexed his swollen hand carefully. It responded sluggishly, but it responded. He gave a long sigh of relief and smiled, genuinely smiled. "I am in your debt, both of you." Then he sobered. "But you're still in danger. Whether by assassin's dart or simply leaving you trapped here, my mother will try to dispose of you as loose ends. It is her way."

"Then I'd rather go down fighting," Trayn shrugged, half drawing his sword.

"I'd rather not go down at all," Jenna said.

"Perhaps the ghost-guardian of this place could be persuaded to fight with us," Trayn suggested. "You do have a way with spirits."

She shook her head. "He doesn't want to move on—I have nothing he wants." Then she paused. "Or maybe I do."

She stepped away from the others to a point where shadows swathed the stones in gray. "Spirit," she called. Pulling out her traveling knife, she pricked her own finger on the point and smeared a line of blood against the nearest wall. Blood, the ultimate power with the dead.

The dwarf-ghost appeared with a *hrrmph*, dropping the temperature in his immediate vicinity. Stepping close the wall, he sniffed at the blood, then put out his tongue to lick the stone clean. Then he turned. "Seems like Mistress Brown Eyes has a few tricks as well as the Sight."

"My talent is working with the dead," Jenna nodded. "Yes, I know many tricks."

The dwarf leered openly. "And you want to bargain for my help now that you're trapped here."

Never bargain with the dead—it was a solid rule of survival for anyone dealing with ghosts. "Not at all," she said. "I want to freely give you a gift."

"A gift?"

"You called this place dark and empty. Perhaps you would like somewhere more interesting to haunt. You said you're bound, blood to stone, to this place. I'm guessing that moving the stone would bring you with it. Of course, I'm only guessing.

You'd have to tell if and how that could be done."

"Funny how this gift of yours means you have to get out of the trap in order to deliver," the dwarf snorted. But he didn't disappear.

"It seems that it does," she nodded. "May I give you my gift?"

The dwarf studied her with narrowed eyes for a long moment. "Yes," he blurted out suddenly. "You're a clever one and I like that."

"So which stone is it?" she asked. The dwarf moved to the center of the cellar and pointed downward. A paving stone with a reddish tint to it, she saw as she drew closer. At least it was a smallish one, not a great slab like some of the others. She pulled a knife from her waist pouch and began picking at the edges with the blade. It didn't seem to be mortared in, just tightly fit into its hole. After a few moments, she worked it loose. She pulled her cloak around herself and looked at the dwarf questioningly...but making no demands. This was a gift, not a bargain.

"The wizards who built this hall were clever," he said with a smirk. "Designed one portal for entrance and a separate one for exit. Trapped more than a few burglars in their time. The second portal is right under that torch bracket there."

Jenna was already moving toward the campfire. "Come quickly—bring everything," she called across the distance, and two knights hurried to her side. Trayn had the saddlebags; Mikhail, a cloak and breastplate with the royal eagle. "I have our way free of here."

She handed Trayn the paver to put in his saddlebag and placed the glowing amulet against the featureless stone wall under the torch bracket. The same shock of bitter cold and they were standing outside in the night on the far side of the clothier's shop. "Any assassins?" she whispered.

Trayn glided forward along the wall, checked the street, then beckoned them forward. They hurried forward, and all of them slipped around the corner on their way to the gate. Only when they had few blocks between them and the gather hall could Jenna begin to breathe normally again.

A quarter hour later, they were in the stableyard retrieving three horses—their two post horses and a larger, milk-white destrier with the royal eagle worked into the leather saddle. "You're coming with us, Highness?" she asked, surprised.

"Just to the turn of the road," Mikhail said, pushing past them both to mount the destrier. "To be sure you are safely on your way. My mother's underlings are nothing if not efficient."

Jenna, already sitting stiff in the saddle, tensed a little more, imagining a knife aimed at her back. But nothing found its way to her ribcage as they rode through the north gate of King's City. They continued down the road through fields of barley until the city was far behind them.

"And there you have it," Mikhail said, reining his horse. "My station doesn't permit the luxury of friends, but I treasure you two as solid acquaintances sensible enough to steer clear of politics."

"We'll consider ourselves treasured, then," Trayn nodded, "but at safe distance from King's City."

"You could come with us, Highness," Jenna added as she handed him the broach talisman. She wanted nothing more to do with it. "It might be safer."

He shook his head, sending his blond mane flying. "I wasn't born to be safe. And someone has to rein in my ruthlessly ambitious mother." He turned and headed back to the city.

"Good luck, Highness," she called.

"Wishing someone who might kill you tomorrow good luck," snorted the dwarf, appearing suddenly in the saddle behind Trayn. "It's amazing you've lasted as long as you have. And your big, brave protector here"—he gave another snort—"I saw who was saving who back there."

She chuckled as they started down the road again.

Trayn gave her a curious look. "It's not over, is it?"

"The politics?"

"That, never," he sighed. "The haunt in the gather hall, I mean."

"There's apt to be more from him," she admitted, glancing at the ghost who was sitting behind him. "How did you know?"

He shivered. "Because my backside is cold as ice."

NUT ROLLS

by Patricia B. Cirone

Marina and her employer, the fake medium Madame Fertaglio, first appeared in Sword & Sorceress 22. It was then that they discovered that Marina actually *is* a medium, a fact that Madame was quick to use for the benefit of her business. Of course, this does not include making sure that her "apprentice" gets the training she needs.

Patricia B. Cirone has worked as a scientist, a teacher and a librarian, but her true love is writing. She has had a number of short stories published, including several in previous *Sword & Sorceress* anthologies, and is currently working on a book. She receives frequent editorial comments on her writing from one of her cats, who considers any hand to be better employed in petting her than in typing.

"Do you have the nut rolls finished yet?"

Marina, her hands busy kneading the dough that would become the nut rolls, rolled her eyes before turning to face her employer. Only when she turned around she realized it wasn't Madame Fertaglio after all. "Oh, it's you," she said, annoyed. "Shoo!"

Perhaps it wasn't the most polite way to speak to Madame Fertaglio's mother, but the Madame would never know. After all, the Madame couldn't speak to her mother, since despite making her living as one, she *wasn't* a medium. Unfortunately, Marina was. And the Madame's mother had taken to haunting her, with criticisms, airs and graces just like Madame Fertaglio's. Marina wasn't quite sure if the ghost was modeling herself on her daughter or if her daughter had picked them up from her mother. One thing was certain: Madame Fertaglio's mother had *not* been the genteel but impoverished gentry woman the Madame referred to occasionally while conducting her séances. The woman dressed and looked like a fishmonger. Swore like one too, when Marina didn't treat her politely. As she was doing now.

Marina sighed and turned back to kneading the dough. Bad enough having to answer to Madame's whims and demands, without getting them from her long deceased mother as well.

"Why me?" she asked herself, digging into the dough a little more vigorously than was needed. Life had been just fine up until that day she had spilled a little of Madame's "special fragrance" on herself when readying the incense for one of the nightly séances. The "special fragrance" had turned out to be a bit of magicked liquid which was supposed to make the séance attendees a little more disposed to believing Madame's show. It had turned out to be a show, all right. Only it hadn't been Madame talking to the spirits—it had been Marina. The exposure to the magic had triggered some latent ability to talk to spirits and she had conjured up the ghost of a Peacemaker who had been killed the night before. Even the other "guests" (as Madame referred to her paying customers) had been able to hear the ghost talking—accusing two of the other attendees of black magic and of arranging his murder. Things might have gone badly for her if another of the guests had not turned out to be a high-up Peacemaker, on the track of the murderers. Yes, it had been quite a show for all the attendees. They had probably dined out on it for months. And ever since then, Marina had been apt to trip over ghosts at odd moments.

Not, of course, during Madame's séances. Madame had wanted her to call up spirits and have them talk the way that poor Peacemaker had—only manage it so it looked as though Madame was doing the calling. After all, she was the one who was the "real" medium—at least she had been making her living by giving séances for years. Only it didn't work that way; for some reason, ghosts didn't come near Marina when she was in the séance room. No, she tripped over them when buying fish at the market, found them sitting next to her when she went to chapel, and spookiest of all, saw eyes watching her when she had to go down to the root cellar for some vegetables. It had made her much more fond of going to the market for fresh vegetables. Daily. And she now had to put up with Madame's mother in the kitchen, in her bedroom and all about the house.

"Wish they'd all just stay dead!" she muttered between her teeth.

"What did you say?" the voice behind her demanded.

Marina swung around, glaring, about to blast Madame's mother, only to find that this time it really *was* Madame Fertaglio. For such a large woman, she could move as quietly as...well, a ghost.

"Pardon?" Marina asked.

"What were you just saying?" Madame demanded imperiously.

"Oh, I was just saying to myself that I wished, umm...the nut rolls were...like bread. I mean that you could buy them in the market..." Marina stuttered.

"Lazy girl. Then what would I employ *you* for?" Madame said and exited the kitchen.

Just about everything else that gets done around here, she thought, glaring at the retreating back of her employer. *Beds, marketing, cooking, séances and cleaning up; by the time I get to bed it's time to get up again and start all over!* Wisely, she didn't say any of it out loud; Madame could have remarkably good hearing at times. And besides—it really was a good job. Not half so bad as working in the markets—or even worse having the kind of job you could get in the warrens. Or no job at all. Marina had been born in the warrens; her mother, sister and brothers still lived in them. Marina had been lucky to find a job outside of them, that paid a wage as well as room and board. It was just the damn ghosts. They were getting on her nerves.

Marina sighed and put the problem out of her mind. If she dallied much longer, she *would* be late in getting the nut rolls—and everything else—ready for the evening. Just as she finished rolling the dough into balls and placing them on the baking sheet, there was a sharp knock on the back door. She wiped her hands on her apron and went over to open it. Her younger brother stood on the doorstep, an anxious look on his face.

"Thomai! What are you doing here?" she asked. "Mom...?"

"Mom's fine. Can I come in?" he asked while already ducking under her arm to do so. He carried a covered basket in his arms, the smell of fish wafting up and replacing the pleasant odors of the kitchen.

"Oh, for heaven's sake, Thomai! Get that smelly fish out of here!" She started to shoo him out the door.

"*Please, Mari!*" he protested, the look on his face getting even more anxious. Marina stopped trying to shoo him out, and shut the door behind him, smelly basket and all.

"What is it?"

"I think I saw something. Well, I know I saw something—I just don't know if I really saw it..." Thomai stuttered.

"What?" Marina asked, totally confused, and starting to feel anxious herself. Her little brother got odd jobs down at the docks, and the docks were almost as bad as the warrens for having all sorts of things go on that you weren't supposed to see. But Thomai, like she herself, was used to that.

"You know that foreign guy you caught?"

"I didn't catch him, the Peacemakers did," Marina automatically corrected.

"You know what I mean. The one they hung for bringing in black magic spells and killing that Peacemaker guy."

"Yes, I know who you mean," she sighed.

"Well I saw him down at the docks."

"You couldn't have, they hung him. And wait a minute, how would you even know what he looked like?"

Thomai looked down at the kitchen floor and muttered: "I went to see them hang him."

"Thomai! You *know* what our Mum says about that."

"I know—but all my friends were going. And besides, I'm growing up now. Seeing things like that is important."

Marina rolled her eyes, but figured it was a lost cause. Boys would be boys, and the hanging of a black magician was a big event.

"Well, it couldn't have been him, since he's dead. What made you think it was him?"

"It was *him* Mari, I swear!"

Marina paused and looked closer at her little brother. Could he be seeing ghosts, too? "Could you see through him?"

"Of course not!" Thomai said, looking at her as if she was daft. "I could see him as plain as you...and I think he might have seen me, too...." he finished in a low mumble.

Marina felt a wave of fear move down her back. If whoever her brother had seen was any relation or associate of the late Ser Kiasie, of the yellow hair and black magic, he was dangerous.

"Quick!" she said, snatching up the fishy smelling basket her brother had brought in with him, opening it and pulling one of the fish out.

"Hey, those are for Mum!" her brother protested. "She even gave me money to buy them!"

"If you get murdered on the way home, she won't get these fish either now, will she?" Marina demanded. She thrust the basket back into her brother's hands. "You take these to the house three doors down, with the yellow shutters, and go to the back door. Tell the cook Marina sent you, that you're the new fish boy. Then go across the corner from there and up two, to the small house with the brown trim and do the same. Haggle a good price from both of them—out on the doorstep if you can manage it. Then duck around the back of the brown-trimmed house as if you were moving up to the next street level, but leave the basket under the porch—the maid leaves others there—and hike yourself fast up the big tree in back. Hunker down and *stay* there, as still as if we were playing catch me up on the roofs at home. Stay there until it's dark. Then work your way back across the street up in the branches of that tree and go into the attic of the house at the end of this row. I'll bring you some food and we'll see about getting you out safely and back home, then. It'll be late, as Madame has a séance tonight, and I have to be there. But I'll come up after that. These row houses are all connected up along the attics, if you know how to find the passages."

"I'm not *sure* he saw me, Mari," her brother protested.

"That man was *evil*, Thomai! Do you want to trust your life to "maybe?" You been out of the warrens too long, if you have!"

"Okay, okay," her brother muttered, and Marina hastened to the door. She just hoped they hadn't been in here too long, in case there *was* a watcher. She flung the door open and called after the "fish boy,"

"You mind, bring some red snapfish tomorrow. And no trying to pass off spalnock as plaice, again, you hear? I know the tests!"

"Alright, alright! You had your say," her brother answered back, hoisting the basket up higher and heading to the yellow-shuttered house. Marina closed the door firmly, as if annoyed and then crept back to the window, trying to watch through the gauze window covering to see if anyone was following her brother. She thought she saw a movement in the shadows, several houses down, but couldn't be sure. It could have been a breeze lifting a piece of debris, or even a cat. She might not even see a follower, if he was using the magic arts. From what she'd heard, they could creep up on you as silent and unseen as a wisp of wind.

"What are you looking at?" a voice whispered behind her. Marina jumped a foot and spun around.

"Oh. It's you."

Madame's mother *again*. She sighed and moved away from the window. She'd done her best, and if Thomai did what she'd told him, she'd be able to get him away up safe to the warrens, where he could lie low for a few days. If whoever he'd seen looked like that Kiasie, then he was foreign and chances were he wouldn't be in port very long.

Did all the foreigners from wherever he'd come from look alike? Is that why her brother had thought he'd seen a dead man? Or what if Kiasie wasn't really dead? Marina shivered again and moved back across the kitchen and opened the stove to put the nut rolls in to bake. The familiar warmth gushing out soothed her, but she still felt cold. If there was one person Kiasie had reason to hate, it was her. *But he was dead!...wasn't he???*

~o0o~

"Those lights are too bright; turn down the flame!"

Marina moved across the room and turned the key on the one in the corner, lowering the flame to barely a flicker.

"What are you *doing*, you stupid girl?" Madame Fertaglio demanded. "I won't be able to see my hand in front of my face, let alone the guests!"

"But you just told me..." Marina stopped, realizing the first command had come from Madame's mother. She gritted her teeth and moved the gas light to its former setting.

"I don't know what has come over you, lately," Madame complained. "You don't do anything right anymore!" She left the room in a huff, the slight train on her gown trailing behind her.

Marina gritted her teeth still harder. She knew she wasn't doing anything different—well, other than having to deal with Madame's mother and other sundry ghosts all the time. Madame was still miffed at her inability to channel any ghosts in her séances and thought she was willfully refusing to do it to spite her.

Despite the lack of any help from Marina, though, attendance at the séances had increased dramatically ever since the incident with the dead Peacemaker appearing. News of that had spread far and wide and Madame now had to maintain a reservation list and limit attendance at each séance to twenty—when she had been happy to get ten at a time before. It was Marina's duty to take the reservations and make sure that those arriving at the door were actually on the list for that night.

She moved to do that now, as the first guest gently rapped the knocker. As each one arrived, she checked their name, took the card sent when they booked their attendance, and locked them, as well as the payment envelopes each guest handed to her in the drawer in the foyer. Each séance had a mix of newcomers, occasional attendees and regulars. One man who had started coming regularly ever since the news of that infamous evening was a slight man with mousy brown hair and nothing really remarkable about him. Marina didn't know what it was about him that bothered her—it was almost as if he smelled peculiar— but she had been close enough to him when taking his coat and payment envelope to know he actually smelled of DestaBrown, a cologne you could get for 10 silvers uptown and for 1 silver in the market down at the docks. In a less fancy bottle, of course.

Maybe it was just because he had started coming so soon after the Peacemaker night and always seemed to avoid her gaze. It made her nervous.

The two Gantry sisters, however, made such a fuss and bother every time they came that Marina quickly forgot the mousy-haired man and had her hands full trying to get them to move along into the sitting room without forgetting their gloves, their payment, or each other in the process.

Finally all of the guests were seated around the sitting room, sipping at the small delicate glasses of wine and nibbling on Marina's nut rolls prior to being moved on over to the large table where Madame seated her guests for the actual séance. The wine, nut rolls and other sweets were Madame's idea and Marina had to admit that both regulars and newcomers seemed to relax and enjoy these few minutes, whether they were nervous about coming to a séance or merely flustered from having to rush here from other business or appointments. It also set the stage for Madame to make her gracious entrance and enquire how each of them were doing and how their day had been and gather all those bits of information she sprinkled back to them, sometimes several séances later. She *was* good at this, Marina thought wryly.

At last they all moved over to the large table, Marina trailing behind and lowering the lights to the level Madame dictated for the actual "event." She then moved over to her chair in the corner, to watch in case someone needed something—or gave Madame any trouble.

Her mind drifted to her brother, wondering if he was still up in the tree or had already managed to creep over to the attic down the way. That was assuming he had made it to the tree in the first place, with no one following him or finding him hiding there. Who on earth had he seen down at the docks? And was he really in danger or had he just been spooked by someone who looked like the man he had seen hanged?

"He done me in, you know," a man's voice complained.

Marina blinked and focused back on the séance. That was an odd thing for one of the guests to have said. Usually they spoke of their "dearly departed" in glowing—and maudlin—terms. Maybe tonight would be more interesting than the usual run. It must be one of the newcomers.

She cast her glance over the men at the table; there were only two who had not come before. But neither were speaking. Indeed, all the attendees had their eyes fixed on Madame Fertaglio, who was humming and swaying in her seat.

"He did, you know, girly," the voice said again. "That man you're scared of up and done me in—I was only in for petty theft, I was." Marina slowly moved her gaze sideways and saw one of "her" guests standing next to her. A ghost. She glanced quickly back at the table, but none of the others seemed disturbed... except for the mousy-haired man, who was watching her. He quickly flicked his gaze back to Madame Fertaglio. So, it wasn't like the last time, when everyone could hear the Peacemaker.

"You don't say!" another voice chimed in. This one she recognized, with dread. Madame Fertaglio's mother had entered the fray. "What did he do, knife you in the cell?" she asked with interest.

Madame Fertaglio's head whipped around. "Marina!" she exclaimed, spots of anger on her cheeks. Obviously, this time, everyone *had* heard the mother speak.

"It wasn't me!" Marina protested.

"Oh, hush, Bertie!" the Madame's mother exclaimed. "I want to hear this gent!"

Madame's eyes grew round. "Mother...?" she asked in a faltering voice.

"Yes, yes, your long-lost mother. Now hush!"

"No, he didn't knife me, you fool! He took my place,"

"Who are you calling a fool, you old hangallows!"

"Marina, are you doing this?" Madame demanded.

"No, I mean, not on purpose! They're just talking. Ummm— can you hear both of them?"

"Both of *who?* All I hear is a voice like my mother's."

"Oh, hush, you old besom!" the man exclaimed. "I came here to tell this girly she's in danger and you keep interfering!"

Madame's look of outrage and confusion didn't change, so it was clear she hadn't heard the "old besom," remark. But her mother certainly had. She shut her semi-transparent mouth like a steel trap and glared at the other ghost.

"I'm in danger?" Marina asked.

"You are if you keep mocking me by imitating my mother's voice!" Madame Fertaglio declared.

"I'm not imitating her voice!" Marina cried. "That's her. And I never knew her, anyway. You know that. She's been dead for longer than I've been alive. And she's been haunting this house for the last three months! What do you mean, I'm in danger—and what about my brother?"

"What brother?" the ghost asked

"What brother?" Madame Fertaglio asked.

"*Her* brother, you fools," Madame's mother declared. "Now hush up and let's hear what the man has to say about danger before we're all murdered in our beds!"

A small shriek emanated from one of the Gantry sisters and the two of them clutched at each other's hands.

"This girly's in danger and a man can't get a word in edgewise around here!" the ghost exclaimed and moved as if to walk away.

"No, stop! Please! Tell me what's happening!" Marina cried.

"That man—that furriner—he did magic on me and changed places. I felt that spell come over me, but didn't know what had happened until they came to take me up to the gallows. Me, who was only in for petty theft—fine and mark on me hand that was all I should've got. But instead they hanged me. Thought I was him—he changed places is wot. I looked like him and he looked like me. And I was in his cell and he was in mine. And I been followin' him ever since, like and now he's come back. And he's after you, girly. For turnin' him in like. And after he offs you, then he's plannin' to stay here and do his black magic stuff, just like before."

Marina felt the blood drain from her face.

"Just like I said, we'll all be murdered in our beds!" Madame's mother exclaimed in satisfaction.

"You fool woman, you can't be murdered in no bed! You're already dead!" the ghost protested.

"Marina, would you kindly tell me *what is going on?*" Madame Fertaglio demanded in a stentorian voice that gathered muted shrieks from both the Gantry sisters.

"I...I..." Marina stuttered, not know what to say.

The mousy-haired man stood up and came around the table. "I think your assistant should move to another room. Perhaps...?" His eyes swept the séance table as if to clear the occupants away. But all the participants held fast to their seats, glued to the events and not budging an inch.

"Yes, perhaps that would be best," Madame Fertaglio declared, and swept her hand towards the door to the kitchen. Marina found herself being helped out of her corner chair by the man with the mousy brown hair and ushered out the door in a manner that seemed totally different from his previous behavior. Not quiet with downcast eyes at all, now.

Marina had a moment of panic, wondering if perhaps this man was from Kiasie, or, or...

"Calm down," the man said softly. "I'm a Peacemaker. My name is Field Agent Lenar."

"What?" Marina exclaimed, not sure whether to be reassured or not. True, the Peacemakers had been nice to her that last time, after arresting the foreigner and thanking her for her part in catching both him and the lord who had been plotting against the King. But still, growing up as she had in the warrens had hardly led her to trust Peacemakers. They were the ones that caught you whether you had done anything wrong or not; that was the way of it.

"I'm here to help you," he said, leading her to a chair in the kitchen and fetching a glass of water for her. "Have been since that last event."

"You're joking!" Marina exclaimed.

"No," he said ruefully. "I was supposed to be unobtrusive, but you've suspected me from the first, haven't you?"

"Not of being a Peacemaker!" Marina declared. "But... well, you stood out."

"I'd like to know how, if you don't mind my asking. I'm supposed to be one of the best at what I do—being unobtrusive, that is!"

"You smelled funny," Marina blurted out, and then blushed. "I mean—I don't mean..."

"Ah!" he said. "So you're one of *those*!"

"What do you mean?"

"A Sniffer!" Madame's mother declared.

"I am *not* a sniffer!" Marina cried. She was starting to be really upset and *nothing* about this evening was going well.

"You are, you know," the mousy-haired man said. "Sniffer doesn't mean Peacemaker, although the force does employ a lot of them. Sniffer is just slang for those of us who have extra gifts—like talking to ghosts or being able to follow trails others just can't."

"Us?" Marina asked.

"Yes, us. I'm one too. There's a reason we get the nickname of "sniffer"—the really good ones can "smell" another sniffer—just like the ones who are good at following trails swear they can smell the ones they're following even hours after they've passed by. Not really smell...but that seems to be the closest any of us can come to describing it. So "sniffer.""

"Oh." Marina sipped the glass of water.

"So what's this about everyone getting murdered in their beds?" Field Agent Lenar asked.

"You didn't hear him?" Marina asked.

"No—though I did realize there was more than one entity in the room."

"Oh!" Marina looked around, startled. "He's gone!" She started to get up.

The Peacemaker pressed her back into her seat. "Just tell me."

Marina did, the words tumbling out one over the other, interrupted by comments from Madame's mother.

"Why can't you haunt your daughter, instead of me!" Marina cried, exasperated.

Lenar snorted. "You're the one that "glows." That's the way they describe it. We give them energy, even those of us who don't always hear them speaking. That's why you feel drained after using any powers—and that's why you need training. But we can talk more about that later. I'm calling in more men to get after this Kiasie and protect this house in the meantime."

After that time moved swiftly, with Madame ushering her reluctant guests out the door and away from all the excitement and descending on Marina to demand answers. Then several Peacemakers came in, asked for the same information, and quickly exited.

"Will they catch him?" Marina asked worriedly. "How will you prevent him from doing the same thing again?"

"Perhaps you would be safer going home to your mother," Madame Fertaglio suggested, as if interested in her welfare.

"Oh yes, shove the poor girl out the door!" her mother's ghost cackled.

"No, it's safer to keep anyone he might attack in location instead of scattering our forces trying to protect all of you," Field Agent Lenar said.

"What?" Madame Fertaglio exclaimed. "I'm in no danger!"

"You might be," Lenar demurred. "After all, it was here at one of your séances that Kiasie was caught. He might consider you just as responsible as your apprentice, here."

Madame opened her mouth and then swallowed whatever comments she had been about to make. If she denied Marina was an apprentice, then she might as well admit she wasn't a medium herself. And the thought that she, herself, could be cast in the role of one of the heroines who had caught the infamous Black Magician both thrilled and terrified her. Her face assumed the stuffed trout look she had when battling between her urge to shout and the need to look genteel.

"And this time, when we catch him, he's going to be handled by the Peacemakers, and not the politicians!" Field Agent Lenar stated firmly.

"What do you mean?" asked Marina

"He means once the nobs get their hands on anything it goes to the fish!" exclaimed Madame's mother.

Marina rolled her eyes, but stopped herself from snapping at the ghost.

Lenar acted as if he hadn't heard the ghost and answered Marina's question.

"Last time we were told to treat him as a gentleman, because of his connections. He was a noble by birth, apparently, and they don't frown on Black magic as much where he comes from. We were told not to create a "diplomatic incident" by rough treatment of him. Which means he wasn't searched as thoroughly or monitored as well as he should have been if he was able to do black magic right in our own prison!" Lenar sounded indignant. "This time, he'll be searched, isolated, and will have very highly trained Specialists monitoring him every minute."

"That sounds good," Marina answered, glancing at the dark window and thinking that they had to catch him first. And then they waited. And waited, for word.

Madame wandered over to the plate of leftover nut rolls and began to eat first one and then another.

"You'll be gaining ten more pounds if you eat all of those," her mother admonished.

Marina winced, waiting for the explosion, but realized, as Madame calmly took yet another nut roll, that apparently whatever had allowed Madame to hear her mother in the séance had stopped and once again she couldn't hear her mother's constant comments. If there was one thing the Madame didn't like to have mentioned, it was her weight.

Almost as if she had heard, however, she spoke up. "I should stop eating these. I had a good dinner. But I never could resist a good nut roll."

Her mother snickered.

"Dinner!" Marina exclaimed. "My brother!"

Lenar looked up. "What about him?"

"He's up in the attic. I was going to bring him something to eat after the séance."

"You have your brother living in my attic?" Madame asked, furious.

"The fat's in the fire, now, girly!" her mother chipped in.

"No, he's not living there. He's the one who spotted Kiasie

216

down on the docks. He's just hiding there until dark. And it's not even your attic."

"What do you mean, it's not my attic! I own this whole house, I'll have you know. Top to bottom."

"Oh, never mind. It will take to long to explain!" Marina leapt up and started to gather together some food—a little left over meat from dinner, some mashed roots and a few of the nut rolls.

"You're feeding *your* brother with food from *my* house?" Madame demanded in ominous tones. "And how long have you been doing that? I *thought* the household expenses seemed high!"

"You can never trust the help!" her mother exclaimed.

"I have *never* fed my brother or anyone else in my family from your household! I'm giving him *my* dinner, which I didn't eat tonight. And you—shut up!" she directed at the Madame's mother.

"I *beg* your pardon!" Madame was truly angry now.

"I wasn't talking to you—I mean it was your mother I told to shut up."

"You still have the effrontery to pretend that my dear, departed mother is *haunting* this house?? My mother would never do something so vulgar! You can consider yourself dismissed. Go as soon as all this," she flapped her hands about the kitchen as if clearing smoke, "is over." She stalked out of the kitchen.

"You can never trust the help," Madame's mother repeated with satisfaction.

"*Ohhhh!*" Marina cried in exasperation, bundled the meager fare together and headed for the hatch that led to the attic. Quickly she pulled it open, stuck the ladder in place and scurried up the rungs.

And stopped dead at the top, staring into the face of Kiasie, the demonstrably *not*-dead Black Magician.

He lunged for her, but Marina kicked her feet off the rungs and dropped half way down, catching her fall with a quick arm through the side of the ladder, and swinging around to the back of it—a move instinctive from years of dodging gangs,

Peacemakers and irate adults while growing up in the warrens.

Kiasie, his lunge ending in thin air, quickly caught himself on the end of the hatch opening and swung down towards the kitchen floor. Lenar snatched a whistle out of his pocket and blew hard, then leapt forward.

"His hands!" he exclaimed to Marina. "Don't let him use his hands!"

Marina continued her swing around the back of the ladder, gained some purchase with her feet on one rung and lunged for Kiasie's back, grabbing and holding his right hand. She tried to pull it up behind his back, but he was too strong for her. Doggedly, she held on, clinging like one of those foreign monkeys the noble ladies liked to carry around as pets. Vicious little things, Marina thought and then decided to imitate them some more. She bit the black magician, hard, on the arm.

He shrieked and started screaming something in a foreign tongue.

Lenar lunged forward and slugged him in the mouth, stopping the chant, then grabbed the man's left hand. The back door burst open and two more Peacemakers lunged in. In moments they had the magician subdued, with a gag in his dangerous mouth and special cords tying his hands behind his back.

One of the Peacemakers who had come in the back door bent over to tie his feet with more of the special cords and Madame's mother cackled: "Now *that's* what I call a fine backside, girly. *Those* are the kind of nut rolls you should be baking in your "oven," girl, not those twirly things made of bread!" she cackled.

Marina turned three shades of red, and completely lost her temper. "You vulgar, wicked old woman, you leave me alone, you hear? I'm sick of your comments, and your swearing, and you, you..." she gasped for breath.

"Stop," Lenar said, putting his hands on her shoulders. "Calm down. Take a deep breath and just calm down."

"But she...but she," Marina sputtered.

"I know, but your emotions just feed her. She gets her energy from you. The more you let yourself get annoyed, the stronger *she* gets. You *really* need training, you know. Or you'll burn yourself out."

"And where would I get *that* sort of training, now!"

"The Peacemakers."

"I'm not becoming any Peacemaker. I've told your lot that before, and I'm telling you again."

"You don't have to join the Peacemakers to get the training. Although it's not a bad job, you know. Especially since it looks like you'll be looking for a new one. But the Peacemakers don't want anyone with talents like yours running around without training, attracting every bad element—both alive *and* dead—in the city. In fact, at this point, you really don't have much of a choice. It's either get training or agree to having your powers controlled by other means. That's one of the reasons I was sent to attend these séances. To see if what happened before was a onetime fluke or if you really did have these powers. And bring you in if you did."

"Other means?"

"Cords, bracelets, monitoring—that sort of control. You're dangerous, Marina—and not just to yourself. Why don't you gather up some things and come down to the station with us tonight. The higher-ups are going to want to question you anyway. If you get through with them before dawn, you can have a room for the rest of the night at the station and I'll help you sort things out tomorrow. I imagine you'll want to stay with your mother while you get training, instead of living at a station, but you can decide all that tomorrow. Let's get this nasty fellow," pointing at Kiasie, "down to a cell and securely locked away."

Marina sighed and looked about the kitchen, then scurried into the back room where she slept and gathered up a clean dress for the morning and a few other things, stuffing them into a bag. She came back to the kitchen in time to see several Peacemakers manhandling the Black Magician onto a wagon.

"Ready?" Lenar asked.

"Yes, let's go," Marina said resignedly.

"I hate to mention this, but weren't you going to bring your brother some food and send him home? Do you want me to come with you to make sure he's alright? After all, Kiase was up in those attics…"

"No, no one Kiase's size, or even yours, could fit through the small gaps along the eaves that connect the attics. Thomai should be fine—just mad at me for being so late bringing him something to eat and getting him out of there." She reached for the bag of food she'd dropped earlier and then hesitated, flushing slightly at the thought of the nut rolls in there. Then she decided her new distaste for the very thought of them would not affect her brother's enjoyment. Besides, their presence might ease her brother's anger over her lateness, and give her a chance to explain what had happened. Except she *certainly* wasn't going to explain her new distaste of nut rolls to him. She just wouldn't be able to watch while he wolfed them down!

WITH THY SIX KEYS ENTER

by Julia H. West

As I said in my introduction to this anthology, my reaction to Disney's *Beauty and the Beast* was that I'd rather have the library than the prince. Here's a protagonist who would agree.

Julia H. West is most often found covered with cats, which makes it very difficult for her to use her keyboard. During the rare occasions she manages to evade the felines, she writes science fiction and fantasy stories, which have been published in such magazines as *Realms of Fantasy* and *Spider*, and the anthologies *Enchanted Forests* and *The Shimmering Door*, as well as three earlier volumes of *Sword & Sorceress*. Most of her previously-published stories, including the tale of a Micronesian navigating a starship through interstellar danger that won her the Grand Prize for Writers of the Future XI, are available from Callihoo Publishing. You can discover more about her writing on her website at http://juliahwest.com.

I perused used books in Bookseller Pukash-Genneti's stall every morning. I usually can't afford them, but he doesn't mind; I buy when I have the coin. He's not one of those who think women shouldn't be scholars.

This morning, Pukash-Genneti had a box of dusty books acquired from some dead aristocrat's estate. He said there had been a donkey-load of them, but Bemmum the Rarities Dealer bought most of them. No humble scribe like me could afford to buy from Bemmum. He catered to nobles and important sorcerers.

I took books from the box one by one. Most were hastily copied versions of classics; I winced at mistakes I saw on the few pages I checked. But one was older, not a cheap copy. Bemmum must have missed this one—it looked like a genuine Meluga. In my head, I counted my coins, and where they must be spent. I'd paid this month's lodging already, and if I ate but two meals a day for the rest of the week. . . .

"How much for this one?" I asked, acting like I was vaguely interested. But Pukash-Genneti knew me well. If I asked to buy a book, it was worth something.

He stroked his beard, peered at the book, then said, "For you, Safji, 20 silver bits."

"Have you looked at the books in this box?" I asked, sounding offended. "Cheap copies full of errors. Not worth two bits each."

"The paper in them is worth more than two bits!" Pukash-Genneti also sounded offended. "If you want to use the blank pages in your trade, you know they're worth more than that!"

We continued in this vein until I realized I'd have to run to set up in my favorite spot near the rugmaker. Perhaps that had been Pukash-Genneti's intention all along. "Eight bits, then, and that's robbery," I said. I wondered how many days I could get by on one meal. I handed over the money, grabbed the book, and ran.

I spent the day as usual, writing a love letter for an over-perfumed elderly lady, another for a pale youth in embroidered robes, doing accounts for a grain merchant, reading a love letter for a blushing girl of about thirteen, who hadn't even blossomed yet. I recognized Sirnos's handwriting on the last. It was obvious he'd given suggestions to the youth sending it—florid and full of banalities, including ebony hair and blood-red lips, neither of which she had. She was thrilled with it.

At last, in the cool of the evening, stomach grumbling loudly because I'd eaten no midday meal, I headed home with my new book.

I pulled the window curtain aside to release the day's heat, settled on my bed mat, and examined the book. If it wasn't a genuine Meluga, it was penned by someone with similar handwriting and attention to detail—a beautiful volume, worth far more than the eight bits I'd paid. It was the second volume of Histories of the Kings, in superb condition. The other books had probably been in a 'show' library of a person who could not read, but owned books to show his importance. He may have inherited *this* from someone who appreciated books for their contents.

As I turned pages, a piece of parchment fell out. It had marked the history of King Neraros's reign, over two centuries ago.

The writing was difficult to read—the pen's nib too broad for the small markings, so they were crowded and smudged. But as I picked out word after word it became obvious this was a set of directions, a guide from one place to another. How old the parchment was I could not say—it was creased and dirty, and the writing archaic. It may have dated from the time of King Neraros, or merely been handy to mark a reader's place when they put the volume down.

On a scrap of paper too small to use for my clients' letters, I copied the directions. Then I held my lamp close and frowned at what I'd written. Some of the description sounded like places near this city of Miyajar. 'Crescent Cliff,' for instance, could be a rock outcropping about half a day away, which my people called 'Demon's Toenail.' It had been years since I roamed the desert with my family, but not so long that I'd forget landmarks.

I was racking my brain for any place that might be described as 'Black Pillars' when my neighbor Dumaishi called outside my window, "Ho, Safji, there's a man here asking for you."

I poked my head out and looked down; a man in a travel-stained robe shifted restlessly from foot to foot. People in need of a scribe seldom came to my room, but I could use every bit I could earn, so I pulled on my headscarf, grabbed my lamp, and ran down the stairs. At the bottom I stopped so I could step into the street with dignity.

The man was a traveler with a letter from a friend telling him where to stay in Miyajar. I could see why he had not waited until morning. I read his letter, gave him directions to the house described, and was about to return to my book when a woman hurried up. "You're a scribe?" she asked.

"I am."

She pulled a small book from under her shawl. "I've inherited this, and want to know what it says and if it's worth anything."

She hovered close as I opened the book. It was old, but the script was clean and dark. Illuminations decorated every other page.

"It looks at least a hundred years old, perhaps older." While she stood almost too close, leaning over to see, I read a few pages. "It talks of King Neraros, who lived over two centuries ago." Odd, that I'd just seen that very name in my book. "I'm no expert, but this book appears quite valuable."

I skimmed several pages, reading about King Neraros, until I realized the woman was getting restive. "Take this to Bemmum the Rarities Dealer, if you want to sell. Don't let him cheat you. I think it's worth a great deal, so if he scoffs and says it's only worth a few bits, pretend you'll leave. That should get him to take you seriously."

The woman, looking anxious, thanked me. She dropped three silver bits into my hand, then hurried off.

I had, in a short time this evening, made back almost what I'd spent on the book. That pleased me greatly. If I hurried, I could still buy supper tonight.

~oOo~

The next day, my business was busier than ever before. I read letters, wrote letters, made contracts, and filled out and stamped permits. I wondered if every other scribe in the market had taken ill; usually the female scribe was the last someone with serious business came to. It was gratifying, but as I worked, my mind kept straying back to the book I'd bought, and the strange note it had contained.

The sun was setting when I headed home, with enough money that I could buy a bowl of lamb kebab. Licking grease from my fingers, I climbed worn steps to my room. During the day, I had solved the puzzle of the 'Black Pillars.' A cluster of columns, which my people called 'Giant's Pipes,' rose from the desert floor a day's walk from Miyajar. When I had been at Miyajar University, I'd heard scholars argue that they were natural, but what in nature made such even, six-sided pillars?

I stayed awake far too late, but before I slept I had a match for each of the landmarks mentioned in the parchment. There was also a name for their destination: Hawzeh. I was certain I'd heard that name before, but recalled nothing about it. In the language of my youth, it meant simply 'field.' What was so important about a field? Unless this scrap of parchment was merely a guide to reach a farmer's home.

I turned the parchment over. I had looked at it briefly before, but it was dirty, and only six words were written there. Rather, six sets of symbols, for they formed no words I recognized. Painstakingly I copied them, holding the parchment close to my oil lamp to assure I had them right.

The next day I sat on my mat beneath the shade of Rugmaker Gurmam's awning. Though I yawned often, I had enough business to keep me awake. Requests for permits were common. Usually Scribe Habuk took these, since his expertise was known throughout Miyajar. Was Habuk ill? I should enquire. I wouldn't want him angry with me for taking his work.

At dusk I bought a bowl of stewed meat and vegetables, eating as I sat quietly in the crowd about Storyteller Shamim. The old woman told the tale of some long-ago hero, enhanced by glowing pictures she drew in the air—either with magic or artifice, I'd never been able to tell which.

When she finished the story, as people tossed copper bits her way, I threaded through the crowd to stand beside her. Without looking at me, she said, "Why do you trouble me, scribe?"

"I seek knowledge," I said, and dropped a silver bit into her palm.

"I encourage those who seek knowledge," she said, finally turning her wrinkled face toward me. Her silver hair gleamed in the darkness with a trace of her magic.

I was blunt. "Do you know tales of a place called Hawzeh?"

She raised her brows. "Why would one such as yourself ask of Hawzeh?"

"I've come across the name in my studies," I said. Shamim had a way of knowing if one told her untruths. From the way she looked at me, she knew that though this was true, it was not the whole story. Perhaps I would tell her of my parchment, depending on what she told *me*.

She turned away, raised her voice and called, "What there was in the oldest of days and ages and times: in those days was a king, a king with seven sons."

The people around Shamim, who began to stand after the end of her last tale, sat back down around her. I settled at her side, listening eagerly.

She went on with her story, which started as many did, but then continued, "The king built a city, the grandest of cities, a city fit for a king of his greatness. He brought in the finest architects, and the most skilled workers in stone, wood, and metal. As construction began, he had the most powerful sorcerers in the land strengthen the buildings and roads with magic. The city was amazing and beautiful, but the king retained the name of the village it had been: Hawzeh."

My silver bit had been well spent. So the Hawzeh my parchment described was—perhaps—this great city.

Shamim went on to describe how the king had moved his family, servants, slaves, and hangers-on to his new city. He transferred the library of his old capital to Hawzeh and spent the rest of his days, when not conquering other kingdoms or ruling his own, adding to this library.

But this king was not to enjoy his grand city for long. Despite the best efforts of his sorcerers, the river that gave life to the city dried up—due, no doubt, to the magical efforts of his enemies. When the king died in a suspicious hunting accident, his sons abandoned drought-stricken Hawzeh and moved to other cities, squabbling among themselves as to who should succeed the king.

"Where did the king's sons go?" asked someone in the crowd before I had a chance.

"The eldest of them moved to this very city where we sit in the cool of the evening. Miyajar. But this happened many years agone, and the strife between brothers was resolved long before your great grandmothers were alive."

Someone else asked about the fight between princes, and Shamim's story veered off into a different tale. I slipped away quietly, my question answered. I knew which king that had been, the one with seven contentious sons. None other than Neraros, whose history my piece of parchment had marked. But his city—

Hawzeh—why did I not remember reading of it?

That night I turned from the parchment to the history of King Neraros in my book. I had not recognized the name Hawzeh because for many years his city had been known as Malun, the cursed city, and thus it was named in this history.

For weeks after that, around my increasing business, I talked to people in the marketplace. I discovered Scribe Habuk was well, and annoyed that I had so much of his business. When I asked what people knew of the city Malun, there were many stories. It was haunted, most said. It had been abandoned all in a night, its treasures and wonders left behind, but those who sought to retrieve them disappeared.

The books I consulted in the University of Miyajar gave me a rather different picture. People left the city gradually as farms around it failed. When King Neraros died the city was finally abandoned. An intriguing note in one of the books said that the king's sons, uninterested in his library, had left it in Hawzeh.

I decided I needed to visit Hawzeh myself. The unprecedented amount of business I had received in the last few months meant, for the first time since I'd left the university, I had money saved. I could take a few weeks, once the weather turned cooler, to seek the library in Hawzeh. For it was, of course, the library I sought. Rare, ancient tomes, I had heard. Several centuries in the desert heat, in a city no doubt mostly covered in sand, may have damaged them, but there should be *some* still readable. If I gave such books to the university, might they accept me back?

I found my guide when she came to me with a letter to read. Short and stocky, tough and practical, Rumah became angry when the letter, from someone who'd hired her to guard a caravan, broke the contract.

I looked at her with interest. "Since you won't be going with his caravan, would you be interested in a short journey, just a few days?"

She was interested.

Rumah knew exactly what we'd need—donkeys, provisions, shelter. In a few short days the journey I'd merely pondered became reality.

We set out before dawn, to travel as far as possible before the day became too hot. I rode one donkey, she another, and we had three more to carry provisions to Hawzeh, and the books I hoped to find back to Miyajar.

I told her of the landmarks, and the place I sought. The fact that some thought Hawzeh haunted gave her no qualms. "I've traveled north and south, east and west, and never seen a haunt," she stated. "It's always the wind, or rats, or someone making trouble."

In three days we were far past Demon's Toenail and Giant's Pipes, traveling through a part of the desert my people had never visited, at least not that I remembered. We found shelter in an abandoned house. I wondered why anyone had built it out here where there was no water, then remembered Shamim's tale of the river near Hawzeh drying up. Had this wasteland been farmland two centuries ago?

The next morning Rumah and I took the donkeys between stone outcroppings, then down into what was surely the dried bed of a long-vanished river. Thorn trees and spiny bushes grew there, suggesting there might still be water beneath the sand and rocky soil.

The donkeys scrambled up a steep embankment, using a trail of sorts, and as we topped the rise Hawzeh was revealed.

It was magnificent, yet eerie. Broad streets, alabaster buildings, spires and towers. But the city gates were missing, and sand buried the streets. Empty doors and windows gave the alabaster buildings a disturbing resemblance to fleshless skulls.

"Are you sure you want to go in, Safji?" Rumah asked, voice muffled by the scarf pulled over her mouth against blowing sand.

In the light of day the city seemed merely sad, not ominous. Well, perhaps not *very* ominous.

"I do," I said firmly, deliberately pushing tales of haunts and demons to the back of my mind.

From our vantage, it was easy to tell where the palace was. On a rise at the center of the city was a fortress, walls seeming intact. The broadest street led straight to its gates—gates that may have closed two centuries before and never opened again.

Now that we were out of the riverbed, Rumah and I found the wind had risen to whip sand around our donkeys' legs. Rumah turned in her saddle to scan the sky. "Storm coming," she said.

We rode quickly through the open gate into broad, sand-drifted city streets. The wind picked up. An ominous stain in the sky meant sandstorm.

Rumah and I jumped from our mounts to peer through gaping empty doorways of the nearest buildings to see if they would provide good shelter. The nearest looked and smelled as if jackals laired in it. Rumah skirted it carefully, brightly painted bow strung, arrow nocked, in case the jackals were still there.

We hurried farther into the city, closer to the fortress in the center. One large edifice, probably some noble's home, had intact walls and ceiling, and we discovered, after we led the donkeys in, that we could close the door.

While Rumah cared for the donkeys, I explored the house. Except for the lobby, where the door had been open, there was no sand anywhere. Light came from small holes in the walls and ceiling, and I wondered why sand had not blown through them. I was puzzled by the small room with basin on the wall and hole in the floor. Why have a privy in the middle of the house? Wouldn't the smell be horrendous? At least time had taken the stink away.

I knew the moment the sandstorm hit Hawzeh. The walls of the building we sheltered in were sturdy, but through those thick walls we heard the howl of wind and patter of sand against the building. Despite its age, the building kept sand out completely. None blew around the edges of the door or through the small holes that let in light.

Glad of shelter, Rumah and I spread mats on the floor and made a meal of dates and flat bread seasoned with salt-cured lamb. The donkeys, in the next room, weren't even restive. They seemed to welcome the relative coolness of the ancient building.

After eating, we curled up on our mats for a nap. When I awoke, it was so cool in the house I thought it night time. But light filtering into the room was so bright that I wondered if I'd slept through the night, and into the next day.

I used the privy; since we'd be leaving this building the smell wouldn't matter. Then I noticed water dripping into the basin on the wall. I had no idea where it came from, but was happy to see it. I washed my hands and then held cupped palms below the drip so I could drink. The water tasted fresh and clean, much better than what we'd been drinking from goatskin bottles for three days.

Pondering the presence of water in the house, I opened the door and peered out into late afternoon, not morning, sunshine. The sandstorm had passed over Hawzeh.

Rumah woke when I opened the door and let in the heat of the day. She rubbed her eyes and came to join me in the doorway. "We slept too long," she said. "Do you still want to search the city? We could wait for morning."

"I'd rather start now," I said, looking toward the city center, where the blank walls of the palace fortress enticed me.

The storm had sculpted the sand in the streets into fantastic patterns as it flowed around buildings. The donkey's hooves made the only sound, echoing oddly between ancient walls.

When we got to the fortress, we left the donkeys inside what might have been a shop, long ago. The gates towered above us, several times our height. I couldn't see any way to open them from outside—no latch or handle, not even holes for fingers. Had the gates always been opened from inside?

There was writing engraved into the stone walls on both sides of the gates. I stepped back several paces to see all the letters. It was old script, words broken in odd places so the writing fit the wall space.

"I was right; this was King Neraros's palace," I muttered under my breath as I read the words. Then, louder, for Rumah's benefit, I read, "Friends and allies may enter, but enemies shall feel the point of the spear, or the arrow through the heart."

I stepped farther back to take in the whole of the gates, and noticed something that made my heart stutter in shock. Nearly buried in sand drifted against the wall was withered flesh over bones—a human hand and arm.

I dropped to my knees, scooping sand away until I found the

skull, the neck, the chest. Right enough, there was an arrow through his heart. I say 'his,' for the corpse was dressed in a robe such as men in Miyajar wear. There was no sign scavengers had been at the body. I stood slowly, eyeing the wall with immense distrust.

"He's not been here two centuries," I commented as I backed away, still watching the wall, looking for movement, ready to run. "Someone must live here after all. Bandits, perhaps."

"Wouldn't we have seen some sign? Footprints, cleared paths?" Rumah backed away, too, and was farther from the wall than I.

"Not after the sandstorm. And we weren't looking before." While Rumah went back to get the donkeys, I began to circle the compound, following the half-buried street at its base, as far from the wall as I could get. I spotted no arrow slits in the wall, and anyone standing atop it should be readily noticeable. Besides, the arrow which killed the man had not come from above, but straight at his back. He'd been killed by someone in the city street.

Rumah came after me, leading the donkeys. They, at least, weren't concerned about bandits.

Halfway around the compound, we came upon a door in the wall. Unlike the huge gates, this was man sized, with a handle to pull it open. "Servant's gate?" I asked.

"Maybe." Rumah and I approached the door cautiously. I kicked at sand drifted against the wall, to see if there was another body, or garbage that would tell us the fortress was still in use. But there was nothing in the sand—not even twigs blown in from the desert.

I turned to Rumah. "Should we try to open it?"

"I don't want to touch it," she said, voice rasping. "This place is uncanny."

I felt it too. Though near dusk, no birds called, no insects buzzed, no wind whispered between buildings. Certainly, if there were people on the other side of that wall, we would hear them.

I took a staff from a donkey's pack and poked it at the door from several arm's lengths back.

Rumah ducked as if expecting a blow. Nothing happened. Either the door was locked, or the feeble tap I had given on the door wasn't enough to open it. But since no one had leaned over the top of the wall to drop a stone upon us, I was bold enough to walk right up to the door.

It was wooden, but hard as stone. I reached out cautiously to touch it, and it felt smooth as the alabaster of the walls. Like the walls, the centuries had not weakened it. Then my fingers discovered what the shadows had hidden before. Words were carved into the wood of the door, small but tidy, in the same old script as the message by the gates.

I leaned in close to read, encroaching shadows and the small size of the letters making that difficult. When I wasn't skewered by arrow or spear, Rumah came up to look over my shoulder. I read the words aloud as I deciphered the text. "O visitor, show respect for King Neraros. Place thy right foot first over the threshold." Since most government buildings and temples had similar rules, that did not seem unreasonable. "Keep to thy place. Neither thou nor thy beasts must stray from the path when thou art within the Palace of the King." Directed at servants, I guessed, or tradesfolk bringing in supplies for the palace. I wondered if they were expected to be able to read.

This inscription said nothing about arrows or spears, so I twisted the door handle and pushed. Once more Rumah cringed, but the door opened without resistance, and I could see into the courtyard beyond the wall.

The sun had set, and the lingering light of dusk did little to illuminate structures beyond the wall. I stepped over the threshold, being certain to use my right foot, and found a smooth stone pathway leading in graceful curves toward a dark building. Perhaps at one time there had been gardens around the path; now there was stone and sand. The path glowed slightly in the twilight, making it easy to follow.

I turned back, and as Rumah brought the donkeys to the door, she took each donkey's right foreleg and assured it crossed the threshold first. In a few moments two women and five donkeys stood within the palace compound of Hawzeh. We strung the donkeys out on the path, assuring they did not stray from it.

"We must be acceptable as friends or allies of King Neraros," I said, trying to make light of a situation that left me a bit shaky in the legs. "No one's shot us with arrows or skewered us with spears."

Rumah did not laugh.

In the light from the path, which strengthened as the sky darkened, it was obvious this courtyard had once been a garden. Dried stalks and weathered tree trunks made grotesque shapes. They had long since lost any virtue; the donkeys were not interested in them.

Though they had not in the city, here the donkeys echoed our nervousness. They crowded together, backs shuddering as if ridding themselves of swarming flies. I saw nothing to cause such alarm. It was a clear, calm evening. No breeze stirred the blasted garden, nor did insects annoy us.

The door of the dark building at the end of the path yielded another set of directions, which I read by the light of a clay oil lamp from a donkey's pack. With Rumah and the donkeys standing well away, I read the antiquated words. "Place thy right hand upon the door handle, then twist it to the left."

I was about to do so when Rumah said, "Wait, Safji." She stared about in the darkness, gaze taking in the roofs of nearby buildings and the statues scattered throughout the dead vegetation. "Do you hear?" she whispered.

There was a sound. A susurration, not wind through the dried stalks or pierced garden walls. "There!" I said, pointing. A stone fountain, its bowl half full of sand, had begun sending a thin plume of water into the air. I stared at it in wonder and more than a little trepidation.

Scenting water, the donkeys started toward it, but Rumah held them firmly on the path.

"Where does the water come from?" I asked. "There was water in the house this morning, too."

"Magic," Rumah muttered.

I remembered Shamim's tale of the construction of the city, when the most powerful sorcerers in the land had assisted. But I thought she meant they used their powers to strengthen the walls, or raise beams too heavy for men—not that they had created magical fountains that spouted water from nowhere.

"Should we try the door?" asked Rumah.

I put my right hand on the door handle, turned it to the left, and it opened without a squeak or rasp of sand beneath it. Light bloomed inside slowly, from no source I could find. I took a deep breath to calm myself, then stepped over the threshold.

The room was a kitchen, a vast space with hearths, cupboards, and tables, all clean as if the cooks had only stepped out for a moment. Bowls, platters, and cooking implements were still in their places. Hearing Rumah's gasp behind me, I walked through, beneath tiled arches as beautiful as any in the temples of Miyajar, to a door at the far end. I squinted at its surface but found no instructions. Carefully I touched it; when nothing happened, I took the handle and twisted to the left.

As the door opened, light streamed out into the courtyard beyond, illuminating benches, fountains, and sculptures much more beautiful than those in the outer courtyard. There was no path, so I hesitated. Would those who worked in the kitchen know of restrictions that visitors were not told? With another deep breath, I stepped into the courtyard.

A fountain began spouting, but there was no other reaction to my entrance. After getting my breathing under control I called to Rumah and told her to come in. She did, and we tethered the donkeys there.

There was no engraving on any of the doors opening into the courtyard, nor on nearby walls. I cautiously opened one to find a hallway, with light that appeared as I stepped through. But there were no cries of discovery, no arrows in the night. After that, I became bolder.

Rumah and I explored. We found living quarters, banquet halls, guard stations—all the needs of a palace. Nowhere was any sign of inhabitants, but most rooms looked as if someone had left them only moments before, expecting to return.

It was deep night when I discovered an alabaster building decorated with friezes of men holding books and scientific instruments. *This must be the library*, I thought, heart hammering with excitement.

I circled it before Rumah joined me, and found a great entrance, double doors decorated with sand-worn paintings. As I approached, the walls around the doors began to glow, and I could see they were covered with engravings. The first set read, in the archaic script I had seen before, "Herein lives wisdom of the ancients, knowledge of scholars, and annals of kings. With thy six keys enter and partake."

Beneath the first inscription was a second set of engravings, in the language of Dhuzah to the east—which had been conquered by King Neraros. I didn't know all the words, but those I could read said, "Gathered here are wonders and shame, marvels and degradation, truth and lies. Use thy keys wisely." Again, a mention of keys. I had no keys. Any keys to this library were probably lost hundreds of years ago. Had I come this far for nothing?

Below the Dhuzahim script was a third, one I had seen before but could not read. And below that, a fourth set of engravings. These I could sound out, for they were written with the same archaic symbols as the rest of King Neraros's pronouncements, but I did not know the words. I sat on the steps leading up to the doors, took out paper, and was uncapping my ink bottle when Rumah came around the side of the building.

"Is this the library?" she asked, voice odd enough that I glanced at her. She stared up at the building with lips firmed and hands clenched, as if to hit something.

"It is, but I don't know how to get in. There are inscriptions in four different languages, and I can only read two of them."

She gave a great sigh, quite unlike the Rumah I had come to know in the last week. I was not sure why. Even if I was disappointed, *she* would get her pay.

"I'm copying this last inscription, to see if I can discover any meaning." I uncapped my ink, dipped my pen, and began carefully copying the symbols.

Rumah sat near me on the steps, turned to look up at the great doors. "Is that picture King Neraros and his seven sons?" she asked.

I paused to look up. "It could be. I don't see any inscription there, though." I found my place in the engraving I had been copying, and stopped, breath catching in my throat. I did not know the next word, but I'd seen it before. It was one of the six unknown words written on the back of the parchment that had started me on this adventure.

Eagerly I scanned the rest of the inscription. It was broken up into six sections, and beginning each section was one of the words I had memorized.

As I copied the rest of the unknown words, I wondered how to use this knowledge. I didn't know those words, what language they were from, or how they should be pronounced. And if I did, what good would speaking words to the door do me now? It was not as if a guard waited on the other side, listening.

I must have made some noise in my frustration, for Rumah asked, "What is it?"

When I explained she said, "The city is magic. Why shouldn't words open the door?"

I stared at her. I had seen so much else in this city come alive—by magic? So why had I not thought of this?

"What would the words sound like, if you said them like you would in Miyajarin?"

I looked up at the doors, then capped my ink and stood. I retreated to a bench in the plaza before the library. If the words *did* open the doors, I didn't want my fumbling for a pronunciation to set off arrows and spears—or whatever else a city that could make light and start fountains flowing after two centuries would threaten me with.

Rumah followed and stood behind me, hands on hips, glaring at the building as if force of will could open the doors.

Hetkaleth, tewketlaf, wedemaney, dewkesna, khethany, yekalema. The pronunciation would be simple if they were in any of the three languages I spoke fluently, but they'd be different for each of those languages. The syllables would be emphasized differently, as would the vowels, and the 'kh' could be any of three disparate sounds.

If I pronounced them as scholars at the university believed Miyajarin had been spoken two centuries ago, would that be correct? What would happen if it was not?

A faint blush of dawn lit the horizon when I finally decided how to pronounce the words. I wouldn't dally any longer and lose my resolve. Pushing myself up from the bench, wobbling on legs that had gone to sleep, I marched up to the base of the steps. Slowly, distinctly, I said the six words.

In the eerie silence of the courtyard, the words seemed to ring on the air. Then, with a whisper of sound, the doors before me parted and swung open. A breath of perfumed air—leather, paper, and ink—found its way down the steps.

Behind me, there was another sound. I recognized it: Rumah stringing her bow. I turned slightly, to see what danger she'd detected, and found her arrow pointed at my heart.

I'd been a scribe in Miyajar for five years, and a scholar for two years before that, but my heritage is of the desert nomads— quick to react to danger. Before she loosed the arrow, I flung myself at her knees.

I heard the arrow whoosh past my head, but was already on her. She was tough, and had survived many fights. But I was decades her junior, and incensed at her perfidy. I knocked her down, and we scuffled, punching and scratching, across that deserted plaza. My blow to the side of her head was mostly luck, but dazed her, and I ran for the library while she scrabbled at my clothing.

When I passed between the doors, they began to close ponderously behind me. I crouched, breathing hard and sobbing, as light bloomed in the great room I had entered. Why? Why had Rumah turned against me? Was it she who had shot that man we found buried in sand by the compound gates?

I didn't have long to regain my breath, nor for these furious questions to pound in my head. The heavy doors muffled noise, but all was so quiet that I heard Rumah recite the words I'd used so short a time before, carefully pronouncing them exactly as I had.

My gaze ran over tables, chairs, racks of scrolls, and shelves of books, but I found nowhere to hide until I saw, at the other end of the room, a great stone staircase. With speed born of terror I bolted up the stairs, then crouched in shadows at the top, staring down at the entrance.

The doors opened, but Rumah did not stand between them, where she would be a perfect target. She knew I had no weapon, but was still wary.

I found myself murmuring those six words. They had woven themselves into my being, carved a niche in my mind that had not been there before. They must be magic; what else could open doors that heavy without even a touch?

The doors began closing, but Rumah slipped through the gap just before they met.

In the cool silence of the library, Rumah's harsh gasps were obvious. I breathed open mouthed, making no sound.

"I know you're there," Rumah called, voice raspy. "You can't get away."

I stayed silent. Until I had a better idea of what had happened, I would not let her know where I was.

Rumah blundered about among the furniture, knocking over chairs, looking under tables. She'd worked herself into quite a frenzy. I crouched behind the mezzanine's railing and again recited the six words, at first under my breath, then in a nearly voiceless whisper.

When Rumah began pulling books from the shelves a great gong shook the building, and she froze with one arm uplifted, still as the statues dotting the blighted gardens outside, as if the air had solidified about her.

Her mouth was still active, though. "Safji, you can't hide forever. Even if I don't return, Bemmum will find other scribes, and keep sending them until he discovers the secret."

Bemmum? The rarities dealer? What had he to do with my quest to find the library of Hawzeh?

"You scribes and scholars are so naive," Rumah rasped. "Give you a puzzle, and you go to great lengths to solve it. Especially when it's assured you can afford to start a quest. But you talk too much. Everyone in the market knows where you are. When you don't return, they'll shake their heads and say the cursed city has claimed another victim. That may make it harder for Bemmum to find another scribe . . . but it hasn't before. You're smarter than the last one was, so you made it into the library, but that won't save you."

I didn't answer. Bemmum. He had bought most of the books from the aristocrat's library. Had he, while picking through the offerings, planted the book I had bought? As Rumah said, everyone in the market must know I stopped at Pukash-Genneti's stall every morning.

Listening to Rumah, I'd quit reciting the six words. I started up again, and let her rant, listening with only part of my attention. When I had a sudden impulse to move farther along the mezzanine, I followed it, crawling so the railing hid me. Rumah's voice became less audible as I moved away.

A narrow staircase led upward from the mezzanine, and I ascended, no longer caring if Rumah could see me. At the top of the stairs was a door. When my hand touched it, a glow appeared, and it swung open just as the great library doors had.

There was already light in the room, a cozy place with three walls covered with shelves, a desk in the center of the room, and a luxurious bed on the fourth wall. Had this been King Neraros's study, or had it housed a librarian? As in the other buildings we'd entered in the palace compound, the room was dust free and the coverings on the bed fresh, as if it had been made up that very day.

A book lay open on the desk, and I leaned over to look at it. In the same untidy archaic hand that had scribed my parchment were written wonderful things. I pulled up a chair and began to read. All was explained: the magic that created Hawzeh, made light and water appear, and did so much more.

~o0o~

Thus began my stewardship of Hawzeh—or my captivity. In the years since Hawzeh was abandoned, it became . . . lonely? Can a city be lonely? It matters not if that is the reason, but the fact remains that I cannot leave, nor can Rumah. I dine on food two hundred years old but fresh as if it had been picked or slaughtered or baked this morning. I wear clothing of a fashion two centuries gone.

The city allows Rumah to live in the servant's quarters but will not let her leave. She knows too much. She curses me every day, though Hawzeh assures she cannot touch me. The donkeys, alas, have long since died of old age.

I have all the knowledge I sought, but it does me little good, for I cannot share it. Everyone else Bemmum has sent to discover Hawzeh's secrets never made it as far as the palace fortress. They were harried by jackals and dust devils, they heard uncanny noises and saw eerie lights, and fled. None has yet found the parchments I have left about, explaining the city and how it trapped me for its caretaker.

I hope someone finds one of my notes before I die here, alone but for an old woman who hates me because she can't kill me and escape to receive her reward.

ALL ELSE

by Pauline J. Alama

Many years ago, MZB wrote an essay titled "Why Prayer Is Not Answered." When we set up her website (mzbworks.com) we put it there, along with her articles on writing. I admit I never expected it to inspire a story, but it did, and here is the story.

Pauline J. Alama is a freelance writer and a lapsed medieval scholar. Despite having lived in New Jersey most of her life, she does not glow in the dark (or at least not so you'd notice). Her high fantasy novel *The Eye of Night* (Bantam Spectra 2002) was a finalist for the Compton Crook/Stephen Tall Award. Since her first professionally published story appeared in *Marion Zimmer Bradley's Fantasy Magazine* in 1994, she has been published in numerous volumes of *Sword & Sorceress*, as well as *Realms of Fantasy, Abyss & Apex, Penumbra eMag*, and several anthologies, most recently *Trafficking in Magic/Magicking in Traffic*.

Anyone could study with the wizard. She would show her spell-book to anyone who could read. If you could not read, she'd be happy to teach you. She would willingly answer all your questions about the role of music in spell-casting; the use of herbs, rare or common; the silent spells cast by a gesture or even a thought. For this she charged no fee: if you offered money, she would laugh. But in all the time I'd known her, none of her students had ever learned to practice magic: the cost was too high.

"Do I have the makings of a wizard?" I demanded one day, enraptured with the sheer poetic beauty of a spell to make apples grow from dead wood.

The wizard did not answer at first. She offered me one of the apples; I took it, inhaling its fragrance worshipfully, the scent of life where no life had been. Without tasting it, I followed her as she hobbled across the street to give an apple to the ragged man begging in the corner of the marketplace, and the rest to a young mother anxiously counting her pennies in front of the bakery. At last she spoke: "Stellina, what makes a wizard isn't something you can *have*."

"Forgive me, Wizard; I put it badly. But I mean—well—it's not everyone that can learn your ways. All my life I've seen your pupils come and go. So many study, but not one of us learns it truly."

The wizard said, "Do you suspect I haven't taught you truly?" I might have thought her angry, but her eyes crinkled with a hint of laughter.

"What I mean is, am I wasting my time trying to learn magic?"

"If you worry that you're wasting your time, then you may be," she said.

"It's not that," I protested, though partly it was true. My parents plagued me about the hours I spent trailing after the wizard when I should have been learning to judge and sort the foreign silks and dyes that made my family's fortune—or, if I lacked the true Gualteri eye for merchandise, seeking a husband or learning to bargain cunningly with money-changers or doing anything useful. "My life isn't rooted in mystery. No one in my family has ever been a wizard. Maybe it just isn't in my blood."

"Your ancestors have nothing to do with it," said the wizard, "except that, having left you much, they left you more to lose."

"But I would be willing to lose so much, if only I thought I had hope of—of this!" I gestured with the apple.

"Ah, but would you be willing to give it all up before you have any hope?" the wizard said.

"Before—? What do you mean?"

She took my arm. "Come, Stellina. Come to the shade of the arbor and sit with me. There are indeed truths I have held back, things I must tell each student at the right time, if that time comes. Today is the right time."

I walked with her toward the arbor where the grape vines, in full leaf but not yet in fruit, shaded a strip of earth like a green-roofed, earth-floored tunnel. Neither the owner of the vineyard nor his workers would resent our presence there, for the wizard had power to make the soil richer, the leaves more vigorous, the blossoms more fertile than before. The wizard lowered her creaking frame slowly to the earth and sighed contentedly as if settling into bed. "Have you ever wondered why, with the power to work marvels—to make apples spring from dead wood, or grapes grow out of season—I have nothing for myself?"

"Having that power, what else would you need?" I said.

She studied my face seriously then. "Have you grasped that? Then, indeed, the time is ripe to tell you how I became a wizard. It is not a matter of learning and knowing, nor is it an inborn gift. It is an act of will. To be a wizard, you must forsake all else."

"I've half forsaken it already. My mother says—"

"Hush. When I say all else, I mean *all:* not just the luxury of sleeping on silk, but the luxury of listening to your own wisdom, the satisfaction of being right. Not just your family's wealth, but your anger at them, your wish for their approval, your pride or shame at being unlike them. Not just the ease of entering your parents' business, but the comfort of feeling you can return to it if wizardry doesn't work for you—and even the hope of wizardry itself. Wizardry will not come to you so long as you cling to anything but one thing."

"Wizard," I said carefully, "what is that one thing, if it's not the hope of wizardry?"

"That," she said, "is not the same for every wizard. For me, it was earth, the womb of seeds and roots and growth. The earth that cradles me now. To work earth, I had to choose it, and choose it with all my being—to have nothing else, to rely on nothing else.

"I gave away everything I owned—not a Gualteri's fortune, but all the little comforts I had slaved for: sandals for stony roads, a broad-brimmed hat against the noonday heat, a leather satchel, a knife, a bowl. I gave away my spare clothes, then the very clothes off my back, and with them my dignity.

"Then I went to the meadow and with my bare hands I dug

myself a grave. I lay in it face down, seeing earth, tasting earth, breathing earth. Loam clung to my eyelashes, dust lodged in the corners of my eyes, many-legged creatures scuttled through my hair, but still I lay there. Some beast came on soft paws and dug in the ground, scattering earth over my back; I did not resist, stilling the fear of suffocation by filling my mind with the rich scents of the soil, the many textures of stone and sand and mud and mould. Night chilled me and day warmed me—at least for the first night and day. Eventually my blood settled into the even coolness of the ground.

"At last the worms that crawled through the dirt traveled not across my skin, but through it. The roots that spread downward passed through me like my own veins. I could feel them growing. I could shape the course of their growth, speed it or slow it or turn it to a richer path of loam. Then I knew I could rise from that trench without forsaking earth, because I *was* earth, and working earth was like moving my own body. And thus I became a wizard.

"I went to my village, but not to my home, because earth did not call me there. I did not touch anything that had been mine before. And it was well I did not, for my own mother would not have known me. My creamy skin had become earth-brown, my fiery hair dark as good planting soil.

"When a neighbor balked at my nakedness, I let her clothe me. Since then, I have worn what others put on me, eaten what others gave me. But I do not choose a garment or a meal for myself. I chose once for my life, and I chose with all my heart."

"Did your family never know you again?"

"I did not stay to see if they would learn to know me in my new form," the wizard said. "Earth called me, and I wandered the dusty road until I found earth that needed working."

"I don't know if I could do that," I said.

"If you told me you knew," the wizard said, "I would not believe you. Time and thought must work their wizardry on you before you know. Mind you, I don't say I was right to forsake all else, even my family. All I can tell you is that this choice made me a wizard. Before it, spells were only words in my mouth, and the rarest knowledge only theory." She stood, reaching up to caress a tendril of the vine, which blossomed at her touch. "You need not decide today, or tomorrow, or this year, or next. You are as free to watch me work, to read my spell-book, to study my ways, as you have ever been. But you know now what it will take to do more than that."

"Thank you, Wizard," I managed to say, though I felt weighted down with lead. I walked slowly home, noticing everything and everyone I passed in the streets: the loaded carts creaking on their way to market, the children scampering, apprentices hustling on errands, couples walking hand in hand. I saw the baker's girl delivering a basket of crusty loaves, smelled the homey fragrance as her load passed me by. I couldn't imagine giving up desiring even such a common comfort as fresh bread—or being so narrow in my devotion that I could not prefer one color over another, like the sparkling blue of a young dandy's sapphire ring or the sunlit turquoise of the ocean I could see from the top of the hill where the Gualteri mansion stood.

Reaching my room with its familiar clutter of books, I tried to imagine forsaking it all for the still and lonesome darkness of an earthen grotto. I had thought I wanted to be a wizard more than anything, but the prospect of having to deliberately give up all else shook me to the core. I doubted I could ever love anything so single-heartedly.

Time to stop chasing rainbows, I told myself. Time to put my hand to a task—whatever task came to me—in stead of pining for a nobler calling. The next day I put on my good twilight-blue skirt and a crisp apron and joined my mother in the shop.

"Heaven defend us," she said, "can that really be Stellina?"

"I thought you wanted me here," I said hesitantly, ready to bolt for outdoors at the slightest sign that she didn't.

"Of course, of course. But do you still remember how to handle the silks? Are your hands clean?"

I held them up for her inspection. Luckily I'd remembered to scrub under my nails.

"Clean enough. You can wind up the bolts I unwind to show the customers." And so I spent the day drifting in her wake as she sailed from one end of the shop to the other.

My mother always shone in the shop, greeting the rich women and busy dressmakers who came to look at our silks, holding a vibrant red up to one woman's face, a delicate green to another, complimenting the fine ladies on their complexions, the dressmakers on their deep understanding of the textures and weights of fabric. Perhaps there is a magic even in this, I thought; perhaps one of these deft-fingered needlewomen could commune with the fabric as the wizard did with the earth, until her soul ran in warp and weft. But it seemed a petty thing beside the wizard's craft, the craft I lacked the courage to take up. How could anyone care so much about the drape of a skirt when in this very city, a woman crouched in the mud stirring dead branches to life?

"*Stellina*," my mother's voice interrupted my thoughts, "where are your manners?"

I realized the customer must have been asking me something. "Pardon, madam," I mumbled to a middle-aged lady wearing a stylish close-fitted bodice and an expression of deep impatience. "You were saying...?"

"The color of your skirt interests me. May I look more closely?"

I let her take a handful of the loose folds and observe the sheen of the fabric. "Twilight blue, we call it," I said. "Deeper than sky blue, with a tinge of purple in it."

"Real Rakovina purple," my mother added. "We use only the best dyes."

The customer frowned at the handful of skirt. "It seems uneven in tone. I might prefer a purer hue."

I wished that she'd let go of my skirt—or better yet, that I could slither out and leave skirt, customer, and shop behind, and be gone somewhere. When she unhooked her fingers from my clothing, I sprang away so eagerly that I backed into a pyramid of carefully stacked bolts of cloth.

Scarlet, vermillion, ember-glow, golden, and canary-colored silk, along with a single precious bolt of the costly Rakovina purple, tumbled down, bounced off me, and rolled on the floor.

"Stellina Gualteri!" my mother cried. Diving to catch the costly purple bolt, she accidentally rammed her shoulder into the customer's middle.

The customer recoiled from her as if from filth. "Pah! I was told this was an elite establishment. Clearly I was misinformed." She stalked out without buying anything.

"Sorry, Mamma," I said.

"Sorry? Is that all you can say? *Sorry?*" My mother drew in a deep breath, and I shrank from the scolding I knew would come—but she only sighed. "Never mind, Stellina. You belong in this shop the way a fish belongs in a stable. Here, carry this note to Uncle Zeppe at the harbor and see if he can make use of you there."

I fled the shop, half delighted to be released, half ashamed of my uselessness. I changed my good skirt for an old stained one, better suited to the grime of the harbor, and left my shoes at home. As I ran downhill toward the water, a moist breeze lifted my hair and, to some degree, my spirits as well. Like a child, I wandered barefoot onto the sand and waded out into the waves, soaking the hem of my skirt. Gulls called their coarse greetings overhead, though the waves' constant thunder muted their clamor. A ragged child begged from me, and I gave him a handful of coins, a trivial thing set against all I could not bear to give away.

Uncle Zeppe smiled to see me. "Stellina! Sent by heaven in answer to my dilemma. See if your sweet young face can do more than all my words to win over Captain Rialdo."

"Why? What do you want from him?" I said uneasily.

"The same deal we had the last time he sailed. He's gotten greedy; he wants a bigger share of the profits if he's to sail for us again."

"If that's what he wants, what could I say that would change his mind? I've never been good at haggling."

"You're a fifteen-year-old girl," he said. "Use your feminine wiles on him."

"Uncle Zeppe!"

"I don't mean anything scandalous. But sometimes the

messenger counts more than the message. He's tired of seeing my face. You look better—even in that bedraggled skirt. Go flutter your eyelashes at him or something."

I found Captain Rialdo at the shipyard, supervising the scraping of Wave Dancer's hull. The ship was careened on dry land, exposing the graceful lines of its hull to the eye, the part you would never see when it was afloat, almost shocking in its nakedness. I gazed a while before I realized I too was being sized up.

"What's worth gaping at here, young miss?"

"Beg pardon, Captain," I said. "Wave Dancer's a beauty, isn't she?"

"You think so, do you? Even seeing her like this, with her hull all over barnacles?" He smiled then. "So do I, girl. So do I. You're a Gualteri, aren't you? You have that look about you—a nose like a prow and that determined chin—but I can't place you. Which one are you?"

"Stellina Gualteri," I said.

"Nesto Rialdo," he said, "But then, you know who I am. Zeppe sent you?"

I nodded, wondering how I could raise the matter I'd been sent for without giving offense.

"He's sending his daughters to haggle over payment now, is he?"

"His niece," I said.

"Ha. What does he think you can tell me that he didn't say himself?"

"That's what I asked him," I blurted out, then fell dumb again, realizing I couldn't admit that I'd been sent to bat my eyelashes at him.

Captain Rialdo eyed me appraisingly. "I have it now! You're the odd one, the wizard's pupil."

Sheepishly, I nodded.

"Have you ever scraped down a hull, Gualteri girl?"

"No, but I'll try, if you show me how." It wasn't exactly feminine wiles, but it seemed to increase my stature in the captain's eyes when I picked up a dull knife and set to work beside him and his crew, watching their motions carefully and imitating them as closely as I'd tried to imitate the wizard's incantatory gestures, with a bit more result.

It was heavy work; my arms ached, my shoulders groaned, and my fingers had been cut by barnacle shells before Captain Rialdo said, "Come away from there a moment, Miss Gualteri. You're not squeamish, I'll give you that. Your Uncle Zeppe's never scraped a hull. You're not a Gualteri of the silk shop or the counting-house."

"I'm not sure what sort of Gualteri I am."

"Your grandfather wasn't afraid to rough up his hands on a capstan bar or a holystone," the captain said, "but your uncle—he doesn't understand, when he asks me and my crew to settle for a small share, what labor and danger it costs us to bring back the things he sells. I want a Gualteri who does. You can tell your uncle this: if he will send you along as one of my crew, doing the same work and earning the same share as any of them, then I will make one more journey at the old rate. Would you agree to that, Miss?"

It wasn't wizardry, but it was something to do that would take me out of the shop, far from the counting house. "Oh, yes!"

And so—a few short arguments with my family afterward—I rose before dawn and boarded Wave Dancer. My cousin Daria went along to manage business in the ports where we sold wine and bought silks and foreign curiosities. I had a bunk in Daria's cabin, away from the crewmen, but that was the only thing that marked me as a Gualteri. I rose with the crew, ate ship's biscuit with them, scrubbed decks, hauled up the anchor, ran the rigging. It was harder work than I'd ever done before, but less tedious than my old chores in shop and counting-house. Here, every task was necessary; our lives depended on the furling of a sail, the pumping of bilgewater from the hold. And if constant labor left little time for dreaming, it also left little time for regrets. At night the rhythm of the sea lulled me; in the morning, I woke to the cries of gulls before the clamor of the boatswain's bell.

Shore leave held less charms for me than for the other sailors, in part because Daria expected me to act like a Gualteri on land, but in part, also, because each trading stop reminded me that the whole voyage was only a matter of buying and selling—not a matter of life, like the wizard's work. It was at these trading ports that I found time to curse myself for giving up following the wizard.

On the Isle of Rakovina, Daria disembarked to bargain with a local grandee for the purple dye that gave some of my family's most sought-after silks their rich tones. The islanders distilled it, they said, from the tears of sea snails. Curious how this could be, I slipped away from my cousin to seek out the divers who caught these extraordinary snails. Their homes were mere tents upon the shore; clearly, little of the price we paid for the dye ever found its way into the divers' hands.

But that day, no one would dive. I found the divers packing their few possessions, their baskets and cookpots, and rolling up their tents to move to higher ground. "The sea and sky make war on the land," one old diver explained to me. "A storm is coming—a Grandmother Storm such as we have not seen in fifty years." She pointed out to sea, where a plume of spray reached from the cloud to the sea like the tail of a giant bird. "I remember, when the waters receded, a fishing boat was left halfway up the hill, stuck through the wall of a rich man's house. If that sky does not lie to me—and it seldom does—then none of this," she gestured broadly around her, taking in the shanties of the poor and the mansions of the mighty, the fishmonger's stall, the dyer's shop, the stand where a woman sold strips of dried fruit, the inn bathed in the fumes of rum—"none of this will be standing a few days from now. It will all belong to the sea."

I gaped, aghast. "What about the ships in the harbor? What will happen to them?"

The diver shrugged; it wasn't her problem. But it was mine. I pelted downhill to the port to find Wave Dancer.

I wasn't the only crew member rushing back to the ship. The experienced sailors needed no one to tell them what the tail of cloud meant. "What are we doing?" I asked one of them as I fell into line hauling on a rope.

"We'll go out to sea if we can, as far as the water lets us."

"Out to sea? Into that storm?"

"Of course," he said. "Would you have us stay here to be pounded to splinters on the wharves—or on the houses behind them, if this storm half lives up to its beginnings?" Already the tail of cloud looked closer and darker. Already rain lashed our faces and wind wrung the palm trees.

We worked as if driven by demons, the jokes and songs that eased our daily tasks silenced by the emergency. Even Daria put her smooth hands to the rough tasks of readying the ship for hard sailing.

We put out to sea, only to be tossed high one moment, cast down the next. Sometimes the waves rose so high that even clinging to the topmast, I saw the water like a cliff beside me. And yet it was not fear that made my heart pound painfully within me, but sorrow. My beloved ocean—the ocean that murmured peace to me when I stretched out to sleep—the ocean that offered life to me when nothing else did—my friend the ocean promised only death to my comrades on ship and the innocent divers on shore. It was like being betrayed by a lover. It was like discovering your own sister plotted murder. Worse: I could have pleaded with a lover or a sister, but the ocean would not love me, no matter how I gave my heart to it.

Through all these anguished thoughts, the scent of the ocean flooded me—the same scent I had come to love. Strange: I never noticed how dearly I'd come to love it till it broke my heart. What could I love if the ocean became my foe? What could I ever want that would be worth half as much as the clean salt spray upon my face, the swell of the wave beneath me?

And so it was the breaking of my heart that taught me what I must choose—what I had already chosen, before I was even aware of it.

When the ship leaned so far that the water lay directly below me, I let go of the rigging and dove.

Soaked linen clung to my limbs, dragging me down. *Naked*, I thought: *the wizard went to the earth naked*. I struggled out of the clinging cocoon of wet fabric and left my clothes to the tide. Now I had nothing but water. I let it close over my head, my hair

251

floating around me like kelp. Brine filled my eyes, my mouth. *"I am yours,"* I told the ocean, speaking not with the breath of my mouth, but the tears of my eyes, the flow of my blood. "Nothing is mine, but I am yours." Sinking deeper, I thrust away the fear of drowning and filled myself with the voice of the ocean, the voice that had spoken comfort to me all through my heart-sore journey. The water pressed upon me, wearing me down as it wears the stones of a jetty—and then my gills opened to the waters of life.

I am yours as you are mine, the sea murmured back to me.

I knew no spell to calm the ocean; all the spells I'd studied had been those of earth. I had no spell-book in the waves. I had nothing—except what I needed. I gathered the angry waves into myself and brooded over them like a seabird over her clutch of eggs until contentment spread across the face of the ocean.

I moved sinuously through the water and cleared the surface with one powerful push of my tail. My crewmates pointed and shouted, "Look: a mermaid!"

"She calmed the waves!"

"Doesn't she look like Stellina?" one of them said doubtfully.

But that name, somehow, was among the possessions I no longer owned. I had the sea, and it sufficed for me. Turning my tail to the ship, my face to unknown waters, I swam where the ocean called me.

GODS OF THE ELDERS

by Jonathan Moeller

Oh, the joys of studying with other girls: the snide comments; the group that invariably surrounds the nastiest girl and follows her example; the spells they aren't supposed to be using on you...and when you try to protect yourself, *that's* when the teachers show up and give you extra work to do.

Jonathan Moeller has written so many books he now requires customized spreadsheets to keep track of them all—including the *Frostborn*, *The Ghosts*, *Demonsouled*, and *The Tower of Endless Worlds* series of fantasy novels. He lives at various locations in the American Midwest (hopefully not all at once), hard at work on more books. Visit his website at www.jonathanmoeller.com to find out more.

"You're a freak," said Adelaide.

Sichilde looked at the taller girl without blinking. Before the Conclave of Araspan had made her an Initiate, Adelaide had been the daughter of a prominent Saranian duke. She still looked the part, even in an Initiate's gray robe. Jewelry and makeup were forbidden Initiates, but Adelaide's hair was arranged perfectly, her gray robe crisp and clean and hung just so. Her usual followers stood around her, both minor noblemen's daughters from across the Nine Kingdoms and the daughters of peasants overawed by Adelaide's illustrious bloodline.

Sichilde was not impressed. She had seen her father call the Jurgur nation to war, a hundred thousand screaming warriors following him over the Silvercrown Mountains to invade the Nine Kingdoms of the west. She had seen the wrath of his blood sorcery, demons rising at his call and striking down his foes.

And she had seen his army shattered, the Jurgur warriors cut down like wheat beneath the scythe.

After all that, a blond seventeen-year-old girl was hardly frightening.

"Most probably," said Sichilde.

Adelaide blinked in surprise.

They stood in the dining hall shared by female Initiates. A silence had fallen over the tables as the other girls watched the confrontation. Even the slaves in orange tunics who served food stopped to watch.

"Look at her eyes," said one of Adelaide's followers, the daughter of a minor Callian nobleman. "Blood-red. She has a demon in her head, I wager. Right now."

Sichilde looked at the girl who had spoken. She could not meet Sichilde's gaze for long. That was one advantage of her eyes.

Among others.

"If I was possessed," said Sichilde, "don't you think the Magisters would do something about it?"

"Oh, she's not possessed," said Adelaide. "She's something much worse. Her mother was possessed. One of Maerwulf's whores. So she's demonborn. A freak." She sneered. "What do you have to say to that?"

Sichilde shrugged. "It is true."

Her mother had fallen motionless upon the frozen ground, her limbs twitching, the snow turning crimson around her. Father had been defeated by then, and the warriors Maerwulf had stationed to guard his wives and children had fled. Sichilde had been alone ever since, at least until Magister Vasily had found her and brought her to the Ring of the Conclave.

"If you were on my father's lands," sniffed Adelaide, "he would have you killed as the monster that you are. Or he would hand you over to the Silver Knights to be burned as a demoniac."

"That would be foolish of them," said Sichilde, "given that I can sense demons. I imagine the Silver Knights would find that helpful."

Adelaide laughed. "Sense demons? You're a Jurgur barbarian! You worship them, like all the Jurgurs do!"

Sichilde said nothing, her hands curling into fists at her side. "See!" said Adelaide. "Look how angry she is! She worships demons, and is upset that we are mocking her filthy gods."

"I do not," said Sichilde, her voice quiet. "I do not."

Adelaide laughed, delighted that she had finally found a weak point. "They're all so afraid of you, but I know better. You're just another demon-worshipping barbarian. Well, you can fool the Magisters, but you can't fool me. You'll slip up sooner or later, and we'll see if your beloved demons save you when..."

Sichilde's fist brought an abrupt end to the taunt.

Adelaide's head snapped back, her face comical with surprise. The women of the western lands, Sichilde had decided long ago, were weak and feeble. To judge from Adelaide's shocked expression, no one had ever laid hands upon her before. Adelaide had grown up in luxury, but by the time Sichilde was twelve, she had seen her father defeated, her mother slain, her people crushed and scattered, and had walked the length of the Nine Kingdoms while half-starved.

"You hit me!" said Adelaide.

"Noticed that?" said Sichilde. She slammed her fist into Adelaide's gut, and the taller girl doubled over. Adelaide's followers scattered, shouting and screaming, and Sichilde felt a flicker of disgust. Cravens, all of them. She caught Adelaide's right arm and twisted it, propelling the taller Initiate towards the table holding the food.

One of the slaves, a gaunt, elderly man with skin like seamed pale leather, stepped before them. "Mistress, perhaps you should not..."

Sichilde looked, and he flinched. Her red eyes often had that effect on people. "You really ought to get out of the way." The old slave stepped aside.

Sichilde dunked Adelaide's head into a pot of cooling potato soup. Adelaide's furious shriek dissolved into a burst of garlic-scented bubbles. She flailed and tried to pull her head out of the soup, but Sichilde held her in place.

One of Adelaide's hands came up, and Sichilde felt the surge of power as Adelaide summoned magic, using a spell of the

Threefold Art.

A burst of invisible force slammed into Sichilde and knocked her to the floor, the breath exploding from her lungs. Adelaide wrenched backwards, potato soup plastering the hair to her head. She trembled with fury, and she raked her hand through the air, blue astralfire blazing to life around her fingers as she began another spell.

Initiates were forbidden from employing spells of the Threefold Art unless supervised by a full Adept or a Magister, but at the moment Sichilde did not care.

She summoned her own strength and started working a spell.

"Cease this at once!"

The voice boomed like a trumpet.

Sichilde saw a middle-aged woman with an ascetic air storming towards them, clad in the crimson robe and black stole of a Magister of the Conclave. Magister Mauriana was in charge of discipline for the female Initiates, and she taught the history of the Nine Kingdoms to the younger Initiates, droning endlessly in her soft, calm voice.

Now she looked anything but calm.

"It is her fault!" shrieked Adelaide, trying to wipe soup out of her eyes and point at Sichilde. "She started it! I..."

"Silence!" roared Mauriana, her eyes glittering in her dusky face. "You will both come with me. Now!"

Sichilde followed the Magister from the hall.

~o0o~

A short time later Sichilde sat in Mauriana's study, listening to the Magister rant.

Though the view from the windows was nice. As a Magister, Mauriana had rooms in a tower of the inner Ring, rooms that offered a splendid view of the grounds, the Ring's outer wall, and the city of Araspan and the sea beyond. Sichilde had first seen the sea six years ago during her journey to Araspan at the age of twelve, and had been enraptured by the sight of it.

But for now, she forced herself to pay attention to Mauriana.

"This is outrageous!" said the Magister, pacing back and forth behind her desk. "You are both senior Initiates! You are a few years away from your Testing, assuming you do not get yourselves killed first. What sort of example is that to set for the younger Initiates?"

"I am sorry, Magister," said Adelaide. She did look miserable. The potato soup in her hair helped with that.

"Understand this," said Mauriana. "The Conclave of Araspan is the guardian of this world. We alone oversee the use of magic, lest mankind repeat the mistakes of the Old Empire in ancient days. And we alone guard the nations from the demons of the astral world. This responsibility is a weighty one. An Adept must be of serious mind and grave judgment...and not the sort of woman who brawls with pots of soup!"

"I am sorry, Magister," said Adelaide, crying now. Sichilde supposed the tears would help wash the soup away.

"Are you?" said Mauriana, looking at Sichilde.

"No," Sichilde said.

The Magister's eyes narrowed.

"She said I worshipped demons," said Sichilde. "That is a lie. The demons led my people to ruin and destruction. If my father had not listened to his high demon's commands, perhaps my people would still be safe in their homeland. I hate them all."

"Indeed?" said Mauriana. "That is fine and commendable. But you are demonborn, Sichilde. You cannot hide what you are. An Adept will know the truth of your nature, but when the ignorant peasants and commoners see your eyes, they will think you possessed. What will you do the first time some farmer sees you and panics, hmm? Or the first time a townsman accuses you of being demon-possessed? Will you attack him? Summon astralfire and burn him to ashes? The commoners and the nobles already hate and fear the Conclave. Will you add to our ill name among the people?"

Sichilde opened her mouth...and then closed it again.

She hadn't thought of that.

"Perhaps...I did not react appropriately to Adelaide's lies," said Sichilde.

"Yes, perhaps not," said Mauriana. She reached behind her desk and lifted a thin cane, and Adelaide let out a little squeak of

257

fear. "To impress the seriousness of your offenses upon you, I shall set penances for you both. First, thirty blows across the back and shoulders. Open your robes."

Adelaide sobbed as she did so, and Sichilde obeyed in silence. The mirror upon the wall, she thought, was a clever touch. It forced the disobedient Initiates to watch as the Magister administered punishment. Mauriana wielded her cane with the skill of long practice, her blows inflicting stinging pain while never breaking the skin. Adelaide cried the entire time, while Sichilde endured in silence, watching her reflection in the mirror. Little wonder people were afraid of her. Her face was gaunt and harsh, her red hair hanging in ragged strings. The irises of her eyes were a deep blood red, eerie and unnatural.She looked much as her mother had, before the end.

The cane cracked against her back, but she had endured worse. The hunger pains as she wandered alone through the frozen forests of Tarrenheim. The cold sinking into her bones as she looked desperately for shelter. The racking cough that had almost slain her. The villagers screaming in fear, throwing things at her.

The terror when she met her father for the first time.

She had indeed endured much worse.

"We are finished," said Mauriana. Sichilde rolled her aching shoulders and tugged her robes back into place. "Adelaide. For the second phase of your penance, you shall clean pots every night for the next week." Adelaide looked horrified. "Go now."

"Yes, Magister," said Adelaide.

She all but fled through the door.

"Shall I join her?" said Sichilde.

Mauriana sighed. "Why bother?"

Sichilde blinked.

"Each Initiate requires a different punishment, you see," said Mauriana. "For Adelaide, the pain of the caning and the humiliation of a duke's daughter washing pots will teach her the necessary lesson. But you, Sichilde...pain means nothing to you, and there is no amount of humiliation that could possibly make a dent in the implacable wall of your arrogance."

Sichilde said nothing.

"Do you truly think so little of your fellow Initiates?" said Mauriana. "You have no friends, I know that. Adelaide picked a fight because you frighten them so much."

"They are weak," said Sichilde.

"Why do you say that?" said Mauriana.

Sichilde shrugged. "I am Jurgur. Pain is to be endured. Weakness is to be overcome."

"And is it Jurgur to worship demons, as well?" said Mauriana.

Anger flared, but Sichilde knew better than to challenge the Magister. "No. My father was a fool. My people were fools. They revered the demons as the gods of our ancestors. But what did those gods bring us? Ruin and death. We were merely more prey for the demons, as they have preyed upon mankind for many millennia."

Mauriana considered this for a moment.

"You frighten me," she said at last.

"Ah," said Sichilde. "Because I am demonborn? Because my mother was possessed when she gave birth to me?"

"No," said Mauriana. "Because of what you might become."

"I...don't understand," said Sichilde. "Because of my father?"

"Maerwulf was a genius, twisted though he was," said Mauriana, "and you have inherited his strength and intelligence. And his hatred. There was nothing in him but fury. And so it is with you. You hate the demons and wish to join the Conclave to fight against them. That drives you as the wind drives the sails of a ship. But Maerwulf almost destroyed the Nine Kingdoms. What might you do if you survive your Testing and become an Adept?"

Sichilde had no answer for that.

"Well," said Mauriana at last, "since neither pain nor humiliation mean anything to you, I am sending you to Magister Vasily." She smiled. "I suspect he will know how to reach you."

"Oh," sighed Sichilde.

~o0o~

Magister Vasily never raised his voice when he got angry, which alarmed Sichilde to no end.

259

Her father had been much the same way. Maerwulf had been prone to spectacular rages. Yet when he had grown quiet, when his voice had become cold and deadly, that had frightened Sichilde.

That meant someone was about to die.

And Vasily always talked like that.

"You disappoint me, Sichilde," said Vasily. He was a Callian man in his middle forties, trim and lean, his black hair and goatee going gray. Unlike most Adepts or Magisters, he always went armed, a sword and dagger at his waist. Some demons were strong enough to suppress even a Magister's magic, and Vasily believed a man had to be prepared.

He had brought her to the Conclave years ago. By now Sichilde realized that the Conclave had many secrets it did not want known in the Nine Kingdoms, and one of them was that the Magisters squabbled constantly. They presented a unified face in public, but amongst themselves they formed into different Colleges to pursue different goals. The College Novitia devoted itself to finding new Initiates to enroll. The College Dominia focused upon influencing the decisions of the nobles and kings for the greater good, while the College Excorisia hunted down demons.

Vasily was one of the chief Magisters of the College Excorisia.

That was how he had found Sichilde. His companions had urged him to kill her, believing her a danger. But Vasily had said...

"Do you know why I brought you here?" said Vasily.

They stood atop one of the towers of the inner Ring, the wind tugging at their robes as they gazed down at the city.

"Because I have magical talent," said Sichilde, "and because I am demonborn. Which means I can sense the presence of demons, even without using a spell. That will make me useful to your work."

"Yes," said Vasily. "The demons that possess corpses and turn them into ghouls are usual easy to find. But some are clever enough to hide themselves in living bodies. Or they have the active cooperation of their hosts, as many of the Jurgurs did, and conceal themselves. Your ability would be invaluable...if you can learn to control yourself."

"I can," said Sichilde. She wanted to become an Adept, join the College Excorisia, and use her magic to help hunt the demons that had brought so much woe to the Jurgur nation.

To hunt the demons that had slain her mother.

"Truly?" said Vasily. "Your actions today do not seem to reflect that. An Adept must have iron control over himself. More immediately, surviving the Testing requires iron control. If you pass the Testing, you become an Adept...and if you fail, you die. Right now, I fear that you would die."

"Then tell me what I will face during the Testing," said Sichilde.

"No," said Vasily. "By the law of the Conclave, those who survive the Testing never speak of it." He stared at her for a long time. Few people could meet her gaze, but Vasily could, and it made her uneasy. No doubt he had seen more frightening things than a gaunt eighteen-year-old girl with red eyes.

"Why do you wish to fight demons?" he said.

"Because I hate them," said Sichilde. "Because my father bound one within my mother, and it killed her."

"Is that all?" said Vasily. "Revenge?"

Sichilde gave a shrug. "Is there anything else?"

Vasily nodded, as if she had confirmed something. "Your penance shall be a week of work with Magister Taldez."

Sichilde winced. "He will want me to organize his library."

"Most likely," said Vasily. "I understand he has recently acquired three hundred new tomes of Orlanish poetry."

"And he will talk," said Sichilde. "And talk, and talk, and talk."

"Undoubtedly," said Vasily. He smiled. "Still, he is so old that you need not worry he will make inappropriate advances."

Sichilde glared at him, but his smile only widened.

"That was a joke," said Vasily.

"It was not funny," said Sichilde.

Vasily shrugged. "Well, humor was never my strength."

"Is that the point of this?" said Sichilde. "To teach me patience? To learn compassion from taking care of a feeble old man?"

"No," said Vasily, "the point is to punish you. Off you go. Do watch out for mice—they tend to burrow into poor old Taldez's books."

Sichilde sighed and walked away.

~o0o~

The next day Sichilde presented herself at Taldez's apartment in the Inner Ring and looked in dismay at his library.

Every Magister received a spacious apartment in the inner Ring, but Taldez had ripped out the walls between his sitting room, his dining room, and his study to create one massive library. Perhaps it had once been organized, but that had been decades before Sichilde had been born. Shelves lined all four walls, and every last one of them had been stuffed to capacity with books, scrolls, loose papers, random oddities, and ancient tablets of baked clay. Three long tables ran the length of the room, curving beneath the weight of more books and scrolls. More volumes had been stacked against the shelves, some of the piles rising so high than they almost reached the ceiling. The air smelled of dust and ancient paper.

Or maybe that was just Magister Taldez.

The old man tottered at Sichilde's side, leaning upon his cane. He was scarecrow-thin, his crimson robe and Magister's stole hanging around him like a tent. The Jurgurs honored their elders, given that the constant internecine warfare between the clans made it rare for a Jurgur man to live past fifty. Yet the Conclave had been founded fifteen centuries past, after the Old Empire had released the demons and destroyed itself, and Sichilde half-suspected that Magister Taldez had already been ancient then.

"Capital, capital," said Taldez, beaming at her. "The Jurgur princess. Capital."

"I am not a princess," said Sichilde.

Taldez blinked his watery eyes. "Was not your father the king of the Jurgurs?"

"He was not," said Sichilde. "He was a blood shaman and a

war chieftain, the greatest my nation has seen. But the Jurgurs have no king." Though it was an amusing thought. Maerwulf had taken dozens of wives and the Divine only knew how many concubines, siring hundreds of children in the process. Sichilde had only met about a quarter of her half-siblings before Maerwulf's defeat, and the thought of hundreds of demonborn bastards struggling to claim a nonexistent crown was darkly amusing.

"Eh?" said Taldez. "Well, no matter. No matter. Whatever you were, you are not now."

"Profound," said Sichilde. Fortunately the Magister was oblivious to her sarcasm.

"You are now an Initiate, which is a far superior calling," said Taldez. "Now, where shall you begin? Alphabetically, I think. By both author and title. And then we must cross-index. By topic and language. That seems logical, does not it?"

Sichilde gazed at the books in dismay. Since coming to the Ring, she had learned the High Imperial tongue, and had become proficient in Callian and Saranian, the chief languages of the Nine Kingdoms. But she didn't speak most of the languages she saw upon the shelves. She didn't even recognize some of them.

"As you wish," said Sichilde, but the old man didn't hear. He wandered into his bedchamber and closed the door behind him, humming to himself.

Sichilde sighed and looked over the books. She did not know if Vasily had intended this to teach her a lesson or as some sort of joke, but it was certainly a vexing punishment. Perhaps she could bribe some of the Initiates working in the Conclave's Great Library to help her catalog the books. Or perhaps Taldez would even forget that Sichilde had been here.

The door to the bedchamber swung open, and a sweet smell filled Sichilde's nostrils.

"Spiced cider," said Taldez, tottering into the library. He set the wooden cup upon a stack of books and smiled. "Keeps the joints warm, yes? Good for this sort of work."

Sichilde smiled back, almost against her will. The expression felt peculiar upon her face. "Thank you."

Taldez hummed again and stepped back into his bedchamber, the door clicking shut behind him.

For a moment Sichilde was so moved that tears almost sprang to her eyes. No one ever brought her hot drinks. Well, her mother had, long ago, before the demon had started eating her mind. Sichilde picked up the cup and raised it to her lips. She would do her best with the library. She might not be able to organize the books, but perhaps she could convince the Ring's seneschal to install extra shelves. At the very least the old man would not be breathing dust and...

She froze.

A familiar smell came from the cup.

It was not cider.

Sichilde stuck her thumb into the cup and rubbed it against her forefinger. She felt the faint trace of grit, of powder floating in the liquid, disguised by the spices.

A drug. She did not know its name, but she knew what it did. Her father had used it to induce trances, to send his mind into the astral world to speak with his high demon. She suspected a Magister of the Conclave would not know of that use...but would almost certainly know that in sufficient quantities the drug caused unconsciousness.

"The old lecher," muttered Sichilde. No inappropriate advances, indeed! Her first impulse was to storm into his bedchamber and confront him. No, that was a mistake. If he knew he was exposed, he would become desperate, and her magic was no match for the spells of a Magister.

But still...

She summoned magic and worked the spell to sense the presence of arcane forces. At once she felt the mighty, ancient wards surrounding the Ring, guarding it from arcane and demonic attack. And she also felt a spell from behind the door of Taldez's bedchamber.

A spell she recognized at once.

Her father had employed it.

Something caught her eye. A gray scrap of fabric, snagged upon the sharp leather corner of a heavy book.

The fabric of an Initiate's robe.

She thought a trapdoor spider lurking in the ground, waiting for a victim to blunder into its trap.

Just how many Initiates had been invited to organize Taldez's library over the years?

Sichilde whispered a curse and pushed open the bedchamber door as quietly as she could. The bedchamber was just as cluttered and dusty as the library. Books leaned against the walls, and the only free space was a path to the unkempt bed, the sour reek of sweat heavy in the air.

The room was deserted.

Sichilde frowned. There was a window on the far wall. It was a hundred and fifty feet to the grounds below, but she supposed Taldez could have levitated himself down with a spell of psychokinesis. Or he could have used a spell of illusion to conceal himself, or an astraljump spell to travel a short distance away. Again Sichilde worked the spell to detect magic. She sensed no illusion spells, nor any of the telltale eddies that lingered for a few moments after an astraljump.

But she felt the familiar spell upon the wall next to the bed, powerful and complex.

And a clear path led through the clutter to it.

Sichilde strode towards the wall, her heart hammering against her ribs.

She knew that spell. It was a powerful spell of blood sorcery, an art forbidden by the laws of the Conclave, but one that Taldez apparently had employed nonetheless. It created a sanctum within the astral world, one only accessible to the caster.

But Sichilde thought she could open this one.

She cast the sensing spell again, probing the structure of the magic upon the wall. Then she nodded to herself, concentrated, and gathered power. She worked another spell, and short bursts of silver astralfire stabbed from her fingers. Silver astralfire could harm neither demons nor mortal men, but it attacked the fabric of spells.

The spell shuddered...and then the wall itself seemed to ripple. A gateway of silver light appeared over the stonework, and a cold wind brushed at Sichilde, tugging at her hair and robes.

The entrance to the sanctum.

Sichilde took a deep breath and stepped into the wall.

The gateway took hold of her.

It felt like an astraljump. A moment of disorientation and blackness. A squeezing sensation, like she was trying to force her body into a garment too small. Then the darkness cleared, and Sichilde found herself standing in a hall of crimson marble, the stone seeming to writhe ever so slightly beneath her boots.

A half-dozen stone tables lined the hall, and unconscious Initiates rested upon them, boys and girls both. Sichilde spotted Adelaide, her eyes closed, her breath rising and falling in shallow gasps. But that was impossible. Sichilde had seen the haughty Initiate just yesterday in Magister Mauriana's study. How had she gotten here?

Then an alien presence brushed against Sichilde's thoughts, cold and malevolent, and alarm flooded through her.

Demons. She sensed demons.

"Well, well. I wondered if you might find your way here."

She turned her head as the wall flowed apart, a doorway appearing, and Taldez stepped into sight. Gone was the affable dreaminess, the lassitude. His face was hard and focused.

And in his bloodshot eyes Sichilde saw a glimmer of crimson fire.

Her mother's eyes had looked much the same way, before the end.

"You," said Sichilde.

"Yes, how eloquent," said Taldez. "But the Jurgurs were not known for their oratory, were they?"

"You're possessed," said Sichilde.

"That," said Taldez, standing on the far side of the table holding Adelaide, "is an oversimplification. I prefer to think of it as a...partnership. A symbiosis." An eerie reverberation entered his words as he spoke, almost like an echo.

Like two voices were speaking through his mouth at the same time.

"There's a demon in your head," said Sichilde, flexing her

fingers as she summoned power for a spell, "and I think you summoned it there deliberately."

"Oh, very good," said Taldez. He smiled, the crimson glare in his eyes brightening. "I thought Vasily might send you. He's been suspicious of me for some time, but Magisters do not accuse other Magisters. It goes against tradition, and the Conclave is nothing if not an ossified mass of obsolete traditions." His smile widened. "Vasily thinks you are clever. Are you clever enough to realize what is happening here?"

"Vasily is part of the College Excorisia," said Sichilde.

"You know about the Colleges?" said Taldez. "Most Initiates do not learn about them until after the Testing. If they survive the ordeal."

"The College Excorisia is devoted to hunting down demons," said Sichilde. "Which means Vasily and the College Excorisia suspect you of consorting with demons." Rather accurately, as it turned out. "But since it is improper for Magisters to accuse each other...he sent me here to investigate. No. To see if I sensed any demons, as I sense a demon within you."

Taldez nodded. "Yes. Very good. Very good, indeed."

"What is all this, then?" said Sichilde, gesturing at the unconscious Initiates.

"Oh, I lured them here, of course," said Taldez. "I could have commanded them as a Magister, but that would have been no fun. And it might have put them on their guard." He laughed. "But they're glad to help old Magister Taldez, so confused and helpless."

"And then you drug them and bring them here," said Sichilde.

Taldez nodded.

"Why?" said Sichilde.

"All in good time, child," said Taldez. "You see, first you have to decide if you are strong enough."

"Strong enough for what?" said Sichilde.

"To see the path of wisdom," said Taldez. He made a dismissive gesture at the unconscious Initiates. "These other fools, they have no vision. They believe the lies the Temple and the Conclave have pumped into their heads for all their lives.

That demons are evil, that demons are the eternal foes of mankind. But you, my dear, are Jurgur. More, you are even the daughter of Maerwulf himself, the most powerful blood shaman the Jurgur nation produced."

"What does that have to do with anything?" said Sichilde.

"Because," said Taldez, "you worshipped demons. You revered them as the gods of your elders."

Sichilde opened her mouth to protest, and then closed it.

He thought she revered the demons of the astral world as gods, as the Jurgur nation had done.

Her father had been a cruel and brutal man, but he had been fond of saying that only a fool interrupted his enemies' mistakes, and Sichilde saw no reason to disagree with that.

"Go on," said Sichilde.

"Revering the demons as gods is mere superstition," said Taldez, "but closer to the truth than the Conclave's hidebound ignorance. We call them 'demons', but in truth they are a different form of life. A resource to be used. The mages of the Old Empire summoned and bound demons, and using their power built a civilization that spanned a continent, an empire of glittering cities and limitless prosperity."

"As I recall," said Sichilde, "the Old Empire burned in the flames of its own hubris. The demons preyed upon us."

Taldez scoffed. "We shall learn from the mistakes of the past. You know of the Colleges, Initiate? There is another College, a secret one. We who are members of the Secret College have sworn to use demons for the greater good, to use their powers to elevate mankind to a new stage of evolution. Alone, a man is weak and mortal. A demon has no physical form. But bound in our flesh...they become something new and powerful."

"Like you," said Sichilde.

Taldez nodded.

"And that is why you have kidnapped these Initiates," said Sichilde. "You are going to use them in your experiments, to bind demons into their flesh."

"Yes," said Taldez. "They are useless fools, and suitable subjects for experimentation. A demon fused to the raw power of an Adept can become quite powerful."

"A foolish plan, though," said Sichilde. "Taking six Initiates at once will draw attention. However much power the demon in your head provides, it will not be enough to stand against the wrath of the entire council of Magisters."

"Entirely true," said Taldez. "But the world is moving on. The Nine Kingdoms stir, and the Conclave will soon totter and fall. From my sanctum, I can make a new gateway to a location far from Araspan and the Ring. Then I shall close the previous gateway to my chambers. To the Conclave, it will seem as if we have disappeared entirely."

"And you want me to come with you?" said Sichilde.

Taldez smiled. "Indeed. The drugged cider was a test. As was finding your way into my sanctum. I wanted to see if you were strong enough...and you are stronger than I expected. So I am extending an invitation to you."

"To do what?" said Sichilde.

"To join the Secret College, to assist in our great and noble work to harness the power of demons for the betterment of mankind," said Taldez. "You would be invaluable to our work. You can sense demons without using spells, which in itself would be a tremendous asset. And you saw your father at work. Maerwulf's efforts were crude, of course—blood sorcery is but a feeble shadow of the Threefold Art. But you saw him imbue demons into the flesh of his followers."

"I did," said Sichilde. She had, again and again. She had heard them scream and sob for mercy, seen them twist into monsters as the demons took control of their bodies and reshaped their flesh. She had listened to her mother weep, watched her die in the snow after Maerwulf's defeat.

Her father, she supposed, had not been so different than Taldez and the other Adepts of the Secret College. He had wanted to reshape the world, too.

"Then aid us," said Taldez. He pointed at Adelaide. "I have heard how she mocked you. Would you like to listen to her scream? You can. She failed to see that you were superior, that she was nothing but cattle to be used to create the new humanity."

Sichilde stared at Adelaide's motionless form for a moment.

"Of course," said Sichilde. "I shall be glad to aid you. To give you everything I have."

"Good," said Taldez. "You can begin by..."

Sichilde lifted her hands and summoned every shred of magical power she could muster.

There were three different kinds of astralfire. Silver attacked spells and wards. Blue astralfire harmed material things. White astralfire disrupted neither material objects nor magical spells. But it harmed demons, and in sufficient amounts it could destroy them.

Taldez's eyes widened, and he raised his hands to cast a spell of his own, but Sichilde was already moving. A shaft of white fire erupted from her fingers and slammed into Taldez's chest, passing through him to splash against the far wall. The spell did no harm to him or to his robes.

But it did upset his demon.

Taldez shrieked, twitching like a man in the grip of a seizure, and the crimson glare in his eyes sputtered. Sichilde had not hit the demon with enough white astralfire to destroy it. But she had hurt the demon, and both of the voices coming from Taldez's mouth howled in fury and pain.

"Side with the fools of the Conclave?" roared both Taldez and his demon in unison. "Then perish! Perish!"

Blue astralfire blazed to life around his hands, and Sichilde felt him summon power, more magic than she could possibly oppose. If she tried to raise a warding spell, his attack would tear through it like a hot iron through a sheet of paper.

So she ran forward and punched him in the face.

Under less dire circumstances, his expression of consternated shock would have been comical.

In many ways, the Adepts were little different than the spoiled daughters of Saranian noblemen. They trained to use magic as their weapons, not their fists or daggers or swords. Sichilde had often been forced to fight and run for her life before Vasily had found her, and the lessons had never left her.

Magister Taldez, it seemed, had never endured a similar education.

He finished his spell, but his concentration had been shattered and his aim was off. The unfocused burst of blue astralfire lashed at her left shoulder, and Sichilde felt a wave of agony spread through her left arm and side. Yet she hit Taldez again with her right fist, and he stumbled. He was taller, but she was young and strong and he was not. She grabbed his head and slammed it into the wall with a loud crack. Taldez's eyes rolled up into his head, and he slumped to the floor.

And as he did, cracks of silver light spread across the crimson walls, and the floor started to shake.

The sanctum. Taldez's spells had created it in the astral world, and his will maintained it. And without his will to sustain it, the sanctum would collapse back into the formlessness of the astral realm.

Sichilde did not know what would happen to anyone still in the sanctum, but she suspected it would be bad.

No reason to stay and find out.

She turned towards the rippling silver gateway, her eyes falling across the unconscious Initiates. A tangle of emotion flickered through her mind. Some spiteful part of her wanted to leave Adelaide and the others behind.

But a far larger part refused to give the demons such a victory.

Sichilde bounced Taldez's head off the floor one more time, and went to work. One by one she dragged the Initiates through the gateway and into Taldez's cluttered bedroom. Her burned shoulder and arm screamed in protest, but she was Jurgur and pain was to be endured. The silver cracks widened as she labored, the vibration in the floor getting stronger, and a low keening noise came to her ears.

The sanctum would not last much longer.

At last she dragged Adelaide across the floor. There were no others left. Just a little farther...

Taldez sat up, his eyes blazing with crimson fire.

Sichilde noticed that he was not breathing, that he remained utterly motionless.

Apparently she had hit him harder than she thought.

It usually took a demon a sunrise and a sunset to seize control of a corpse, which was why every village of any size in the Nine Kingdoms had a crematorium. But the demon had already been inside Taldez...and it had raised his corpse as a ghoul.

"Daughter of Maerwulf," said the ghoul, its voice deep and inhuman. "Do you think to defy us? Your world shall be ours. The gates shall open. You..."

"Shut up," said Sichilde, raising her hand and summoning power. The ghoul scrambled to its feet, but her blast of white astralfire caught Taldez's corpse in the belly. The crimson blaze in Taldez's eyes dimmed, and the ghoul lost its balance with a bellow of fury. The silver cracks spread down the wall and across the floor, the sanctum unravelling around them.

Sichilde seized Adelaide's arms and threw herself backward. They both fell into the rippling gateway as the sanctum shattered in a blaze of silver light and crimson shards. She glimpsed Taldez's corpse spinning away in an infinite storm of silver light, the demon screaming in fury, and then she felt the familiar squeezing sensation.

Sichilde fell into the bedchamber, dropping Adelaide as she did so, and landed on one of Taldez's reeking blankets. She coughed and got to her feet, head spinning, and the door to the library burst open. Magister Vasily and Magister Mauriana stormed into the bedchamber, astralfire crackling around their fingers, and Sichilde saw more Adepts ready in the library.

For a moment the Magisters stared at the scene in shock, looking at the unconscious Initiates upon the floor.

Sichilde tried to think of something to say.

"I suspect," she said at last, "that organizing Magister Taldez's library would now be a waste of time."

~o0o~

The next day, after the Magisters had finished questioning her, Sichilde stood with Vasily atop the ramparts of the Ring.

"I must apologize again. I did not know," said Vasily, shaking his head. "I truly did not know. I suspected, yes, that Taldez was consorting with demons. But if I had known in the truth, I would

272

never have sent you in there. I had hoped that you would sense any demons he summoned." He sighed. "I did not know his plans were so far advanced."

Sichilde shrugged. Her shoulder hurt, but she ignored it. "Life is pain, Magister."

Vasily snorted. "And there is that famed Jurgur fatalism. But Magisters voted to give you the official thanks of the Conclave. A mere Initiate has received that exactly three times in the last century." He smiled. "I think you shall come through your Testing fine, and I think you shall make a formidable Adept."

"Thank you," said Sichilde, unable to think of something to say.

"Go," said Vasily. "You are excused from duties for the rest of the day. Amuse yourself as you think best. The Divine knows you deserve much more."

Sichilde nodded and walked along the curve of the outer wall, thinking. She did not know what to do with herself. Duty filled her life, and she certainly had no friends. Well, perhaps she could spend the time in the Great Library, reading as she saw fit. Certainly the Library held more books than she could read in a lifetime...

"Sichilde?"

She turned and saw Adelaide climb onto the rampart.

"Aye?" said Sichilde, wary. Adelaide looked nervous. Perhaps she had suffered such a loss of face before her friends that she had to challenge Sichilde once more. Or maybe...

"Thank you," said Adelaide.

Sichilde blinked. "For what?"

"For saving my life, of course," said Adelaide. "And...I want to ask your forgiveness. I treated you very badly. I didn't see it before, but...by the Divine, I was a fool. I wouldn't have blamed you for leaving me behind."

Sichilde said nothing. She had fought Taldez and saved the Initiates because she hated demons. That had been her motivator, and she had rescued the Initiates to spite Taldez's demon.

And yet...

Sichilde was glad she had saved their lives. Even Adelaide's.

Perhaps Vasily was right. Perhaps there were reasons to fight other than hatred.

"I have liberty for the day," said Adelaide. "Would you...like to visit the shops with me? I can have some of the Swords escort us. Or we could play checkers..."

"Checkers?" said Sichilde. "I've never heard of it."

Adelaide beamed. "Oh, you'll love it. It's a game. Everyone in Saranor plays. I must teach you."

"Very well," said Sichilde, and Adelaide led the way.

Perhaps it would not be so hard to find something to do after all.

BRONZE BRAS AND MORE!

by Melissa Mead

We always like to end the anthology with something short and funny. Here is a story about an advertising campaign in search of its proper audience.

Melissa Mead lives in Upstate NY. *Sword & Sorceress* was the first place she submitted a story, and she still hasn't broken the habit. Her web page is at http://carpelibris.wordpress.com/melissa-mead.

As they had every morning for the past three months, the women of the King's Royal Guardiennes woke not to sunlight, but to the sudden flash of a magic mirror coming to life.

"Bronze Bras, 50% off!" proclaimed the banner behind the glass, followed by images of buxom, scantily-clad Valkyries modeling said bras. The Guards groaned.

"50% off? They probably have only one cup," Bellatrix LaRouge muttered. A snicker ran through the barracks.

Since the mirror took up most of the wall, the constantly-shifting images were impossible to ignore.

"At least it doesn't have sound," said another guard.

"Oh, the King wants it to, believe me! But the royal wizards haven't found a sound-spell that won't shatter glass."

By the time Bella finished dressing, the mirror had touted not only bronze bras, but also dragon-burn ointment, eight-league boots (A Step Beyond The Rest!), Genuine "Unikorn" Horn, and dates with half a dozen Prince Charmings.

The dining hall had a mirror too, of course. So did the armory, the training rooms, and even the privy. Bella had heard rumors that the infirmary was still mirror-free. She'd briefly considered breaking a bone, just to get a few days away from the glass menaces.

It was bad enough that the King required all his Guards to keep these mirrors in their quarters for "strategic purposes." Bella would've liked to break a mirror over the head of whoever had suggested renting them out for advertising.

According to His Majesty, the point of the magic mirrors was to give him a way to contact all his guards instantly in an emergency.

"Wars are emergencies," Bella muttered, planting a throwing knife in the eye of a target carefully painted to look nothing like the king whatsoever. "Or earthquakes, or fires, or floods. Or the barbarian horde camped less than a mile from our gates at this very moment. *Not* cheap armor or"—she glanced at the mirror—"Potions to double your bodice size."

Bella yanked her knives out of the target and headed for the stables. Ravenheart *did* need exercising, and not even His Majesty could expect her to carry a full-length mirror while riding a galloping horse.

Just as she was about to leave, Lady Hyacinth ran up, smiling and waving. Bella sighed inwardly and smiled back.

"Have you got your compact yet, Bella?" Lady Hyacinth held up a little round powder box of painted ivory. She flipped it open to show the mirror inside—complete with advertisements. Bella groaned.

"Guards don't have much call for makeup on while on duty, my lady. And a pretty little mirror like that would only get lost or broken in battle. So no, I don't."

"Oh, what a shame! I'm going to ask the wizards to make one that you can carry into battle."

"No! I mean, don't trouble yourself, Lady Hyacinth. You shouldn't go to all that bother on my account."

"Oh, it's no bother at all! I'll go ask them right now, while you go for your horse ride. Toodles!"

Bella spurred her startled horse into a gallop, wishing she could leave all this nonsense behind her for good. Makeup boxes, when Bronzefist the Bloody and his men were waiting to storm the city! Mirrors in battle. Mirrors with stupid advertisements for bronze...

Bella reined her poor baffled horse to a halt and rode back to the castle. She rubbed Ravenheart down, gave him an apple by way of apology, and hurried to talk to the wizards herself.

~oOo~

The King's Royal Guardiennes rode up to the barbarian camp. Every woman carried a shining new shield.

"Glass shields!" Bronzefist the Bloody guffawed. "Very pretty, girlies. Sparkly, even. But you'll cut your lovely faces when we shatter all that glass. What a shame."

"Ah, but these shields are magic," Bella retorted.

"So they won't cut you all to shreds? So much the better. My men always appreciate good-looking..."

He stopped. His jaw dropped. *Yep*, thought Bella. *This is the real audience for those bronze bra ads.*

Every barbarian stood mesmerized. The wizards had programmed all their shields with a special set of advertisements for custom-fitted armor, Rapunzel brand hair conditioner, belly-dancing lessons, and more. The barbarians didn't even notice when the woman laid their shields on the ground and began a slow retreat.

"She's talking to me! What's she saying?" I wanna hear!" shouted one barbarian.

The lipstick ad. Get ready to run—Bella signaled.

"Hey, lookit! It says 'For sound, touch the center of the shield'."

The Horde bent over to touch the glass shields. For just a moment, a squadron of sultry voices echoed across the field. "...luscious cherry flavor..."

Then the shields exploded.

ABOUT SWORD AND SORCERESS

by Elisabeth Waters

The *Sword and Sorceress* anthology series started in 1983, when Marion Zimmer Bradley, complaining that she was sick and tired of sword & sorcery stories where the female character was "a bad-conduct prize" for the male protagonist, persuaded Donald A. Wollheim of DAW Books to buy an anthology of sword & sorcery with strong female characters. The book was published in 1984.

The original title, *Swords and Sorceresses*, was changed during the production process when it was discovered that nobody could pronounce it in a conversation. So the first book was titled simply *Sword and Sorceress*. It was a success, so the following year we got *Sword and Sorceress II*.

It is my personal belief that if either Marion or Don had realized how successful this series was going to be, they would not have used Roman numerals, but they did, and DAW published the series through *Sword and Sorceress XXI*. (That's #21, for the non-Romans among us.)

Norilana Books picked up the series with volume 22, and because Marion was no longer alive to edit it, Vera titled the book *Marion Zimmer Bradley's Sword and Sorceress XXII*. This led to five titles that were listed on the royalty reports as "Marion Zimmer Bradley's" with the only thing different being the ISBN.

We changed to Arabic numerals with *Sword and Sorceress 28* and have now reissued volumes 22 through 27 as *Sword and Sorceress 22* through *Sword and Sorceress 27*. We hope that our readers will find this less confusing. We know that we will.